A Girl Called
Summer

LUCY LORD

HARPER

Harper
An imprint of HarperCollins*Publishers*
77–85 Fulham Palace Road,
Hammersmith, London W6 8JB

www.harpercollins.co.uk

This paperback edition 2014
1

A catalogue record for this book
is available from the British Library

ISBN: 978-0-00-744176-1

Set in Meridien by FMG using Atomik ePublisher from Easypress

MIX
Paper from
responsible sources

FSC
www.fsc.org   **FSC˚ C007454**

For my brother, Nick, with love and thanks

She had thought of him as a brother, once.

She'd grown up on the beach an only child, happy and free with loving hippy parents. She rarely wore shoes, and her overriding memories were of sunshine, kind faces and cheerful voices – laughing, or singing along to her dad's acoustic guitar. Swimming in the sea, even in mid-winter, during storms and clean, cold sun, was as natural to her as breathing.

He was three years older – eight to her five when he turned up on the beach, motherless, but not an orphan. He always looked after her during the storms, racing her to safety, or carrying her in his skinny arms to shelter under the rocks if the rain became too heavy.

She had loved him for as long as she could remember, so it was only natural, when he started to look more like a man than a boy, that her young emotions had been stirred still further.

She'd hated his first girlfriend – a dark-haired, dark-eyed girl who looked so different to her. It always seemed as though they were mocking her, as she tried to run after them across the sand, always several steps behind, despite her legs, which everybody said were long for her age.

When she was fifteen, he started to look at her differently. She could still remember how tender he was the night he had given her what she'd been aching for. Naturally, it was on the beach.

For nearly a year they were as happy as young lovers could be. Kissing, hidden behind sandy dunes, laughing till they could laugh no more, the exquisite sun bathing their exquisite bodies in heat, and light, and lust. They were perfect for each other; everybody said so.

Until that dark, ugly night when her innocence was shattered for ever.

1

'Are we completely bloody insane?' asked Bella, as the jeep lurched along the uneven dirt track that led to their new home. It was pitch-black outside, and raining, the downpour so heavy that the water bounced right off the jeep's roof, sounding inside like a volley of gunfire.

'Bit late to start thinking about that.' Andy smiled at her, and took one hand off the steering wheel to give her knee a reassuring squeeze.

Bella looked anxiously over her shoulder to the back seat, where their daughter, Daisy, was sleeping soundly, utterly oblivious to the noise and bumpiness of the journey. Her heart swelled with love as she gazed at the perfect, untroubled little face, and she smiled too. Daisy had just turned one, and her birthday-cum-farewell-to-England party, a pretty riotous affair, had been the last time they'd seen all their London friends. Had it only been a week ago?

'See?' said Andy. 'Daisy's completely unfazed by it all. Stop worrying – everything's going to be fine.'

'Daisy's not fazed by anything.' Bella smiled again. 'And I'm not fazed, really, either. But it would have been nice not to have been arriving in the dark. Bloody MonAir.' The plan had been to arrive shortly before sunset, but their flight from Gatwick had been delayed by four hours. 'And bloody rain. This is meant to be *Ibiza*!' It came out as a wail. 'This is what we emigrated to escape from!'

'It's April, Belles. It's a freak storm. It'll pass. Now come on, old thing, where's your sense of adventure? This is the beginning of a whole new chapter in our lives. It's meant to be exciting.'

'Less of the old, please! But yeah – sorry. It is exciting.' Bella used to be up for anything, but the responsibilities of motherhood had somewhat tamed her sense of adventure – which was probably just as well, considering some of the things she'd got up to in the past. 'I can't wait to see Ca'n Pedro again.'

Ca'n Pedro was the four-hundred-year-old finca that Andy and Bella had first laid eyes on the previous summer, their first holiday with little Daisy as a newborn. It was set in incredibly picturesque surroundings, in the middle of nowhere, and they had fallen in love with it immediately. Such was its state of disrepair that when they'd idly asked a local estate agent how much she thought it was worth, the price had been so low that they'd realized they could actually afford to buy it if they sold Bella's tiny Notting Hill flat, which had soared in value in the years she'd lived there, and was far too small for a couple with a baby. There was even some money left over to do the finca up themselves (apart from the kitchen and bathrooms – for all their attributes, neither Andy nor Bella could claim much knowledge of plumbing).

And so what had been the germ of an idea, conceived excitedly over a long, lazy lunch on a beach, had now become reality.

Gulp.

Eventually they drew to a halt, the jeep's headlights the only illumination for miles around.

'Well, here we are then,' said Bella. The ancient finca looked less romantic than daunting and terrifyingly remote in the darkness and pounding rain. 'Our new home.'

'Our new home,' Andy repeated. 'Right then, I'll go and open up, put some lights on, and then you can bring Daisy in.'

'God, I'm glad we got the rewiring done in advance. Imagine turning up on a night like this with no electricity.'

'That would have been grim.' Andy smiled. 'OK, I'll make a run for it. I've got the torch, but can you keep the car's lights on until I'm in?'

Bella watched as he ran towards the heavy wood front door, jacket pulled up over his tousled head of dark hair to protect him from the rain, and put one of the keys that Carmen the estate agent had left them at the airport into the lock. After three attempts, he found the right one. As he opened the door, he turned back and waved at her, grinning, before disappearing into the house.

Bella waited, properly excited now at the prospect of seeing their new home's interior again. She vividly recalled the ancient wooden beams, flagstone floors and white-washed (if distinctly grubby) walls that more than made up for the dilapidated old kitchen and bathrooms that hadn't been updated since the Seventies.

And she waited.

Just as she was getting slightly worried, Andy emerged into the beam of the headlights, and ran back towards the car. Bella leaned over to let him in. He was panting and soaked already.

'Well?'

'I can't get any of the lights to work. I don't know – maybe there's a central switch somewhere . . .'

'. . . or maybe the storm's buggered up the electricity?'

'Good point.'

'Shit.'

They both stared at the dark old house, which was looking more spooky by the second.

'Well, we've got the torch,' said Andy, and Bella nodded. It wasn't the end of the world, but it wasn't exactly how she'd envisaged their first night in their new home. 'Shall we brave it, then? Get Daisy tucked up, go to bed and sort it all out in the morning?'

'As long as the bed's been delivered . . .' They'd had the pretty wrought-iron French antique shipped over weeks ago, but you never knew.

'Carmen did tell us it had.'

'Carmen also told us the electricity'd been sorted.'

They looked at one another.

'Only one way to find out.'

'OK, let's go for it.'

Bella sat in the dark as she waited for Andy to return with the rest of Daisy's stuff, and anything else that might make their first night a bit more comfortable. He had offered to leave her the torch, but she'd said no. Sitting with your baby in the dark wasn't as bad as negotiating your way up unfamiliar and slippery stone steps, encumbered with nappies, bottles and the rest of the gubbins, with bugger-all illumination. They couldn't keep the jeep's lights on all night.

Their bed had arrived, thank God. And thank God, thought Bella, that her daughter was such a heavy-sleeping little angel. Like mother, like daughter, she supposed (angel bit aside). The only sounds in the creepy darkness were Daisy's steady snuffling breath from her carrycot, and the rain still pounding down outside. Bella longed to pick her up and cuddle her, to smell her sweet powdery baby smell, but knew she shouldn't break her blissful slumber.

Despite everything she'd read (and been told by her own mother), she hadn't believed it was possible to love another creature so much. From the minute the slimy, wriggly little thing had been put in her arms, the previous agonizing twenty-four hours all-but-forgotten, her life had changed for ever. She knew she was biased, but Daisy was an enchanting little girl, with an extraordinarily sunny disposition. She rarely cried, preferring to observe things solemnly through her enormous brown eyes, until something made her gurgle with spontaneous giggles.

What with the bonus of Andy being a pretty good approximation of a hands-on father (he had his moments, but then, he was a man), and now their move to Ibiza, her favourite place in the whole world, Bella felt exceptionally lucky.

Darkness, shmarkness. Rain, shmain!

She had her baby, her man and their new home, and that was all that mattered. Though it *was* starting to get a tad chilly. Daisy seemed comfortable enough, wrapped up snugly in her fleecy layers, but Bella wished she'd thought to wear something warmer than the optimistic ensemble of sundress and flip-flops she'd thrown on back in London that morning.

The sound of Andy's familiar tread up the stairs was accompanied by the glimmer of torchlight. He entered the room, and dumped three heavy bags on the floor.

'Hello, you.'

'Hello, you, too.' Bella smiled. 'What's in the other cases?'

'Sheets, blankets – it's a bit chilly, isn't it?'

Bella nodded, trying not to shiver. Andy pulled a tartan blanket out of one of the bags and wrapped it around her shoulders. She kissed him gratefully.

7

'And this!' Triumphantly, he produced a bottle of duty-free Cava and a couple of plastic glasses from one of the bags. 'Got to toast our new home.'

'Of course!'

'Our new home,' said Andy as he poured the cheap fizz.

'Our new home.' And they clinked their plastic cups, smiling happily in the torchlight.

The following morning, Bella opened the shutters that led out onto the stone balcony outside their bedroom and gazed, slightly dazed, at the sunshine flooding in. The overgrown garden had thrilled them when they'd visited the previous summer, but now, in spring, and sparkling from last night's downpour, its beauty was overwhelming.

Lush bougainvillea climbed all the way up to the balcony on her left, its purply pink flowers clashing vividly with the cornflower-blue sky. She would probably paint the shutters to match the sky, Bella thought excitedly as she observed their peeling state of grey. The decent-sized pool, empty now, and mouldy, was surrounded by orange, lemon and almond trees, the citrus already starting to bear fruit, the almond in full bridal blossom. A few palms thrust their spiky heads skywards, and a couple of gnarled and silvery old olive trees stood guard, the patriarchs of the arboreal clan. Scarlet poppies grew wild in the undergrowth, and even from here she could smell the rosemary, lavender and thyme creeping their way up the hill the other side of the pool. If she stretched far enough to peer around the side of the house, she could make out the glittering deep blue sea, over a few acres of densely populated pine forest.

'Andy, come and look,' she whispered, trying not to wake Daisy. But when she glanced over at their daughter, she saw that her eyes were starting to open, the long lashes that had been brushing her cheeks now starlike as they blinked into life. 'You can come and look too, darling,' she said quietly, lifting her up and kissing her, before carrying her out onto the balcony.

'Wow,' said Andy, walking up behind them. He put his arms around Bella's waist and kissed the top of her head, leaning over her shoulder to kiss the top of Daisy's silky blonde head too.

They stood in silence for a few more seconds, breathing it all in.

'Well, I think we made the right decision,' said Andy eventually.

Bella laughed.

'I think so too. What d'you reckon, Daisy? Did Mummy and Daddy make the right decision? Do you think we're all going to be happy here?'

Daisy gurgled, a cheerful grin lighting up her little round face.

Andy had driven into San Carlos, their nearest village, for breakfast provisions, so Bella was giving Daisy a tour of the finca. They'd do a proper supermarket shop later that day.

They still hadn't been able to work out how to turn the electricity on, and had left several messages with Carmen, but she hadn't got back to them yet. Unable to face a cold shower, Bella had struggled into an old denim miniskirt that used to hang off her hips, and a baggy T-shirt that she hoped hid the remnants of baby weight around her middle. She'd managed to lose most of it, but that final half-stone was proving a bugger to shift. She'd washed her armpits and tied her long dark hair up into a ponytail, but was still feeling pretty grubby and travel-soiled. Never mind, the electricity (and her flab) would be sorted soon enough, she thought optimistically as she carried Daisy into the room opposite their bedroom.

The finca was laid out simply over two floors, with four rooms on top, two facing each other either side of a fairly wide corridor.

'So this is going to be your nursery. Quite a big room for a very little girl, isn't it? But it means that when you get bigger it can carry on being your bedroom.'

Bella walked across the room to the large window and fumbled with the shutters with her left hand, balancing Daisy on her hip with her right. 'And look – you've got a proper sea-view, which is more than you can say for Mummy and Daddy. Although Mummy and Daddy have got the balcony, and the garden view, so they can't really complain.'

I am rambling, she thought. *Does everyone speak to their baby like this, or am I losing the plot?*

'Anyway, I was thinking yellow-and-white gingham curtains in here, which will go with your yellow cot, and look lovely against all your Beatrix Potter stuff. You can always go for pink when you're old enough to choose, but for the moment Mummy's taste goes.'

They continued into the room next door.

'This is the spare room. Now, I know Daddy wants to keep everything traditional, and I'm with him on that – the sleek, minimalist thingy may be cool, but it's not for us. *However . . .'* Daisy looked up at her expectantly. 'When our famous friends come visiting from Hollywood, it needs to be a little bit funky, so I was thinking this room could have a bit of a colonial vibe, with an overhead fan, rattan furniture and some great big yuccas – which means I'll be able to smuggle in some animal print in the form of cushions and maybe even a couple of throws. What do you think of that, then, my angel? Isn't Mummy clever?'

Bella tickled Daisy under her chin until they were both helpless with giggles.

'OK, so this is the bathroom. And it needs a *lot* of work. But I suppose that's fairly obvious, isn't it?'

Mother and daughter gazed at the shabby avocado green fitted bathroom suite, complete with leaky showerhead and mildew on the walls. 'I imagine it was very trendy at the time, but I'm afraid it's all got to go.'

Daisy nodded solemnly.

'Someone else is going to come in and take all this out – it's not something Mummy or Daddy should even think about attempting – and we're going to replace it with a freestanding Victorian claw-footed bath, a proper, thundering power shower in that corner over there, creamy white tiles, like the ones you get on the Paris metro, and an old wooden wardrobe filled with lavender-scented linen and lovely fluffy towels. That should impress our groovy Hollywood friends, shouldn't it, my darling?'

It occurred to Bella that she was perhaps obsessing a little too much about impressing her stratospherically successful old mates – but hey. There was nothing wrong with wanting to make your house as nice as you possibly could, was there?

Bella shifted Daisy to her left hip, so she could clutch the wrought-iron bannister as they descended the steep spiral stone steps that led to the ground floor.

'We're going to have to be careful of these stairs once you start walking, aren't we? In fact, I don't think I'll be able to let you out of my sight for a minute. Oh—'

Bella finally shut up as she turned right into the kitchen.

The ground floor was divided into two large spaces – the kitchen, and what would eventually be their sitting room, via a large archway. There was another, smaller room leading off the sitting room, which they planned to turn into a downstairs loo and wet room.

The kitchen was an extremely good size, but other than

that had few redeeming features. Doors were hanging off hinges on the plastic units that had clearly been installed in the Seventies – or possibly even the Sixties. Orange and brown wallpaper peeled off one of the old stone walls, the cooker had two electric hobs, and the tiny fridge had given up the ghost a long time ago, judging by the dodgy-looking spiral wires, springing from all angles and leading nowhere.

'I'd forgotten quite how awful it is.' Bella kissed Daisy on the nose. 'And we won't really know what we're going to do with it until someone's ripped out all this horridness. There may be some wonderful treasures lurking beneath – who knows? That would be a lucky break for us all, wouldn't it, my angel? But never fear, it'll be spectacular once we've finished with it. Now . . . moving swiftly on . . .'

They walked back under the archway and Bella caught her breath. This was one room she hadn't forgotten. OK, so the whitewashed walls were filthy and covered in graffiti, but its proportions were fantastic, with original wooden beams still intact, and light flooding in through the floor-to-ceiling French windows that led to the garden and pool.

Carmen had told them that the finca had been used as a hippy commune in the late sixties and early seventies – hence the graffiti, which comprised CND signs, badly drawn sunflowers and rainbows, and even 'MAKE LOVE NOT WAR' written in large loopy letters, with hearts where the Os should be.

'It almost seems a shame to paint over it,' Bella mused, more to herself than to Daisy this time. 'So evocative of its era. But Daddy wouldn't hear of it, of course.' This bit *was* directed at her daughter. 'And it's going to take an awful lot of white paint. Mummy's right arm will be killing her once we've got this room into shape. Oh but, God, it's going to be worth it.'

She gazed around, her artistic mind already imagining the lovely, airy room, complete with wafty white cotton voile curtains, welcoming white linen sofas, bookshelves, rugs and a load of mis-matched bluey/greeny cushions to break up the all-whiteness, and bring some of the outside colours in.

'Right – are we ready to go and have a look at the garden now?'

Daisy nodded. Bella had no idea whether her daughter actually understood a word she said to her, but her nods, grins and giggles encouraged her to carry on.

It was funny how your priorities could change in the space of a couple of years, she thought. She'd always been a bit of a good-time girl, often to be found disgracing herself in nightclub loos or the kitchen at parties. She'd had enough fun to last anybody a lifetime. But much as she'd loved her old life, she had never been happier than she was now; in Andy and Daisy she had everything she could possibly want.

2

Being in the garden was even better than looking at it from the bedroom window. The smells! The colours! The tiny birds flitting from tree to tree! It was a shame about the mouldy state of the pool, but Bella was already seeing it sparkling turquoise, full of bobbing heads and happy faces.

She was pushing Daisy around it when they encountered their first orange tree. She reached up to pick one and inhaled deeply, savouring its sweet, fragrant tang.

'Smell that, darling.' She crouched down and held the ripe fruit to Daisy's little nose. The baby grinned and gurgled in appreciation.

'What a delightful sight,' said a heavily accented French voice. Bella jumped to her feet, startled. Standing in front of her was a smiling old gentleman with a handsome, lined face. Wearing an artist's smock, loose linen trousers, and a battered straw hat with a floral silk scarf acting as a flamboyant hatband, he fitted the surroundings beautifully.

'I am sorry, *mademoiselle*, I did not wish to frighten you – oh *pardon*, I should say *madame*' – he indicated Daisy in her buggy – 'but you look so young.'

Bella grinned. Compliments were gold dust when you were a relatively new mother. Everyone said how beautiful your baby was, of course, but the most personal comments that people managed tended to be 'you're looking well', or a slightly forced '*great!*' – which Bella took to mean 'fat'.

'Well, actually I'm not married, so technically, I suppose, I am still *mademoiselle*.' The Frenchman frowned. 'But I'm not a single mother,' Bella added hurriedly. 'Andy – that's Daisy's father – and I moved in yesterday. We're from London. I'm Bella.' She extended a hand and the Frenchman gallantly held it to his lips.

'*Enchanté*, Bella. *Enchanté*. I should introduce myself also. I am Henri, your new neighbour. I live up the hill – a mere ten-minute walk. My son and I heard that finally some English people had come to live in Ca'n Pedro – such a waste, for such beauty to be deserted for so many years – so we thought we should come and say '*allo*.'

'How very neighbourly,' smiled Bella, seeing no sign of the son and wondering if the old man may perhaps be a little doolally.

And then a dark-haired young man appeared from behind their largest almond tree; he had, until now, been obscured by both his father and the abundant blossom.

Bloody hell, he was good looking. Limpid dark-brown eyes looked up at her through ridiculously long and thick black lashes. His olive skin had that deep russet hue of a man who has lived his whole life in the sun, and full pink lips parted to reveal even white teeth as he smiled at her. He wasn't particularly tall (well, you couldn't have every-thing) but his sleeveless black T-shirt revealed the well-defined biceps of somebody who does something manly in the great outdoors. A gardener, perhaps, or a . . .

Bella shook herself internally. She loved Andy. No, she didn't only love him – she worshipped him, adored him.

They were soulmates, and as happy as two people ever could be in one another's company. But there was no harm in appreciating a bit of beauty, she excused herself. All the same, she did wish she'd been able to have a shower and do something with her hair before her new neighbours' unexpected arrival, and was overcome with a sudden insane compulsion to give her armpits a surreptitious sniff.

'*Buenos días*,' said the young man. He held out his hand and Bella shook it, keeping her arm as close to her side as she could.

'*Buenos días. Me llama Bella* – um . . .' She did know quite a bit of Spanish, having spent a large chunk of her childhood in Majorca, where her father still lived, but it had become pretty rusty of late.

'It's OK. We can speak English if you prefer,' grinned the handsome young man. 'Hi, Bella. I'm Jorge.'

'Hi, Jorge, and thanks,' Bella smiled back. 'I really should be practising my Spanish, now we're actually living here, but for the first couple of days, to ease myself in . . .

'I like to practise my English too. Maybe we can take it in turns?'

'Your English sounds pretty good to me, but yeah, sure – it's a deal! And in the meantime some kind of weird English/French/Spanish Esperanto?'

'*Bienvenue a Ibiza*,' said Henri. 'This form of communication is very common here. *Mostly* we understand one another.'

Bella laughed and lifted Daisy out of her buggy.

'In that case, I think I should introduce you to Daisy. We're hoping she'll grow up bilingual. Tri- would be even better, of course.'

As he looked at the baby, Jorge went into raptures, tickling her under the chin, stroking her silky white-blonde hair and exclaiming, '*O que rubia, que linda, que bonita*!'

Henri smiled sadly. 'My son loves the children. I think maybe it is because his own mother died when he was small. She was a local Ibicenco girl – very beautiful . . .'

'Oh, I'm so sorry to hear that,' said Bella. 'But I'm not surprised to hear she was beautiful, looking at you two.'

Ewww. Did that sound like the compliment she'd intended, or slightly slimy lechery? Jorge had to be at least five years younger than her.

Henri opened his mouth to say something when Andy appeared at the French windows, laden with flimsy carrier bags so full they looked as though they might split any second.

'Andy darling!' She waved over at him with relief, totally forgetting the armpit situation. 'Come and meet our new neighbours. We're speaking English – for the time being, at least.'

Andy, smiling, put the carrier bags in the shade and made his way around the pool.

'Hi, I'm Andy. Nice to meet you.'

'Henri.' The old man held out his hand.

'Jorge.' The young man held out his.

Andy courteously shook both hands. 'We were about to have some breakfast – I've bought plenty. Would you like to join us?'

Bella looked at him proudly. Andy had *such* good manners.

'*Non, non*, it is very kind of you, but we have already eaten,' said Henri. 'And I am sure you would rather have your first *petit déjeuner* here without unwelcome strangers!' Neither Bella nor Andy knew what to say to this, so they carried on smiling stupidly. 'But I was thinking,' Henri continued, 'tomorrow – if you are free – maybe I could show you around the locality, show you some places of interest – the farm where we buy the best eggs, the most beautiful

17

secluded beach, which will also be safe for *la bébé*, the shop that sells the best *hierbas* . . .' He winked and gave a wicked grin as he mentioned the island's potent local hooch.

'Well, Andy has to go into town tomorrow, for some business stuff, but Daisy and I would love to take you up on your offer. It's really kind of you. That should be OK, shouldn't it, darling?' Bella looked up at Andy.

'Of course. And as Bella says, it's very kind of you, *monsieur*.'

'*Parfait*.' The old man smiled at them from under the brim of his battered straw hat. 'Do you know Bar Anita, in San Carlos?'

'Oh yes,' said Bella, smiling as the memories hit her. 'I've known Anita's for years.'

'*Formidable*! *Donc* . . . shall we say Anita's at – would eleven in the morning suit you, *mademoiselle*?'

'That sounds great. Thank you, *merci* and *gracias*.'

The following morning, Andy was driving into Ibiza Town, a large smile creeping across his face as he turned up the volume on Rodrigo's *Concierto de Aranjuez*, one of his and Bella's favourite pieces of classical music. It was another beautiful day and he could still hardly believe they'd actually done it.

Andy had always been the sensible one, had had to be after both his parents were killed in a car crash when he was a teenager. Bella was his best friend Max's little sister and he'd had a crush on her ever since he'd first set eyes on her – she was seventeen, visiting Max at Cambridge, where he and Max both studied. He'd never considered himself in her league though – the wild child London art student, with her enormous, Bambi-lashed brown eyes, pretty face and messy long dark hair. What on earth would she see in an earnest, speccy geek like him?

But what he hadn't known at the time was that Bella's wild-child behaviour was the only way she could deal with the shyness that had afflicted her for most of her life; that underneath it she was sweet and kind and funny. When they eventually fell in love, he was engaged to marry his long-term Cambridge girlfriend, who he subsequently found out was cheating on him the day before the wedding. His antipathy towards marriage, as a result, was as solid as his commitment to Bella and Daisy.

When he and Bella got together, Andy had been an award-winning journalist on one of the better broadsheets. He was known for intelligent and insightful pieces exposing people-traffickers, practitioners of female-genital mutilation and child pornographers. He'd worked extremely hard for nearly two decades, his sense of burning injustice that the drunken truck driver who'd killed both his parents outright escaped with a suspended sentence spurring him on to write about things that disgusted him.

It was inevitable, of course, that writing about the things that disgusted him involved constant exposure to brutal, sadistic people who disgusted him, and the summer before last, before Daisy was conceived, he'd come to the conclusion that he couldn't bear much more of the seedy underbelly of life. So he'd approached an agent with an idea for a history book.

Bella had been delighted – both of them working from home was ideal, as far as she was concerned; she worried incessantly about Andy's accumulative knowledge of things more horrible than anybody needed to know, and she'd never been hung up on where the next penny might come from.

The idea to move to Ibiza had been hers – she'd been spending holidays there for as long as she could remember, and loved the island. By the end of a long, boozy lunch on Benirrás beach the previous summer she had managed to convince him that it was the right thing to do, that Daisy would have a far better upbringing there than in London.

Dear Bella, he thought, his smile widening further as he steered the jeep into the outside lane in preparation for turning off the motorway. Her arty impulsiveness was exactly what he needed in his hardworking, somewhat strait-laced life.

None of this would have happened without her, and for that – as though he needed further reason – he would love her for ever.

Anita's was Ibiza's original hippy bar, *the* place for the assorted long-haired peaceniks, draft-dodgers, artists, writers and plain old pleasure seekers to hang out in the Sixties and Seventies. Bella, whose imagination had always been fired by that era (she loved the music, the clothes, the whole make-love-not-war thing), liked to think that several of them would have been living in Ca'n Pedro.

It was still wonderfully atmospheric, with rickety wooden tables and chairs laid out under a vine-covered trellis, leading to a narrow bar at the back and an indoor restaurant that was generally deserted at the height of the season, when everybody wanted to sit outside. Now, a couple of months before the summer madness started, the inside was more bustling than out – though Bella, after yet another miserable English winter, was relishing the partially covered outside area.

An old defunct phone box, which had once been the only one on the island, and a whole wall lined with individual post-boxes (many of them still in use) bore testament to the fact that the bar had acted as a kind of *poste-restante* – the only way for anxious parents to contact their wayward offspring – and added to its authentic charm. Anita's was much more than a period piece though; its whitewashed walls were plastered with daily-changing posters advertising club nights from Pacha to Space, Ibiza Rocks to DC-10, Amnesia and the rest.

The people who worked there were efficient and friendly. The waiter who had brought Bella her coffee, as she waited for Henri under the vines with Daisy on her lap, had recognized them both from the previous summer and greeted them with warm enthusiasm, exclaiming how Daisy had grown, and commenting on her beauty just as Jorge had the previous day: '*Que linda, que bonita, que rubia!*'

It appeared that Spaniards adored blonde babies. Bella wasn't quite sure how she and Andy had managed to produce one, both being dark-haired and dark-eyed themselves, but she imagined her daughter's hair would grow darker as she got older – the same way her own had, in fact.

San Carlos, their local village, was small but perfectly formed. Aside from Anita's, it boasted a simple whitewashed church, a little grocery that sold all the essentials (but was shut between 1 and 5 p.m.), a couple of very good restaurants, a pharmacy and a pedestrianized area lined with boutiques, an antique shop, a few more bars and a health-food store that also offered ayurvedic massages. Everything was beautifully kept, and the locals, who all seemed to know one another, were as friendly as the waiters at Anita's.

It was also cool. One of Kate Moss's best friends had had her wedding at the local church several years previously. Bella knew that it was extremely *un*-cool of her a) to know about this and b) to care, but there it was. She was living in rural bliss in one of the coolest villages in Ibiza, and loving it already.

'*Hola*, Bella!'

Bella looked up from Daisy, at whose face she had been gazing with her usual rapt adoration, to see not Henri standing in front of her, but Jorge, his handsome son. Today he was wearing white jeans and another sleeveless, bicep-revealing T-shirt.

'*Hola*, Jorge.' She smiled and stood up to kiss him on both cheeks. 'How lovely to see you again. But . . .?'

'Papa asked me to give you his apologies, but he has important business to attend in Santa Eulalia. So I shall show you around instead.'

'Well – thank you,' said Bella. 'If you're sure you've got time. What about your work?'

'Oh, it's OK, I can take an hour or two off. I am my own boss,' said Jorge with a gleaming grin that lit up his deeply tanned face. 'I design people's gardens, fix things that are broken – I suppose you could call me an "odd-job man", but there is a lot of call for it around here. Many foreigners buying up old properties.' He winked at Bella and she laughed. 'I don't do too badly,' he added modestly.

'I'm sure you don't.'

Well, she'd almost been right about him being a gardener.

Jorge had very flash wheels for an odd-job man. As he drove Bella and Daisy around the winding tree-lined roads in his white convertible BMW, pointing out Las Dalias, where the hippy market was held every Wednesday (Bella already knew this, but didn't have the heart to tell him), and various farmsteads, butchers and isolated, but apparently amazing restaurants, they chatted easily about the events that had led Bella and Andy to the island.

'Andy's a writer,' she told him proudly.

'Clever man. What kind of books?'

'History books.'

Jorge let out a low whistle. 'Wow. *Very* clever man.'

'Yes, very! His first one, a political history of the Balkans since the Second World War, did brilliantly, so he was given a much bigger advance for his second one, and we thought we might as well go for it. Our flat in London was too small for the three of us, and we couldn't buy anything like Ca'n Pedro for the same price there . . .'

'. . . and you were lured by the magic of the White Isle.'

'Well, yes.' Bella laughed. 'Got it in one, in fact. I've been coming here for years and have loved it more every single time.'

'And you, Bella?' Jorge briefly took his eyes off the road to look at her. 'What did you do, back in London?'

'I was . . . *am* an artist. I paint in oils mainly, but haven't done much since Daisy was born. I was hoping that living here would start to give me some inspiration again . . .'

'*Mais non*!' Jorge reverted to his father tongue, slamming the flat of his hand on the steering wheel and causing the car to swerve slightly. '*Lo siento*. But Papa – Henri – is also an artist. *Quelle coincidence*! You are right about the island providing inspiration – the light, the colours, the sky and the sea . . .' He took one hand off the steering wheel again to gesture around at the silvery olive groves and colourful spring flowers bordering the road, and up at the cloudless blue sky.

'Exactly! And that's wonderful about your father – I have to say he looks the part.' Bella laughed.

'Oh yes, he likes the artistic image.'

'I'd love to see some of his work.'

Bella was thrilled. Day two and already they'd met a local artist. Soon they'd be surrounded by fellow writers, and musicians, and sculptors, and poets . . . Her imagination was running away with her again.

'In that case, I know exactly where to take you now.' Jorge did a sudden U-turn in the middle of the road – his driving was erratic, to say the least. Bella looked over her shoulder at Daisy, strapped into her car seat, but she was grinning away as ever, apparently loving the impromptu fairground ride.

A couple of minutes later the car took a sharp turn to the left, down a steep, winding dirt track that was clearly leading to the coast. Dirt track wasn't exactly the right expression though, thought Bella, not when the 'dirt' in question was white sandy rubble, bordered either side by thick, highly scented pine forest. These paths, leading to unspoilt coves of almost invariable beauty, were among her favourite things about Ibiza.

'So where *are* you taking me?'

'The Art Resort. It's a beach bar and holistic health centre, run by a Swedish couple – the Larssons. They like to display paintings, photographs, sculptures – anything creative by local artists. Henri's work is there, most of the time. I am sure they would like to meet a *new* local artist.'

'Gosh, thanks – I mean *merci*, or *gracias* – I promise I'll stop speaking English soon . . .'

'No hurry.' Jorge turned to smile at her again. 'As we always say here, *mañana* . . .'

'*Mañana*,' Bella repeated, feeling even happier. Such a beautifully lazy sentiment.

As they descended the track, a girl came into view. She waved, and Jorge drew the convertible to a halt.

'*Hola*, Summer!'

'*Hola*, Jorge,' smiled the girl. 'Hi,' she added to Bella in one of those indeterminate, yet educated, slightly Americanized European accents. 'I'm Summer.'

Never had a name been more appropriate, thought Bella.

Summer was about five foot nine, a good three inches taller than Bella (who felt distinctly stumpy in comparison), with long, streaky blonde hair tied back in a simple plait. Her unmade-up face was perfectly proportioned, with high cheekbones, a pretty mouth that turned up naturally at the corners and large, wide-apart, dark-blue eyes that held you in a direct gaze. She was slim but not skinny, with beautifully shaped arms and shoulders revealed by a faded indigo vest top. Bella imagined that her long legs, hidden at the moment by a tiered white cotton maxiskirt, were equally exquisite. Her skin had that enviable golden hue, without so much as a hint of pink, that suggested Scandinavian genes.

'Hi.' Bella smiled back. 'I'm Bella.'

'Great to meet you, Bella.' Summer reached over the half-up window and into the car, and they shook hands. The handshake was warm, dry and strong. She was liking this girl already.

'And who is this?' Summer looked over at Daisy, strapped into her little car seat. 'Wow, she's so beautiful!'

'Thanks! I have to say I agree with you, but then I guess I'm biased.' Bella peered back at Daisy, who was grinning up at Summer with glee. 'Hey, Daisy, meet Summer. Summer, this is Daisy.'

'Hi, Daisy,' said Summer. 'Is it OK if I hug her? I won't take her out of her seat.'

'Of course,' smiled Bella, and opened the car's back door to give Summer better access to her daughter. The girl leaned in and gave Daisy a gentle squeeze, showering her little face with kisses. Daisy grinned and gurgled some more from under her white, lace-bordered sunhat. 'It looks as though she's taken to you already.'

'All the *pequeños* love Summer,' said Jorge. 'It is her job to look after them.'

'Really? Where?'

Summer dragged herself away from Daisy to smile at Bella.

'My mother teaches yoga on the beach, at dawn. There are very many "yummy mummies" here . . .' Bella could hear her putting the words in inverted commas, as she rolled her cool, dark-blue eyes. 'So I look after the babies, at the crèche . . .'

'If I came down to the beach at dawn, to do some yoga, and get rid of my bloody baby weight . . .'

'I see no baby weight,' said Jorge. Bella smiled at him gratefully, even though he was lying through his perfectly white teeth.

'. . . you could look after Daisy?'

'For sure. It would be my pleasure.' Summer handed Bella a card. 'Call me.'

'We're on our way to meet your *padres* anyway,' said Jorge. 'Bella's an artist . . .'

'Oh, they'll love you,' smiled Summer. 'I must go now, but hope to see you – and Daisy – soon on the beach.'

And she continued to walk up the sandy white track, turning once to give them another friendly wave.

'So how do you know Summer?' Bella asked, reluctantly dragging her gaze away from the gorgeous girl walking up the hill.

'We were childhood sweethearts. You know – first love . . .' Jorge shrugged nonchalantly.

'*Really?*' Bella wondered why she was so surprised – they were certainly good-looking enough for one another. 'So why didn't it last?'

'Does first love ever last? I suppose we both grew up.'

'She's very beautiful,' said Bella wistfully.

'Yes, she is. But there are many beautiful people in Ibiza.'

And Jorge turned to her with his dazzling white smile again.

3

Tamara Gold pouted at herself in the mirror as she applied a third layer of mascara. The mascara was unnecessary, as the long, fluttery eyelash extensions were individually applied on a weekly basis, but Tamara had yet to learn the meaning of 'less is more'.

Tamara had been a cute kid whose red hair, pretty freckled face and slightly goofy grin had landed her many a movie role and legions of fans. The child star was smoking weed by the time she was twelve, snorting coke at thirteen and had been in rehab three times by the age of fifteen. She had been clean for nearly ten years now, and intended to stay that way.

The grown-up movie star bore almost no resemblance to the child actress; so successful had her transformation been that few people remembered the goofy little redhead. The tiny frame that had enabled her to carry on playing ten-year-olds into her mid-teens had not blossomed as well as she'd hoped, so Tamara – encouraged by her unscrupulous parents – had paid for her first breast implants herself the day she turned sixteen. The teeth came next – Hollywood perfect veneers corrected the gappy grin shortly after the boob job, and 'preventative' botox three times a year kept her crooked dermatologist in the expensive brandy and cigars he favoured.

Freckles were out of the question for a movie goddess, so Tamara kept out of the LA sun and had her slender, boobalicious body spray-tanned twice a week by one of her many beauty therapists. The ginger hair was dyed a lustrous chocolate brown that now fell in heavy waves down to her most recent breasts, and contact lenses in a vast range of greens gave the impression that she had extraordinary eyes that lightened or darkened to match her mood. Only her parents and Jack, her fiancé, knew that they were really a sludgy shade of hazel. Tamara's sexy, bee-stung pout was pure collagen, and two hours a day with a personal trainer gave her delicate frame the muscle definition that Hollywood now required.

In short, pretty much everything about Tamara Gold was fake. But the effect was stunning, and she knew it.

'Tamara! Surely you must be ready by now?' Jack Meadows, her fiancé, was rapping at the bathroom door impatiently. 'Our first guests have arrived.'

'Go greet them, then.' Tamara checked herself out again in the multi-mirrored bathroom. 'You're good at that, with your *educated charm*.' The final words were laden with bitter sarcasm.

She and Jack had met on the set of their first movie together, an enormously successful remake of *Antony and Cleopatra*, in which they'd fallen deeply in lust with one another. Their on- and off-screen romance had been so widely publicized – the new Liz Taylor and Richard Burton – that they now rivalled Brad Pitt and Angelina Jolie as Tinseltown's most high-profile couple. 'Jamara' didn't have quite the same ring to it as 'Brangelina', though. 'Tack' didn't even bear thinking of.

Tamara thought she loved Jack – as much as she could love anyone, damaged little girl that she still was – but sometimes he could be a real pain in the ass. He had been educated at Dwight, one of the most prestigious boys' schools in New York; Princeton, and then – to cap it all – the Lee Strasberg school of acting. He was respected, with or without her.

Whereas she had been a classic Hollywood car-crash kid, endlessly mocked in the tabloids, paparazzi constantly with their cameras up her skirt – even *after* she'd got clean, for chrissakes. Being with Jack gave her kudos. His kindness and decency also gave her the sense of security that had been lacking for most of her life. So she needed him.

But there were times when she thought, *Screw you, Jack, I can do this on my own.*

Now, having slithered into a tiny emerald green satin bikini that matched the brightest of her contact lenses, she looked into the mirror that reflected the mirror behind her, which gave her a great view of her perfect, tight little bottom.

'Kiss my ass, Jack,' she said, thrusting it out, kissing her own hand and patting it, and then kissing her reflection in the mirror. 'And all you fuckers out there can kiss my ass too.'

She took one more look at herself and smiled. Yes, she looked *beyond fabulous*, as her gay hairdresser was wont to say.

She was ready to face her public.

Jack Meadows was thinking about a phone conversation he'd had with his mother that morning. His mom, who couldn't stand Tamara, had been trying to persuade him to call the wedding off, and while she could be a little overbearing at times, Jack knew his mom always had his best interests at heart. The conversation had ended with Jack saying, somewhat weakly, 'Dad likes her,' and his mother finishing, triumphantly, 'That's a ridiculous argument, and you know it. Your father likes all pretty young girls who wear next to nothing.'

Which was a fair description of his dad, rock legend Filthy Meadows.

When he and Tamara had first met, in the hothouse environment that was a movie set, they had taken an instant shine to one another. Tamara, for all her faults, was clever and witty. Jack also sensed the vulnerability beneath the veneer, and had the urge to protect her. OK, so he wanted to get her into bed, too, but who wouldn't? She was gorgeous.

The chemistry between them was something that couldn't be faked, and one of the reasons that *Antony & Cleopatra* had been the highest-grossing movie of the year. There had been some narcissism on both sides, too. Jack, who at six foot three was about half a foot taller than most movie stars, had the same green eyes and lustrous black lashes as his fiancée – though his were real. His curly mop of black hair had been cropped short for the film, while hers had been hidden by the bobbed wig obligatory for anybody playing the Queen of Egypt. As they gazed into one another's eyes for yet another close-up, it was almost like looking into a mirror.

Jack had been aware of Tamara for years – how could anyone not be? She was rarely out of the tabloids – but their paths had never crossed until the epic movie, mainly because of his mother's insistence that her only child had a proper education. He'd been a straight-A student at his New York boarding school, studied English Literature at Princeton, and had only got into acting by chance. Despite (or perhaps because of) being surrounded by veterans of the film and rock world while growing up, he'd never wanted to pursue either route himself, and spent most of his school holidays lying in his favourite hammock, his face buried in a book.

In Jack's final year at Princeton, Chad Junior Martell III, one of his best buddies, was meant to be playing Hamlet in the end-of-year show, but had got so hammered at a frat party that he was hospitalized for a couple of weeks – a combination of liver damage and head injuries.

'Go on, Jack, do it for me?' Chad had pleaded from his hospital bed. 'I know you know the play inside out and back to front.'

'Me? Act?' Jack didn't even like speaking in public. 'Are you crazy, dude?'

'For me?' Chad had repeated. 'There's nobody else who could learn the lines in time, and I'm in enough crap as it is. If the show's cancelled because of my bender, I could be out on my ass.' He sensed Jack's hesitation. 'And I think you'd make a great Hamlet, with your goddamn annoying intelligence and introspection.'

Chad's words proved prophetic. Jack made the best Hamlet that any Ivy League college had seen for years and, having conquered his initial stage fright, realized that he loved acting. If he wanted to act, he had to do it properly, though – which was why he'd enrolled at Lee Strasberg. It probably would have been easy for him, with his rock-star parentage, LA contacts and extraordinary good looks, to get crappy parts in crappy movies, but that wasn't Jack's style.

His first role had been in a critically acclaimed indie film about the Spanish Civil War; its juxtaposition of tragedy and wry humour had earned comparisons to the Coen brothers. That had been nearly ten years ago, and now he was a big, blockbuster star, while still retaining credibility. Johnny Depp – although quite a bit older than him – was about the only other movie star who could command lust and respect in equal measure. Men wanted to be him, and women wanted to fuck him.

And now he had Tamara.

He had proposed to her as she'd been giving him a particularly great blow-job, looking up at him with those long-lashed green eyes, so similar to his own (or so he believed at the time). By the time he'd come in her mouth he was already regretting it, but the studio loved the engagement, and Tamara had been so adorably, kittenishly grateful that he hadn't had the heart to renege on his offer. As soon as news of their engagement hit the Press, their joint bankability had soared overnight.

And Tamara was beautiful, sexy and funny – when she chose to be. He was very fond of her, and most men on the planet would give their right arm to be in his shoes (if that wasn't the most ludicrous mix of metaphors he'd ever entertained).

But he did know, with horrible certainty, that his mother was right.

'Will her highness ever make an appearance, I wonder?' Natalia Evanovitch languidly looked over the top of her enormous Chanel sunglasses at her friend Poppy Wallace.

The pool party was heaving now, Jack's Spanish-style villa thronging with stars, starlets, rockers, groupies, agents, producers and money men – all clamouring to be heard under the blazing California sun.

'Course she will, and who cares how late she is anyway? It's her party and she can do what she wants to.' Poppy sat up from the adjacent sunlounger to take a sip of her frozen Margarita through a kitschy neon pink straw.

'She always does what she wants to. Little bitch.'

'Aww come on, Nat – you don't have to be so harsh on her. I think she had a pretty rough time growing up . . .'

Natalia, whose cold, dark childhood in Kiev had been more than 'pretty rough', snorted. 'Oh, the poor little darling, struggling to handle all that wealth and adulation from such an early age. My heart *bleeds* for her!' She clutched her chest dramatically, and Poppy chuckled, leaning back against the sunlounger again.

They were an amazing-looking pair of blondes.

Natalia, nearly ten years older than Poppy's thirty-four, was a little over six foot tall, with the longest, most elegant legs you were ever likely to see outside airbrushed photos in magazines. Diamond-encrusted clips held her platinum blonde hair off her exquisite, high-cheekboned face in a glamorous up-do. Her high-cut, halter-neck, silver swimsuit was also cut out at the sides, emphasizing her still-slender waist.

Poppy, by contrast, was the epitome of LA surfer girl chic – even though she was originally from the English Home Counties and had spent most of her adult life in London. *Her* blonde hair was loose and free-flowing around her shoulders, her Heidi Klein string bikini casual and sporty, and her tan (whisper it) was *natural*. She knew she shouldn't, but she loved the feeling of the sun on her body, without any greasy gloop to stop the rays penetrating her skin.

She'd endured enough gloomy English winters to think 'fuck it' now that she was living in LA – whatever her agent, manager and dermatologist told her.

'Do your best, you evil, ageing UVs,' she said, happily turning her pretty face up to the sky. It was only slightly disingenuous – she was vain enough to spritz a weightless SPF-15 over her gamine features if ever they were at risk of burning.

'You'll regret it when you're my age,' said Natalia, whose all-over application of Factor-50 every morning was almost religious.

Poppy laughed again.

'Oh sod off. You know you look fantastic.'

Poppy and Natalia had met a few years previously in London, at the launch of Poppy's best friend Bella's first art exhibition. Natalia, who had made a lot of money in her former life as a high-class hooker, had bought the majority of Bella's paintings, and subsequently lent Poppy her ultra-modern, uber-luxurious villa in Ibiza as the venue for her wedding reception.

As Natalia smiled her feline smile, Poppy's iPhone beeped.

'Oooh, look Nat – it's from Belles. Photo of my god-daughter. Isn't she gorgeous?' She passed the phone over, and Natalia, who had never had any maternal urges, smiled again.

'Uh-huh. Daisy is cute.'

'*So when are you going to visit us in our run-down rustic hovel?*' Poppy read out, as Natalia passed her phone back to her. '*I know it's not up to your levels of glamour, but it's sooooo pretty – or it will be, once we've got everything sorted. Go on, Pops, surely you're rich enough now to be able to pop over to the White Isle whenever the mood takes you? I miss you xxx.*'

'Sweet girl, Bella,' said Natalia.

'Yeah, and I miss her too. I also miss Ibiza.' Poppy's mind drifted back, both to her wedding, and also to all the fun they'd had before success had hit them – some more strato-spherically than others. 'I'd love to go back this summer.'

'What about your *work*?' Natalia put the word into ever so slightly sarcastic inverted commas and Poppy smiled. She knew she had the easiest job in the world.

'Well, we're shooting Coachella next weekend, and loads of crappy awards ceremonies for a month or two, but I'm sure Damian and I could pay them a visit after that. What about you and Ben?'

Poppy worked as a roaming TV reporter, covering all the coolest things happening in California, and her husband

Damian was a screenwriter. Ben, Natalia's other half, was a movie star almost as famous as Jack Meadows, and equally handsome – though his was the pouty, blond, blue-eyed variety of male beauty. He had starred in his first movie with Jack, and their Matt Damon/Ben Affleck-esque 'bromance' had done no harm whatsoever at the box office.

Jack had also persuaded one of the biggest studios to turn Damian's first screenplay into a major motion picture. So in many ways Jack was their lynchpin in LA. And it had been fun when it was only the five of them hanging out: Poppy, Damian, Ben, Natalia and Jack. Natalia, with her dodgy past, was happy to do the glamour thing at private parties like this one, but avoided the red carpet as much as she could – she found that, provided you didn't court publicity, on the whole you were left alone. So Ben and Jack often turned up at the premieres and awards ceremonies together, joshing and laughing and playing up their bromance.

But now this little cow Tamara had turned up and ruined everything. Her brattish and demanding ways had destroyed the equilibrium of the easy friendship the five of them had shared. The Jack and Ben show had been replaced by the Jack and Tamara show, so Natalia had been forced to act as Ben's dazzling consort on the red carpet on more than one occasion.

And after years of hard graft, Natalia liked to call the shots herself. Having transformed herself from teenage Kiev street whore to one of the most in-demand call girls in boom-time Nineties Moscow and London, to canny property investor and uber-glamorous socialite, she felt it was the very least she deserved.

Tamara certainly knew how to make an entrance.

Filthy Meadows, Jack's father, started strumming the chords of one of his greatest hits – 'Sexy Green-Eyed

Woman' – as three male models, naked from the waist up, carried her horizontal, emerald-bikini-clad body over their heads, out from the French windows to the terrace at the top of the wide marble steps leading down to the mosaic-lined pool.

'*Sexy green-eyed hellcat. I want you so bad, but you can never be mi-y-y-iiine . . .*'

'A little inappropriate, don't you think?' said Natalia, turning her slanting ice-blue gaze on Poppy.

'Yeah, I'll give you that,' Poppy laughed, wondering if she could steal the introduction for her Coachella shoot. Her eyes were green too, and it would probably only take two blokes to lift her; she didn't have the weight of Tamara's fake breasts, after all.

Jack remained silent, but inside he was seething. *What the fuck had Tamara been thinking? His* dad?

Filthy came to the end of the chorus, and the beefcakes put Tamara on her feet. The assembled glitterati applauded lustily, and Tamara ran down the steps to give the rock star a huge kiss on the lips.

'Thanks, *Dad!*' She grinned up at him, and there were ripples of sycophantic laughter through the crowd. 'Hey, Jack – get me a drink won't ya? Virgin Margarita?'

Not wanting to make a scene, Jack did as he was told, absolutely furious. His ego wasn't half the size of most Hollywood stars, but this was meant to be *their* party. The Jack and Tamara pool party. Not the Tamara Gold show. And as for his dad serenading her in that repulsively lecherous way? It was wrong on so many levels.

'Here,' he said quietly as he thrust the drink into Tamara's outstretched hand. 'But don't you *ever* show me up like that again. And Dad . . .' He turned to his father. 'What the *hell* were you thinking?'

'Uh?' Filthy's face, all plumped-up lips and weird facial

topiary under his shock of dyed black hair, was the picture of bemusement. 'Tamara told me you'd agreed this, the two of you. My greatest hit, her greatest assets . . .' He grinned roguishly.

Jack sighed. 'Tamara—' he started.

'*Whatever*, Jack,' she snapped. 'Now you must excuse me. I gotta greet my guests.'

'*Our* guests, Tamara. *Our* guests,' Jack repeated, as he took her firmly by the arm and steered her away from his father.

Poppy and Natalia, who had by now been joined by Damian and Ben, were within earshot. The four of them exchanged glances, eyebrows raised, then burst into slightly guilty giggles.

'Wow,' said Poppy. 'Just – wow.'

'Poor Jack,' said Ben, who was very fond of his movie-star buddy – the bromance was genuine.

'I told you she was a little bitch,' said Natalia.

'I think Jack's old enough and ugly enough to stand up for himself,' said Damian.

They were now sitting at a circular glass table, with a white leather padded circular seat that went all the way round, underneath a huge white parasol.

'Darling . . .' Poppy turned to Damian, laying a hand on his arm. 'Before that entertaining little charade, I got a text from Bella.' She didn't bother to mention the photo of Daisy – men were *so* not interested in baby photos. 'She's dying for us to visit her in Ibiza. And I have to say, I'm dying to see their new place. What do you think? This summer? Feasible?'

'Eminently so, I'd say.' Damian's teeth flashed white in his dark face as he smiled at his pretty wife. His half-Indian, half-Welsh genes were an odd-sounding but winning combination. 'God, I'd love to hit Ibiza again. It seems like years . . .' His mind drifted back, the way Poppy's had earlier. 'Yeah, let's do it. We could even try to combine it with the opening parties, like we used to.'

'Shall we all go?' said Natalia. 'You can stay at my villa . . .'

'Thanks, Nat, but I think Bella will expect us to be staying with her,' smiled Poppy.

'Of course!' Natalia hit herself on the forehead in one of her characteristic dramatic gestures. 'Stupid me. Still . . . Let's look at our diaries and see what we can all fit in. Ben, sweetie, you should be able to take some time off this summer, no?' She gazed adoringly at her movie-star boyfriend, who was looking more handsome than ever today in Hawaiian printed boardshorts, his streaky light brown/blond hair, still wet from his swim, flopping into his delicious blue eyes.

'If you're all going to Ibiza without me, I'll bloody well make time.' The longer Ben stayed in LA, the more posh English his RADA-created accent became. 'Ooh, Nat, we could even take your boat out, little trip round the Med – Greek islands, St Tropez . . .'

Natalia smiled at him, remembering the magical time they'd had in St Tropez, where they'd first met.

'What's this about St Tropez?' Tamara slinked over and kissed Ben on the lips, leaving a sticky residue of lip gloss. 'My God, Ben, I swear you get more handsome by the day.'

Poppy kicked Natalia under the table, willing her not to rise to the bait.

'Hi, Tamara,' she said, getting up to kiss her on both cheeks. 'Great party.'

'Thanks.' Tamara smiled. 'Nice to see you, Poppy.' Poppy was one of the few women in Hollywood she didn't feel patronized by. 'But *tell me*, what's all this about St Tropez?'

'Hi, Tamara,' said Damian, getting up to kiss her too. 'We were actually planning a trip to Ibiza, but then Ben got carried away and started talking about cruising round the Med – which was how we ended up at St Trop—'

Tamara, who'd seen the photos of P Diddy's yacht and realized that Mediterranean cruises were *cool*, smiled slowly. 'In that case, you can count me in. *Jack*,' she yelled over her shoulder. 'How d'ya feel about a European vacation this summer?'

Natalia, behind her back, rolled her eyes and mimed slitting her throat.

4

'Yeah, I know. Bloody men don't understand how *exhausting* it is, being a full-time wife, mother *and* entrepreneur – *Scheherazade stop that!'* India Cavendish nodded sympathetically as her friend Saffron paused from her moaning to snap at the children. *'Leave Francesca alone!'*

Summer Larsson sighed as the two thirty-something yummy mummies approached the beachside crèche with their squabbling children. India and Saffron were both married to extremely rich and good-looking men, living in beautiful villas with extensive staff, and were constantly going on about how arduous their lives were. Physically, they were almost indistinguishable, although India's streaky light-brown hair, currently held up in a messy bun, was slightly less blonde than Saffron's, which today hung to her shoulders in insouciant plaits. Skinny and tanned, they conducted their lives in short, floaty kaftans that showed off thoroughbred legs, glittery flip-flops and large, round designer shades. Both had high-cheekboned faces that had probably been rather beautiful before the botox.

India, with the backing of her husband Jamie (who had been a hedge-fund manager in London before they'd moved to Ibiza – all a bit dodgy), had just launched a Fairtrade kids' clothing company. Saffron made jewellery from bits of driftwood and pebbles that she found on the beach.

'And can you please *stop that, Milo!*' India grabbed her son by the scruff of his Fairtrade T-shirt, and frogmarched him into the crèche. 'Hi, Summer,' she said. 'Rather you than me. He's been an absolute little horror all morning. The nanny's threatening to resign and God, do I need some me-time.' She gave a weary smile.

'Hi, India, hi, Milo!' Summer smiled back. The little boy's face lit up at the sight of her.

'Summer!' He jumped up into her arms.

'Yes, well,' said India. 'I suppose the change of scene does him good. Right, I'm going to get changed. See you on the beach, Saff,' she added over her shoulder to her friend, who was vaguely ushering her twin daughters into the crèche.

'What? Oh, right, yeah.' Saffron bent down and picked a twig up from the ground. 'Wow, that could make, like, the most incredible statement piece. What *is it*, Francesca?' she snapped at one of the little girls, who was tugging at her arm. 'Mummy's being creative. Oh, you want to go to the loo – well, go on then, you know where it is. Nobody's stopping you. Honestly,' she added to Summer, 'Kids. Who'd have 'em?'

'Oh, they're great girls,' smiled Summer, because, in all honesty, most of the children were fine as soon as they were away from their mothers.

'Whatever. God, I'm looking forward to this class. I can't *tell you* the stress I've been under this week.' And Saffron made her way to the changing rooms, pausing to do a couple of limbering stretches, without so much as a backward glance at her daughters.

Summer sighed again as she busied herself making sure

all the children had everything they needed, wondering, not for the first time, if running the crèche three mornings a week was worth it. She loved the kids – most of them – but some of the mothers were so horrendous that it took every last bit of willpower she possessed to smile politely at the inane, self-centred crap they came out with. Still, since she'd opened the crèche a couple of years ago, her mother's yoga classes had soared in popularity; she owed it to Britta to keep it going, she supposed.

Summer's main job was food and drink columnist on *Island Life*, an extremely hip and glossily produced English-language website chronicling every aspect of life in Ibiza, from fashion, to festivals, to new restaurant or club openings. Its offices were in Ibiza Town, though she didn't have to set foot in them much, filing most of her copy from the Mac in her little apartment, high up in the Old Town.

Summer loved Ibiza. She'd grown up in her parents' hillside villa, which had direct access to the unspoilt beach that now housed the Art Resort, via steep stone steps. Naturally athletic, she loved swimming and hiking and cycling in the great outdoors. Still, she'd tried to flee the nest: she'd studied Modern Languages at the University of Barcelona, with a vague idea of becoming a journalist in New York, or London, Stockholm, Paris or Rome (her French and Italian were now as fluent as her Swedish, English and Spanish). But after travelling around the world teaching languages for a couple of years, she'd realized that she was always happiest on the island of her birth.

Much as she adored the house overlooking the beach, she couldn't live with her parents for ever, and had been delighted, on her return, to find a quirky little flat in the Old Town that wasn't too extortionate to rent. From time to time, recommended by her childhood friend Clemency, who ran an upmarket Ibiza concierge service, Summer cooked fabulous meals for rich tourists in their villas. Her gift for languages and sensational good looks were as much a factor as her excellence in the kitchen when it came to the high fees she commanded. The varied and unstructured nature of her professional life suited her perfectly. Life *was* pretty cool, she reflected, although the David situation was becoming a bit tiresome.

'Summer!'

She looked up from Milo to see Bella, pushing Daisy along in her buggy.

'Hey. So glad you decided to brave the yummy mummies on the beach.' Summer gave Bella a warm hug, and Bella felt instantly nervous.

'How yummy are they?' she asked.

'Some of them are OK, but some of them – well – don't get me started.'

Bella laughed as she took Daisy out of her buggy and, showering her face with kisses, handed her over to Summer.

'You'll be OK with Summer, darling, I can tell. She will, won't she?' Bella sounded as anxious as she felt. The only person she'd ever left Daisy with before was her own mother.

'Don't worry, Bella. Daisy will be fine with me.' Summer smiled, wishing that all the mothers with whom she had to contend showed as much consideration for their little ones.

Bella had never been more glad that ninety minutes were over. The white sandy beach, lapped by clear tourmaline water and backed by dense, highly scented pine forest, was on the east coast of the island, perfect for the rising sun. Britta, Summer's mother, was a delight – a very blonde, very hippy-ish woman in her late fifties who took her job as a yoga teacher seriously; she took the time to readjust the postures of every single one of her clients, all of whom she knew by name.

Bella, who was wearing old baggy yoga pants and an even baggier T-shirt, had sweated profusely during the exhausting workout. The other participants were clad, almost uniformly, in short lycra shorts and tiny vest tops that showed off their absurdly neat little bodies as they contorted themselves into shapes that were way beyond her abilities. The yummy mummies to whom Summer had referred – India, and particularly Saffron, had made her feel horribly uncomfortable as they acknowledged her presence with a snooty once-over, turning to one another with raised eyebrows. She was sure she'd heard Saffron sniggering as she'd failed, yet again, to go smoothly from a downward into an upward dog.

However, as she lay on the sand, looking up at the morning sun and reflecting that the only time she'd ever been up in Ibiza at such an ungodly hour in the past had been post-clubbing, Bella smiled, feeling strangely peaceful yet elated. Maybe she'd finally grown up. She only wished she wasn't so red-faced and sweaty.

'Hey!' Summer approached her, Daisy in her arms. 'I think your daughter wants to say what a cool mom I have, to have gotten through Britta's yoga class.'

'That's sweet of you, Summer, but I don't think I excelled myself.' Bella dusted the sand off her body, every muscle burning. 'I was the bloody class dunce.'

Summer laughed. 'Be easy on yourself. My mom does put people through their paces, and you did OK for your first time. Don't you think so, Daisy?'

Daisy gurgled and grinned.

'See? Daisy thinks you did just fine.'

'You're an angel.' Bella stood up on very shaky legs and took her daughter from Summer. 'I think I'd better go and have a shower now, though.' She hugged Daisy and planted a kiss on the top of her head. 'I must look horrendous. I don't s'pose you could look after her for ten more minutes?'

'For sure.' Summer stretched out her arms to take Daisy. 'And then, maybe you'd like to join me for breakfast in the café?' She nodded over her shoulder at the whitewashed stone building at the back of the beach, fronted by white-painted wooden tables laid out under rainbow-striped parasols in the sand.

'Thanks.' Bella smiled. 'I'd love to.'

'You lived *there*?' Bella paused from her breakfast of free-range eggs, scrambled with wild spinach on organic spelt bread, to gaze up at the little white house halfway up the hill, with its steep stone steps leading down to the beach. 'Wow, what a location.'

'Uh-huh. My parents still do. Pretty handy for work, huh? Not much of a commute.'

Bella laughed. 'So where do you live now?'

'I've an apartment up in the Old Town. It's small, but cute. I like it. I only work here three mornings a week,' she added, pausing to take a mouthful of her eggs – she'd opted for the same breakfast as Bella.

'What do you do the rest of the time?' Bella was expecting something along the lines of model or dancer.

'Mainly I write a food column. I don't suppose you've heard of a website called *Island Life*?'

'God, yes! The last few months in England, I became completely addicted to it, getting myself thoroughly over-excited about our move here! I've read your column. It's fab!' Bella knew she was beginning to gush again, but she couldn't help it. She felt completely starstruck by this beautiful, clever, friendly girl. 'So how did you get such a fantastic job?'

'Ah.' Summer gave a slightly embarrassed smile. 'Pure nepotism, I'm afraid. The old editor was a friend of my dad's and he took a chance on me. That was a few years back though – there's a new editor now.' Something changed slightly in her tone of voice. 'Anyway, I'm glad he did – it was a great break, and I love writing about food.'

'I love reading about it. *And* eating it.' Bella grimaced. 'I felt sooo out of shape during your mother's class. How do those bloody women stay so skinny?'

'They don't eat. *At all*. Stupid stupid stooopid. As long as you eat good fresh food and take plenty of exercise, there's no need to starve yourself.'

As Summer wiped a stray strand of blonde hair back from her glowing golden face, Bella thought that she couldn't have been a better advertisement for her words. Mind you, being childless, twenty-five-ish, and possessed of excellent Scandinavian genes probably helped too.

Summer was driving her little Fiat back to Ibiza Town, still pondering the David situation, when a cluster of green spears, just off the side of the road, caught her eye.

She checked her rear-view mirror to make sure that no other cars were on her tail, and pulled in, taking her iPhone out of her handbag as she did so. She snapped several photos of the wild asparagus, before picking a handful and putting them onto the passenger seat.

'You, my babies, will be both my lunch and my next post,' she said in Swedish, as she revved the Fiat into action once more.

The view from Summer's flat, right at the top of Dalt Vila, the oldest bit of Ibiza Town, was, in its own way, as spectacular as the one from her childhood home. From here she could see, over slanting rooftops and higgledy-piggledy backstreets, all the way down to the vast array of boats in the harbour. On an exceptionally clear day she could see all the way to Formentera.

It was starting to get hot already, so Summer took her Mac out onto her little stone balcony, and uploaded the pictures of the wild asparagus that grew by the road.

This is what makes Ibiza special, she typed. *As much as Pacha, or Space, or even Playa Las Salinas. I found this wild asparagus less than an hour ago, growing freely by the road from San Carlos to Santa Eulalia. It's probably best simply steamed or chargrilled and served with melted butter and plenty of black pepper, but you can be a little more creative. For example . . .'*

Summer was interrupted by David, who'd let himself in and climbed the stairs up to her balcony. He was looking at her with that irritating puppy-dog expression he'd been adopting of late.

'Hey, Dave.' She tried to brush him off. 'I'm filing some copy.'

'Fuck your copy.'

'Wow, very professional attitude.' Summer turned back to her Mac. 'For my *editor.*'

'Fuck your copy, because I want to fuck *you.*' David put his short, hairy arms around Summer's waist and started to kiss the side of her neck. Feeling her weakening, he reached around to touch her between her legs. His thick fingers knew exactly what they were doing, and soon she was lying, naked and prone, on the sun-warmed stone terrace.

'Oh yes, baby, lie there like that and let me look at your beautiful body.' David, her editor on *Island Life,* gave her clitoris a gentle lick. Despite herself, Summer gave a soft moan of pleasure.

'Dave, you can't do this to me, it's not fair . . .'

'What's not fair, honey? You want it, and I want it . . .' He started to go down on her again, his stubbly beard rubbing against her as he thrust three fingers inside her.

Summer gave in and went with it, enjoying every moment of his mouth on her, his tongue lapping at her, his fingers probing ever deeper inside her. She had a very pragmatic, Swedish attitude towards sex. If it gave her pleasure and hurt nobody, then – *why not?*

'Oh God,' she moaned, more loudly now, as she felt the first waves of orgasm washing over her. David was relentless, pushing his hand into her even more deeply, never taking his mouth from her bucking body as she moved helplessly against him, again and again and again. When he was satisfied he'd milked the last drop of pleasure from her, he looked up at her flushed, sweaty face and smiled.

Summer smiled back, all her misgivings about the situation temporarily forgotten. 'That was great,' she said (well, credit where it was due). Seeing the bulge in his jeans, she sat up and started to undo his belt buckle, pushing him gently to the floor. His hard-on was enormous – his large, thick cock was out of proportion to the rest of his body – and Summer gasped as she lowered herself down onto it. David reached up to stroke her beautifully shaped breasts, the pinky-brown nipples already hard and sensitive to his touch.

'Fuck me, Summer. Fuck me hard.'

So she did. She rode him and rode him in the morning sun, increasing her tempo until he too was crying out, calling her name over and over. As soon as she felt him starting to pump inside her, she was overcome by a second, intensely powerful orgasm, before collapsing, damp and utterly spent, on top of his hairy body.

Oh shit, I've done it again.

When David had taken the place of her dad's friend as editor on *Island Life*, Summer had found herself weirdly attracted to him. The Jewish New Yorker was clever – probably smarter than anybody she'd met in her life – and even though he was shorter than her, and actually old enough, at forty-seven, to *be* her dad, she had been unable to resist his charm, wit, and – as she was soon to discover – amazing ability in the sack. The intensity of those dark, intelligent brown eyes as they'd roamed over her face and body, the first night he'd taken her out to dinner (ostensibly to congratulate her on a particularly good piece she'd written about paellas) had won her over completely.

'So, babe . . .' David stroked her face with a stubby finger. 'When are we going to go public? We're so good together.'

'We can't. OK?' Summer kissed his hairy chest to soften the blow. 'Fucking my boss is not cool.'

'Cool enough for you to do it, though?' David's voice was angry. It wasn't as if either of them was married, or even in relationships with other people. 'I don't get you. You act like you don't give a fuck about me, but I make you come, I make you laugh, I . . .'

Oh Jesus, he wasn't about to start crying, was he?

Summer had experienced this all too many times before. She loved sex, and her wanton abandonment to it gave the impression that she loved the men with whom she was having it. But they always got so *clingy*. One of the boys in Barcelona had left his girlfriend for her, when she hadn't even been aware that he'd had a girlfriend. There was no way she'd knowingly take another woman's man to bed. Again, it was the Swedish pragmatism that had led her to this conclusion – it wasn't worth the hassle. Why ruin somebody else's relationship when there were plenty of single people in the world?

Sometimes she wondered if there was something fundamentally wrong with her; why else would this sense of suffocation creep over her whenever a lover got too keen? She was fond of them, of course, but she'd never met anybody she felt a reciprocal passion for. Apart from Jorge, but that had been a long time ago – and it certainly hadn't been worth it.

Her thoughts returned to David, who appeared to have worked himself up into quite a state.

'I guess you think I'm not good enough for you. I'm just some dumb Jewish schmuck, old enough to be your dad. Why would a beautiful young girl like you want to be associated with me?'

The self-pity was worse than the anger – and *definitely* more of a turn-off. Summer tried to be kind.

'Oh, Dave, it's not that, of course it's not.' And it wasn't – not really. Summer sat up and wrapped her arms around her knees, gazing out at the view down to the harbour. David was right – there wasn't any reason for them not to make their relationship public. It wasn't as if anybody could accuse her of sleeping her way to the top – her position on *Island Life* had been secure well before David had joined the company. In fact, probably more secure than it was now, which was one of the things worrying her. She didn't *think* he'd use his power over her to make life difficult if she didn't comply with his wishes.

But he *could*. And she didn't like it one bit.

5

'Shhh darling, it's OK,' said Bella, rocking Daisy in her arms and wishing that somebody had given her lessons in how to be a mother. 'Shhh, darling, shhh.' She felt so bloody ineffectual on these rare occasions.

Daisy had been so little trouble ever since she was born that Bella realized she'd become a tad blasé about motherhood. She was no use whatsoever when her angel refused to sleep for more than half an hour a time, for *the entire night*. It was now mid-afternoon and mother and daughter had been awake, with intermittent naps, for over thirty-six hours.

'Maybe we'll feel better if we go and have a walk around our lovely garden,' said Bella optimistically. Daisy's response was an even louder wail.

'OK then, maybe it'll make *me* feel better if we go and have a walk around our lovely garden,' added Bella, trying to sound firm. Her voice crumbled before she got to the end of the sentence, but she managed to carry her daughter outside, halfway around the empty pool, where Andy had set up a couple of sunloungers, side by side.

She sat down on one of them, leaning back against the

headrest with a weary sigh, pulling Daisy to her chest and stroking her silky blonde hair, continuing to murmur 'Shhh, sweetheart, shhh.'

Through the incessant wailing, Bella's phone beeped and buzzed from one of the many pockets in the old combat-style miniskirt she was wearing with a faded black T-shirt.

'Oooh, maybe it's Daddy,' she said, her heart leaping, as it always did, at the prospect of a text from Andy. Or, indeed, at any contact with the outside world. Andy had driven off in the jeep that morning on a round of meetings with banks, IT people, the water man and others who were meant to make their life at the finca more comfortable.

She shifted Daisy into the crook of her left arm and pulled out her phone.

'It's from Poppy, darling, isn't that nice?' she said to Daisy, who continued to sob, albeit at a slightly lower volume. She opened the message.

Fantastic news, Belles, we're definitely coming to see you this summer! So exciting, it'll be just like the old days. Sa Trinxa, Pacha, DC-10 . . . I'm shooting Coachella next week, which should be a laugh, but nothing beats Ibiza for full-on hedonism, right? Loads of love to Andy and my beautiful god-daughter, Pops xxx

Bella gave a disbelieving snort. Poppy was on another planet sometimes. Full-on hedonism? DC-10, the club that only started after all the other clubs had finished? Did she seriously think life carried on completely unchanged once you had a child? And as for the way she so casually mentioned that she was 'shooting Coachella' – Bella had been dying to go to Coachella ever since she'd first read about it in *Grazia*, several years ago. Glastonbury in the desert, with guaranteed sunshine and hot and cold running celebs . . .

For a minute or two she let her mind drift back to the wild times of her past. The Glastonbury she'd shagged Ben had been a particularly good one. It had all ended in tears, of course, was bound to, but she had fond memories of that debauched, sun-drenched long weekend – and it was lucky they were all friends again. It could still have been horribly awkward, but Ben had Natalia, she had Andy, Poppy had Damian, and everything had worked out for the best.

Now she'd started though, she found she couldn't stop, and soon she was reminiscing about the Ibiza of her past, the ridiculous things they had got up to, the absolute freedom of it all . . .

The time she'd nearly shagged the Manumission dwarf until he put her off by boasting too much about past conquests . . . the time somebody pinched her dress when she was bonking that fit American in the loos at Pacha and she had to spend the rest of the night clad only in a towel . . . She gave a slightly guilty giggle – God, she'd been a slapper, back in the day – that turned into a wistful sigh.

Suddenly she realized that Daisy had stopped crying and was looking up at her with big, enquiring eyes.

'Sorry, darling, Mummy's just being silly. We've all got to grow up some time, haven't we, and you are, *without a doubt*, the best thing that's ever happened to me.'

She rained butterfly kisses all over Daisy's petal-soft little face until her daughter was gurgling with happy giggles. Bella gazed up at the cloudless blue sky, then over at the ancient finca, at the vivid bougainvillea climbing the white-washed walls, the charming wooden shutters that she'd started painting to match the sky, and began to laugh too.

What a bloody idiot she was being! Her life was idyllic, and having the freedom to nearly shag a dwarf really wasn't comparable, on any level.

Upside down on the sunlounger next to her, her phone started to ring.

'That'll be Daddy,' she said happily, giving Daisy one last kiss before picking up the phone again and turning it over to look at the screen. But no.

'Summer, how lovely to hear from you. How are you?'

'Hey, Bella, I'm fine, thanks. Listen, I'm down at the Art Resort with Mom – do you fancy joining us for a drink? Maybe you could bring some of your paintings and we'll think about displaying them in the gallery?'

'God, I can't tell you how much I'd love to.' Bella sighed. 'But I'm stranded. Andy's taken the car and won't be back for hours.'

'Shame,' said Summer. 'Never mind, there will always be other days. I have that list of useful phone numbers for you, too – would you like me to email them over?'

'That's really sweet of you, thanks,' smiled Bella, as Daisy started to cry again. 'Bugger, I'd better go. Daisy's not a happy bunny today. But thanks so much for the invite – please bear me in mind next time.'

'Of course. See you soon.'

'See you.'

As she put the phone down and Daisy's crying got louder, Bella started to cry too. She couldn't help it – she knew she should be counting her blessings, but she was so tired, and it would have been great to have a drink and a chat with Summer and her mother – *especially* a chat about her paintings. She couldn't remember the last time she'd thought of herself as an artist.

'*Hola*, Bella!' somebody shouted through the wrought-iron gates at the bottom of the garden.

'*Hola*, Jorge,' Bella shouted back, hastily and disgustingly wiping her sodden face on the back of her arm. 'The gate's open – come in!' Much as she liked the casual way people seemed to pop round to say hello in Ibiza – something that had never happened in all her years living in London – there were times when being caught off-guard wasn't so great.

Jorge sauntered across the garden, ludicrously handsome in tight white jeans and a fluorescent pink T-shirt with cutaway armholes and 'Blue Marlin Ibiza' written in slick capitals across his broad chest. Rather than looking camp, the pink simply served to emphasize his caramel tan, pink lips and startlingly virile masculinity.

As he got closer to Bella and Daisy, the smile on his face was replaced by a look of concern.

'Hey hey, what's the matter?' he asked, sitting down at Bella's feet on the sunlounger. Bella threw her legs over the edge and shifted up to make room for him. In response, he put a well-muscled arm around her shoulder and started to tickle Daisy under the chin with his other hand.

At his ministrations, both mother and daughter gradually stopped crying.

'Do you want to talk about it?' he asked gently.

'Oh no, it's nothing, I'm just being silly. I'm probably over-tired – Daisy hardly slept a wink last night – then Summer invited me to go and have a drink and a chat about displaying some of my paintings at the Art Resort, only I can't go because Andy's got the car, and I suddenly felt . . . well, trapped, I guess.'

She laughed slightly shamefacedly and looked up at him through dripping eyelashes. 'I told you I was being silly.'

'*Non, non*, I understand perfectly. You miss having the freedom, yes?' Something in the way he said it made Bella wonder if he guessed the nature of her recent reminiscences.

'Well, sort of, yes, I . . .'

'*Pero no es problemo*,' Jorge smiled. 'I can give you a lift. I have some errands I must make near the Art Resort anyway. Then I pick you up, and give you a lift back in – what – one hour? Two hours?'

'Could you really? Are you sure it would be no trouble?'

'No trouble at all. You go and fetch whatever you need – I would like to see your paintings, very much – and I shall look after Daisy. Go go go!' he added, shooing her towards the finca.

Her canvases were stored flat in a couple of old suitcases in the guest room, and now she quickly rifled through them, picking out ten that she thought would be most suited to the Art Resort, and transferring them to a smaller, lighter zip-up holdall. Then she nipped next door into her bedroom to check her reflection in the small unframed mirror she had propped up on top of a chest of drawers.

Jesus Christ, she looked horrendous, her eyes redrimmed from crying and puffy from lack of sleep, her face blotchy, hair lank and greasy in its habitual ponytail. The faded black T-shirt did absolutely nothing for her complexion, and after a moment's thought she swapped it for a white vest top, which also necessitated a change of bra. After shaking her hair out of its ponytail, spraying on some dry shampoo, mussing it up with her fingers and retying it, she studied herself in the mirror and grinned reluctantly. At least her cleavage drew attention away from her face.

When she walked back outside, Jorge was sitting with Daisy grinning happily on his lap. He let out a low whistle and kissed his fingertips.

'Wow, what a transformation. *Que bella*, Bella!' Bella tried to ignore the happy warm feeling suffusing her at the compliment. 'You have everything you need? Everything Daisy needs?'

'What do you think?' Bella indicated the mountain of baby essentials she had lugged outside and they both laughed.

'OK then, let's go. *Vamos a la playa!*'

'God, this is heavenly.' Bella took a sip of white wine and gazed out at the waves lapping the shore. Ambient chill-out music wafted out from inside the Art Resort to where she and Summer were sitting under a rainbow-striped parasol at one of the whitewashed wooden tables set up in the sand. Daisy was at long last sleeping soundly in her buggy and all seemed right with the world. 'I was going a bit stir crazy, stuck on my own in the finca with a screaming baby – even though it's a beautiful finca, and I love my screaming baby more than life itself. That doesn't sound too horribly selfish, does it?'

'Of course it doesn't. You've gotta get out from time to time.'

'Thanks so much for thinking of me. And thank God for Jorge, too,' Bella added, smiling at the thought of him.

'Oh, I'm sure he had something else to do around here,' said Summer with a dismissive wave of her hand. 'Jorge would never put himself out for somebody unless there was something in it for him.'

Bella looked at her curiously, but decided to leave it for the moment. No point in arguing when Summer had been so incredibly kind and helpful, compiling that long list of useful emails and phone numbers and talking Bella through each of them. They had also been through her paintings, and Summer and Britta had deemed them all worthy of hanging in the gallery, which was enormously gratifying. Now Britta had gone to do some work on her computer – 'the business can never be left to take care of itself,' she had said with a wry smile as she went inside to her office – leaving her daughter and Bella to bond.

'And you must tell Andy to make sure his phone is charged if he's going to abandon you and Daisy all day, taking the car with him,' Summer added sternly. Andy's phone had gone straight to voicemail every time Bella had tried to call him from Jorge's car, and she'd had to conclude that his battery had gone. 'What if there had been an emergency?'

'Yes, you're right,' said Bella, starting to feel slightly angry now she thought about it. What if there *had* been an emergency? 'He'll be feeling the edge of my tongue when he gets back,' she added, like a comedy battleaxe or fishwife; something pre-feminist from a Fifties black-and-white movie.

'Awww, don't be too harsh on him. He's only a man.'

'True. And he's *my* man, and I love him to bits.' She looked over at the radiant blonde sitting opposite her. 'What about you, Summer? Is there a man in your life?'

'Nobody.' Summer pulled a sad face, too ashamed to tell her new friend about David.

'But you're so beautiful! I can hardly believe it. I suppose, when you look like you do, you learn to be awfully choosy.'

Summer had to bite back her laughter, still thinking of David.

'I wouldn't say that. I don't know. Sometimes I wonder if there's something wrong with me. I don't believe I've ever been in love, not properly.'

'Not even with Jorge?' Bella teased, then stopped when she saw the look on Summer's face. 'Oh, sorry, I . . .'

'Jorge was a long time ago.' It was clear that that was all she had to say on the matter. Then she smiled again. 'It's weird, though. The keener they get, the more I go off them. Is that normal?'

'I've no idea.' Bella laughed. 'I'm certainly no expert on relationships.'

'Well, you seem to have a pretty good one with Andy.'

'True.' Bella gave a happy sigh as she looked out at the

tranquil bay, feeling the spring sunshine warm on her shoulders.

'But what about before? Were you ever "in love", the way it's shown in books and movies?' Summer persisted, suddenly desperate to know. Despite being generally well liked, she had few female friends, and had always found it hard to get close to people. But it felt natural, somehow, to confide in Bella.

'I thought I was, once.' Bella leaned forward conspiratorially, glad to be able to share this bit of gossip – she might be a boring old mother now, but she had at least gone out with a film star, back in the dark ages of her past. 'You know the actor Ben Jones?'

'Ben Jones?' Summer furrowed her lovely brow. '*The* Ben Jones? Gorgeous blond movie star Ben Jones?'

'The very same. It was years ago, before he was famous – well, he was starting to be a little bit famous – and still living in London . . .'

'No way!' said Summer. 'Wow, that's so cool. So what happened?'

'I walked in on him in bed with . . .' Bella had been about to say 'my best friend', but Poppy would be in Ibiza over the summer and she didn't want to give Summer a bad impression of her before she'd even met her. It had taken a lot to forgive Poppy, but there were mitigating circumstances, her remorse was total and it had been water under the bridge ever since Bella had fallen in love with Andy. '. . . somebody else.'

'Shit. Every woman's worst nightmare.'

'Yup,' said Bella. 'Without a doubt one of the most awful moments of my life.'

'So how did you meet him?'

'We'd been friends for ages, but I'd always thought he was way out of my league. I was slimmer then, though . . .'

'Oh, Bella, enough about your weight,' laughed Summer. 'You look great.'

'Thanks,' Bella smiled, feeling the waistband of her miniskirt digging into her flesh and not believing a word of it. 'Anyway, we first kissed at Glastonbury – God, it was good . . .' She shut her eyes and breathed in the smell of the sea, lulled back into the memory by the rhythmic sound of the waves licking the shore, the late afternoon sun now seeping deep into her bones.

'And?'

'And the rest!' Bella opened her eyes and giggled guiltily, feeling disloyal to Andy. 'I never was one for playing hard to get. And then – well, we were an item for a while . . .'

'So what was it like, being in love with somebody almost famous?'

Bella paused to think. Summer was so sweet and open that she wanted to give her a proper answer.

'To start with, it was incredible,' she said, remembering the absolute ecstasy she'd felt at the knowledge that Ben Jones, of all people, felt the same way about her as she did about him. Well, kind of. Then she remembered all those evenings spent home alone, waiting for him to come back from drinks with models after shoots, the permanent anxiety gnawing away at her, the feeling that she could never quite trust him.

'And then, to be honest, it was shit,' she added, and both girls burst out laughing.

'Hi, honey, I'm home!' shouted Andy, pushing open the finca's heavy wooden front door. He couldn't wait to see Bella and Daisy, and was furious with himself for not noticing his phone battery had been so low. He normally charged it overnight as a matter of course, and he and Bella liked to stay in touch with hourly texts on days they were forced to be apart.

'Bella!' he called, more loudly this time. 'I'm home!'

She was probably putting Daisy to bed, he thought, bounding up the spiral stone staircase and bursting into the sunny little nursery, his arms outstretched to give her a hug. Seeing no sign of them, he frowned. They must be in the garden, although surely it was past Daisy's bedtime now?

It might not have been all that easy for Bella to get her to settle, of course. Andy guiltily remembered turning over and going back to sleep, several times, after being woken by Daisy's crying during the night, leaving Bella to deal with it. His own justification that he had to be up early for the first of today's many meetings rang slightly hollowly in his ears now, and he vowed to be a more hands-on father if tonight was another sleepless one.

'Bella! Daisy!' he called as he walked out through the French windows, starting to worry ever so slightly. Why wasn't Bella responding?

Once he'd searched the whole garden, his long legs making short work of the luscious, overgrown grounds, he was out of his mind with fear. Where were they? Even though it wasn't far to San Carlos, their nearest village, probably a half-hour walk at the most, it was a half-hour walk down a steep winding road around whose corners cars screeched with foolish haste. Not a walk any mother pushing a buggy would consider attempting in a million years.

Automatically he reached into his pocket for his phone, before remembering that it was out of juice. They hadn't got around to sorting out a landline yet. Damn, shit and bugger. He rushed inside to plug it into the charger, his mind spinning. Now, think logically. Somebody must have given them a lift somewhere. A woman and a baby couldn't simply disappear into thin air. But if that were the case, why hadn't she left him a note?

Worry now having settled into his stomach in a tight knot, he opened the front door again and looked out at the beautiful rural landscape in despair. Where were they? At that moment, to his immense relief, he heard a car rumbling up the steep dirt track of their drive. But his joy at seeing Bella, chatting and joking about something in the passenger seat, as the convertible BMW ground to a halt, turned to anger as soon as he saw who was driving the car.

'Bella, where the hell have you been? I've been out of my mind with worry.'

'Shhh, darling, Daisy's finally got to sleep, and we don't want to wake her. Thanks so much for the lift, I'd have been lost without you,' she added, kissing Jorge on both cheeks before leaning over to open the car door. But Jorge was too quick for her, gallantly getting out first, walking round to open her door for her, then reaching into the back to unfasten Daisy's car-seat.

'Here, let me take Daisy,' said Andy. 'Thanks,' he added as an afterthought, attempting a tight smile.

'*De nada.*' Jorge smiled. 'I merely came to the rescue of a damsel in distress.' At this both he and Bella started laughing, which irritated Andy for reasons he couldn't possibly start to explain.

'So where *have* you been?' Andy asked, more quietly this time, as he walked back inside, carrying Daisy.

'At the Art Resort, with Summer. They've agreed to hang some of my paintings in the gallery, and Summer's put together a list of useful contacts for us. Isn't that sweet of her?'

'Yes, very,' Andy was forced to concur. 'But you could have left me a note or something. I've been worried shitless.'

'I thought I'd be able to tell you, but your phone's been dead all afternoon. By the time I realized that, we were halfway to the Art Resort and it was too late to leave you a note. Anyway, I thought I'd be back before you. I guess I was having such a lovely time that the hours just flew by,' she said, facing him defiantly, knowing that these words would annoy him.

Looking at her, it dawned on Andy that he hadn't seen Bella look so animated and – yes, *sexy* – for some time. She'd caught the sun, her nose spattered with freckles, cheeks flushed pink. Her eyes sparkled, and several strands of hair that had come loose from her ponytail in the open-topped car journey now fell seductively around her face.

'Since Daisy's finally got to sleep,' he said, 'how about we put her to bed, then make the most of having a bit of time to ourselves?

'I think,' responded Bella, smiling, 'that's the best idea you've had in ages.'

6

'How bloody amazing is this?' Poppy grinned at Damian from the passenger seat of his convertible vintage Mercedes as she cracked open another beer and gestured around at the spectacular Southern Californian scenery. The car was snaking its way through winding roads, overlooked by vast mountains the exact shade of Burnt Sienna that Poppy had had in her paintbox as a child. Desert palms stood ramrod straight in the searing late afternoon sun – no breeze here to ruffle their fronds – and spiky cacti dotted the scrubby landscape in a pleasingly Sergio Leone manner. She whistled the theme of *The Good, the Bad and the Ugly* to emphasize her point.

'Pretty bloody amazing.' Damian smiled back at his wife, who was dressed for Coachella in tiny denim cut-offs, a tie-dye bikini top, Stetson and heart-shaped Lolita shades. 'Oh fuck it, I'm sure I can risk a beer – we're nearly there now.'

'I'd say a beer was mandatory,' said Poppy, leaning over to reach the coolbox on the back seat. 'Your patience, thus far, has been that of a saint!' She was on her fourth already. She cracked open Damian's and handed it to him.

'Thanks, gorgeous.' Damian took a swig. 'I have to say, I'm looking forward to this – and we can be pretty sure it's not likely to rain.'

'I know.' Poppy gazed out again at the mountains and palms and cacti. 'It makes all our past Glastonbury excitement look a bit pathetic, doesn't it?'

'No! Come on, Pops, we had some incredible times – even if we were knee-deep in mud and shivering to death.'

'You're selling it well. But yeah, of course we had some incredible times.' Poppy looked over her shades and smiled at Damian. 'Remember that night in the Green Fields . . .?'

'I'll never forget it.' Damian smiled back fondly, remembering. 'SHIT!'

They had rounded another bend, and the previously open road stretched out before them with the worst traffic either of them had ever seen. As they got closer, it became apparent that everyone was en route to Coachella. Cars backed up against rainbow-painted camper vans, myriad genres of music pounded from thousands of iPod speakers and you could almost taste the excitement in the air.

'Oh God, I've got to get some pre-festival footage,' said Poppy, taking out her phone to video the scene. She was meeting the crew at Coachella itself, but as the Merc drew almost to a halt behind a Jeep full of giggling, stoned twenty-somethings, she realized she might have a bit of TV gold on her hands.

'Hey, guys – how'd you like to be on TV?' she shouted over at them.

'Dude, you don't shoot TV shows on your *phone*,' drawled a boy with a goatee and a woolly hat pulled down low over his ears. He must have been absolutely sweltering. 'D'you think we're like dweebs?'

'Not at all,' smiled Poppy. 'My crew's waiting for me at the festival but I think our techie people should be able to get *something* off my phone footage, even if it is a bit grainy. It'll add to the atmosphere.' She continued to smile brightly and Damian looked at her admiringly. His wife was nothing if not persistent, and extremely good at her job.

'Omigod, I recognize you!' yelled one of the girls, who was wearing a denim waistcoat over a floral maxidress, her dark brown hair hanging to her shoulders in hippy-ish plaits. 'You're Poppy Wallace! She's not shitting us, guys. We're going to be on MTV!'

'Something like that, yeah.' Poppy smiled again. 'So you're happy for me to video you?'

'Uh-huh!'

'Sure thing.'

'Fuck, yeah!'

All the jeep's passengers had now turned, waving and giggling madly, to face Poppy. She knelt up on her seat to get a better angle.

'So have you come far today?'

'University of Berkeley,' they chorused, with much whooping and cheering.

'And is this your first Coachella?'

A few hundred metres down the road Filthy Meadows surveyed the scene from the air-conditioned luxury of his enormous tour bus.

'Told you we should have taken the jet,' said Grizz through a haze of dope smoke. The roadie was one of Filthy's oldest friends, a giant of a man whose thick black beard and multiple tattoos belied his gentle nature.

'I kinda like it,' said Filth. 'Old school. Those kids are having a great time.' He gestured out through the tinted windows. Roaches were being passed from car to car, new friendships forged, flirtatious banter exchanged under the blazing desert sun. 'Wish I could be part of it really.'

'Bored with our company already?' Grizz took a swig of bourbon and grinned. The other two occupants of the bus were Len, Filthy's manager, a small bespectacled man who was currently engrossed in a battered old paperback of *Moby Dick*, and Sam the driver, not a fellow renowned for his witty banter.

Filthy laughed. 'How could I be bored with you three? No, I just wanna get down with the kids. Hey . . .' His eyes lit up. 'I'm havin' an idea . . .'

Grizz looked at him warily. Filthy's 'ideas' were invariably hare-brained and distinctly impractical.

'Shoot.'

'Amp me up, Grizz, I'm goin' up top.'

Poppy's questions were drowned out by a sudden loud cheer from the cars and vans a little further up the highway from them.

'What is it? What's going on?'

The Chinese whispers finally reached the jeep, and the girl with the maxidress and plaits excitedly shouted to Poppy,

'It's Filthy Meadows! Look, up there, standing on top of his tour bus. It looks like he's gonna play something . . .'

And on cue, the first chords rang out across the desert.

Poppy stood up in the seat of the convertible to get a better view.

'Careful, Pops,' said Damian.

'Don't worry, darling, I've a phenomenal sense of balance.' Poppy grinned. 'Oh, look at Filth! Isn't he a legend?'

Filthy was giving it his all on top of the tour bus, treating his fans to an impromptu gig that they'd never forget. Poppy and Damian were edging nearer now, as their lane of traffic was moving ever so slightly more than the one the tour bus was stuck in, and Poppy trained her video phone on the gyrating bare-chested, leather-jean-clad figure as he screamed out the chorus of one of his greatest hits. All the festival-bound hipsters and hippies screamed along with him.

Soon the Mercedes had drawn up next to the tour van, the traffic in both lanes at a complete standstill now.

'Filth!' yelled Poppy, waving wildly at him from behind her video phone. 'Over here! It's Poppy! Poppy Wallace!'

'Poppy?' Filthy broke off mid-song to smile at her. Poppy had been able to wind him around her little finger ever since Jack had first introduced them a couple of years ago at an awards after-party. 'Fuck, man, you look hot!' He winked. 'Hey, you filming for your TV show?'

Poppy nodded.

'Wanna join me up here? The view's great . . .'

'*Really?*' Poppy couldn't believe her luck. Her bosses were *so* going to love this.

'Help her up, Grizz,' Filthy shouted over to his friend, before launching back into song.

'See you later, darling,' Poppy grinned at Damian, handing him her beer before clambering over the Merc's wound-down window into Grizz's enormous arms.

Once on top of the tour bus, she took around half a minute's footage of all the people cheering from their cars, of the mountains and the desert, before training her phone back on herself.

'This is Poppy Wallace, reporting from the road to Coachella, and boy, have we got a treat in store for you. I'm standing on top of Filthy Meadows's tour bus – yes, you heard that correctly – *the* Filthy Meadows – and he's treating us all to a free desert concert! See for yourselves.' She turned the phone on to Filthy, who had come to the end of the song.

'Thank you, ladies and gentlemen, boys and girls,' he shouted. 'Nothing like a captive audience, huh?' A ripple of laughter ran through the crowd. 'I'd like to dedicate my next one to this lovely lady standing right next to me up here on top of the world. Poppy Wallace, this is for you.' And he launched straight into the unmistakable chords of 'Sexy Green-Eyed Woman'.

This is one of those moments that you'll remember for the rest of your life, Poppy told herself, unable to stop the enormous smile spreading across her face, but keeping a steady hand on her phone, professional to the last.

Damian, watching her with pride and awe, finished both their beers. And then he thought: *Fuck. Tamara's going to go apeshit.*

Tamara, 20,000 feet in the air above them, was blissfully unaware that her father-in-law-to-be was serenading another woman with what she had come to think of as 'her song'.

Jack's private jet was luxuriously appointed, with thick cream carpets and large armchairs upholstered in the softest cream leather. Jack and Ben, sitting towards the front of the plane, were getting excited about the festival and drunk on champagne.

Natalia, not wanting to make small talk with Tamara, was flicking through the latest *Vogue* as she sipped her champagne. Her silk Pucci minidress with its signature brightly coloured swirly patterns was not what you'd call Coachella-chic, but Natalia didn't do dressing down – not since that brief blip when she'd gone incognito in Thailand a couple of years back. She couldn't have cared less about the festival, but she realized it was important for Ben to be seen there with his Hollywood buddies; she intended to stay in the background as much as she could.

Tamara, bored and petulant as she stared out of the jet's window at the desert and mountains below, wasn't excited about the festival either. Jack and Ben were engrossed in boy chat about which rock bands they were most psyched about seeing, and hadn't paid her nearly enough attention for the duration of the flight. But the main reason she wasn't looking forward to Coachella was that everybody got so fucking wasted at festivals. And when you were sober, there was nothing more boring than being surrounded by drunken, drugged-up assholes.

Tamara remembered the hell of drying out – *three times* – all too vividly. Even though she'd been incarcerated in the most expensive rehab centres in the States, no amount of freshly laundered linen, no number of sparkling swimming pools could compensate for the nightmares, nausea, shakes, sweats and sheer physical pain she had endured in order to get clean. There was no way she'd risk going through that again; even one drink could be enough to send her straight back on the road to misery.

But the Coachella pantomime had to be played out. Tamara had to appear in all the magazines looking cool as she and Jack outdid their Hollywood peers with gratuitous public displays of affection. Even if it did mean putting up with a load of drunken garbage over the next few days.

She took a Chanel compact out of her flashy Gucci handbag and checked her reflection, which cheered her up a bit.

'Hey, Natalia, how do I look?'

Natalia glanced over the top of *Vogue*.

'Great,' she said.

Like a cheap Vegas slut, Natalia thought, conveniently forgetting her own background for a second.

Tamara had gone down the shorts, boots and bikini top route that a lot of girls followed for Coachella. But her silver chainmail bikini top barely covered her fake boobs, her white denim hotpants showed way too much butt cheek and the green suede platform boots that matched the darkest of her contact lenses reached halfway up her smooth fake-tanned thighs. It was hardly the insouciant festival look that Poppy had nailed so effortlessly.

Jealous old bitch, thought Tamara, turning to stare moodily out of the window again.

'Pretty cool, huh?' smiled Jack, as he and Tamara walked into what was to be their bedroom for the next few days.

Manny Brookstein, *Antony & Cleopatra*'s producer and one of the richest men in Hollywood, had lent Jack his holiday home for their Coachella vacation. Built in Palm Springs' Fifties heyday, the sprawling modernist mansion was a monument to mid-century design. With its clean lines, walls made of glass, interesting geometrical quirks and emphasis on indoor/outdoor living – the entire low-lying edifice was built around a vast pentagonal swimming pool – the 'Brookstein House' was a classic example of what had become known as 'desert modernism'. Jack could imagine Frank Sinatra hanging out with his Rat Pack buddies here, flirting outrageously with beautiful women as they drank potent cocktails by the pool.

'Oh my God, it is!' Tamara suddenly sounded excited, girlish even, and Jack was reminded, not for the first time, how much of her childhood she had lost. 'It's awesome!' He watched indulgently as she ran through the ultra-cool Fifties suite, throwing cupboards open, bouncing on the huge double bed and putting an original vinyl LP of Patsy Cline singing 'Crazy' on the vintage turntable next to it.

She ran over to the sliding glass doors that led to a crazily paved patio, complete with pentagonal bubbling hot-tub that looked out over mountains now glowing deep red in the setting sun. Tall palm trees cast long shadows over the desert.

Jack followed her out, his eyes never leaving her as she danced beside the jacuzzi singing along huskily to Patsy Cline, her lovely body silhouetted against the spectacular view.

'Come dance with me, Jack.'

Jack put his arms around her and together they swayed and spun across the terrace, smiling into one another's eyes, every nuance of the music exaggerated by the magnificence of the scenery.

'Hey, this is just like being in a movie,' Tamara joked and Jack laughed out loud, pulling her closer to him.

'I know the next few days are going to be hard for you,' he whispered into her freshly washed hair. 'I'm proud of you for being so strong, and thought this place might cheer you up some, when we escape the craziness of Coachella.'

Tamara smiled gratefully. That was thoughtful of him, she had to admit.

Jack bent his head to kiss her and her arms entwined themselves around his neck. After a few seconds she pulled away, and before Jack had time to catch his breath, she was standing in front of him fully naked, save for her green suede thigh-high boots. She hadn't been wearing anything underneath the tight white denim hotpants, which were held together by poppers that went all the way between her legs, so she'd been able to whip them off easily. The friction against her bare skin, and anticipation of Jack's reaction had been turning her on all day.

Jack felt himself getting hard immediately. God she was sexy, with that lustrous dark hair tumbling over her slender shoulders, those amazing breasts, slender waist, hips and thighs, the green suede boots leading his eyes straight to ground zero. Her long-lashed green eyes were doe-like now as she gazed up at him with barely concealed mischief.

'Oh God, Tammy, we don't have time for this . . .' They had agreed with Ben and Natalia that they'd dump their bags in their rooms, have a quick freshen up and join them aboard the helicopter they were taking for the final leg to the festival.

'I think we do,' Tamara put one finger inside herself, lifted it to her lips and sucked provocatively, still looking him in the eye.

Just as Jack was starting to weaken, his phone beeped in his jeans pocket.

What's taking you so long? he read. *Nat and I are on the chopper already. Can't wait to get there now.*

He put the phone back in his pocket with regret.

'Ben and Natalia are already on the chopper. We shouldn't keep them waiting . . .'

The sting of rejection was more than Tamara could bear, a metaphorical slap in the face.

'Shouldn't keep *them* waiting?' Her eyes narrowed. 'What about keeping *me* waiting? Oh no, silly me. Nothing's more important than darling Ben. Are you in love with him, Jack? Is that what it is? Is that what your fucking *bromance* is all about?'

The shriller her voice became, the more swiftly Jack's hard-on deflated.

'C'mon, Tammy. I'm sorry, but it's their first Coachella. We can always do this later . . .'

'You'll be too fucking stoned to get it up later.'

'I'm sorry,' Jack repeated, meaning it. 'C'mon, honey, let's put on some warmer clothes and get out there. It's cold in the desert at night.'

Damian kissed Poppy's damp forehead and rolled off her with a groan.

'Great though that was, it's probably wiped me out for the rest of the day.'

'Where's your stamina, darling?' She raised herself up onto her elbows to look him in the eye, then collapsed back onto the pillow. 'Fuck it. Think I spoke too soon.'

'Spent. Utterly spent.'

Their first night at Coachella had been a wild one. They'd ended up backstage with Filthy, several other of the headlining acts and their entourages. The predictable quantity of quality intoxicants had been ingested, and now they were paying the price.

'You realize we're going to have to do it all again later?'

'Let's just enjoy our surroundings for a minute.' Damian put his arm around his wife and gazed up at the ceiling fan whirring overhead. 'Do you think this is actually the coolest hotel in the world?'

The Ace Hotel was certainly the coolest hotel in Palm Springs. An original motel, built in the same era as the Brookstein House, and revamped and overhauled as a kitschy boutique hotel, it had a reputation as *the* hipster hangout in Palm Springs. Poppy and Damian were in one of the Ace Suites, which were decorated in earthy shades and a quirky combination of modernism and Navajo-chic. Mid-century leather furniture sat on cowhide rugs, the whitewashed breeze-block walls of their outdoor shaded patio were adorned with large Native American hangings, and the patio's semicircular stone fireplace kept out the nightly desert chill. Bottles of every type of booze that one could feasibly require lined the shelves of the little kitchenette – several already a tad depleted after Poppy and Damian had toasted love, life and the mountains on their return from Coachella in the early hours of the morning.

'Possibly,' smiled Poppy. 'It sounds like the party's started out there.' She nodded her head in the vague direction of the pool, where the jolly sound of laughter, loud voices and DJs spinning classic house confirmed what she was saying.

'Shall we clear our heads with a swim, then get some breakfast before we head off?' suggested Damian. 'I'm starving. You don't have to start filming for a couple of hours yet, do you?'

'Nope, we've got plenty of time. Oooh, they were thrilled with the Filthy footage, weren't they?'

'They certainly were, you clever thing.' Damian leaned over and kissed her again.

'I'd say more lucky than clever – *in this instance only* – but thanks anyway!'

'Tamara wasn't quite so thrilled, of course.'

'No.' Poppy grimaced. 'Oh well, it was only to be expected. She needs to get over herself. I'm bloody glad we're staying here, however glam their modernist mansion sounds.' She started to rise to her feet. 'Come on, let's head out. A swim and breakfast are sounding more and more appealing by the minute.'

In the Brookstein House, Ben and Natalia were preparing to go their separate ways.

'Sure you don't mind, sweetie?' asked Natalia. 'But it's *so* not my scene.' Her Ukrainian accent now had a slight Valley Girl twang. 'All those people, that stupid little bitch, and today the paparazzi too?' She shuddered.

'Don't worry, Nat.' Ben smiled and shut her up with a kiss. 'I know it's not your thing. You enjoy yourself by the pool.'

Tamara had been at her most poisonous the previous night, flirting outrageously with Ben, Damian and pretty much every random male in the VIP area: she was clearly trying to make Jack jealous, though nobody could quite figure out why. She'd been insufferably rude to Natalia, with constant barbed references to her age and background. And once she'd found out that Filthy had serenaded Poppy with 'Sexy Green-Eyed Woman' ('her' song – even though her eyes weren't really green), she'd lost it completely, stamping her green suede feet, screaming and refusing to have anything to do with any of them, finally demanding that Jack take her back in the chopper immediately. Natalia hadn't been too bothered to leave the festival so abruptly, but both Jack and Ben had, and the (thankfully brief) flight back to the Brookstein House had been fraught with tension. Once they'd landed, Tamara had flounced off to bed, leaving Jack, Ben and Natalia to play cards under the stars and avail themselves of their host's well-stocked drinks tray.

'Oh, I intend to.' Natalia was looking forward to a day on her own, reading under a parasol. She'd already been down to check out the pool area that morning, and the sunloungers looked unbelievably comfortable. 'Thanks, sweetie. I hope you have a *vooonderrrful* day.'

Ben laughed as she hammed her old accent up. 'It'll probably be OK. But something tells me you've picked the long straw here.' He gestured out of the floor-to-ceiling windows at the spectacular surroundings, the sparkling pentagonal pool flanked by desert palms and overlooked by those rugged snow-capped mountains.

'But this is your *first* Coachella,' Natalia couldn't help teasing him. 'I thought you were, like, *so excited*!'

'I am.' Ben grinned boyishly.

Natalia wasn't particularly bothered about the temptations that might confront him at the festival. He faced far worse at work, and there had, in fact, been one near indiscretion since they'd been together. It was only to be expected, beautiful people acting out sex scenes with other beautiful people, and Natalia, of all people, knew how men could be tempted away from their other halves. She had been a professional temptress, after all.

Having got wind of excessively flirty behaviour on set, she'd thought about approaching the girl, but reconsidered.

In his job, there would always be other girls. No, much better to go to the source.

'Sweetie,' she'd said, one evening when Ben had returned late, yet again, from a cast after-party. 'I am very happy that you are becoming so successful . . .'

'Thanks, darling.' Ben had smiled.

'. . . but if you *ever* . . .' Natalia's voice had risen steadily '. . . do anything to hurt me . . .' Ben's grin had faded '. . . I shall disappear. And this time it will be for ever.'

'Oh, Nat—' He had put his arms around her, but she had shaken him off angrily.

'You told me that you loved me, that I would never be unhappy again . . .'

Ben had been overcome with remorse as he remembered all the promises he'd made only a year or two previously; the absolute need he'd felt to protect Natalia, having learned the dreadful details of her past.

'I promise you, Nat, I promise,' he'd told her. 'And I'm sorry.'

Natalia had rewarded him with a night of sex he'd never be able to forget, and he'd realized that whatever the temptations, she really was too special to lose. He'd had no doubt that she'd act on her threat if he strayed, and he'd come to the conclusion, as Paul Newman had so memorably put it, 'Why go out for a hamburger when you have steak at home?'

For Ben, most of his past conquests had been little more than ego boosts, a reflection of his own gorgeousness; now he had the adoration of millions of fans, he didn't need to risk losing Natalia for one more meaningless ego boost.

Now he looked over in the direction of the helipad, and saw Tamara and Jack approaching. Jack was holding an enormous parasol to protect Tamara's face from the searing noonday sun.

77

'Shit, Nat, I've got to go. Much as I'd love to keep Madam waiting, it's not fair on Jack. We'll make up for it later, though. I'll miss you today.'

Natalia shrugged. 'Never mind. I'll miss you too. Now run along . . .' She kissed him on the lips and he took her face in his hands, leaning in for a proper snog that went on for nearly a minute.

'I said run along.' Natalia grinned. 'You don't want to anger it.'

Tamara and Jack walked hand-in-hand around the sun-drenched VIP field, whispering sweet nothings and giggling like a couple of lovesick teenagers. Every few minutes they stopped to gaze into each other's eyes and kiss, giving anybody who was interested a number of perfect photo opportunities. Today Tamara was a little more appropriately dressed, in a short printed dress and cowboy boots, with a Navajo-style headband tied around her long glossy hair. Jack was bare-chested in a pair of old Levis, his lean, well-muscled torso with its scattering of dark hair drawing admiring glances from all the females in the vicinity.

After an hour or so of this charade, Jack pushed a lock of hair behind Tamara's left ear and whispered into it, 'OK, I think we're all acted out. There should be enough material to keep them in magazine sales for months. I could use a beer now.'

'OK, honey.' Tamara smiled back sweetly, her heart sinking. Let the drinking commence. They pushed their way through the heaving crowds of funkily dressed people towards the bar, which was being propped up by Ben, Poppy and Damian, all three of them already doing their best to confirm people's worst preconceptions about British drinking habits.

'Jack! Tamara! There you are! What can I get you both?'
Ben cried effusively, downing his enormous plastic schooner
of lager in one.

'One of those for me.' Jack grinned. 'Hell, make it two.
This is Coachella, right?'

'Right!' Ben high-fived him, and Tamara suppressed a
groan. God their buddy-buddy stuff could be tiresome.

'Diet Coke for me,' she said, wondering how she was
going to get through the next few hours.

Five hours later, everybody was wasted except Tamara, who
was bored and restless. Jack and Ben had been smoking
weed, and while it seemed that Ben could handle his dope,
it tended to make Jack irritatingly silly, giggling like a lunatic
over the least funny things. Poppy and Damian, who'd been
snorting lines of coke in the loos (which couldn't have been
more different from the portaloos at Glastonbury), were
hyper and over-chatty, interrupting other people's sentences
with rambling streams of consciousness about themselves.

They'd moved on from beer and were now sharing a
bottle of JD as they lounged in large leather sofas in the
shaded VIP tent. Glamorous girls with long brown legs,
long flowing hair and retro Seventies-style shades flitted
about, drinking beer from the bottle and talking at the tops
of their voices. Handsome bare-chested dudes with ludicrous facial hair and even more ludicrous (given the
weather) beanie hats lounged on the grass, smoking dope.
There was a strong smell of weed in the air.

'Well, guys, it looks like we're going to need another
bottle,' said Ben, picking up the nearly empty bottle of JD.
Jack started giggling as though this was the funniest thing
he'd ever heard.

'Another bottle,' he spluttered. 'Ha ha ha ha ha,
awesome, dude!'

Tamara looked at him with annoyance. Why couldn't he be more like Ben? It was a real turn-off when guys couldn't handle their poisons. Had she thought about it a little more deeply, she'd have realized that the reason Jack couldn't handle his dope was that he was generally a pretty wholesome kind of guy, not nearly as used to booze and drugs as his more hard-living English friends.

At that moment, though, it was just a turn-off. And Ben – well, as she looked at him through narrowed eyes, she had to admit that he was something of a turn-*on*. He really was quite staggeringly beautiful, even in today's slightly grungy outfit of faded black T-shirt that contrasted nicely with his floppy golden hair, and khaki knee-length shorts that did nothing to disguise his gloriously muscular golden body.

As he got up to go to the bar and replace the bottle of Jack, Tamara found herself also getting to her feet.

'I'll help ya,' she said, smiling sweetly.

'Oh thanks, Tammy,' said Ben in surprise. 'I could do with a hand with the Cokes.'

As she followed him through the crowds, unable to take her eyes off his broad back and perfect bottom, Tamara felt the familiar relinquishing of control. It was happening again, and she was powerless to stop it. When they got to the bar, almost as if she were in a trance, she began rubbing her breasts up against the back of his T-shirt.

Not realizing that it was deliberate, Ben moved forward slightly. Tamara followed suit, increasing the pressure.

Ben looked over his shoulder and frowned.

'Tamara? What's going on?'

In response she put her arms around his back and reached forward to stroke his crotch through the khaki shorts. It was so crowded in the VIP tent that nobody else could see what she was up to.

Ben jumped, then reached down and took her little hands in his big ones, moving them deliberately away from him. He turned around to face her.

'I don't know what you think you're doing,' he said, his cobalt eyes serious as they searched her face for answers. 'But you're barking up completely the wrong tree. Let's pretend that didn't happen, shall we?'

Tamara nodded, her cheeks burning, head cast down like a naughty schoolgirl being chastized by a teacher.

Feeling sorry for her, flattered and guilty that she'd turned him on, just a little bit, Ben added, 'Right then – let's get these drinks in!'

Later that evening, backstage with the bands, the party was rocking. Wild-eyed groupies hand-picked by flint-eyed roadies were flirting with Filth and the band while trying to catch the eye of Jack Meadows and Ben Jones over their shoulders. Jack and Ben, oblivious to the attention of the glamour girls, were pissing themselves at Poppy and Damian's approximation of twerking in the corner, taking imaginary selfies with their smartphones.

They were all so off their tits that nobody noticed when Tamara slipped quietly out of a back exit and joined the student jock who'd approached her earlier, asking for her autograph. She'd conquered her other addictions – the booze, the drugs, *nearly* the fags. But her sex addiction was as full-on as it had ever been, and that incident with Ben at the bar had lit a fire that could only be extinguished one way.

'Hi.' She smiled, grabbing him by the hand and leading him to the empty tent she'd noticed in her wanderings, one of those used to store the bands' instruments when they weren't on stage. She was taking an enormous risk, but that was all part of the thrill.

'You want to screw me, you do it on my terms. Understand?' she said, still smiling sweetly.

'Uh – sure. Yeah, definitely,' said the jock, unable to believe his luck. He'd had posters of Tamara on his wall since high school, and now he was going to get to fuck her? Whatever her conditions were, he could live with them.

'My terms are simple: total secrecy. I am very litigious and I have a lot of money. If any word of this gets out, I will sue the ass off you for defamation. Understand?'

The jock gulped, then shuddered as she put her hand in his pants and started stroking his balls. 'I understand.'

'Great.' She smiled, leaning in to kiss him. 'You won't regret it.'

7

Bella had been coming to the beach yoga classes twice a week for a good six weeks now, and neither Saffron nor India had seen fit to acknowledge her presence. Summer told her not to worry about it, that they were a couple of ill-mannered bitches, but it still stung, especially as she was the only other English participant.

'*Namaste*,' said Britta, straight-backed in the lotus position.

'*Namaste*,' repeated her pupils as the class came to an end.

Bella opened her eyes and let her gaze rest on the sun rising, far above the horizon by now. The sea stretched out in variegated shades of turquoise, deepening to a dark navy. A couple of white sails bobbed in the distance.

This was by far her favourite bit – in fact it made the whole agonizing ninety minutes worth it. That cleansed, wholesome, at-one-with-nature feeling really did have a lot to recommend it. Bella couldn't help but give a wry smile at the contrast between this life and her old one.

At the front, Saffron and India were comparing abs and congratulating one another on how well they had held the most difficult vinyasas, even though Britta was always reminding them all that you should be striving for your own personal best, not comparing yourself to others. Which was hard, Bella thought, when others could balance standing on their heads while you were struggling with a shoulder stand.

Not everybody had been as unfriendly as the English women. Gabriella, a wonderfully un-grand sixty-something Italian *contessa*, was a delight; Leila, a sporty American realtor, had been unremittingly chirpy from the minute she'd handed Bella her card; and Junko, who ran a sushi restaurant in Santa Eulalia, kept inviting her and Andy around for dinner. They hadn't been able to take her up on the invitation yet, but they would. Having left all their friends in London, it was nice to start to feel part of a community – even though, so far, it was mainly ex-pat.

Bella, still gazing out to sea, was overcome by a sudden urge to run into it. She was sweating repulsively from the class, and there was nothing she would have liked better than to take a quick dip. She hadn't had a chance to taste the water yet; what with the constant renovations going on at Ca'n Pedro, Andy tearing his hair out over his new book, and somebody always having to look after Daisy, there hadn't been the opportunity.

'Hey.' The lovely smiling form of Summer loomed up behind her, Daisy in her arms. 'Good workout?'

'Great, thanks. Hello, my angel.' Bella got to her feet and kissed Daisy on the forehead. 'I was just thinking how much I'd love a swim now.'

'Why don't you have one? I can lend you a bikini if you don't have yours with you – I keep a couple down here.'

'Oh, I don't think I could possibly fit into your bikini.' Bella felt embarrassed, yet compelled to tell the truth.

'Nonsense.' Summer smiled. 'Mom's classes have definitely been having an effect on you. You get in that water, if you want to. I can look after Daisy . . .'

'Really?' Bella looked at her in delight. She loved the sea – she'd been able to swim before she could walk, and was intending to teach Daisy as soon as their pool was ready. 'Are you sure we've got time?' She and Summer had arranged to have breakfast together in Ibiza Town, followed by food shopping in the Saturday market.

'Oh, sure, sure.' Summer gave an airy wave of her hand. 'Relax. This is Ibiza.'

It was with some trepidation (and closed eyes) that Bella climbed into Summer's navy-blue string bikini in the Art Resort's nicely kept changing rooms. She hadn't looked at herself naked in a full-length mirror since moving to Ibiza (partly as she and Andy didn't own one – yet). Tentatively she opened one eye, and then the next.

My God, I've got a waist again!

Slowly she smiled, then turned around to inspect the rest of her body as best she could. Bloody hell, Summer was right – the yoga classes actually had been having some effect. Yippee! She did a little dance in the changing room, then picked up the sarong Summer had also kindly lent her. She may have got her waist back but she was still not (and never would be) in the same league as Saffron and India; she wasn't about to give Saffron, who was definitely the queen bitch, an opportunity to sneer at her.

Bella didn't relinquish the sarong until she was at the water's edge. Then she ran, without a backward glance, into the gently lapping waves, going in head first as soon as it was deep enough, gasping as the cool, refreshing water engulfed her. She swam underwater for a couple of minutes before turning back and waving ecstatically at Summer and Daisy on the shore, Summer waving Daisy's little hand back at her.

She was in the sea. She was home. And it felt great.

'So are you planning to stock up on groceries today?' Summer asked Bella, as they sat under large red parasols on the pavement outside Café Madagascar, Daisy gurgling away happily in her buggy beside them. The café, an Ibiza Town institution, was bustling with locals reading the papers over their morning coffees. At the table next to them, a couple of transvestites – clearly still up from the night before – nursed balloon glasses of *hierbas*. Their make-up was starting to run in the morning sun.

'Actually, no, though I would like to make a habit of doing a weekly market shop. We've got lunch guests today, and I thought I'd try my hand at a paella. I've never made one before, but surely it can't be too hard?'

'No way!' Summer laughed. 'I have written so many articles about paella! I can give you all the tips you need.'

'Oh, brilliant! Thank you. I want to do a mixed one – with shellfish, chicken, chorizo and peppers. I'm assuming you fry the chorizo first with the onions, garlic and peppers, so it gives off its spicy oil, then add the rice, then the stock – a bit like a risotto – then all the other bits, according to how long they take to cook?'

'That's pretty much it. You don't need my help at all.' Summer took a sip of her freshly squeezed orange juice. 'Of course it all depends what the fishermen have in stock, and one thing I'd add is don't forget the lemon, saffron and *loads* of parsley. They make all the difference.'

'I'm sure I'd have forgotten at least one of those.' Bella smiled. 'So you do have your uses. What would you serve it with? A simple green salad and some bread?'

'I guess. Though it depends how many of you will be eating, of course.'

'Just the four of us – we've invited Jorge and Henri to join us.'

Summer looked taken aback. 'Jorge and Henri? Have you been seeing much of them, then?'

'Oh yes. Jorge's been so helpful – today he's delivering this enormous antique mirror we found to go in our bedroom. And Henri's a lovely old chap. So this lunch is a kind of thank you from us.'

'I see,' said Summer, frowning slightly.

'What is it? Don't you like them? I thought you and Jorge were childhood sweethearts?'

'Is that what he told you? Well, yes, I guess it was something like that. Oh, sorry, don't listen to me. You're right about Henri – he is a charming man. And Jorge. Well, Jorge's . . . Jorge. Just be a little bit careful around him, huh?'

'Is there something I should know about him?' Bella was starting to worry a bit now – though it was difficult to feel worried about anything much on such a lovely day.

'No, no – of course not. Sorry, I shouldn't have said anything.' At that moment the waiter arrived with their food and Summer seized gratefully on the interruption. 'Ah *tortilla*! Breakfast of the gods!'

They had both ordered slices of *tortilla Española*, with a large platter of juicy fuchsia watermelon chunks to share.

'Oh *yum*. Heaven.' Bella took a bite of the tortilla, which oozed savoury, just-set egginess.

'Uh-huh. And a perfectly balanced meal in itself.'

Bella laughed.

'I mean it. You get protein from your eggs, carbs from the potatoes, and *plenty* of vitamins and minerals – not to mention *thousands* of antioxidants – from the onion and garlic.' She grinned. 'As I said – a perfectly balanced meal in every bite.'

'You make healthy eating sound so simple.' Bella found something more to like about Summer every moment she spent with her.

'That's because it is simple.' Summer's golden face glowed under the red parasol. In flat sandals and a gossamer-light short, floaty cotton dress in shades of indigo, navy and white, with her streaky blonde hair loose around her shoulders, she was the epitome of laid-back island chic. Bella, looking at her, felt suddenly dowdy in her denim miniskirt and T-shirt. It was about time she had some new clothes.

'Hey, Summer!' A short, swarthy man wearing knee-length combat shorts and a linen tunic top was waving enthusiastically and approaching their table. Summer suppressed a sigh.

'Hi, David,' she said coolly, proffering one smooth brown cheek to be kissed. 'This is my friend Bella, and this is Daisy.' She smiled as she nodded towards the buggy. 'They live in San Carlos, moved here from London – what? A couple of months ago?' She raised her eyebrows at Bella.

'Yes, nearly. Hi, David.' Bella smiled, holding out her hand for him to shake.

'Welcome to Ibiza,' said David. His accent was educated NY, his handshake firm and dry. 'I'm Summer's editor on *Island Life*.'

'Cool, great to meet you! I love your website! I was completely addicted to it in London before we moved here.'

'Wow, a fan!' David grinned wolfishly and Bella grinned back. 'Do you mind if I join you for coffee?' He sat down in an empty chair.

'No, of course . . .' Bella started, but Summer cut her off.

'Sorry, David, but we've nearly finished and then we're hitting the market. See you on Monday, huh?'

David's grin faded.

'Yeah, well, I don't have time to hang about anyway.

Fashion show at Ushuaïa this afternoon. I might find me a hot model.'

'You do that,' said Summer.

'Sorry it was so short and sweet,' said Bella, smiling.

'I'm sure our paths will cross again,' said David, and stomped off in the direction of the harbour.

Shopping in the market with Summer had been great fun, thought Bella as she pushed Daisy's buggy through the ancient winding streets behind the harbour to where she had parked the jeep. The buggy had been worth the extortionate amount of money they'd spent on it, as it doubled now as an extremely capacious shopping trolley, laden with colourful fresh produce.

All the stallholders knew Summer, and she had bartered to get the best price for the spankingly fresh clams, mussels, squid and langoustines for Bella's paella. 'Hey, smell this,' she'd exclaimed, as she held an enormous lemon, burstingly ripe and fragrant, to Bella's nose. 'Hey, smell this, Daisy!' The baby had grinned and gurgled in appreciation.

Yes, thought Bella, it had been her lucky day when Jorge had introduced her to Summer.

Now she meandered happily through Ibiza Town's back streets, lined with restaurants, bars, chic boutiques and a surprising number of pharmacies. The tourist season hadn't started properly yet (the club opening parties at the beginning of June heralded the start of the summer craziness), but there were plenty of cool- and not-so-cool-looking local residents going about their weekend business. The sky above the tall buildings was a cloudless blue, but the warren of streets was cool and shady.

Bella stopped as something caught her eye in the window of one of the island's many impossibly chic clothes shops.

Bloody hell, that dress was to-die-for! Bella stood and stared at it for a full minute before saying to Daisy, 'What do you think, darling? Could Mummy get away with it, do you think? Or is she too old and fat? Well, only one way to find out.' And she pushed the buggy into the shop.

'*Hola*,' smiled the pretty young shop assistant. All the shop assistants (and bartenders, and policemen) were young and pretty in Ibiza. '*O que bonita!*' She rushed over to Daisy and crouched down by the side of her buggy, blowing raspberries at her.

'*Hola*.' Bella smiled back, watching the girl fondly. The Spanish did love their babies. '*Um – habla Ingles*?' She was going to brush up on her Spanish if it killed her.

'Uh-huh. Sure.'

'I'd like to try on that dress in the window – the white one. Sorry – hardly narrows it down, does it?' The girl laughed. Everything in the shop was white. 'The long floaty one, with the embroidery on the bodice.'

'Oh, that's a beautiful dress,' said the girl. 'You'll look great in it. Size – medium, I guess?'

'I hope,' Bella joked.

The empire-line maxidress was made of the sheerest white cotton voile, with a double-layered fluted skirt that swished around Bella's ankles. The intricately embroidered bodice tied, halter-style, at the back of her neck. Bella finished tying the ties, shook her hair out of its ponytail, so it fell to her shoulders, and finally allowed herself to look in the mirror.

Yay! Pre-pregnancy, all of her favourite dresses had had halter-necks, but she hadn't worn one for over eighteen months now, feeling too fat and flabby. It seemed that the yoga classes that had worked wonders on her waist had worked wonders on her arms too. The flesh actually stopped moving when she did! The empire line gave a fabulously flattering silhouette and the white was great against Bella's dark hair and eyes, to say nothing of the tan she'd already picked up from living in such a glorious climate.

'How does it look?' asked the girl.

Bella pushed the curtain open and walked into the shop, smiling.

'Wow! You look beautiful!'

'Thanks! I love it! What do you think, Daisy my darling?'

'Doesn't your *mama* look pretty, huh?' said the girl.

'I feel like the Cadbury's Flake girl,' Bella mused, more to herself than to the girl, on whom she assumed the cultural reference would be lost. 'OK, I'll take it. Actually, can I keep it on? I never want to take it off!'

It would be nice to wearing something decent in front of Jorge, for once. Of course she wanted to look good for Andy, too, but he'd seen her at her best *and* worst, and there was nothing wrong with craving a bit of ego-boosting attention from somebody who wasn't the father of your child. Especially if that somebody looked like Jorge.

'Been shopping then?' said Andy, as Bella walked into the outhouse at the bottom of the garden, which he'd turned into his study, Daisy in her arms. 'Wow! You look like a film star. Hello, darling!' He took Daisy from her, kissing the top of her head, and Bella did a little twirl.

'Thanks! Isn't it pretty?' She grinned. 'Have you had a productive morning?'

'I have actually.' Andy's intelligent eyes gleamed with excitement behind his glasses. 'I've finally cracked something that's been bugging the hell out of me for weeks. At least, I think I have.' He smiled ruefully and Bella kissed him on the cheek.

'Fantastic. Aren't you clever? Now you can relax and enjoy lunch properly.'

'Lunch? Oh shit, I'd completely forgotten . . .'

'How can you have forgotten? We talked about it this morning. Such an absent-minded old professor.' Bella put her arms around him and Daisy and kissed them both affectionately. 'I've got all the ingredients for a fabulous paella. Jorge and Henri won't be here till two thirty, but I'd better get cracking all the same. Come on, my sweet angel, let's go and have some lunch.'

Bella took Daisy back and floated out of the door in her long white dress, leaving Andy staring, somewhat despondently, in their wake. His book was never going to get written at this rate.

They had made great progress on the house in the last couple of months, although the biggest rooms – the downstairs living area and the kitchen – remained resolutely unfinished. Bella had decided to tackle Daisy's nursery first, and now the sunny little yellow-and-white room, with its gingham curtains, bookshelf full of Beatrix Potter hardbacks and Beatrix Potter mobile hanging over the painted wooden cot, was the stuff of childhood (or possibly more accurately, motherhood) dreams.

Next up had been Bella and Andy's bedroom. The initial decision to keep everything white had been thrown by her discovery of a glorious patchwork quilt at the antiques fair in Santa Eulalia. In shades of red, white and cream, the multi-patterned floral patchwork looked fabulous against their French antique wrought-iron bed, on top of which Bella had piled more cushions in vibrant scarlet silk, red-and-white stripes, gingham, the lot, telling herself that there was nothing wrong with a bit of red for passion in the bedroom. Against the plain whitewashed walls, floaty white voile curtains and dark wooden floorboards, the effect was wildly romantic.

Bella had painted the spare room, and put up curtains, but they had yet to acquire any furniture for it. Still, plenty of time for that before Poppy et al turned up in July. The upstairs bathroom hadn't been touched, so they had to content themselves with the downstairs wet room, which was an absolute joy, with its huge window looking all the way down to the sea.

The kitchen had been gutted, and Bella had been thrilled to discover an original fireplace hidden behind one of the horrible plastic Seventies units. A large Belfast sink had been fitted, and the new cooking range and American fridge delivered, so it could actually function as a kitchen, while they waited for the rest of the units to turn up. Bella also wanted to buy a big wooden kitchen table, eventually, but as they were eating all their meals outside at the moment, there was no rush for that.

So now, still in her beautiful new dress, she was chopping her onions, garlic and red peppers at an old plastic table, in a huge empty room with a brand-new sink, fridge and cooker in it. Daisy was sitting in her high chair next to her, and she had positioned the table so that they could look out of the window, at the glorious view down to the sea, as she chopped.

'It's lovely living here, isn't it darling? Aren't we lucky lucky lucky, as Kylie used to sing?'

Daisy giggled as her mother launched into song.

'*Hola*! Bella!' Bella heard the voices and the tentative tapping at the heavy wooden front door as she stood at the stove, stirring her paella. Daisy was sleeping peacefully upstairs in the nursery.

'It's open! Come in!' she shouted. Wiping her hands on the apron she'd belatedly thought to throw on to protect her delicate white dress from greasy red splats of chorizo oil, she turned to face her guests.

Jorge, in tight black jeans and yet another bicep-revealing sleeveless T-shirt, was bearing a bottle of rosé wine and a large smile. Henri, standing behind him, was clutching a lovely bunch of flowers that looked as though they'd been picked from his garden.

'Oh, they're beautiful. Thanks so much.' She buried her face in the bouquet and breathed in the heady scent of lavender. 'Hi, Henri; hi, Jorge, how lovely to see you.' She kissed them both. 'I'll just put these in some water, and this in the fridge, and then we can all go and have drinks outside. The paella's almost ready and it won't do it any harm to rest for a bit.'

'What about your mirror?' Jorge smiled, his black eyes gleaming as they roamed lazily over her face and body. 'It is probably best we bring that in now, *si*? We may not have the energy after lunch!'

'Good point.' Bella laughed, her cheeks ever so slightly flushed. 'I'll get Andy to give you a hand. Thanks so much for doing this – it's hugely appreciated.' She made towards the French windows to get Andy from his study, but he was already approaching them, having heard the arrival of Henri's pick-up truck.

'Hi, Henri; hi, Jorge,' he said, shaking hands with them. 'Great to see you both. Right, shall we bring this bloody mirror in then? Bella's gone a little bit over the top with her romantic interior vision this time, but hey – what can you do?'

But by the time the enormous, ornately framed (and very heavy) antique was propped up against the wall opposite the bed, all three men had to admit that Bella's judgement had been correct. The room looked more than twice the size, with the mirror reflecting both the gorgeous bed and the colourful view out over the balcony into the luscious garden.

'Oh God, it looks fabulous! Thank you so, so much.'

'Yes, thank you,' smiled Andy. 'She may be full of highly impractical flights of fancy, but Belle does seem to know what's going to look good.' He gave her a little squeeze and kissed the top of her head.

'She has an artist's eye,' said Henri.

'This is a room made for passion,' said Jorge, flashing Bella a glance.

'Yes – well. That was certainly thirsty work,' said Andy. 'I don't know about you guys, but I'm ready for a drink.'

'*Mon dieu*,' said Henri, wiping his mouth on a napkin. 'You cook like a French woman.'

'Thanks!' Bella beamed at the compliment. 'But Summer gave me the best tips. I'm sure I'd have forgotten the saffron, or something else, if she hadn't been there in the market today.'

'You were with Summer today?' Jorge looked a tad uneasy as he took a sip of his rosé wine.

'Yeah, I had yoga this morning – *and* my first swim of the year. It was gorgeous!' Bella, happy and replete after the delicious lunch and half a bottle of rosé, smiled at the memory. 'Summer looked after Daisy. Then we went for breakfast in Ibiza Town before hitting the market.'

'And hitting the shops,' laughed Andy.

'Only one shop! Besides, this is the first thing I've bought for myself since giving birth to Daisy.'

It was true. Feeling fat and frumpy wasn't terribly conducive to clothes shopping, so Bella had poured all her shopping urges into the acquisition (mainly online) of garment after exquisite little garment for Daisy. Minuscule dresses, tiny cardigans, T-shirts, jumpers, hats, booties, dungarees – all of which she grew out of in a couple of months, but Bella didn't care. The very sight of the adorable little scraps of fabric was enough to turn her heart to marshmallow.

'That dress you are wearing now, it is your new purchase?' asked Henri, with a twinkle in his eye. 'But you look ravishing, Bella – *très, très jolie!'*

'Thanks.' Bella smiled again at the second compliment. She could get used to this.

'Très jolie,' repeated Jorge, grinning. Andy stopped smiling and Bella was suddenly aware of how much tanned cleavage her new dress revealed, not to mention the smooth expanse of bare back and shoulder. She shifted in her chair and looked away when Andy tried to catch her eye.

They were sitting around the garden table on the stone patio, immediately outside the French windows that led from the house. A slightly chipped blue-and-white jug containing Henri's bunch of wild flowers sat in the middle of the table, over which Bella had thrown an embroidered white cloth. The bougainvillea-covered balcony that led out from Bella and Andy's bedroom jutted out overhead, providing shade from the afternoon sun. Beyond the patio lay the romantically overgrown garden, with its orange, lemon and almond trees, spiky palms, wild poppies, lavender, rosemary and thyme, all surrounding the magnificent turquoise-tiled pool – still empty, but clean now, and devoid of mould.

'I can't wait to get the pool filled.' Bella tried to divert the subject from how *jolie* she was looking. 'That swim this morning made me realize how much I'm missing it. It will be ready by the time Poppy and Damian come to stay, won't it, darling?'

'Don't worry, it'll be ready in plenty of time for your glamorous Hollywood friends. Honestly, you've known Poppy most of your life.' Andy turned to Henri and Jorge. 'Bella and Poppy have been best friends since they were at school, but now Poppy's a little bit famous, Bella's got this bee in her bonnet about showing off to her that we've got this *perfect life* and *perfect home.'* Bella stuck her tongue out at him, laughing.

'That, I can understand,' said Henri kindly. 'It is only natural, *hein*?'

Jorge was leaning forward eagerly, his ears fully pricked. 'Hollywood? Famous?'

Henri smiled. 'My son, he loves the celebrity gossip.'

'Poppy's not that famous,' said Bella. 'Poppy Wallace?' Both men looked blank. 'Never mind. She's a TV presenter – her show probably hasn't reached Spain yet. But her husband Damian's a screenwriter – he co-wrote the screen-play for *Antony & Cleopatra*.' Jorge let out a low whistle, and rubbed his fingers together in the internationally recog-nized gesture for filthy lucre. 'Exactly. *Rolling in it.* Our other friend, who should be coming with them, is more famous though – Ben Jones?'

'*The* Ben Jones?' Jorge's eyes were out on stalks.

'Oh yeah.' Bella was enjoying the effect her name-dropping was having on her guests. She wished she could tell them that she and Ben had been an item once, but didn't want to rub Andy's nose in it. 'And there was even talk of Jack Meadows and Tamara Gold joining them here.'

'*Jamara*?' Jorge's voice rose by two octaves.

'Yup! There's not room for them all to stay *here*, of course – Ben's other half owns a fabulous villa down on the south-east coast, near Playa s'Estanyol – but you can see why I'd quite like to get the renovations finished before they arrive?' said Bella, shooting a triumphant glance at Andy.

'Sure I can see that!' Jorge leaned back in his chair, evidently having decided to play it a bit cooler. His smile lit up his tanned, handsome face. 'So do you actually know Jack and Tamara?'

'Not personally, but they all seem to have become pretty close. I get regular updates from Poppy. I have to say that Tamara sounds an absolute nightmare!' Bella did love a good gossip.

'She is very sexy, though.' Jorge's chocolate brown eyes gleamed. 'Mmmm.'

'Fake,' said Henri dismissively.

'Bit of both, I'd say,' said Andy, and they all laughed.

'Anyway, we'll be having a pool-warming party when they're here, and you're both very welcome – I'll let you know the exact date nearer the time,' said Bella. 'Though of course I can't *guarantee* Jack and Tamara will grace us with their presence. I must say, I'm dying to meet Jack.'

She had been planning the pool-warming party ever since Poppy had confirmed her holiday plans. She already had quite a few guests in mind: Jorge and Henri; Summer (of course) and her parents – oooh, maybe she'd also invite David, whom she'd met over breakfast that morning; Gabriella and the other ladies from yoga; Pilar, the smiley cat-faced young waitress at Anita's, and Carlos, the good-natured older waiter; Poppy, Damian, Ben and Natalia – her guests of honour; and she was secretly hoping that Jack and Tamara would accept the invitation too. Surely word would get around the island that Tinseltown's golden couple had been at their pool party? Bella wasn't particularly proud of her delight at the prospect of wiping the smug smiles off those bitches Saffron and India's faces.

Summer had offered to help with the catering, and Bella was planning to turn the currently run-down and dilapidated outhouse at the opposite end of the pool to Andy's study into a Balinese-style folly, complete with daybed, lush plants and brightly coloured silks. She hadn't yet confided this to Andy, anticipating more good-natured mockery, but Daisy was fully aware of her plans and approved whole-heartedly.

Bella could just imagine all the happy, glamorous faces lapping up her sunshiny hospitality. She couldn't wait.

8

Summer's kitchen was small, but light and airy, with the same view from the window behind the gas hob as that from her balcony, all the way down over the higgledy-piggledy streets to the boats bobbing on the harbour below. The compact galley with a few tongue-and-groove cupboards above and below, painted in soft shades of dove grey, white and eggshell blue, gave more than a clue to her Nordic heritage; the vivid blue-and-white-tiled splashback, terra-cotta tiled floor and hand-embroidered cloth on her little round kitchen table were pure Ibiza.

She padded barefoot out onto the balcony and picked a generous handful of parsley from one of her colourful window boxes, smiling as the warmth of the sun hit her bare skin, before heading back inside to chop the herb and scatter it over the large pan of spaghetti vongole she'd just prepared. She'd picked up fresh clams from the market after waking early and deciding to make the most of the beautiful morning with an energetic hike in the hills north of Ibiza Town.

She'd certainly worked up an appetite, but even she couldn't eat this much, she thought with a rueful smile.

Normally she'd save some for her dinner, but this evening she and David were going to the opening of a new restaurant close to Cala Jondal. It was awkward that she had to accompany him to these openings, but she *was* food and drink columnist on *Island Life*, and she guessed she'd brought it upon herself.

You made your bed, now you must lie in it. The phrase popped unbidden into her mind and prompted a spontaneous giggle.

Oh well, she'd simply take whatever she didn't manage to eat down to the office this afternoon – there were always grateful takers amongst Summer's colleagues for her delicious leftovers.

She spooned a generous portion of the fragrant, steaming pasta into a shallow bowl and carried it outside onto her balcony with a plate of green salad simply dressed with olive oil and lemon. Returning with a glass of iced water she sat down and contemplated her lunch with satisfaction and a healthy modicum of greed.

Once she'd wolfed most of it down, though, she sighed. Yes, her life was good. No doubt there were a lot of people who would happily change places with her right now – would in fact, she thought, with typical candour, deem her a stupid, spoilt bitch for not being thankful, every day, for the gifts life had bestowed on her.

Yes, the David situation was far from ideal, but the sex was great, she told herself, trying to be fair to her boss. OK, so maybe he had been a little creepy recently, but it wasn't as though she hadn't given him any encouragement. It was about time she took herself in hand and tried to cool things a bit between them.

She sighed again, taking an absent-minded forkful of crisp Romaine lettuce, trying to work out the cause of her niggling dissatisfaction.

What her life was missing, she suddenly realized, laughing at herself, was a bit of old-fashioned excitement. She had been right the first time: she was just a silly, spoilt bitch. Her natural cheefulness having returned, she started to clear up her plates, before washing up and decanting the leftovers into tupperware pots for her colleagues.

Summer ambled through the winding streets of the Old Town, down to the elegant nineteenth-century building, in a gracious tree-lined square, that housed the *Island Life* offices. Wearing a peach cotton spaghetti-strapped playsuit, trimmed with creamy broderie anglaise, her streaky blonde hair held partly back from her face with a simple leather thong, she looked both demure and effortlessly sexy.

'*Hola*, Jose!'

'*Hola*, Summer!'

The ice-cream vendor who sold her a rich chocolate cone broke into a broad grin as she greeted him – a grin that faded into a wistful smile as he watched her walk away, wondering what it could possibly feel like to have such a woman, even if only for one night.

Summer reached the office before she'd finished her ice cream so she stood on the pavement outside, making easy conversation with the doorman, who watched her with the same mixture of fondness and lust as Jose the ice-cream vendor had. She bade him farewell and made her way inside, then up in the beautiful, creaky art nouveau lift to the second floor.

The *Island Life* offices had been modernized a couple of years ago and were now completely open-plan, except for a glass cubicle at the far end from the entrance that housed the editor's lair. Summer knew that David relished sitting inside, able to keep an eye on what his staff were up to while he hid behind his 24-inch Mac.

There were moodboards pinned to most of the walls – glossy pictures of beaches, restaurants, yachts, enticing piles of colourful fruit and veg, bohemian wedding dresses – in fact, there was a *lot* of boho wedding inspiration. The Ibiza wedding market was at all-time saturation point, and you now had to book your venue months, if not years, in advance.

'Hey, guys,' said Summer as she made her way to the desk she shared with the part-time weddings editor. 'Having a good day?'

'Hey, Summer,' they chorused.

'Don't,' groaned Valentina, the very posh half-English, half-Spanish editorial assistant, whom David liked to treat as his personal dogsbody. 'He's been in a foul mood all day – won't even let me out for lunch until he gets back from his, and I'm *starving*. Don't know why he always has to take it out on me.'

Summer guessed that David had a chip on his shoulder, a massive inferiority complex about the dark-eyed little beauty who spoke and carried herself with such aristocratic bearing, but she didn't let on. No point in stirring things up as far as David was concerned. Instead she put an arm around Valentina's slim shoulder and said, 'In that case, you're in luck. I have three portions of spaghetti vongole in here . . .' She patted her leather satchel, grinning, and Valentina's face lit up. 'First come, first served!' she added to the room at large, making her way to the kitchen. Several of her colleagues leapt to their feet to follow her with unseemly haste.

'Darling, could I ask you a massive favour?' asked Valentina, through mouthfuls of garlicky vongole.

'Depends what it is,' smiled Summer.

'I left my iPad in David's office after the editorial meeting this morning. You couldn't go and get it for me, could you? I don't think I could face him biting off my head again today, and he's never as harsh on you as the rest of us . . .'

Summer flinched, instantly on guard, but Valentina's remark appeared to have been innocent, her attention now back on her food. 'God, this is good. I wish I could cook like you.'

'Yeah, sure, I'll get it for you. Do you know where you left it?'

'Probably on his desk.'

The iPad's whereabouts was not immediately apparent, so Summer walked around David's messy desk, shifting papers so she could look underneath. As she did so, she accidentally touched his mouse, causing his screen to light up. A folder full of files appeared on it, all with the prefix NY: NY1, NY2 etc, all the way down to NY63.

Briefly wondering (but not caring much) what was inside them, Summer jumped out of her skin as David loomed up in front of her.

'What the *fuck* do you think you're doing?' he hissed.

'Oh, uh, hi, David, I was looking for my iPad . . .' David's eyes narrowed. 'Oh, here it is!' Summer saw it, grabbed it and held it close to her side, not wanting to get Valentina into trouble.

David shut the door behind them, and speaking far more evenly, said, 'OK. Just get out of here. But don't think because we share a bed you can walk around like you own the place. Don't ever touch my stuff again' – he indicated the rest of the office with a flick of his head – 'otherwise I might let everyone here know *exactly* what has been going on between us. You wouldn't want that, would you, *honey?*'

Summer stared at him mutinously, unable to believe that he was speaking to her this way.

'I told you, get out,' he snapped.

*

Summer had no sooner stepped out of the shower than the doorbell rang. She frowned. David was more than half an hour early. What was he playing at? Still pissed off about the earlier incident in his office, she wrapped a towel around her wet body and walked out of the bathroom into her tiny sitting room, dripping all over the terracotta-tiled floor. Impatiently she buzzed him up.

In less than a minute David had climbed the three flights to her flat. He had dressed up for the evening in a cream linen suit and was flushed and out of breath.

'You know, it's just as bad manners being early as it is late,' said Summer. 'Look at me – I'm not nearly ready.'

David's pupils dilated as he looked at her, taking in the long wet hair dripping down her back, showing off her perfect bone structure, her cool blue eyes. His eyes lingered over the tiny towel that barely covered her glimmering brown body, taking in her beautiful long arms and legs, then he smiled.

'I am, though.' In one swift move, he'd whipped off the towel and taken one full, pert breast in both hands, bending his head to the rosy nipple, which hardened immediately under his lips. Involuntarily, and hating herself for it, Summer threw back her head and moaned.

'That's it, baby. You like that, don't you? Oh *yes*, you like that.' His right hand had now strayed down between her legs and found her hot and wet for him already. The more he played with her, the hotter and wetter she became. Looking up into her eyes, David pushed her gently to the floor, never taking his right hand from between her legs.

He parted her thighs further and gazed at her beautiful body before bending his head and giving her a gentle lick. He was about to increase his tempo when he had another thought.

Summer watched through glazed eyes as David untied the yellow silk tie around his neck. Leaning over her, he grabbed both her wrists and secured them above her head with the tie, fastening the other end to the foot of her desk. He pulled on the knot until it was tight.

'I can do whatever I want with you now. Do you like that, baby? Do you?'

He slid two fingers inside her, using his other hand to gently massage her clit until she was panting and writhing underneath him. Suddenly, abruptly, he stopped.

'What are you doing to me, David?' Summer's voice was hoarse.

'I want you to beg for it, baby.'

Now he was kissing her breasts again, still fully clothed himself and in total control of the situation. Reaching up to the desk, he found what he was looking for. The scented candle was the perfect size and shape, and Summer moaned even more as, ever so slowly, he slid it inside her. When he moved his mouth from her breasts to her pussy, her hips rose from the floor, bucking helplessly against him as he slid the smooth candle in and out, in and out.

'Oh God, oh, David, I, oh God . . .'

He slid the candle out.

'Oh God, David, what? What do you want, Summer? Tell me . . .'

He looked intently into her eyes.

'Oh please just fuck me. Please, please fuck me.'

'Please just fuck me, *David*?' David stressed his own name. 'Please, *David*, I want to feel you inside me?'

'Please, David. I want to feel you inside me. Pleeeease . . .'

'Why didn't you say so before?' With a wicked grin, David undid his belt, opened his flies, and without even pushing his trousers down, thrust his big cock deep inside her. He was bigger and thicker than the candle, and remorselessly, relentlessly he ground into her, again and again, until he felt her start to contract around it. Keeping his cock buried inside, he reached down to touch her clitoris.

The orgasm seemed to go on for minutes.

Summer was furious with herself. She'd allowed him to do it *again*, even after the way he'd spoken to her in his office earlier. And now, at the super-swanky opening of yet another new beachside restaurant, he kept giving her those annoying half-smiles, furtive glances, as though they shared a particularly amusing secret. Which they did, she supposed. His ankle kept pressing against hers under the table, too.

David, for his part, couldn't believe his luck. Summer was looking utterly gorgeous in a short white crochet dress, with her hair tied back in a loose plait. Despite the shortness of the skirt that showed off her beautiful brown legs, the effect was demure – virginal even. As he remembered tying her up, her begging him to fuck her, he felt himself getting hard under the table. That was one to save for the wank bank.

The opening of Aqua, Ibiza's latest beautifully designed, beautifully thought-out 'concept space' was as glamorous as it was predictable. They'd feasted on canapés of wittily styled salmon roe and supped at blue cocktails, before being seated at the large round table that was reserved for the great and the good of the island. The mainly open-air restaurant was perched on a clifftop around the corner from Cala Jondal, the idyllic sandy white beach that was home to the famous Blue Marlin beach bar. The uninterrupted view down to the clear blue sea below was spectacular enough, but to get to this table, the A-list table, you had to walk down a whitewashed wooden walkway that led out onto a whitewashed platform that had been built onto a jutting promontory, totally open to the elements. The sound of the sea gently lapping the shore twenty metres or so below, the background buzz of cicadas and the odd seagull's cry complemented the ambient house music coming from speakers hidden in the rocks.

In the summer months to come, the reservations would be for celebrities – mainly yacht-owners, as it was accessible from the water – but now, at the end of May, all the people around the table were either local media, or silly-rich residents, like Jamie and India Cavendish. It was weird that Jorge Dupont was there too, but that strange, slippery boy seemed to get everywhere.

Now he was talking to India Cavendish, who was pushing her delectable seafood starter around her plate and glugging back the champagne.

'You must know Bella?' Jorge was saying. 'I'm sure Summer told me you do yoga together?'

'Oh, you mean *that* Bella.' India yawned slightly. 'The fat one with the sweet baby?'

Summer, who had heard this, interjected: 'Bella's not fat. She looked great in my bikini the other day.'

India laughed out loud. As the mirthless ripples spread across her bony body, her husband Jamie said, 'I think you've probably had enough, darling.'

Summer studied the two of them, coolly. Much as she disliked India, Jamie was even worse. Tall, with slicked-back dark-brown hair and mean little eyes in a blandly handsome face, he exuded arrogance and insincerity from every over-privileged pore in his body. He hadn't eaten anything, and was now smoking a fat cigar – even before the main course had been served.

What a bastard, thought Summer.

He was also leering at her. She was used to this – he'd leered at her ever since she'd been hired to cook lunch at one of the Cavendishes' private parties, several years previously. That time, he'd tried to snog her, and had sneered when she had pointed out, horrified, that his wife and baby son were outside.

'You have a wife. Don't be disgusting,' Summer had said in her pragmatic, Swedish way.

'My wife is now a mother. She's not fit for anything in bed. But I bet you're lovely and tight and juicy.' He had shoved his hand against her then. 'Aren't you, Summer?'

Resisting the temptation to tell him to fuck off, Summer had removed his hand shakily and said, 'That's for me to know and you to never find out,' before walking back outside, bile rising in her throat.

'Oh, I don't think that Bella is fat,' said Jorge. 'She looks kind of – what's the word? *Voluptueuse*? But the big gossip is that she has some film stars coming to stay.'

'Film stars?' This seemed to perk India up slightly.

'Uh-huh. And not any old film stars – Hollywood royalty!'

'Jack Meadows and Tamara Gold. And Ben Jones,' Summer finished for him.

'You knew?' Jorge looked perplexed. 'Why didn't you say something?'

'It's no biggie.' Summer, who had catered for film stars – if not such illustrious ones – in the past, shrugged. 'Bella asked me if I'd help with the food at her pool-warming party. Oh, look at you, all star-struck,' she teased. The rest of the table laughed too, and Jorge felt himself flushing. Only Summer had the ability to make him feel like a silly little boy.

'I'm looking forward to that party,' said Gabriella. Tonight she was every inch the *contessa* in a scarlet jewelled kaftan, her rich brown hair piled up in an elegant chignon with no hint of grey to betray her age. Real diamonds sparkled at her earlobes and throat. Most of the time Gabriella conducted her life in yoga pants or scruffy jeans and a ponytail, but when she decided to pull the stops out, she went for it. 'I remember Ca'n Pedro from the old days – such a beautiful house. Small, of course, but the garden was always exquisite. It will be interesting to see what they have done with it.'

'What is this party, and why haven't I heard about it?' demanded India.

'Bella's going to have a pool-warming party when her Hollywood friends are here,' said Summer. 'She's hoping that their arrival will coincide with the old pool finally being fit for purpose. But I don't see why you think you should have heard about it – you're hardly bosom buddies.'

'Well, she should have made it her business to know about it,' said Jamie, looking at his wife with disdain. 'Good God, woman, all you have to do is look nice and meet the right people, and you can't even manage that! We should be invited to that party.' He could see himself hanging out with Jack Meadows and Ben Jones, three Alpha males together. He wouldn't mind having a shot at Tamara Gold, too. She looked like a filthy little thing.

'Jamie, you know full well that I am a full-time business woman, *on top of* being a wife and mother.' India glared at her husband through large, hurt blue eyes. He threw his head back and guffawed.

'Business woman? That's a good one. Your "business"' – he made air quotes – 'is nothing but a very expensive hobby, funded by me.' Everybody looked at Jamie with horror. He really was a nasty piece of work. 'Anyway, *darling*, how about you make it your "business" to get us invited to that party?'

'I'm sure I can get you invited to the party, if it means that much to you,' said Summer, feeling sorry for India.

Then she thought, *Shit, what have I done?* Bella didn't want these horrible people at her party.

'Now that's a bit more like it.' Jamie smiled lecherously in her direction. 'Why can't you take a leaf out of Summer's book, darling? Looking particularly luscious tonight, too.'

India, hurt as ever by Jamie leering over other women, even though she knew she should be used to it by now, straightened her back and blinked away the tears that were threatening to spring into her eyes.

Summer ignored Jamie and turned to Gabriella.

'So you know Ca'n Pedro? What's it like? I haven't been there yet, but I know they've been working very hard trying to get it ready before their guests arrive.'

'When I knew it, it was a hippy commune,' said Gabriella. 'Man, the parties they used to have there were wild. Free love and every drug under the sun.'

'You used to go to drug-fuelled orgies?' asked David, trying to picture the elegant sixty-something contessa forty years younger, being roasted by a couple of long-haired hippies. It was surprisingly easy to envisage.

'We all did, darling,' said Gabriella. 'It was Ibiza in the Seventies. What do you imagine we got up to?'

'Well, I don't think Bella's pool party will be a drug-fuelled orgy,' laughed Summer. 'Though it should be a lot of fun.'

'More's the pity,' said Jamie. 'I wouldn't mind going to a drug-fuelled orgy with Tamara Gold.'

'I think you'll find Tamara Gold has been clean for years,' snapped India, pushed almost to the limit of her endurance by her husband's constant sniping, and the painful implications that other women were so much more attractive to him than she was.

'Did you read that in *Heat*?'

'Common knowledge. And fuck you.'

Gabriella raised her eyebrows at David and Summer and continued, 'Funnily enough, I think I met Bella's father at one of those parties.'

'Bella's *father*?'

'Yes, Justin Brown – the photographer? He lives in Majorca, but he was all over the Balearics in those days. A *verrrry* naughty man.' Gabriella smiled. '*Verrry* naughty, but a lot of fun. I made the connection only a few days ago.'

'Have you told Bella?' asked Summer.

'Well, of *course*. I told her this morning at yoga. She didn't seem too surprised.'

'It sounds like this Bella is pretty well connected,' interrupted Jamie. 'You *have* been slack on the social networking front, *darling*.'

'How was I to know?' India sounded sulky again. 'I mean, she looks like she dresses from charity shops. I wouldn't *immediately* associate her with film stars.'

'Hey, can you stop being so rude about my friend?' said Summer.

'Sorry, *sorreeee*.' India looked as if she might be about to cry and Summer felt awful for her, despite everything. It couldn't be easy, being married to such a detestable man. 'I'm not myself tonight,' India added, trying to pull herself together.

'You could do with a bit more meat on your bones, for one thing,' said Jamie. 'Just look at you.' He prodded one of India's thin brown shoulders, protruding out of her exquisite pale yellow chiffon Alberta Ferretti cocktail dress. 'I know I told you not to let yourself get fat, but you didn't have to lose your tits too.'

'I cannot tell you how much I hate you,' India said slowly. She turned to the table at large and added, 'I wish my boy had a nicer father.'

There was silence, punctuated by a couple of nervous giggles. The Cavendishes were clearly out of their tiny minds on something, all normal awareness of what was acceptable to say in public long gone. Summer was pretty sure she knew what they'd been taking *and* who'd given it to them.

'For all I know, he does,' Jamie drawled back. 'Little sod doesn't look anything like me, and you never could keep your legs closed. Before you got old, of course. No one would touch you with a bargepole now.'

'Jamie, that's enough,' said David. 'Don't say things you'll regret in the morning.'

'Are you telling me what I can and can't say to my own wife? I don't take orders from jumped-up little Jews. Oh, fuck the lot of you. This is one of the most boring evenings I've ever had. I'm going out to have some fun.' Jamie downed his champagne in one and stalked away from the beautiful table in its fabulous location, up the whitewashed walkway and into the night. In the silence that followed, the waves lapping at the rocks below sounded much, much louder.

India sat stone-still for about half a minute before bursting into tears. Summer leapt up, ran around and put her arm around the other woman's thin, shaking shoulders.

'I hate him so much,' India sobbed. 'How did I end up married to such a bastard?'

'He's had too much to drink, that's all,' Summer said, trying to soothe her. She didn't want to defend Jamie Cavendish but reckoned it was the kindest course of action at this stage of the evening.

'Yeah, and the rest of it,' India snorted through her tears. 'Thanks, Summer, but you don't have to defend him. I know he's a complete cunt – he's probably gone off to some hooker bar in San Antonio, and you must think I'm mad for staying with him, but' – her shoulders sagged – 'it's not that simple.'

'Surely—'

'It's OK. Go and sit down. I'll be fine after another line, but the bastard's got our stash. Jorge . . .?

The look of panic that flashed across Jorge's handsome face gave Summer a brief moment of satisfaction. Most of the people at the table knew about his 'other job' but he didn't like it being made quite so public.

Jorge was one of the most popular dealers on the island. And on an island like Ibiza, that meant a very tidy income indeed.

At that moment, Aqua's proprietor, Shane Connelly, arrived, strolling down the whitewashed walkway towards them, his six-foot-four frame elegant in white jeans and an open-necked white shirt. Summer, watching from her seat next to David, was glad to see him. Shane was a sweetheart as far as she was concerned, and even better looking at the age of fifty-one than he'd been in his Eighties heyday (she'd seen the photos), when his starring role in an Australian soap opera had given him international fame and legions of fans. Then, he'd had a mop of surfer-boy blond hair; now, incipient baldness had compelled him to shave it all off, with impressive results. His high cheekbones, fierce jawline, piercing blue eyes and muscular physique made him a hit both at the gay gym in Ibiza Town and also with the island's beautiful people.

After earning *heaps of dosh*, as he'd termed it, back in the day, Shane had moved to Ibiza in the Nineties, come out, opened his first bar in San Antonio – *'the horror'* as he now felt allowed to be camp enough to describe it – and lived high on the hog ever since.

'Everything bonza?' It had been his old catchphrase on the soap.

'This is fabulous, Shane,' said Summer, putting her fork to the side of her plate. 'Tell me the secret of the stuffing, pleeeease?' The sea bass had been stuffed with a mixture of herbs, citrus zest and nuts, which sounded a bit Christmassy for late spring, but somehow tasted summery due to the lightness of the chef's touch.

'If I told you I'd have to kill you.' Everybody laughed, sycophantically. 'Anyway, I don't know. Ask Juan. I'm only the boss.'

'OK, fair enough,' said Summer, smiling. 'I will. It wouldn't do you too much harm, would it, Shane, if I leaked one of Juan's delicious recipes? Nobody will be able to make it nearly as well as he does, so they'll all be flocking here. Win win!'

'Win win, indeed,' grinned Shane, high-fiving her. 'My clever Swedish doll.'

He walked around the table and sat in the seat recently vacated by Jamie Cavendish. 'So what do we think, guys? Is Aqua gonna be a hit?'

'Everything is exquisite,' said Gabriella, gesticulating in a pleasingly Italian manner. 'Look . . .' She indicated the table, the surroundings, the sea below, with a waft of her graceful hand. 'Listen . . .' Such was her magnetism that even the ghastly Russian oligarchs stopped shouting for a bit and listened, yet again, to the sound of the sea lapping the rocks. 'Taste . . .' She took a bite of her stuffed sea bass. 'Ambrosia from heaven – and whatever you say, Summer, I do not think you can replicate it.'

Summer shrugged good-naturedly, smiling. 'Surely that is what I said?'

Gabriella continued. 'Smell!' As one, the people sitting around the table inhaled, getting a lovely mixture of ozone and delicate herbs. 'And *feel* . . .' This time she clutched her heart in a dramatic yet tongue-in-cheek swoon. 'You,

Shane, have created one of the best sensory experiences Ibiza has ever seen!'

'And you, Gaby, are one of the coolest birds I've ever met.'

Gabriella gave a smiling half-bow.

'I think it'll be a great success,' said Summer. 'I'll give you a glowing write-up – as well as leaking a couple of Juan's recipes.'

'Cheers, babe.'

'What you need is celebrity endorsement,' said Jorge, his eyes lighting up. 'Jack Meadows and Tamara Gold will be here in July, and *some of us* are going to meet them! We could . . .'

'Hey, Jorge, don't get carried away,' said Summer. 'We don't know for sure that they'll be going to Bella's party yet.'

'Jack Meadows and Tamara Gold?' Shane said thoughtfully. He had his fair share of celebrity friends, but it would certainly be a coup if Hollywood's golden couple was papped arriving at Aqua. He could even arrange a boat to deliver them to this table.

It was something to bear in mind.

9

Natalia's yacht was anchored about 200 metres offshore from St Tropez's Pampelonne beach. It was small by the standards of some of the monstrous gin palaces that dotted the bay, but perfectly formed, all shiny polished oak, gleaming brass fittings and navy and white linen upholstery. Natalia, Ben, Poppy and Damian had finished lunch – *salade Niçoise* washed down with several bottles of chilled rosé wine – and were now relaxing happily around the large round table on the boat's rear deck.

'*Merci*, Jacques.' Natalia smiled as a member of her crew came to clear their plates away.

'That was delicious. Thanks, Nat,' said Poppy. 'This is the life.' She stretched her limbs out happily in the afternoon sun.

'It certainly is,' smiled Ben. 'We've come a long way from the valleys.' He could only utter such a sentiment among close friends; his public image now was posh, posh, posh.

'The valleys seem a lifetime away,' concurred Damian, who had grown up with Ben in Wales – two small boys who'd pledged to be best friends for life. He had always wanted to be a writer, and Ben, pretty little show-off, had always wanted to act. It seemed almost inconceivable that they'd both done it, so successfully, and were at the top of their respective games now.

Both men were wearing Vilbrequin swimming trunks and not much else. Damian – dark, lithe and graceful – reminded Poppy of a panther. Ben, who was taller, blonder and with much broader shoulders, was the lion. She wouldn't trade them for the world – she had, once, and it had been the biggest mistake of her life.

'Kiev seems several lifetimes ago,' said Natalia, with a bleak expression in her eyes.

'Oooh look!' squeaked Poppy, pointing over in the direction of their nearest enormous gin palace. It was close enough to be able to see exactly what was going on, on board. 'He's taken his trunks off! Oh yuck . . .'

Its owner was an enormously fat, mahogany-tanned, elderly man with several gold chains nestling in abundant grey chest hair. Every other person on board was young, female and topless.

'Do you think they all have to service him?' Poppy was watching in fascinated horror as one of the girls stood up, revealing high young buttocks bisected by a tiny gold thong, and started to rub oil into the billionaire's fleshy shoulders.

'No, some of them only have to look decorative,' said Natalia with authority. 'Not all of them will be hookers.'

'What are they then?'

'Good-time girls, party girls . . .'

'Isn't that the same thing? Pretty bloody shameless at any rate . . .' Poppy regretted the words as soon as they came out of her mouth.

'For most of them it is the chance of a lifetime to experience such luxury.' Natalia's Ukrainian accent surfaced whenever she was irritated. 'If all they have to do is sit around with their tops off, probably it doesn't seem too much hardship.'

'I'd do it,' said Ben.

'Yeah, but you're a total man tart!' said Poppy, and they all laughed, relieved. It was slightly awkward talking to Natalia about things like this. Nobody referred to her past directly, but there it lurked, elephantine on occasion.

'Anyone fancy a cognac?' asked Ben. 'Yacht, St Tropez . . . Silly not to . . .?'

'Go on then, boyo,' said Damian happily. He had reecntly sold his third screenplay and couldn't be more pleased with life. He was rich beyond his wildest imaginings, married to the beautiful woman he had loved for years, slightly drunk on a yacht in the Med, with the sun beating down on his bare shoulders. It was a good combination, by anybody's standards.

'Not for me,' said Poppy. 'I do fancy a swim, though. Anyone else?'

The other three shook their heads, and she walked, slightly unsteadily, to the edge of the boat. Holding her nose, she leapt off, landing with a splash in the deep blue sea. They smiled over at her as her golden head popped back out.

'The water's gorgeous!' Poppy waved and went under again, in the direction of the gin palace.

'I think I shall take a small nap,' said Natalia. 'I want to be well rested for dealing with The Bitch.' The plan was to join Tamara and Jack at Nikki Beach later that afternoon. 'Enjoy your cognac, boys.'

She kissed them both and went down the polished steps to her cabin.

Ben opened the cognac and they both heaved a happy sigh. Man time.

'Cheers.' They clinked balloon glasses, the amber liquid glowing in the late afternoon sun. After sitting in companionable silence for a few seconds, Ben turned to Damian.

'Mate. There's something I need to discuss with you.'

Damian raised his eyebrows. 'Sounds ominous.'

'No, not really, but I can't talk about it in front of Nat – she'd flip.'

'Jesus Christ, Ben, what – or should I say *who* – have you done now?'

'I haven't done anything!' Ben raised his arms, a mock-hurt look on his face. 'Fantastic that you assume *I've* done something wrong . . .'

'Well, you do have form . . .' Damian was referring to Ben's fling with Poppy and they both knew it.

'Yeah, yeah I know. Touché, you cunt. But I'm a changed man now.'

'What's the problem then?'

'Tamara's been coming on to me.'

Damian grimaced. 'Awkward.'

'Yes, very.'

'Are you sure though? She's a bloody flirt with everyone.'

Ben rolled his eyes. 'I *do* know that. It drives Nat crazy when she sits on my knee and talks in that stupid baby voice. No, I would definitely class her recent behaviour as beyond the acceptable bounds of friendship.'

Damian grinned. 'I'm intrigued now.'

'Well . . .' Ben drew it out. 'Do you remember that day at Coachella when Nat stayed at the villa and we all got wasted?'

'Fun day.' Damian grinned again.

'Yeah,' Ben grinned back. 'Anyway – remember how, before we got wasted, Tamara was playing up to the cameras with Jack, doing her loved-up "Jamara" act?' Damian nodded. 'Well, *act* is exactly what it was. She groped my balls at the bar.'

'Shit.'

'Yeah. And it gets worse.' Ben picked his phone up from the table, tapped the screen several times and then gave it to Damian.

'*Double* shit. Fucking hell, mate. She's taking a massive risk.' He was looking at a pair of amazingly firm, round, naked young breasts. 'I'm assuming they're hers?'

Ben nodded. 'She sent the message this morning.'

'She must be barking mad,' Damian laughed. 'Nice rack, though.'

'So, do I tell Jack or not?'

'Hmmm. Tricky one.' Damian took a swig of cognac and looked out to where Poppy was frolicking in the sea, doing underwater backwards somersaults. 'I don't think you should, at this stage. She's pretty fucked up, and you know what they say about shooting the messenger. Probably better just to hope she sorts herself out.'

'That's what I was thinking. I wouldn't want him to think I've done anything to encourage her. I mean, it's not as if I can help being irresistible.'

'You are one vain cunt, Ben Jones.'

'Tell me something I don't know. So what do I do?'

'Tell her it's not on, and if she doesn't stop, you'll tell Jack.'

'Yeah, sounds about right.' Ben took a contemplative sip of cognac.

'I do think you should tell Natalia, though. Surely honesty's always the best policy, and – for once – you haven't done anything wrong.'

'You are joking, right? Nat can't stand Tamara as it is – this would make things completely impossible between us all. She'd *definitely* tell Jack. And even though Tamara is madder than a box of frogs, I do quite like her. No – trust me on this one. I know Nat, and some things are best kept quiet.'

Nikki Beach was the flashiest, glitziest bar on Pampelonne Beach. Even though Club 55, the original St Tropez beach bar, which dated back to 1955, was infinitely cooler and chicer, the wildest, most hedonistic, bling-tastic parties now all seemed to be held at its newer rival. Today was no exception. The large terrace surrounding the smallish, turquoise pool thronged with beautiful people – some lounging on enormous white linen-upholstered daybeds, sipping cocktails or rosé wine from white glass goblets, others roaring with mirth as they sprayed one another with vastly overpriced champagne. Palm trees were festooned with hot pink and orange garlands – a cheerful sight under the unblemished denim-blue sky.

The next stop on their sybaritic Mediterranean jolly was Ibiza, but for the time being the Côte d'Azur was suiting them just fine.

Tamara and Jack were holding court at the bar, surrounded by sycophantic admirers. Tamara was wearing a tiny leopard-print Melissa Odabash bikini with scarlet satin ribbon ties that matched both her lipstick and the glossy varnish on her fingers and toes. Her chocolate-brown hair fell in lustrous waves to her shoulders, and a large diamond sparkled in her navel, drawing attention to her flat, lightly muscled stomach and tiny waist. As she twinkled and charmed those around her, flirting and cracking filthy and surprisingly hilarious jokes, nobody could have guessed the turmoil churning inside her.

Why the fuck had she sent Ben that photo of her tits? The longer she went without receiving a response, the more panicky she became. She had been sure he'd reply instantly. How could he not want her? Everybody else did, and she was far hotter (and younger) than that dried-up old cow Natalia. But what if she'd been wrong? And – even worse – what if Ben told Jack?

Tamara's latest act of recklessness was directly linked to some news she had received late the previous night. Her mom and dad had been on *David Letterman*, once again selling the story of their daughter's troubled teenage years, milking their only child dry for profit as only they knew how. It had been *beyond* sickening to watch as they sat there holding hands, apparently as loved-up as the day they'd met, telling the world about Tamara's most private and painful times.

No wonder I'm a screw-up, she thought bitterly. *My parents have only ever seen me as a commodity.* Years of therapy had encouraged her to use that sort of language when talking or thinking about herself.

She hated herself when she behaved this way. Sure, Ben was gorgeous – even more so than Jack – and she was certain that he'd be fantastic in the sack. But it wasn't fair on Jack, whom she did love, deep down. She guessed she was trying to punish him for something, though she wasn't sure what. Maybe it was because she had thought that being engaged to him would magically take away all the pain and resentment she'd been carrying around for so many years. When it didn't, she acted in a manner deliberately calculated to appal him, were he ever to find out. But she didn't want to be found out.

Jack, sitting on a stool next to her at the Polynesian-style bar, smiled his sweet smile and leaned over to ruffle her hair. Tamara felt guiltier than ever. He had seen how distraught she'd been last night, and had been gentle and loving with her all day, clearly proud of the way she was holding it together. He was looking tanned and handsome in his navy and white Tommy Hilfiger trunks, his curly black hair still damp from his last swim (he was one of the very few people to have used the pool that day, most – Tamara included – were far too concerned about their appearance even to countenance getting wet).

'Awww, don't they make a cute couple,' said Barbara, one of the hangers-on, the blonde fifty-something wife of a billionaire studio head, who'd had so much plastic surgery her face looked as if it had melted. Tamara thought it unlikely Barbara was capable of genuine human emotion, but smiled back sweetly nonetheless.

Come on, get a grip, Tam. Think of something funny to say.

'Did I tell you about the time I . . .' she started.

'Jack! Tamara!' Crap. The moment of truth. It was Ben, making his way through the glamorous crowds with the others in tow behind him. Heads turned to gawp at the drop-dead gorgeous movie star as he passed. Jack bounded up to greet his friend.

'Hey, buddy!' he said warmly, embracing him in a man-hug and slapping him heartily on the back. Jesus Christ, they'd only seen each other yesterday. This bromance was seriously starting to get on Tamara's tits.

'Tamara.' Ben gave her a brief hug. 'Nice bikini.'

What the fuck was *that* supposed to mean? She looked at him enquiringly, silently begging him not to tell tales. Ben said nothing else, just gave his head the slightest shake, as if to say, 'Not now'.

The others joined them at the bar and ordered drinks, and soon the mood was livelier than before, Tamara no longer the centre of attention. She hated it when it got to this time of day, when, with the drinking catching up on them all, they became louder, sillier and much more annoying.

Poppy, nursing a margarita across the bar from Tamara, and wondering what the hell had got into her this time, suddenly felt a heavy hand on her shoulder.

'I would recognize that back view anywhere,' said a deep voice. 'Poppy Wallace.' She turned.

'Lars!' she squealed, jumping off her stool and flinging her arms around an enormous blond man. 'What are *you* doing here?!'

'What do you think? That I am on business?' The huge man gave an equally huge, hearty laugh. 'I am on holiday, of course! The same, I guess, as you?'

'Sorry sorry, stupid question, but – oh, I can't tell you how fabulous it is to see you! Damian, look who it is – Lars is here!'

A big grin spread across Damian's handsome brown face and he walked round from the other side of the bar to give the larger man a hug that practically swallowed him up.

Lars was six foot seven, most of it muscle, and pleasing to look at, with even, Scandinavian features, clear, honest blue eyes, a large, square head and straight, blond hair that he kept cropped short. He had met Damian a couple of years previously when they were both in their early thirties and newly unemployed in New York, and had proved a very loyal friend to both him and Poppy when their marriage hit a rocky patch. As well as providing a vast shoulder to cry on, he had mediated between the two of them, to the extent of joining Poppy and Bella on a road trip across the States in hot pursuit of Damian, who had taken off on his own to find himself ('When did my bloody husband become such a fucking idiotic hippy?' Poppy had sobbed at the time).

You knew you could rely on Lars, whether in a crisis or to have a good time, and Poppy and Damian – and Bella too, after their eventful road trip – were extremely fond of him.

'How long are you here for? Have you got time to join us?' Poppy was babbling, dragging Lars across to meet the others. 'You remember Ben and Natalia, don't you? Oooh, I'd better introduce you, not that they need much introduction. Lars, these are our friends Jack and Tamara. Jack, Tamara – our very good friend Lars.'

As Lars looked at Tamara, it was as though time itself had stopped. Luckily, nobody else seemed to notice.

Several hours later, they'd repaired to Bar Senequier in the Vieux Port of St Tropez village. Natalia, Ben, Poppy and Damian had made the journey back in the yacht; Jack, Tamara, Lars and a couple of his friends had travelled by chauffeur-driven limo and rented Mercedes, respectively.

With its distinctive red awning and white tablecloths, Bar Senequier was a St Tropez institution, situated right on the seafront where the most expensive yachts were moored – *the* place to watch the constant promenade of the rich and beautiful. Naturally the rich and beautiful were more interested in watching the table occupied by three extremely famous movie stars, but they gave them no trouble – it simply wouldn't have been chic.

Lars, who was sitting next to Poppy and Damian, reminiscing about old times, had recovered his equilibrium, but still hadn't quite got over the enormous jolt he'd felt on seeing Tamara. Of course he knew what she looked like – he'd watched *Antony & Cleopatra*, seen her face on countless billboards, and had been vaguely aware of the car-crash child star when she was growing up.

But in the flesh, she was exquisite, irresistible. The tilt of her head as she smiled, her delicate jawline, tiny frame, cat-like green eyes, retroussé nose and full, luscious lips aroused feelings in Lars he'd managed to repress for several years, after a particularly messy and painful break-up had made him vow never to feel that way about a woman again.

Don't be ridiculous, he told himself sternly. *You are behaving like a star-struck imbecile. She's a world-famous movie star, engaged to be married to another world-famous movie star. This is nothing more than common lust, and you must not make a fool of yourself.*

So he did his best to ignore her, extremely glad of Poppy and Damian's company, but couldn't resist sneaking the occasional glance in her direction.

Tamara, for her part, was by no means oblivious to the effect she was having on the Swedish giant, and was thrilled. At least *somebody* appreciated her. She'd stopped being centre of attention hours ago; both Poppy and that bitch Natalia, she had to concede grudgingly, were looking far too attractive tonight for her liking.

While Tamara knew she looked beyond fabulous in a backless – and practically frontless – violet Versace silk minidress, Poppy was channelling Bardot in a ridiculously cute outfit of blue-and-white sleeveless gingham shirt that tied under her bust, paired with fraying denim cut-offs. With her hair now streaked white by the sun and her teeth gleaming in her (naturally) tanned, slightly freckled face as she laughed, Tamara could see that none of the men at the table were immune to her charms. Even Natalia looked good *for her age*, she supposed, elegant in a midnight-blue chiffon minidress that showed off her endless legs.

Ben, sitting next to her, saw that Natalia was engrossed in chatting to Jack on the opposite side of the table, and decided that now was the time.

'Tamara,' he said quietly. She looked up at him through big, innocent eyes. 'Quit the innocent act. I don't know what you think you're playing at, but if you don't stop, I'm going to tell Jack. *Capisce*?'

Tamara nodded, her bottom lip quivering. *Capisce? Who did he think he was, Don fucking Corleone?*

Ben noticed the quivering lip and said, a bit more gently, 'Jack's my mate, and I love Natalia. Whatever you're hoping to achieve, it's not going to happen, so . . .' Something made him look up. Natalia was looking across the table at them intently. 'Nat, darling,' he added smoothly. 'I was telling Tamara about the first night I met you – how you were sitting just over there, and how I was mesmerized by your beautiful back. Wasn't it magical, my love?'

It had been here, at Bar Senequier, that he and Natalia had met. Ben had been on location filming his first film, and Natalia, attracted by the loud chatter of the movie people sitting outside the restaurant, had wandered ashore from her yacht. The attraction had been instant, but had turned into something much deeper for both of them.

Natalia smiled, looking relieved. 'Magical!' She blew him several kisses across the table and Ben blew several back. Tamara felt sick, and humiliated.

'Hey, *garçon*!' She suddenly shouted, clicking her fingers like some demented flamenco dancer. 'Over here! *Vite*!' Her Californian accent grated against the soft and balmy night air.

'*Oui oui*, Mademoiselle Gold? 'Ow can I 'elp?' One of the white-aproned waiters, who were generally laid-back to the point of rudeness, rushed over immediately.

'I asked for my salad with the dressing *on the side*.'

'*Mais, mademoiselle*, I brought it to you on the side. Look!' The waiter picked up the small white jug that still contained around half the vinaigrette. Tamara had poured the other half over her salad.

'Well, it's not on the side any more, is it?'

Natalia, across the table, raised her eyebrows to heaven.

'I want a fresh one – and don't bother bringing any dressing this time – your dressing sucks.'

'Of course, mademoiselle,' said the waiter, taking her plate away.

'Well, that was grown-up,' said Ben.

'Oh fuck you.' She glared at him, daring him to say more, but he merely shrugged and turned to the chap on his right, a friend of Lars's.

'So it's really taken off, your eco-tourism business?'

127

Poppy was saying to Lars. 'That's so cool! I'm pretty sure that, last I heard, you were only covering the States . . .'

'Uh-huh,' said Lars. 'It seems that many people, even in a global recession, want to travel responsibly, and we do not charge much more – in some cases considerably less – than other travel companies covering the same places.'

'Where are you expanding to?' asked Damian, in between mouthfuls of buttery soft steak tartare, sharpened with cornichons and capers.

'For the moment – Mexico, Ecuador, Venezuela. Not far.' Lars's modesty was endearing. 'But next year, maybe Africa. I am in talks with some responsible safari guys. And of course I have contacts in Sweden. Winter safaris would be cool.'

'They would indeed,' smiled Poppy. 'It suits you. You seem so much happier these days.'

'I am happier.' Lars glanced, ever so briefly, in Tamara's direction. 'Even if I could have gone back to banking, it never suited me the way this does. I was made to explore the world.'

'You certainly were,' laughed Damian. 'You great big Viking, you.'

'Hey – enough with the Viking jokes.' Lars stared at them seriously, a hurt expression on his big square face. 'You think that living with a heritage of raping and pillaging is easy?'

Poppy and Damian looked gobsmacked.

'Hahahaha! I got you guys going! This is the Swedish sense of humour!' Lars was booming with laughter so good-naturedly that it was impossible not to join in. 'And I am sorry, because I have you guys to thank for my new life. It was chasing you on that crazy road trip that reminded me how much I love to travel.'

'Oh, how cool!' beamed Poppy. 'Isn't that fab, darling?!' Damian nodded, smiling.

Poppy continued, brazenly, 'So, to thank us, I think you

should – please, please, please? – take us skiing in the Swedish midnight sun? I've always wanted to do that!'

'She doesn't change, does she?' said Damian fondly.

Lars shook his head with an equally affectionate smile. 'It'll have to be once we've stopped jet-setting around the Med, pretending we're film stars, of course . . .'

'Hey, Lars,' Tamara interrupted, leaning forward across the table so he could get a better view of her breasts, barely concealed in the violet silk minidress.

'Yes?' Lars, doing everything he could not to stare at the invitingly packaged cleavage, looked her determinedly in the eye.

'Do you like the movies?'

Poppy kicked Damian under the table, amused by Tamara's blatant attempt to bring the conversation around to herself.

'Uh, sure,' said Lars, mesmerized by her feline green gaze.

Tamara, feeling her heart starting to beat faster at the lust she was certain she could read in his clear blue eyes, gave him an almost surreptitious, and extremely sexy wink.

'So what's your favourite genre? Let me guess – you don't look like a black-and-white arthouse kinda guy. I'd say something more *masculine.*' She emphasized the word, smiling coquettishly. 'Action, adventure, maybe some comedy? Am I right?'

'I'm afraid you're wrong,' said Lars, desperate to escape her thrall, even though he was as fond of action movies as the next guy. 'My favourite director is Ingmar Bergman.' And he turned his back on her to resume his conversation with Damian and Poppy.

Tamara, furious and baffled by the snub, was relieved when her phone started to ring. A genuine smile crept across her pretty, petulant face as she took the call.

'*Omigod!*' she screamed as she hung up.

'Jesus, what can it be this time?' said Damian, *sotto voce.*

'That was my agent!' Tamara was brandishing her phone triumphantly, thrilled that at last she had a reason to be centre of attention. 'Miles Dawson's here – *here, in the South of France* – and he knows that *I'm* here, and he wants to meet me to talk about possibly starring in his next movie! Isn't that *fantastic*?' She looked around, eyes shining, and everybody agreed that it was, indeed, fantastic. Miles Dawson was a highly respected director of indie films – the kind of movies, in fact, that Jack had starred in at the beginning of *his* career. For Tamara to land a role like that would give her credibility, with or without Jack.

'That's wonderful, honey,' said Jack. 'When does he want to see you?'

'A few days' time, I think. He's in Cannes at the moment. Isn't that cool? He'll be coming from Cannes, to see *me*!' She sounded so excited that Lars had a sudden urge to kiss her, despite her horrendous narcissism.

'We're meant to be leaving for Ibiza the day after tomorrow,' said Jack mildly.

'Ibiza can go screw itself.' Everybody laughed weakly, and Tamara raised her voice. 'I mean it – Ibiza *can go screw itself!*'

'Why are you being this way, Tammy?' Jack's voice was concerned. She wasn't drunk, hadn't been for nearly ten years, but she behaved more like an irrational alcoholic than all the people around the table, most of whom had been drinking all day.

'Being what way? I finally get a break, and you're concerned about jetting off to some crappy little island? Are you scared that I'm going to be top dog in this relationship? Is that what it is, *Jack*? I don't know why you can't be more supportive. I'm staying here, whatever happens. You can fuck off to Ibiza on your own.'

'You know what?' All of a sudden Jack sounded immensely weary. 'I might just do that.'

10

Bella stood back to inspect her handiwork, exhausted. It had taken five layers of whitewash to obliterate the graffiti on her sitting-room walls, her right arm felt as though it was about to fall off, and she was spattered in paint from head to toe. But it had been worth it.

'What do you think, darling?' she asked Daisy, who was sitting up in her chair at the far side of the room (to avoid the paint splatters), watching with interest. She clapped her little hands, grinning.

'I'd love to pick you up and give you a kiss, my lovebird, but I don't think I'm going to be picking up anything heavier than a glass of wine for the next couple of hours. Thank God Jorge's coming to help move the furniture back in.'

It would have been nice if Andy had been around to help move the furniture back in, of course, but his book seemed to take bloody precedence over everything. Yes, she knew it was irritating when the Wi-Fi went off, but he was working to a nine-month deadline, not daily ones, and a bit of appreciation on the daily front wouldn't have gone amiss.

Jorge had been an absolute godsend, though.

Before she had time to think about it any more deeply, she tried to remember where she'd left her make-up bag. It had been so long since she'd bothered to do her face that it was nearly ten minutes before she found it underneath Daisy's cot.

'This is silly,' she said out loud as she applied a couple of layers of mascara and a tiny bit of blusher, squinting at herself in a grubby old compact, cross-legged on the floor next to Daisy's high chair. 'Who on earth do I think I'm trying to impress?' Then, seeing Daisy gazing at her with her huge, round innocent eyes, she added, slightly guiltily, 'It's not about impressing people though, is it, my honey-love? It's simply about not letting one's standards slip.'

The finca was very nearly ready for Poppy and Damian's arrival the following day.

The guest room was immaculate, with a romantic, colonial feel to it. With Jorge's help, Bella had found an enormous wooden sleigh bed with intricately carved headboard, a couple of Balinese enamel-inlaid bedside tables, with a matching chest (now full of freshly laundered, lavender-scented linen), and two rattan armchairs, which sat either side of the big shuttered windows, with their view over pine and olive groves all the way down to the shimmering navy-blue sea. The bed linen was pure white, offset by a tumble of animal-print cushions (leopard, zebra and cow), and more cushions with vibrant Moroccan silk covers brightened up the rattan chairs. A huge mirror hung above the Balinese chest, and white voile curtains wafted in the breeze created by the large wooden ceiling fan whirring overhead. A jungle of yucca and rubber plants stood next to a dark wooden wardrobe and added to the exotic atmosphere. Bella had put an enormous vase of pink and orange roses and orchids on the chest, along with a pile of new and very fluffy white towels, and a selection of the latest English glossies – *Vogue, Elle, GQ* and *Esquire* – which had cost a fortune from the English newsagent in Ibiza Town. In fact, none of this had come cheap, but she still had some money left over from the sale of her Notting Hill flat – London prices had reached ridiculous levels – and never having had a guest room before, she was determined to be the hostess with the mostest.

The bathroom opposite was the one room in which Bella had been able to stick to the original plan of white (ish), and she was thrilled with how the claw-footed Victorian bath looked against the dark wooden floorboards and cream Paris metro tiles. The kitchen units had finally been delivered, she had found (again with Jorge's help) the perfect rustic wooden kitchen table, and the kitchen now felt like the cosy heart of the family home she had always dreamed of. All that remained was to rearrange all the furniture, which had been shifted outside for the last couple of days, back into the freshly painted sitting room. She'd left the most tedious, arduous task – painting over the graffiti – till last.

There was also the filling of the swimming pool, of course. Bella grinned to herself in excitement. It was actually happening this afternoon, and she couldn't wait.

'So, darling, was Mummy completely mad to even think of this folly, or is she an artistic genius? What do you think, eh?' Bella's arm was still aching so much from the painting that rather than carrying Daisy, as was her wont these days, she'd fallen back on the trusty buggy.

The run-down outhouse this end of the pool had been built, in contrast to the one that Andy was using as his study, out of a combination of whitewashed stone and wood, which meant that Bella had been able to knock down three wooden walls, leaving only the back stone wall, the stone ceiling, raised stone platform, and two stone pillars at the front, facing the pool. This left a shape perfect for an approximation of a very wide four-poster bed, flanked on either side by exotic-looking date palms.

Now boasting two white linen-covered double mattresses and mountains of large white linen cushions, it was hung with vibrant Indian silks in shades of pink, red and orange. Bella had attached lanterns in jewel colours to the front pillars, arranged tea lights in Moroccan coloured glasses either side of her extravagant folly, and cleared away the weeds so there was a comfortable enough path leading to it. Andy had burst out laughing when he'd first seen it in its full glory, but it had been tinged with awe, and he had followed it up with a big kiss and the words, 'It's beautiful. You really are a clever, artistic thing.'

Today he was in Santa Eulalia. Their Wi-Fi was down again and he was waiting for an urgent email – which was a shame, but it couldn't be helped. Bella couldn't wait to see him later, when the house would be practically finished, and *the pool filled*.

'Bella!' called Jorge as he walked into the garden via the back entrance. He'd been around enough times by now not to have to knock at the front door.

'Hi, Jorge,' Bella replied cheerfully. 'What do you think? I only put the finishing touches on yesterday.'

Jorge stopped dead. *'Madre de dio,'* he said. 'Wow! It looks amazing. You, Bella, are one creative lady.' He gave her a big hug and kissed her on both cheeks. *'Hola,* Daisy,' he added, leaning into the buggy to kiss the little girl too. 'Are you still the most beautiful little girl in the world? Are you?'

Bella smiled indulgently as he tickled her daughter under the chin. She loved the way Jorge was with Daisy. That juxtaposition of manly brawn with soft, baby-like innocence reminded her of the iconic Athena poster that had hung above her, and millions of other, teenage beds.

'Hey, what's this?' Jorge nodded over to the pool, which was being tended to by three muscly men accompanied by a lot of loud machinery and hoses. 'Today is pool-filling day, too?'

'Yup,' said Bella, unable to keep the excitement out of her voice. There was already about ten centimetres of water in the pool, and it was filling up fast. Well, slowly, actually, but she wasn't going to let a little thing like that ruin her enjoyment of this big day.

'Just in time for your famous friends, huh?' Jorge teased. 'They're coming tomorrow, *es verdad*?'

'You have got a good memory. Yes, Poppy and Damian are arriving tomorrow, and Ben and Natalia too, but I'm not sure about Jack and Tamara. Apparently they had a fight or something.'

Jorge's face dropped. 'But they *could* still be coming, right?'

'I suppose so.' Bella wasn't too bothered either way. Of course it would be fascinating to see these famous people, and fun to show off in front of Saffron and India (who had been bizarrely nice to her recently), but what she was really looking forward to was catching up with her old friends. 'Anyway, do you want a drink before we get started? Coffee? Wine? Brandy?'

Jorge laughed. 'I think a brandy would not be such a good idea, but a glass of wine – *¿porque no?*'

Andy raked his fingers through his thick black hair in despair. The Wi-Fi in his favourite bar in Santa Eulalia was almost as temperamental as the Wi-Fi at the finca, and he watched with mounting irritation as his laptop failed, yet again, to connect. He knew he should have bitten the bullet and driven into Ibiza Town, but Santa Eulalia was so much closer to home, and the traffic into Ibiza Town was generally hellish at this time of year. Besides, he liked Santa Eulalia. It had a genteel, almost staid charm that was entirely different from the rest of the island.

Yes, it was touristy, the main street lined with bars, restaurants and shops selling flip-flops, postcards and sarongs, but it was a gentler type of tourism than the full-on hedonistic glamour that pulsated through the veins of Ibiza Town. Santa Eulalia was popular with families with young children, and this bar, overlooking the marina, was deserted mid-afternoon. It would have been the perfect place to get on with his work had the bloody Wi-Fi behaved itself.

The heat was almost overwhelming at this time of day. Taking off his glasses, which were sitting uncomfortably on his sticky face, Andy got up to order himself a beer. Much as he loved his new home, things weren't working out quite as smoothly as he'd hoped. Rural bliss was all very well, but when you were trying to write a book to help pay for living the dream, it was extremely frustrating not to have all the mod cons at your fingertips. As he thought this, he laughed at himself for the old-fashioned expression; what did people call mod cons these days?

And Bella was so enraptured with every aspect of her new life that she seemed entirely oblivious to his concerns. Of course he was happy that she was so happy, and it was great that she was making new friends – especially Summer, about whom he couldn't think anything bad at all . . . Andy had been so caught up in his book that morning that he hadn't really been listening when Bella had told him that Jorge would be coming round to help her move furniture. If he had remembered, it would no doubt have increased his irritation and guilt that he wasn't there to help her himself.

As it was, he told himself to snap out of it. It wasn't Bella's fault that they lived in a technological desert. He loved her, and she was a fantastic mother. The thought of Daisy's happy little face made his heart swell, and his frustrations faded almost into nothingness. Taking a swig of his beer, he tried to reload his screen for the fifth time. Nothing. Oh well, nothing else for it. He would have to brave the traffic into Ibiza Town after all.

'We've done it.' Bella let out a happy sigh and looked around her beautiful new sitting room. 'Actually, no – *you've* done it. Thank you so much, Jorge, you've been fantastic.'

'All I provided was the muscle,' said Jorge, flexing one of his impressive biceps, and Bella laughed, averting her gaze, trying not to look at the muscle for too long. Lifting anything heavy had made her right arm hurt so much that Jorge had insisted on moving all the furniture himself – except for the two white sofas, which Bella had dragged ineffectually with her left hand while Jorge heaved, lifted and pushed.

'But all this beauty came from you. Beauty from beauty.'

'Thanks,' she said, her gaze still averted. *Beauty from beauty*? Much as she liked the comment – it was great to start feeling attractive again – she wasn't sure how appropriate it was when accompanied by the lingering looks Jorge had taken to giving her of late. But that was just the Mediterranean way, she told herself. All perfectly harmless!

One of the walls, the one that had always been free from graffiti, was completely lined with bookshelves, but they had been in situ before today, and Bella and Andy had already filled them. The *Oxford Dictionary of Quotations*, Bella's art books, Andy's history books, beautifully bound works of Shakespeare, eighteenth- and nineteenth-century hardback novels, the complete works of Oscar Wilde (illustrated by Aubrey Beardsley) and anthologies of poetry took pride of place on the most visible shelves. The Twenties and Thirties hardback schoolgirl books (Angela Brazil, the Chalet School, early Enid Blyton – all with their original dust covers) that Bella had collected as a child, when they were cheap as chips at the book fairs to which her mother had taken her, occupied an entire shelf above them. Next up were Penguin modern classics, literary fiction, cool vintage paperbacks – original James Bonds and the like – and some obscure foreign literature that made them look intellectual. The books that they actually read – Andy's crime thrillers and Bella's bonkbusters – were right at the top, where nobody could see them.

On the wall opposite the bookshelves, the one which had previously borne the nostalgic graffiti, hung three large paintings – two of Bella's oils, and a beautiful watercolour seascape, a present from Henri, Jorge's father. Its aquamarine hues lent themselves perfectly to the room's slightly nautical vibe, with its mishmash of turquoise, cornflower and navy-and-white-striped cushions, battered old reclaimed driftwood coffee table that sat between the white linen sofas (which Bella had asked Jorge to position in an L shape) and warm flagstoned floor. The light flooding in from the floor-to-ceiling French windows ensured that the overhead beams never seemed too oppressive.

'I absolutely adore it.' Bella smiled. 'You've worked so hard – let's celebrate with a drink.'

'That would be good – *muchas gracias*,' said Jorge, who was pouring with sweat after his exertions, even though it was early evening now – Ibiza in July was always too hot for manual labour to be actively enjoyable. Bella went to the kitchen to retrieve the bottle of wine they'd had a couple of glasses from earlier, poured some olives and salted almonds into a bowl, and took them out onto the bougainvillea-shaded patio, where Jorge was sitting with his feet up on the wrought-iron table, watching the workmen completing their job on the pool. The water was almost at the level it should be.

'Merci, gracias, thank you Bella.' He grinned, helping himself to a couple of olives and an almond. 'How I wish they had finished their work, so I could jump in and cool off.'

'You must be sweltering. Have a shower, if you want – the wet room's fab!'

'Thanks, but it's OK.' Jorge turned to give her the full wattage of his smile. 'I should go soon anyway.'

'Bella?' It was Andy, who had walked through the garden, clearly en route to his study, rather than coming to say hello to her and Daisy first. She bristled slightly at his priorities. 'What's going on?'

After an incredibly frustrating day of technological hitches and gridlocked traffic, all Andy could see was the mother of his child, wearing little but a paint-spattered T-shirt over her bare brown legs, being chatted up by that slimeball Jorge Dupont, who had the cheek to have his legs up on *his* table, drinking *his* wine. He was looking greasier and sweatier than ever, too.

'Hi, darling.' Bella got up to give him a kiss. 'We're just celebrating a bloody good day's work! Look!' She pointed into the sitting room and Andy's eyes widened slightly in apparent admiration. Soon they narrowed again, though, as he saw that Jorge hadn't even taken his feet off the table.

'Yes, well, thanks, I'm sure you've been very helpful, but I'd like to have some time alone with my wife now.'

'I'm not your wife,' said Bella through gritted teeth. 'You've never asked me to marry you. Sorry about my incredibly rude *boyfriend*, Jorge. And thank you so much again for today. See you on Saturday, yeah?'

'De nada. Saturday's cool. I was about to go anyway.' Jorge got to his feet at a leisurely pace, kissed Bella on

both cheeks and sauntered through the garden towards the back exit. '*Hasta luego*, Andy.'

'What the fuck do you think you're doing?' asked Bella, furious. How dare he march in here like some bloody Victorian husband, when he'd done little, if anything, towards getting their home as they wanted it to be?

'What do I think *I'm* doing?' Andy's voice was incredulous. He picked up the bottle of rosé, which was empty, although both the glasses Bella had poured were still full. 'Who's been looking after my daughter while you've been boozing all day with that slimy little toe-rag?'

'How dare you?' Bella was furious. 'She's *our* daughter, and she's having her evening nap, as you'd know if you were ever around to witness anything to do with her, or me. We had a glass of wine each when Jorge turned up, after lunch, and I'd just poured another one, after about three hours' work, before *you* stormed in, being so fucking rude and unpleasant. If you must know' – she was on the verge of tears now – 'I couldn't have done it on my own, my arm's hurting too much, and Jorge—'

'Jorge did what?' asked Andy sarcastically. 'Did he kiss it better?'

'*What?* Oh, this is ridiculous! Haven't you even noticed how amazing it's looking in there? You should be *thanking* Jorge, he's—'

'Ah, *señor, señora* . . .' One of the workmen interrupted them.

'*Señora*, yeah right, like I'm ever going to be *married* to you, even though I'm the mother of your daughter,' Bella muttered under her breath, still furious, but not wanting to make too much of a scene. How depressingly English.

But Andy's ire seemed to be evaporating as he gazed over at their swimming pool, full, at last, with clear cool water.

'Look, Belles! Isn't this what we've been waiting for?'

Bella followed his gaze and smiled reluctantly. The pool was perfect, and completed the picture of the garden she'd had in her head for such a long time.

'*Muchas gracias*,' Andy was saying to the workmen as he over-tipped them, willing them to leave him and Bella to it. '*Muchas gracias*.'

'*De nada*.' The head pool chap smirked as he pocketed the euro notes, before heading back to gather up all his equipment.

'I'm still not happy with Jorge hanging around you all the time . . .' Andy started quietly.

'Why? Look at me, and stop being such an idiot.' Bella pointed at herself, laughing. She was wearing an old sleeveless smiley-face T-shirt that barely covered her bum, was daubed in paint splatters from head to toe and had scrunched her hair up in a messy blob (to call it a bun would be stretching it) on top of her head – but she was tanned, and she'd lost all the baby weight. 'He's hardly going to be after my body, is he?'

Andy suddenly realized that she wasn't seeing what he saw and what Jorge undoubtedly did. 'If he's not, then he's an idiot,' he said, taking her face in his hands and kissing her.

After a bit, Bella came up for air. 'That's better.' She grinned. 'I've got my Andy back. Now, isn't it about time we christened that pool?'

As if on cue, the unmistakable sound of Daisy's little voice made its way down the stairs.

'She's waking up,' said Bella. 'She doesn't like to miss out on anything, does she?'

Andy smiled. 'Well, it seems only fair that she should witness the pool christening, too.'

They walked upstairs to Daisy's bedroom hand-in-hand, both relieved that the row was over. They rarely fought, and when they did, it knocked them both for six. Daisy was standing up in her cot, holding onto the railing and chattering away unintelligibly, her eyes wide and starry.

'Did you have a lovely sleep, darling?' said Bella, leaning into the cot to pick her up. 'Owww!'

'What's the matter?' asked Andy.

'I told you my bloody arm hurt. It was painting out the graffiti that did it.'

'Oh God, I'm sorry, you poor thing. Here, let me take Daisy.'

Back down at the pool, Daisy looked on from her buggy as her parents, naked and giggling like schoolchildren, took a running jump right from the end of the garden and landed – with an almighty splash – in the pool together.

'Oh my God, it's wonderful,' said Bella.

'It's more than wonderful – it's perfect,' said Andy, taking her wet face in his hands and kissing her as they trod water. 'You, Daisy, this . . .' he gestured around at their exquisite surroundings. The sun was starting to set now and the west-facing garden was cast in a rosy glow. 'I must be the luckiest man alive.'

Bella felt unaccountably nervous as she sat under the vines outside Bar Anita the following afternoon, sipping at a small San Miguel as she and Daisy waited for Poppy and Damian. It was ridiculous. Poppy was her oldest friend. Why did she care so much about impressing her? But care she did, which was why she was wearing her favourite dress – the white halter-neck maxidress she'd bought in Ibiza Town; and why she'd rearranged the cushions in the guest room at least five times; and why she'd been up at the crack of dawn to buy the biggest, freshest langoustines and sea breams for their supper tonight. She'd dressed Daisy in her best new frock too – it was smocked, in the palest yellow cotton, and embroidered, appropriately, with daisies. Bella thought she had never seen anything so adorable.

'Belles! We're here!' In a flurry and a whirlwind, Poppy raced into the bar, turning all heads, and flung her arms around her oldest friend. Damian followed, smiling, at a slightly slower pace.

'Oh my God, you look fantastic! You've lost so much weight! So tanned, you're like a proper local! And Daisy – how's my beautiful god-daughter?' Poppy picked her out of her buggy and swung her up in the air, making her giggle with delight, before blowing raspberries all over her face, until the little girl was cackling. 'She's grown so much! Oh it's so good to see you both – where's Andy?' Finally Poppy was out of breath, and she sat down in a rickety wooden chair opposite Bella, bouncing Daisy on her knee.

Bella laughed. 'It's wonderful to see you too, Pops. You're looking gorgeous as ever.'

Poppy was wearing a battered straw trilby on top of her silky blonde locks, Havaianas, and a teeny tiny strappy mint-green cotton slip-dress that kept slipping off one slim brown shoulder. She looked more Ibiza-chic even than India Cavendish, and Bella marvelled at the way she always, without fail, managed to get it right.

Bella looks beautiful, Poppy was thinking, taking in the sun-streaked long brown hair, happy tanned face and air of maternal contentment. OK, so she was covered in splats of white paint, but that was Bella for you.

'Hi, Bella,' said Damian, kissing her on both cheeks. 'It's so great to be here at last. You're looking fabulous. Hello, Daisy!' He waved at the little girl sitting on Poppy's lap.

'Right, do you want a drink here, or shall we get going? I've nearly finished this.' Bella indicated her beer.

'Oh, let's get going,' said Poppy. 'I'm dying to see your house. And I bet you've got a fridge-full of booze, right?' She winked.

'I did stock up, knowing you two were coming, yes,' said Bella primly and Poppy and Damian laughed. 'OK, let's go.' She downed her beer, plonked some cash on the table, took Daisy from Poppy and put her back in her buggy. Poppy watched in amazement. She looked so . . . capable.

'*Adios – gracias*!' She called over her shoulder. '*Hasta Sabado*!'

'*Hasta Sabado*!' called back Pilar, the charming waitress she'd invited to the party.

Bella drove the jeep along winding roads, through silvery olive groves, and finally the rubbly white dirt track that led to Ca'n Pedro, chatting excitedly all the way. The sun was high in the sky, but the wind in their hair kept them cool.

'I still can't get over you driving,' said Poppy.

'I know – weird isn't it? Driving, having a baby, giving up smoking . . . I might, just maybe, have grown up.'

'Naah – that's going a bit too far,' Poppy laughed. 'Anyway, you didn't answer my question – where's Andy?'

Bella made a face. 'Santa Eulalia. Our Wi-Fi's down again – one of the disadvantages of living in the sticks – and he's got "urgent business"' – she took one hand briefly from the steering wheel to make air quotes – 'to attend to.'

'Surely he can email on his phone?' said Damian.

'Not reams and reams of impenetrable historical prose, no.'

'Oh well, fair enough,' said Poppy. 'Looking forward to seeing him later, though.'

'How was St Tropez?'

'Fun, and weird – so much to tell you. We bumped into Lars!'

'Oh, that's fab! How was he?'

'He . . .' Poppy finally shut up as the jeep turned a corner and Ca'n Pedro came into view. 'Is this your house?'

Bella nodded, unable to stop the big smile creeping across her face.

'Oh my God, Belles. It's abso-fucking-lutely beautiful!'

Later that evening, they were sitting out under the stars. They'd moved the table out from under the balcony so that they could look up at the sky as they dined by candle-light, and were all feeling very happy with life.

'This is truly wonderful,' said Damian sincerely. 'You two have got it made here.'

'It's been bloody hard work,' said Bella.

'Well, you've done a great job. Really.'

'I can't get over our room,' chimed in Poppy. 'I don't think I've ever seen a lovelier spare room!' She knew the way to Bella's heart.

'Thanks, Pops.' Bella smiled happily. 'OK, so fill me in again on the complicated lives of our Hollywood stars?'

'You do it. Go on – prove you've been listening,' said Poppy.

Bella took a swig of her wine. 'OK, so . . . Jack's lovely, Tamara's a nightmare, though she can be lovely too, Tamara's been coming on to Ben, but he's keeping schtum for the sake of harmony all round, but especially where Natalia's concerned, because she *loathes* Tamara . . .'

'Ten out of ten so far,' said Damian.

'Jack and Tamara had a spectacular row, so Jack's come to Ibiza without her,' said Andy, picking up the baton, and they all looked at him in surprise. 'I'm not immune to a bit of gossip, you know.' He laughed. 'And we're meeting Ben, Natalia and Jack for lunch at Benirrás tomorrow.'

'I can't wait to meet Jack,' said Bella.

'You won't be disappointed,' said Poppy.

11

Tamara tilted her head to one side as she considered her reflection in the ornate gilt-framed mirror hanging in her suite at the Byblos hotel. She was meeting Miles Dawson for lunch at Club 55, and needed to look the part. Of all the things you could accuse Tamara of, stupidity wasn't one of them, and she realized that her usual in-your-face glamour probably wasn't what the indie director was looking for. Her agent had told her that the film was going to be set in the dust storms of the Mid West in the Depression of the 1930s. So Tamara had gone easy on the make-up for once, smudging just the tiniest amount of black kohl around her eyes, which were today a subtle pale green, and so thickly lashed that mascara was unnecessary. Pink blusher on her lightly fake-tanned face, and a light slick of pale pink lip gloss kept her façade young, vulnerable and incredibly pretty. She'd pinned some of her dark hair back, but allowed the rest to tumble loose and wavy (with the obligatory wispy tendrils framing her face), and was wearing a simple short white kaftan that showed off her slender brown legs.

Young, innocent, ethereal. It was good, she thought, giving herself a wink, thumbs up and a wicked grin.

After their row at Senequier the other night, Jack had remained cold and distant with her, choosing to hang out on Natalia's yacht with the others until it was time to leave for Ibiza. Tamara was more hurt by this than she was willing to admit to anybody, least of all herself, but her excitement about meeting Miles Dawson had helped to mask the hurt. It was also quite a relief, after her dreadfully mis-judged faux pas with Ben, to have a bit of space from the others. She just had to keep her fingers crossed that Ben wouldn't stitch her up.

Her Swarovski crystal-embossed iPhone beeped inside the buttery-soft Marc Jacobs tan leather handbag she'd elected to take to today's lunch meeting. She smiled as she read the message.

Good luck today, Tammy. I'm thinking of you. Let me know how it goes. Jack xxx

Miles Dawson sat at an unobtrusive corner table under a tamarind tree at Club 55. Everything at this legendary St Tropez watering hole was chic and beautifully thought out, all faded blues, cream linen and sun-bleached wood. He was slightly apprehensive at the prospect of meeting Tamara Gold; her reputation certainly preceded her, and after several days of difficult negotiations with money men in Cannes, he wasn't sure he felt up to any prima-donna shenanigans.

He thought he saw vulnerability beneath the brash exterior – she had tugged at the heart strings in *Antony & Cleopatra* – but he could be wrong. He also remembered, from her childhood roles, that she had natural comic timing, which was going to be essential for anyone playing the female lead in *Dust Bowl*. Using one of the bleakest periods of American misery as the backdrop for a black comedy was risky (especially during the current recession), and the casting of Amy, the plucky oldest daughter in a motherless family of seven, was to be pivotal to the movie's success.

'Mr Dawson?' a shy voice enquired. Miles looked up from his menu to see Tamara, looking pretty and virginal as a snowdrop, smiling and holding out her hand.

'Please, call me Miles.' He jumped to his feet and shook the outstretched hand, which was small, dry and firm. 'I'm so pleased you could make it.'

'I wouldn't have missed this opportunity for the world.' Tamara gave him what looked like a genuinely warm smile and he felt his doubts starting to fade. They both sat down and Miles picked up the bottle of sparkling mineral water that was sitting in an ice-bucket on the sky-blue linen tablecloth.

'Water?'

'Thank you.'

Tamara considered the geeky-looking chap sitting opposite her. With his round, wire-rimmed glasses, goatee beard, scruffy light-brown hair and unprepossessing outfit of knee-length combat shorts and a baggy T-shirt, he could have been straight out of UCLA. None of their fellow diners would suspect that this was one of the most influential young film directors of his generation.

Half an hour later, Miles Dawson was completely smitten. Tamara had had him in stitches as she recounted life on the set of *Antony & Cleopatra*, complete with well-timed one-liners and wicked impressions of her co-stars (including Jack). She had also done her research in the few days since her agent had briefed her on *Dust Bowl*, downloading several Steinbeck novels onto her kindle and familiarizing herself with the period.

Lars, who was having a jolly lunch with his old Merrill Lynch pals at the next table, was trying to pretend that he hadn't noticed Tamara. She certainly hadn't clocked him, all her attention was focused on the clever director, and having heard snippets of their conversation, Lars was reluctantly impressed. Could this demure, charismatic, *witty* young beauty, so far removed from the arrogant, petulant glamour girl of his first encounter, be the real Tamara, the sweet young woman beneath the brittle façade?

Surprised and slightly alarmed by how happy the thought made him feel – she was so out of his reach it was laughable – he redirected his attention to his pastel-coloured polo-shirt-wearing buddies.

Tamara, sitting in the back of her air-conditioned limo, stuck in the atrocious traffic that brought the road to St Tropez pretty much to a standstill for most of June to September, was twitchy with excitement. Miles had all but offered her the part! Well, he wanted her to accompany him to Cannes to meet the money men – they wanted *way* too much say in the artistic side of things, as far as he was concerned – but he assured her that that was a mere formality, that she'd knock their socks off. She'd also have to do a read-through with her leading co-stars when she was back in LA in a couple weeks' time. But again, Miles had given her his word that this was a mere formality, that he had nobody else in mind, and the part was hers for the taking.

Tamara gleefully reached into her handbag for her phone, and touched Jack's name on the screen. It rang for at least thirty seconds before giving up the ghost. Irritated, she tried again. This time he picked it up on the third ring.

'Tamara? Hey, how'd it go?'

'Why didn't you pick up before?'

'I didn't hear it. We're having lunch on the beach, and reception's awful.' Tamara felt irrationally annoyed and

149

tried not to let it show in her voice. After all, hadn't she just been having lunch on the beach? 'So how'd it go? What was he like?'

'Geeky, nerdy, *insanely talented*. And he loved me!' Tamara was grinning with glee again. 'The part's mine, Jack – save for formalities.'

'That's wonderful! Hey, guys, Tammy got the part! Isn't that great?' Tamara could hear murmurs of congratulation in the background and smiled to herself. 'So does that mean you can come join us now? You'll love it here – it's *way* cooler than St Tropez – and Bella's giving a big party tomorrow—'

'Um . . . *no?* I told you there are some formalities. I have to go to Cannes to meet the money guys.' Tamara loved saying this. Cannes had kudos.

But Jack didn't seem to see it that way, sounding genu-inely disappointed as he said, 'Shame. The party should be a blast. But, hey – the film's more important, right? Listen, honey, you're cracking up on me – reception's crap here. I gotta go. But I'll call you this evening, huh? Congratulations again. I'm so proud of you. And I love you.'

'Love you too,' said Tamara in a small voice, before hanging up, deflated. Why couldn't Jack get what a big deal this was for her? And who cared about some crappy party, given by somebody she didn't know? She and Jack spent their entire lives at parties. She wanted to call someone else, but couldn't think who. She'd already left a message with her agent, who'd been in a breakfast meeting. Her money-grabbing parents were out of the question. She realized she'd spent so much time hanging out with Jack and his buddies that she didn't have any real friends her own age left – and anyway, the heiresses and Hollywood princesses she'd grown up with had soon gotten tired of her after she got clean. There was the usual gang of sycophants that hung around her like flies around a steaming pile of shit, but none of them would realize how much this meant to her – and it was way too early for any of them to be up in LA, even if they did.

Tamara played with the beautiful diamond-and-emerald engagement ring that Jack had given her, all of a sudden acutely aware of how lonely she was. She lit a cigarette with her gold Cartier lighter and took a few grateful puffs. She was meant to have given up, but fuck it. After a few more puffs, she opened the car window and chucked the fag out, then opened Twitter on her phone. She had hundreds of thousands of followers – at least *they'd* be interested in her news. Cheering up a bit, she took a photo of herself in the back of the limo, then started to compose a new Tweet.

'Hey, buddy, am I hallucinating or can I like actually see Shangri-La?'

One of Lars's less couth old friends from Merrill Lynch was pointing up the skirt of one of three nubile young lovelies dancing on a glittery podium next to their bottle-rammed table. It had cost the all-male party €10,000 to book the table at Les Caves du Roy, St Trop's absurdly jet-set nightclub, which was located in the basement of the Byblos, and another €1,000 for every subsequent bottle of champagne (the initial fee was supposed to cover the first). It was impossible to get past the enormous bouncers unless you were famous, incredibly rich or ridiculously beautiful – preferably all three.

Already that evening, Lars had spotted Claudia Schiffer, Miranda Kerr, Katy Perry and all of the Black-Eyed Peas – he'd even caught a glimpse of that geeky film director that Tamara Gold had been lunching with earlier. A couple of Russian oligarchs were enjoying the company of five beautiful girls several decades younger than them, and the large group of sheikhs paying little heed to the teachings of the Koran at the next table probably owned half the Middle East.

Lars tried to hide his boredom. He didn't feel he had much in common with his old banker buddies any more. In all fairness, they weren't that bad, and it had been fun hanging out with them in the daytime at 55 and Nikki Beach, where the sheer beauty of the sunny surroundings made it impossible not to have a good time. Here, it was different. Since Lars had set up his eco-tourism business, he had started to feel more and more claustrophobic when in crowded places, underground or surrounded by meaningless excess. Les Caves du Roy? Not his ideal environment. 'I don't think so,' he said now, apropos the visibility of the girl's nether regions. 'She's probably wearing underwear. Watch my drink, will you, Steve? I'll be back in five.' He pushed his way through heaving, thronging, sweaty bodies (you'd think with the obscene amounts they charged for drinks, Les Caves would manage to get the aircon working) to the men's lavatories. He was taking a piss in one of the opulent cubicles when he heard a female voice panting from the next-door cubicle.

'Oh God, yeah . . . Oh God, that's good . . . Don't stop, don't stop, don't stop, *don't stopppp* . . . aaaah.'

Oh well. At least someone was having some fun.

He zipped himself up, exited the cubicle and was washing his hands when the other cubicle door opened, and the couple who had been in there crept out. The girl was saying 'shhhh' with her finger to her lips, and giggling.

It was Tamara.

Gone was the demure, sophisticated, professional young actress he had seen on the beach earlier that day. In her place was a mad-eyed little starlet, with scarlet lipstick smeared across her face, hair tangled into a wild bird's nest and skin glowing with sweat and sex. Her gold sequinned dress was so short and so tight that if you didn't know she was Hollywood royalty she could easily be mistaken for one of the many expensive hookers that frequented this horrible place.

As soon as she saw Lars, her eyes widened in panic.

'Shit. You won't tell, will you?' she pleaded.

'Come with me.' Lars was furious, though whether with her for not living up to the sweet image she'd put in his head that afternoon, or with himself for falling for it, he wasn't sure.

'Hey, who are you – her dad?' asked the handsome young Lothario who'd just had his wicked way with her.

'I'm a friend of her fiancé.' Lars glowered menacingly into the boy's eye. 'You ever mention a word of this – you're dead. Understand?' The boy looked at the gigantic Swede and nodded, gulping. Lars grabbed Tamara by a small reluctant hand and dragged her out of the gents, along the thickly carpeted corridor and outside, to a dark, quiet area around the back of the pool.

'Who the hell do you think you are?' Tamara demanded quietly, more furious than scared now. 'You're no friend of Jack's – you've met him *once*, for chrissakes. Get off me, you great big bully.'

'I'm doing this for your own good, you stupid girl.'

'What are you talking about?' Tamara stared at him, her hands on her hips in a show of defiance.

'I saw you at 55 today, having lunch with that film director. It was very convincing, your Little Miss Innocent act . . .'

'*What?* Are you like some crazy stalker, or something?'

'You're the crazy one,' said Lars bluntly. 'St Tropez is a small place. Did it not occur to you that the film director might come here, tonight? It is, *like*, the hottest club in town.' Sarcastically he imitated her intonation.

Now Tamara did look frightened. 'M-Miles is here?'

'Uh-huh. He's sitting with a load of people inside there.'

'Did he say anything about me?'

'How am I supposed to know?' Lars sounded exasperated. 'I don't know the dude. But if I were you, I'd go back to your room – I'm assuming you've got a suite here?' Tamara nodded mutely. 'And go to bed.' He was finding it very hard to look at her when she glared at him with that half-angry, half-scared defiance. He was trying not to admit to himself that as well as wanting to protect her, there was a strong element of good old-fashioned jealousy contributing to his anger. Not that he'd want to screw her in a toilet, of course – their first time would be more special than that, but . . .

'Why did you take such a stupid risk?' he continued, trying to ignore his whirring thoughts (*First time? What the fuck?*) and jumbled emotions. 'You don't seem drunk, or high. You're not, are you?' He grabbed her narrow wrists again and she shook him off.

'No, I'm not. And I still don't get what it is to *you*. Unless . . .' A self-satisfied edge had crept into her voice. 'It's because you want me, isn't it? You couldn't stop staring at me the other day, at Nikki Beach, and then at Senequier . . . Do you want me, Lars? Do you want to *kiss* me?' She gazed up at him through glittering green eyes, standing up on tiptoe to get closer, her lips slightly parted.

She was teasing him, but the longer she looked into his eyes, the more she felt an intense connection growing – despite her recent encounter in the toilet. Her heart started pounding. For a second or two, Lars gazed back, mesmerized.

'I met your fiancé, and I liked him a lot,' he said abruptly, jerking his head away. 'I don't like girls who play games with men. Now get out of here, before I change my mind and tell Jack, that director guy, and every goddamn gossip columnist in St Tropez what I've just seen.'

Tamara stared at him for around half a minute more, then laughed in his face.

'Nobody would believe you if you did. But I'm tired now, and think it's time to hit the sack. Goodnight, Lars. It was nice to bump into you again.'

As she sauntered off into the warm night air, Lars had to admire her chutzpah. He only wished his cock wasn't pushing so painfully against his jeans.

12

The day of the pool-warming party dawned – not unusually, for Ibiza – hot, bright and clear. Bella woke early, as was her wont these days, as excited as she used to feel as a child when it was her birthday, or Christmas. Andy had already risen, presumably to get some writing done before the festivities started, so she put on a pretty, short cotton nightie and went to check on Daisy before making her way downstairs. First things first: breakfast. She had guests to feed.

But once she got to the kitchen she saw that her old friend had beaten her to it.

'Morning,' grinned Poppy, as she bustled about the enormous sun-filled room, pouring orange and grapefruit juice out of cartons into jugs, cutting up ripe, highly scented nectarines and brewing delicious-smelling fresh coffee on top of the stove. She actually seemed to be doing all three simultaneously, bless her efficient little heart. 'Thought I'd give you a break – you've got so much on today.'

'Thanks, Pops, that was thoughtful of you.' Bella smiled. 'Oooh and you bought *ensaimadas* – yum!' She indicated the basket of delicious icing-sugar-sprinkled sweet pastries that were indigenous to the Balearics.

'You can thank your husband for that.'

Bella raised her eyebrows.

'Oh shit, sorry, keep forgetting,' Poppy continued. 'But you two are sooo married. Anyway, sod it – let's leave it for today, yeah? Your lovely *other half* gave me a lift down to the *panadería* in San Carlos. We thought that pastries, fruit and yoghurt would cause less mess and washing up than eggs and stuff. Now you go and get showered, sort Daisy out, and leave this all to me.'

'Such a bloody bossy boots,' grumbled Bella, still smiling. Poppy was a godsend.

By midday, they'd laid out mis-matched towels in every colour of the rainbow on sunloungers all around the pool, with plenty more stacked up in a neat pile next to the French windows; made jug after jug of fruit-laden red and white sangria, which now filled the fridge almost to bursting point; filled the bath upstairs with ice, cava, wine and beer; put vases of fresh flowers on every available surface; set out rows of glasses on one of the garden tables; filled blue-and-white china bowls with almonds, olives and little cubes of tortilla, plates with jamon Serrano and baskets with bread, all sitting in the cool of the kitchen, covered by tea-towels to protect them from wasps and flies; and last but not least, stocked up the downstairs wet room with large bottles of Aveda shower gel, shampoo and conditioner – nice for guests to be able to wash away the chlorine with delicious-smelling unguents if they fancied it. All that still needed doing was the paella, but nobody was arriving until at least two o'clock, and they didn't want to make paella too far in advance and risk ruining the seafood.

Bella and Poppy, who had been working in the kitchen, were wearing cotton sundresses over their bikinis; Andy and Damian, who had been sorting things out around the pool, were in their swimming trunks; Daisy, sitting in her high chair where Bella could keep an eye on her, sported her best daisy-embroidered frock. Occasionally she commented on the adults' progress with words that were known only to her.

'Hellloooo?' called a friendly voice. 'Anybody home?'

'Hey, Summer, come in!' Bella shouted from the kitchen. 'The door's open.'

Summer, looking lovely in a halter-neck indigo maxi-dress, walked into the kitchen carrying an enormous basket filled with fresh seafood.

'Oh, you are an absolute angel,' cried Bella, rushing over to give her a hug and a kiss. 'Thank you so much for doing this – it's saved me so much work!'

'Hey – no biggie,' smiled Summer. 'It would have been stupid for you to drive all the way into Eivissa to pick up the fish when I live on the market's doorstep. Hi,' she added to Poppy, holding out a friendly hand. 'I'm Summer.'

'Hi, Summer, I'm Poppy.' Poppy smiled, but she was wary. She didn't want anyone taking advantage of Bella, and everything she'd told her about Summer sounded a bit too good to be true.

'Hi, Poppy, great to meet you. Hey, Daisy darling!' Summer went to pick Daisy up out of her chair and give her a hug and lots of kisses. Daisy grinned and giggled – she loved Summer.

'How are you getting on?' Summer asked Bella. 'It looks like you have everything under control.'

'We do. Come and see what you think of the garden.'

'I'll stay here and keep an eye on Daisy,' said Poppy, plopping several ice cubes into her first gin and tonic of the day.

'It is even more beautiful than I remember from the old days,' said Gabriella, sipping from a glass of cava as Bella

158

gave her a tour of the garden. She stopped by a large rosemary bush to rub the pungent needles between her fingers, sniffing the heady aroma. 'You have worked wonders.'

'Thanks.' Bella shifted Daisy onto her left hip. Soon it would be time for her daughter's afternoon nap, thank God. She was never any trouble, but Bella was looking forward to relaxing with her guests for a bit.

'You don't mind that I brought Shane?' added Gabriella, who was wearing a floppy wide-brimmed hat, elegant palazzo pants and a loose linen shirt over a strapless one-piece swimsuit – all in white. 'He's a good man – and a good contact to have on this island, owning all those bars.'

'Not in the least,' smiled Bella. 'I did ask you to bring a guest – and Shane seems fab.' They both looked over to where Shane was chatting with Andy and Damian, the three men bonding, by the look of it. Only a handful of guests had arrived so far, and nobody was swimming yet, but it was already quite clear that the party was going to be a success.

'I hear India and Jamie are coming too,' said Gabriella, with a slight tinge of disapproval in her voice.

Bella shrugged. 'She dropped so many hints that in the end it was easier to give in. Can't see what harm it can do.'

Gabriella frowned. 'You don't know Jamie Cavendish. He is a truly horrible man. Beware of him – that is all I say.'

'So you must come to Aqua – dinner on the house?' Shane was saying to Andy. 'It's the least I can do to thank you for your hospitality.' Like Gabriella, he was dressed in white, in his usual uniform of linen shirt over immaculate jeans, with a sailor's cap protecting his shaved head from the sun.

'Thanks – that would be great. Slightly premature to thank us for the hospitality, though – we haven't even eaten yet!'

'Oh, I know Summer's food is always wonderful. And I'm sure your wife's is too,' Shane added hastily.

'She's not my wife, but yeah – Bella's a bloody good cook. It should be fantastic.'

'Hi, Andy,' said Poppy, walking towards them out of the French windows, now clad only in a tiny yellow bikini that showcased her tiny brown body to perfection. 'Do you think we can christen the pool yet, or does Belles want to do some kind of "I declare this pool well and truly open" thing?'

'Oh, I don't think so. In fact I'm positive – she wants everything to be laid-back and fun and casual. Have you met Shane, by the way?'

Poppy shook her golden head.

'Shane, this is Poppy, Damian's wife – the annoyingly handsome dark-haired guy we were chatting to earlier? – and Bella's oldest friend. Poppy, this is Shane – owner of one of the coolest new restaurants in Ibiza, by all accounts.'

Poppy was looking at Shane with a huge grin on her face.

'You're Shane Connelly, aren't you? *Bonza, mate!*' She held up her hand, and Shane high-fived her, grinning back. 'I used to have a massive crush on you when I was at school!'

'Thanks,' said Shane. 'But ouch. Anyway, I know who you are too. Poppy Wallace, right? *Poppy Takes Manhattan?*' Gay men always loved her shows.

'That's right,' said Poppy, trying not to look or sound too pleased. After hanging out with Ben, Jack and Tamara for so long, it was nice to have a bit of bloody recognition for once.

*

'*Muchas gracias,*' said Ben, taking some euro notes out of his wallet to pay the cab driver.

'Thanks, buddy. I'll get it on the way back,' said Jack.

As soon as they got out of the air-conditioned taxi at the end of the white dirt track that led to the ancient finca, the heat hit them afresh.

'Pouf, it's hot,' said Natalia, fanning her face with an elegant hand.

'I know. Can't *wait* for a swim,' said Ben. 'Sounds like the party's in full swing already.' Finding the heavy old wooden front door ajar, they went into the house – Bella had invited them for dinner a couple of nights before, so they were familiar with its layout. Ben and Natalia were making to turn right, towards the garden, when Jack tapped Ben on the arm.

'These need chilling.' He held up the plastic carrier bag containing three bottles of very good, unflashy vintage champagne. 'I'll take them to the fridge. See you out there.'

He turned left and made his way into the kitchen, which smelt deliciously of garlic and seafood. A tall, slim girl with long blonde hair was standing with her back to him, stirring something on the stove. She looked over her shoulder at him, and he saw her eyes widen in recognition. He was used to this, and hoped she wouldn't start to gush.

'Hi,' she said, smiling and wiping her hands on the apron she was wearing over a long, dark-blue dress. 'I'm Summer. If you're looking for Bella, she's upstairs putting Daisy to bed for her afternoon nap.'

'I wasn't actually looking for Bella, just somewhere to chill these?' He held up the carrier bag. 'I'm Jack, by the way.'

'No kidding,' laughed Summer, her clear dark-blue eyes crinkling ever so slightly at the corners, perfect white teeth gleaming in her smooth brown face. Jack's heart seemed to stop in his chest. She was absolutely beautiful. 'Nice to meet you, Jack.'

She held out a lovely, long-fingered hand, and Jack shook it. When their fingers touched, his heart started beating again. But soon she had turned away from him and was opening the fridge.

'Not much room in here, I'm afraid,' she said in that sweet, slightly sing-song voice. 'But if you take *this*,' she handed him a jug of white sangria. 'We can probably shove them in.' Jack passed her the bottles, one by one, and watched as she made room in the overcrowded fridge to slide them in on top of one another. Her back was bare, brown and smooth underneath the silky sheet of flaxen hair.

'So – would you like some?' Summer nodded towards the jug.

'Uh – yeah. Yep. Great. Thanks.'

Oh great, great, *Jack, impress her with your eloquence, why don't you?*

'Glasses are outside. I have to finish the paellas, but I'll join you out there later. Good to meet you, Jack.' She smiled again and Jack couldn't help but smile back.

'Good to meet you too, Summer.'

'Hi, India, so glad you could make it,' lied Bella. 'And you must be Jamie. Where's Milo?' She had fully expected them to bring their son with them and had made provision, food-wise too. Children, even groovy Balearic-bred ones, tended not to be huge paella fans.

'We thought it would be better to leave him with the nanny today,' said India, who was looking gaunt and fragile in her oversized Gucci shades and kaftan. 'He was playing up a bit this morning.'

'And we didn't want the little sod spoiling our fun,' said Jamie, sniggering nastily at his own joke. His eyes narrowed when he realized neither Bella nor India were laughing with him. 'So you're the famously well-connected Bella, eh?'

'Hardly,' said Bella, embarrassed. 'Anyway, what can I get you? Beer, wine, cava, sangria?'

'Oh, a glass of sangria would be great, thanks,' said India.

'I'll have a beer.'

'There's some sangria on the table over there, India. I'll nip upstairs to get you a beer, Jamie. The rest of the drinks are on ice in the bath, so help yourself when you want another one.'

'How very student-chic,' sneered Jamie.

Bella popped into the kitchen on her way upstairs to see how Summer was getting on.

'How's it going? Sorry to abandon you like this, but everyone's arrived at once. I've just had the pleasure of meeting Jamie Cavendish.'

Summer laughed. 'Charmer, isn't he? Well, these are about ready to go.' She nodded at the four big paellas steaming away on the hob. 'So is everybody here?'

'Everyone except Jorge and Henri.'

'Oh, no need to wait for them,' said Summer dismissively. 'Jorge's always late.'

'OK, I'll start sending people in with their plates as soon as I've fetched the delightful Mr Cavendish his beer.'

Summer laughed again. 'By the way,' she added casually, 'Jack Meadows seems nice.'

'Even more gorgeous in the flesh, isn't he? Lucky Tamara, that's all I can say.'

'Lucky Tamara,' repeated Summer.

'This is great,' said Gabriella, taking a mouthful of paella and looking around the exquisite garden, the party in full swing now. Bella smiled happily. Mid-afternoon, her pool-warming was exactly as she had envisaged it. The sun was high in the dark-blue sky, casting a fierce light on the brightly coloured beauty of the garden. Every colour, every sense seemed heightened, from the vivid turquoise of the pool to the deliciously garlicky, lemony, sweet salinity of the paella.

Bella was sitting on a bright pink towel on a sunlounger, with Gabriella lounging gracefully on a pristine white lounger opposite her. Poppy was splashing about in the pool with Shane, who seemed to have taken a huge shine to her, both of them showing off as they did handstands and swallow dives, challenging one another to races.

Ben, Natalia and Jack were larking about in Bella's folly with the waiters from Anita's, who couldn't believe they were at a party with Jack Meadows and Ben Jones; Jorge and Jamie were engaged in deep conversation outside Andy's study; Andy was sitting with most of the others at a large table on the other side of the pool. He looked over at Bella and smiled broadly.

'It's perfect!' he mouthed, giving her a double thumbs-up. She smiled happily back at him.

Bella and Poppy had had lots of fun the night before compiling a playlist of late Sixties and early Seventies music to be played today, in homage to the finca's previous incarnation – everything from the Small Faces' 'Itchycoo Park', to the Kinks' 'Sunny Afternoon', the Beatles (of course) singing 'Here Comes The Sun', and – now – Carly Simon's 'You're So Vain'.

'My God, this takes me back,' said Gabriella. 'I'm sure I used to sing this to your father, Bella.'

Bella laughed, shrugging. 'Sounds about right.'

'You've brought this house to life again,' Gabriella added. 'This is like old days – well, apart from the sex and drugs of course.'

'Thanks, Gaby. Is it OK if I call you that?'

'Of course,' smiled the older woman graciously.

'God, it's hot today – not that I'm complaining. But I'm going to need a dip very soon . . .' As she was saying it, the unmistakable sound of Daisy's little voice, chattering away incomprehensibly, came floating down over the late afternoon air. She laughed. 'Should have known it was too good to be true. Daisy's waking up.'

Summer, helpful as ever, started to carry plates to the kitchen. Within less than a minute, Jack Meadows had appeared at her elbow.

'Hey, you've been working hard all day,' he said. 'Let me do that.'

'It's OK, I'm happy to do it,' Summer said automatically. Then she looked at him and reconsidered. 'Though it's nice to have a helping hand. We can do it together.'

'That paella was fantastic, by the way,' said Jack. 'You're an amazing cook.'

'Thanks. It's my passion.'

Between them, they ferried all the dirty plates back to the kitchen.

'What a wonderful young man,' said Gabriella. 'So polite, so handsome.'

'Yup, he's gorgeous all right,' agreed Bella. 'OK, I can't wait another second!' And she set off towards the pool steps.

The kitchen seemed suddenly cool and dark after the intense heat and light of the garden.

'Thanks so much for doing this,' said Summer, as she scraped the plates into the bin. 'It's not the sort of thing you'd expect from a famous movie star.'

Jack laughed. 'It may sound ridiculous, like every inter-view you've ever heard from a fatuous Hollywood A-lister, but I am, really, *just a regular guy*.'

Summer laughed too. 'Yeah, just a regular guy who happens to command millions of dollars for every movie performance.'

'Billions for *Antony & Cleopatra*, actually.'

As Jack scraped another plate into the bin, his bare shoulder brushed Summer's. Immediately, they leapt apart from each other. And then, at exactly the same time, they both laughed again.

'Okaaaay – slight over-reaction,' said Jack.

They gazed at each other for what seemed like minutes, but was probably only seconds.

Up close, Summer could see the hazel flecks in Jack's thickly lashed green eyes as they roamed over her face, the scattering of freckles across the bridge of his elegant straight nose, the softness of his full lips.

'Time for a swim, I think,' she said, snapping herself out of it. 'There's a party out there – this can wait till later.' She meant the tidying up, but the words hung over them.

'I'll join you,' said Jack. 'I could use some cooling off.'

Back outside, Jack tried not to stare as Summer undid the halter ties of her maxidress and let it drop to the floor, revealing her beautiful long-limbed, subtly curvaceous body in a faded blue string bikini. Without looking back at him, she performed a clean dive into the deep end, then swam the whole length of the pool underwater. Not giving himself time to think, Jack dived in after her.

The water was wonderfully cool and soothing against his burning skin, purging him of unclean thoughts. Except it wasn't. What the hell was happening to him? He had drunk quite a lot of the sangria, he rationalized to himself, as he swam after Summer under the water. And the sun could be going to his head. But when he came up for breath, and found himself face to face with her, he realized that it wasn't nearly that simple.

Her blonde hair, wet against her head, shone golden in the Balearic sun and emphasized her lovely bones and wide laughing smile. She looked him in the eye for a millisecond, before swimming back under.

She looks like the sun, he thought as he followed her. And, try as he might not to make the comparison, he couldn't help but think of Tamara, unwilling ever to put her face in the sun or her head underwater. He carried on swimming, eyes closed as he was wearing his contacts. As one hand encountered a slender ankle, he allowed himself to caress both legs, ever so slightly at first, and then, gently but more firmly, further up the thighs.

Suddenly, they kicked back at him, absolutely not the reaction he'd been expecting.

When he re-emerged this time, he was face-to-face with Poppy.

'Get your hands off me, you bloody perv,' she giggled. 'Don't think I was your target, though, was I? She's over there.' She nodded towards the far corner of the pool. 'You must have the worst sense of direction ever.'

'Sorry, Pops.' Jack was hideously embarrassed. 'What the hell did Bella put in that sangria?'

'Maybe it was a luuurve potion.'

'Please stop it.'

Jack looked so agonized that Poppy thought she should give him a break.

'None of my business, mate.' She thumped him on the shoulder. 'My lips are sealed!' Her high voice rang out, bell-like, over the water.

'Well, you have put my mind at rest. I don't think I've ever met anybody more discreet.'

'Sorry,' said Poppy, quietly this time. 'But maybe you should try to be a bit more discreet yourself.'

'OK. Point taken.' Jack searched for something else to say as he bobbed, treading water. 'Great party, huh?'

Poppy looked out at all the happy faces. After a quick

dip, Bella had nipped inside for a brief shower and come back down with Daisy in her arms. She was sitting on her sunlounger with the little girl on her lap, as her new friends cooed over her. Andy had his entire table in fits of giggles – he could be very funny, in his dry way, when he chose. Several people had started drunken dancing by the edge of the pool to an old Stones hit – Jorge was getting quite touchy-feely with Pilar, the waitress from Anita's, Poppy noticed – and Ben and Natalia were still lounging in Bella's folly.

'It's fab, Belles!' she shouted, waving over at her friend. 'Jack's just been saying what a brilliant party this is!'

'Thanks, Jack!' Bella called back happily. 'Glad you're having a good time.'

'A great time!' Jack cast one last, longing glance in Summer's direction. 'OK, so I've done my cooling off,' he added to Poppy. 'I think I'll go hang out with Ben and Natalia now.'

'Probably the safest course of action,' said Poppy. 'I'm staying right here. This pool is pure heaven.' And she dived back down under the water.

From the other end of the pool, Summer watched as Jack hauled himself out with strong tanned arms, noticing the way the muscles rippled in his back as he did so. He shook his black curly head to get some of the water out. His broad shoulders tapered to a narrow waist and hips, and Summer's stomach twisted with longing as he strode on long, well-muscled legs back to the folly.

Inside the folly it was cool and shady, with an almost ethereal light cast by the whitewashed stone of the ceiling onto the white linen-covered mattresses and cushions. The Indian silk drapes in vivid shades of pink, red and orange fluttered in the slight breeze, lending it an exotic air. Natalia was reclining against the cushions, one long leg pointed straight out in front of her, the other bent at the knee. Dressed in a ruched white silk swimsuit, with her white blonde hair piled on top of her head, she could have been Grace Kelly acting the part of a Grecian goddess.

Ben, dazzlingly handsome next to her in his sunny yellow Vilebrequin trunks, was swigging from one of the expensive bottles of champagne Jack had bought and making Natalia laugh. Now, as Jack approached, he offered him the bottle.

'Thanks, buddy, but I'll use this.' Jack held out the glass he had picked up en route from the pool, so Ben could fill it. 'Jeez, whatever happened to the famous British sense of decorum?'

'I think you'll find it's the famous British sense of humour, actually,' said Ben.

'I have been telling him he's *dreadfully uncouth*,' Natalia added. 'But I think he thinks it makes him look *cooool*.' She winked and Jack laughed, because, in all fairness, Ben *did* look kind of cool, in a decadent, golden-boy sort of way. A bit Robert Redford in *The Way We Were*, now he came to think of it.

'Mind if I join you?' asked a slightly hesitant voice, and Jack turned around to see Summer standing behind him, her long golden hair dripping down her back, droplets of water already drying on her shimmering brown body. She smiled, almost shyly, for her.

'No! No, not at all! Come meet my friends. Summer, this is Ben and Natalia. Ben and Natalia, Summer!' Jack could hear the over-hearty jocularity in his voice and winced internally.

'I know who you are, Ben.' Summer laughed, and Ben did too, preening himself slightly. 'It's great to meet you. And you too, Natalia.' She held her hand out, smiling, and the older woman smiled back. It was impossible not to warm to Summer.

'Let me get you a glass,' said Jack, striding off in the direction of the house and giving himself a chance to breathe. He found Summer's proximity quite overwhelming.

'So how do you know Bella and Andy?' Ben asked, trying not to gawp at the beautiful girl. He wasn't being lecherous, but Summer was so exquisite that it was difficult not to stare.

'I run the crèche at my mother's beach yoga classes. Bella's been coming for the last couple of months, and we've become friends.'

'So you look after the kids?' said Natalia, thinking that this girl had to be every man's wet dream made flesh.

'Only three mornings a week. Most of them are soooo cute, but the mothers – ugh, don't get me started.' Summer rolled her eyes, and Ben and Natalia laughed. She looked guiltily over her shoulder. 'Shit, I should keep my voice down – a few of them are here.' Ben and Natalia laughed again, warming to her more.

'But it's not my main job.' Summer sat down on the edge of the folly, careful not to get her wet bikini bottom on the linen-covered mattress. 'Mainly, I write a food column.'

'Cool,' said Ben, looking at her with respect as he edged his way towards Natalia inside the folly. He liked writers. 'Hey, Jack,' he added, as his friend returned with a wine glass and another bottle of champagne, 'Summer's telling us about her work.'

'You're a cook, right?' said Jack confidently as he uncorked the champagne.

'Oh no!' Summer smiled. 'Well, yes, actually, sometimes I do cook for private parties, but that's not what I'm doing here today. I was helping Bella out, as a friend.'

'You made that delicious paella?' said Ben. 'I *thought* Bella had upped her game.'

'We made it together.' Summer's voice was firm. 'Bella's a great cook. Thanks.' She took the glass from him. 'I'm a journalist. I have a food column on a website called *Island Life*. I don't suppose you've heard of it.'

'Not yet, but that's easily remedied. Chuck me my phone, Ben?' They'd put all their phones in a pile inside the folly, to protect them from the sun. 'Thanks.' He caught it expertly, in one hand.

'Good catch,' said Summer.

'I played baseball for Princeton.' Jack smiled back into her eyes. For a second, as he drank in her golden sunshiny beauty, it was as if nobody else had ever existed. The idea – the fact – of Tamara was there, but it was as if he was . . . oh God, he was going into cliché overload. What kind of pathetic loser was he? He was engaged to Tamara, and had known this girl for less than an hour. For chrissakes.

From inside the folly, Ben groaned, breaking the spell. 'Is there no end to your talents, you smug bastard?'

'Not really, no.' Jack snapped himself back into reality. 'OK, so . . . *Island Life*, you say?'

'Yes, but there's no need —' Summer protested.

'I want to see it.' Jack briefly looked up from his phone, into her eyes again, and Summer looked back, her heart starting to beat faster. 'Wow, cool site. *Very* nicely produced. OK . . . Food and drink . . . Oh *here* you are . . . Summer Larsson . . .' He looked up at her again. 'You're Swedish?'

Summer nodded. 'Uh-huh. Born and bred in Ibiza though.'

'Explains a lot,' said Ben, and Natalia gave a snort of laughter.

'Hey, this is great. You write beautifully.' Jack was reading Summer's review of Aqua. 'Aqua . . .? Isn't that the restaurant owned by that Shane guy we were introduced to earlier?'

'That's it.'

'He was offering us a free meal, any time we like over the next couple weeks,' said Jack, trying to ignore the perfection of Summer's face, and the sweet expression in her dark-blue eyes. 'I wasn't that keen before – though he seemed a nice enough guy – but having read this, I think I'll take him up on it. The sea bass sounds fantastic.'

'It is manna from heaven,' said Summer. 'And you should take him up on the offer – the restaurant is fabulous. But you must pay for your meal,' she added sternly. 'He has a business to run, and I'm sure you can afford it.'

'Ha, that told you!' chortled Ben, taking another swig from the champagne bottle.

'Yeah, like *you've* never accepted any freebies. Honestly, Summer, this guy is the biggest freeloader in Hollywood. But you're right, of course. We'll go – *and* we'll pay.'

'Cool. I'll drink to that.' Summer raised her glass, smiling, and Jack clinked it with his, smiling back at her.

'Right, on that note, with my reputation in tatters,' Ben announced dramatically, his RADA accent verging on the Ian McKellen, 'I'm buggering off for a swim. Going to join me, Nat?'

Natalia stretched lazily. 'Hmmm, I don't know. It is *verrrry* comfortable here . . .'

Ben gave her an unsubtle nudge, nodding over at Jack and Summer. After Tamara's recent nightmarish behaviour, he reckoned his mate deserved some fun, and what could be more fun than a beautiful, free-spirited Swedish chick? He did feel a bit sorry for Tamara, but God only knew what she was getting up to in St Tropez, and as far as Ben was concerned, what was good for the goose was good for the gander.

Natalia, catching on immediately and feeling no loyalty whatsoever towards Tamara, changed tack. 'But that water looks *vonderful*! Yes, I shall join you, my darling. See you guys later,' she added to Jack and Summer, throwing her long legs across the side of the folly and standing up to her full six foot, stunning in her white silk swimsuit and enormous Chanel sunglasses.

Jack and Summer watched as the couple sauntered towards the pool, Ben still clutching his champagne bottle by the neck.

'Now that,' laughed Summer after they'd left, 'is Hollywood glamour.'

'Hey!' Jack was mock-hurt. 'What about me?'

'I thought you were *just a regular guy*,' Summer teased him, and he laughed.

'I guess I asked for that.'

They looked at one other some more, each acutely aware of the other's nearly naked body next to them. Summer had no idea why she was behaving like this. She had never, in her entire, charmed life, knowingly shown interest in a man who was involved with someone else. Too messy, too chaotic, too much potential for pain. Yet now, here she was, gazing into the no-doubt faithless eyes of one of the most famously attached men on the planet.

'Don't think about Tamara,' said Jack, reading her thoughts. 'I won't be here, in Ibiza, for long. I promise not to do anything bad – anything that would make you uncomfortable. I just feel that I really, *really* want to get to know you. I felt like you *got* me, as soon as you saw me. You saw Jack, not Jack Meadows . . .'

'I saw Jack Meadows,' Summer smiled. 'Of course I did – who wouldn't? But maybe I am starting to see Jack, now.'

He looked at her, sitting there in her faded indigo bikini, her golden skin and hair such a beautiful contrast to the scraps of purply-blue cotton. There was no denying the intense attraction between them. But it was more than lust

– Jack was slightly ashamed that the fact she was a journalist, not only a cook, had attracted him to her even more. Not that there was anything wrong with being a cook, of course – he'd loved her paella, and in his business he rarely came across women who took unapologetic pleasure in food. But Jack had studied English at Princeton and was probably guilty of a touch of intellectual snobbery. A cook *and* a writer? What could be more perfect?

'I want to know everything about you,' he repeated. 'Your childhood, your family, where you went to school, how you got into journalism, your loves, your hates . . . Actually, you don't look like you hate much.' As he said this, Jack had to physically restrain himself from reaching out to stroke her cheek.

'Oh, you'd be surprised,' Summer laughed shakily.

'You're not married, are you?' Jack added, shocked by how much pain the thought gave him. He knew he had no right whatsoever to feel like this.

'No, not married, not seeing anybody.' Summer conveniently brushed the little matter of David aside. 'But you are . . .'

'I know, and it's something I'll have to sort out. But please, can we spend some time together – alone? Please? This party is far too public.'

Summer could only nod mutely, gazing back at him through sincere blue eyes.

'Tomorrow,' she whispered. 'Tomorrow I'll show you Ibiza – *my* Ibiza . . . Oh shit,' she suddenly added.

'What is it?'

'Jamie Cavendish is heading in our direction. He's a horrible, horrible man – a bully and a thug . . . Hi, Jamie.' She smiled as the man himself strode up to the folly.

'You two look very cosy.' Jamie smirked. 'Aren't you going to introduce me to your famous friend, Summer?'

'Well, you know who he is, so introductions probably aren't necessary. Jamie, Jack. Jack, this is Jamie Cavendish.'

'Hi, Jamie,' said Jack, reaching out to shake the man's hand.

'So where's the lovely Tamara?' asked Jamie pointedly.

'She had to stay on in St Tropez for a few days – possible part in a new movie,' Jack said, not liking the overfamiliarity of the Englishman's tone.

'What a shame. I was looking forward to meeting her – she looks a right goer. You're a lucky man, Jack!' Jamie slapped him heartily across the back, roaring with laughter.

'I'm sure she'd be thrilled by the compliment,' said Summer. 'Anyway, we've been monopolizing this bit of the garden for far too long. I think we should get back to the party. Are you coming, Jack?'

'Sure.'

And they walked towards the pool, leaving Jamie Cavendish standing alone at the folly.

'Thanks for inviting us today, Bella,' said India, smiling. 'I've had a lovely time so far. And even Jamie seems to be behaving himself, for once.' She laughed, slightly brittly, and Bella was amazed at the difference in the woman who'd started off being so unfriendly. Her face was actually rather lovely – delicate, with big soulful eyes and a sweet smile that had been conspicuous by its absence in the few months Bella had known her.

'I'm glad you're enjoying yourselves.' Bella bounced Daisy on her lap. 'We like our guests to feel at home, don't we, darling?'

'Yes,' said Daisy.

'Oh my God! Did you hear that? She's just said her first proper word. Say it again, Daisy! Yes yes yes yes yes!'

'Yes,' repeated Daisy, her little round face wreathed in

smiles. As if the effect hadn't been sweet enough, she giggled for good measure.

'Oh my God!' repeated India, smiling again. 'I am so glad I witnessed that.'

'Andy!' Bella yelled. 'Come over here! Daisy's just said her first proper word!'

'Oh, wow! Sorry,' Andy added to the rest of his table, 'but I've got to hear this.' And he raced over to where Bella, Daisy and India were sitting on the sunloungers.

'Say it again, darling. Say it for Daddy. *Yes!*'

'Yes,' repeated Daisy, and all three adults laughed in indulgent delight.

'Not sure how well this bodes for the future,' said Bella as an afterthought. 'Hope we haven't spawned a girl who can't say no.'

'I think it's terribly sweet and positive,' said India, reaching out to stroke Daisy's silky head. As she did so, the voluminous sleeve of her kaftan fell back, revealing her inner upper arm, which, from elbow to armpit, appeared to be one enormous multi-coloured bruise – or, more likely, several bruises, meted out over several weeks, melding into one. She quickly pulled the sleeve back down, but it was too late: from the horrified looks on their faces, both Bella and Andy had seen the evidence.

'How did you get those bruises?' asked Andy quietly. 'They look very painful.'

'Oh, I fell over. Too much to drink the other night.' India tried to laugh it off.

'I can't see how you could bruise that bit of your arm by falling over,' said Andy. 'Even Bella's not that clumsy.'

'Thanks,' said Bella. Then she turned back to India. 'He did it, didn't he?'

India stared at them both for a couple of seconds, before realizing it was useless denying it. 'Oh, all right, yes he did, but it's nothing, honestly. Sometimes he doesn't realize his own strength. Please don't say anything, Bella. Andy? Please? My life won't be worth living . . .'

She stared at them both with huge, scared blue eyes.

'He should be arrested,' said Andy, furious. He had made a career of exposing men who were violent towards women, and few things made him angrier.

'Andy, if India doesn't want us to say anything, then I don't think we should,' said Bella. 'But you don't have to put up with being treated as a punchbag.'

India's entire body seemed to sag. 'It's not that simple,' she said wearily. 'Jamie's stupidly rich, with half the corrupt politicians on this island in his pocket. I can't leave him. He'd never let me have custody of Milo, even though I don't think he likes his son very much.'

'I think that any judge, seeing those bruises, would know exactly who should get custody,' said Andy.

'You don't know Jamie,' said India. 'He's very clever. And I'm OK, *honestly* – as long as I've got my boy. Jamie doesn't hurt me all the time, either. He's not that bad really. Please . . . promise you won't say anything?'

'We won't say anything,' said Bella, thinking of the unimaginable horror of having Daisy taken away from her. 'But we're always here if you need us.' She reached out to clasp India's thin hand. 'Remember that.'

Jamie locked the upstairs bathroom door behind him and walked over to the loo, where he emptied half a wrap of coke on top of the cistern. This party wasn't working out nearly as well as he'd hoped. No Tamara Gold, and he had the distinct feeling he'd been snubbed, by both Jack Meadows *and* Ben Jones, to say nothing of that snooty Eastern European tart, Natalia. Who did she think she was, the miserable old bat? He chopped out a hefty line and took a straw out of his wallet. Ah, that was better. He checked his reflection in the mirror and smiled with satisfaction. He was a good-looking bastard, he had to give himself that.

Jamie and India had been happy, once. They had met through the Notting Hill trustafarian boho scene, on which they'd both been major players – India by virtue of her slender, high-cheekboned beauty; fey, hippyish style, and – oh yes – small trust fund set up by her aristocratic country family. Tall, handsome Jamie, who had attended a minor public school, tried to pass himself off as the same class, but was, in fact, mainly self-made. His dodgy investments had gone from strength to strength, funding the lavish, cocaine-fuelled lifestyle that he and India both enjoyed. Once, they had been partners in crime, snorting lines in the backs of cabs, giggling en route from one glamorous party to the next.

Things had begun to go wrong after Milo was born. As soon as pregnancy had started to change India's body, Jamie had lost all sexual interest in her, but India had reassured herself that things would get back to normal after the birth. They hadn't. It seemed that motherhood had rendered her physically repulsive to him, even though she'd worked her damnedest with yoga, running and starvation to get her body back to the way it once had been.

India, beautiful all her life and never short of admirers, was angry and hurt at what she saw as Jamie's cruel rejection. The fact that certain of her friends (bitchy, dim Saffron in particular) liked to boast, with horrible smugness, about how much their husbands had *loved* their bodies during pregnancy, helped not one jot. Her paranoia about younger women was off the scale, and she'd have had no compunction at taking a lover herself were she not so permanently depressed and exhausted.

Then there had been the business with the dodgy investments, which had meant they'd had to leave the UK, fast. Ibiza, where they'd spent most summers for years, seemed the obvious choice for relocation, but Ibiza's draw for the Cavendishes was also their Achilles' heel: the ubiquity of class-A drugs, and cocaine in particular. Not for nothing was Ibiza known as the White Isle.

It was perfectly possible to lead a wholesome, drug-free existence here, but the club scene was a huge factor in Ibiza's allure, and in certain circles the use of narcotics was even more prevalent than it had been back in West London, where for the most part, snorting coke was limited to weekends. Not so Ibiza in the summer, when hundreds of thousands of pleasure-seekers descended on the island and party followed party on a daily and nightly basis. It would have taken a far stronger couple than Jamie and India to resist the lure (and it was lucky for little Milo that they'd hired a very good nanny).

As the couple's joint dependency on the drug increased, so their relationship plummeted. What had once brought them together now pushed them apart, until they could hardly bear to be in the same room. Jamie wasn't proud of his occasional violent outbursts, but God did India ask for it sometimes.

Jamie's phone beeped. It was Tiffany, his twenty-one-year-old bit on the side. Tiff, who was originally from Croydon, worked as a podium dancer at Manumission and lived in a crummy studio flat on Playa d'en Bossa; she always appreciated the expensive gifts that Jamie liked to bestow on her. She was a common little tart, of course, with her dyed red hair, heavy make-up and thick false eyelashes, but she certainly knew how to turn him on with her gorgeous young body and uninhibited attitude to sex. Tiff knew Jamie was married and didn't give a fuck about India, as long as the presents and expensive dinners kept coming. She relished the power she had over the posh, skinny old bitch to whom Jamie had once introduced her, when they'd bumped into one another at Pacha. Jamie had clearly relished the encounter, telling India that Tiff was his new PA.

'I might have guessed,' had been India's tart response. 'Taste has never been your strong point.'

Jamie read the message.

U cumin round l8r? i want you Tx

He immediately stiffened, and grabbed himself for a quick wank, picturing Tiffany on all fours, her arse high in the air as he took her from behind. But the coke he'd just snorted made it impossible to come, and he banged the wall in frustration, chipping one of Bella's beautiful new cream tiles as a result.

'Hey! What's going on in there?' called out a high, girlish voice. 'Some of us are getting desperate out here!'

'Coming!' Jamie shouted, shoving his aching cock into his trunks and trying to will his hard-on to go away. He ran his forefinger over the final crumbs of coke and rubbed them on his gums, before unlocking the bathroom door.

'Crumbs *all* around your nose,' said Poppy, leaning against the wall in her yellow bikini. 'Dead giveaway.'

'Want some, sexy?'

'Actually, no. But thanks for the offer.'

'Oh, come on,' Jamie sneered. 'What's with the goody-two-shoes act? You can't tell me you've never done it?'

'No, I can't, so I won't. But there's a time and a place, and I don't think a complete stranger's house, right opposite a baby's nursery, *is* the place. If you'd asked Andy or Bella's permission, it would be different, but I very much doubt that you did.'

The way the little bitch was talking to him so sternly turned him on as much as her slender half-naked body. Still buzzing from the enormous line he'd just snorted, Jamie pushed Poppy against the whitewashed wall and ground his mouth against hers, trying to force it open with his tongue.

'You like that, don't you, you tart?' he breathed into her face.

'You are such a pathetic loser,' said Poppy, breaking free and slapping him hard across *his* face. 'If it wasn't for the fact that I don't want to make a scene at Bella's party, I would be downstairs now, telling everybody, including your wife, what you've just done. Actually, if you don't leave this minute, that's exactly what I *will* do.'

Jamie, thinking of Tiffany waiting for him in Playa d'en Bossa, and reckoning that this crappy party wasn't nearly what it had been cracked up to be, shrugged.

'I was going anyway,' he said. 'Don't even know why I bothered coming to this shithole in the first place.'

'Bye, guys,' said Summer. 'Thanks so much for a fantastic party, Bella. It's been such fun. And thanks, Andy – you two are the hosts with the mosts!'

'Thanks, Summer,' said Bella, giving her a hug. 'But without your help with the paella, it wouldn't have been nearly so great.'

'Oh, c'mon, you'd have been able to cook that on your own . . .'

'Yes, I think I would,' said Bella. 'Though it wouldn't have been so yummy, and I wouldn't have had nearly as much fun, stuck on my own in the kitchen all day. So thanks, lovely. We owe you.'

'It was a pleasure,' smiled Summer as she made her way out. 'Kiss Daisy goodnight for me, please.'

181

The minute the heavy old front door was closed, Bella and Andy looked at one another and laughed.

'Bloody hell!' said Bella. 'I reckon I've got a girl crush. What do you think about me channelling my inner lesbian?'

'Threesome?'

'Yeah, like that gorgeous twenty-five-year-old would want to do stuff with us,' said Bella. 'Besides, I love you too much to want to share you with anyone, however gorgeous and lovely she is.'

'Yup – me too,' said Andy, giving Bella an enormous hug and kissing the top of her head. 'However gorgeous and lovely she is.'

Outside, Summer was waiting for her taxi, inhaling the olive- and pine-scented air that she'd breathed most of her life, but which still never failed to make her happy, when Jack Meadows walked stealthily out of the back garden gate, looking over his shoulder in a nervous, furtive manner.

'Hey.'

'Hey.'

They walked towards each other in the semi-darkness, hearts beating fast.

'You told me you wanted to show me the real Ibiza, *your Ibiza*, but you didn't tell me how,' said Jack.

'This is how,' said Summer. 'I needed to know you meant what you said. Did you really think I'd give my number to some movie star who's about to get married?'

'I meant what I said.' Jack did what he had been longing to do all day, which was to stroke her peach-like skin. It was even softer than it looked, and as he touched her, Summer closed her eyes, relishing the sensation of his fingers on her face.

'Mmmm.' The way she said it was almost like purring.

She opened her eyes again, and Jack looked into them.

'Are you sure?' he asked. 'You know there's loads of stuff I have to sort out . . .'

'I'm sure,' said Summer.

Jack took her in his arms and kissed her like she'd never been kissed before. She kissed him back, feeling like a teenager, when kissing had meant something and could go on for hours, the end rather than the means.

All too soon, they heard the taxi rolling up the dirt track.

'I must go,' said Summer, giving Jack another kiss. She handed him a club flyer, on the back of which she'd drawn a makeshift map with a large cross on it. 'I guess you don't want to be seen anywhere too public, so meet me there at midday tomorrow. It's the road down to my parents' place. Should be pretty private.'

'Your *parents'* place?'

Summer laughed. 'I said *the road to* my parents' place. We're not going to hang out with Mom and Dad – what kind of pervy Swede do you take me for? As I told you, tomorrow I'm going to show you Ibiza.'

She gave him one last kiss on the lips. Then she got in the cab and was gone.

13

Jack sat in the back of the hire car, looking out of its tinted windows at the sunny sylvan landscape unfolding around him. The hire-car company was the one used by all celebrities visiting Ibiza, and its drivers could be counted on for their discretion. Jack was wearing non-descript long shorts and a baggy grey T-shirt, a baseball cap pulled down low over his face and dark glasses. Short of putting on a burka, it was as good as it was going to get, incognito-wise.

He was enormously excited about seeing Summer again. The previous night he had lain awake for hours thinking about her lovely sunny smile, sweet-natured dark-blue eyes and slightly sing-song voice. When he had finally fallen into a fitful sleep, it was full of disturbingly erotic dreams about her. He knew he was treating Tamara horribly, but he had already decided that as soon as they got back to LA, he was going to call the engagement off. Even if this whole Summer thing came to nothing (and he couldn't, in all honesty, see how it could come to anything, with her living here and him living in LA), the fact that he was experiencing such strong feelings proved that he didn't love Tamara. He didn't think that she loved him either, really, though she had definitely needed him in the past. But now she had the *Dust Bowl* role, her career would be going from strength to strength and she'd be a fully credible leading lady in her own right.

Thus Jack justified his actions to himself as he sped through Ibiza's olive-tree-lined roads to adventure and almost certain infidelity.

The car slowed down as they approached a turn-off that led down in the direction of the sea. A large white wooden arrow with the words 'Art Resort' painted in rainbow-coloured faux-naïf lettering pointed down yet another rubbly white track, flanked with highly scented and very tall pine trees either side.

After driving for a couple of minutes down the track, the hire car drew to a halt.

'This is where it say, on the map,' said the driver, leaning around to show Jack the flyer that Summer had given him the night before. Jack looked out of the window. They were still on the simple dirt track, with nothing to be seen but pine forest for miles around. Oh well, he guessed Summer knew what she was talking about.

'OK, thanks,' he said to the driver. 'How much do I owe you?'

'One hundred euros.'

It seemed you paid for discretion on this island, but Jack didn't have to worry about money, so he fished the notes out of his pocket and handed the driver an excessively generous tip, for good measure.

'How are you going to get back?' he asked. The track wasn't nearly wide enough to turn around. The driver shrugged.

'I carry on to the bottom, and turn around there. Is nothing.' If he thought it odd that Jack was getting out here, he certainly wasn't going to show it. It was not his job to ask questions.

Jack got out of the car and the heat hit him afresh. He was used to year-round sunshine in LA, but here it was different. The fact that they were sitting on a rock in the middle of the sea, not far from Africa, might explain why everything felt more intense in Ibiza. He watched the car continue down the track, blowing up a cloud of dust in its wake, and wondered what was going to happen next.

He didn't have to wait long.

'Hey,' said Summer, emerging from her hiding place behind a large pine tree. Jack caught his breath. She was looking even more stunning than she had yesterday, if that were possible, sporty and casual in white denim cut-offs that showed off her beautiful brown legs, grey Converse and a simple grey marl strappy vest top. She'd tied her blonde hair up in a high ponytail to keep her neck cool in the heat of the day, and the style emphasized her lovely bone structure.

'Hey.' Jack walked towards her, suddenly unsure of what to do. He wanted nothing more than to kiss the life out of her, but guessed he should let her dictate the pace. 'We gotta stop meeting like this,' he joked, and Summer laughed, the tension between them broken.

'So – I guess you're wondering what we're going to do next,' she said.

'Darling, I am dying of curiosity,' said Jack in a camp voice and Summer laughed again.

'Come with me,' she said, holding out her hand. Jack took it, trying to ignore the electric jolt he felt at the touch of her fingers, and followed her into the woods. Hidden behind another pine were two bicycles, a man's and a woman's, and a little way beyond them was another stony white track, leading off to the right.

'I told you we were going to explore Ibiza my way,' said Summer. 'I hope you like cycling.'

'Are you kidding? I LOVE cycling!' Jack's smile was wide. 'I try to get out on my bike at least once a day in LA.' It was true. Like Summer, he was naturally athletic and the Los Angeles climate made it easy to stay fit in an enjoyably outdoorsy way.

'That's great! Shall we go?'

'Try stopping me.'

They mounted their bikes and set off along the dirt track, side by side.

'So where are we going?' said Jack, already enjoying the exercise and the feeling of the wind in his hair. 'It doesn't look as if this track leads down to the sea.'

'Not yet, it doesn't, though we'll see some beaches eventually, never fear.'

Jack laughed. 'I trust your judgement entirely.'

'This track is almost totally unused, and by coming this way we can bypass all the main roads until we hit the northern beaches,' Summer explained. 'The coastline is really beautiful and rugged up there, and I even know a couple of coves that, on a good day, are . . . deserted.'

Summer paused a fraction before saying the word and turned to look at him. Jack felt his heart start to beat faster again at the implication.

'So tell me about your childhood,' he said, changing the subject. 'I guess it was pretty cool, growing up on the beach?'

As they cycled, they chatted. Summer told Jack all about her childhood, growing up on the beach with her hippy parents; Jack, in turn, had her giggling helplessly with his impressions of *his* parents – the renowned Filthy Meadows and flashing-eyed ex-groupie Maria Gonzalez. They talked about Summer's time at the University of Barcelona, and Jack's at Princeton, and how Jack got into acting almost by mistake. Summer told Jack about her global travels, and surprised and impressed him with her knowledge of the world – he had kind of assumed she'd led a happy but sheltered island life. Jack filled Summer in on the latest Hollywood gossip, some of which had her in fits of astonished laughter. They talked about music, and art, and literature, and by the time they reached the turn-off for one of the northern beaches nearly two hours had passed and they felt like they'd known each other for ever.

'This is great,' said Jack, thoroughly exhilarated by the exercise and the beauty of their remote surroundings. 'You were right – it's a fantastic way to get to see Ibiza.'

'Just you wait,' said Summer, getting off her bike. 'Leave the bikes here for a bit, and come with me.'

Jack did as he was told and followed her. As they emerged from the forest, he saw that they were on the edge of a cliff, looking down at a vast expanse of glittering sea several hundred metres below. The sea was patterned in two distinct colours – dark blue where rocks lay beneath, and a brilliantly clear turquoise that indicated pale sand under the waves.

'See down there,' Summer pointed at a tiny sandy little cove, bordered with rocks on either side. 'That's where we're going.'

'Wow.' Jack whistled. 'Beautiful.' Then he laughed. 'And you did promise me remote. But how do we get to it?'

'When we get to the bottom of the track, there's some hiking involved,' said Summer. 'You're not afraid of a bit of climbing, are you?' she added, teasing him.

Jack smiled at her. 'Bring it on!'

'So we made it,' said Summer, her face glowing from exertion as they scrambled down the final boulder and landed on soft white sand.

'We made it,' repeated Jack, looking around at the idyllic

surroundings. The cove was tiny – barely six metres wide – and bordered on either side by rocks, although the hillside above it was populated by dense green forest. The sugar-like sand stretched into the sea for some distance, so it was quite a way before the clear turquoise water faded into indigo, then deep navy.

'So,' said Summer, starting to feel slightly nervous now that they were actually here. She'd been so buoyed up on adrenaline and excited by her plan as she'd prepared the picnic that morning, she'd barely had time to consider the possible consequences. Despite their getting acquainted with each other during the two-hour bike ride, she didn't *really* know this man from Adam. But it was too late to turn back now. 'What would you like first? Lunch or a swim?'

Jack started to laugh. 'You brought *lunch*?' Could this woman be any more perfect?

'Uh-huh. What did you suppose was in that?' She indicated the rucksack that Jack had gallantly been carrying for her as they'd clambered down the rocks. 'You didn't think I was going to let you starve, did you? You're my guest for the day.'

'I feel honoured,' smiled Jack.

'But you still haven't answered my question.'

'Oh, a swim first, definitely. It was pretty hot work getting down over those rocks.'

'I agree,' said Summer. 'And the sea here is absolutely delicious.'

So are you, thought Jack. *So are you.*

'You know,' said Summer. 'As these beaches are so deserted, we don't tend to bother with bathing suits up here. It's so cool to feel the water on your naked body. But if you're not comfortable with that, then . . .'

'No, no, I'm totally cool with nudity,' said Jack hastily,

thinking that Summer had just answered his question: yes, she *could* actually be even more perfect.

'OK then, race you in!' Summer grinned and started to pull her vest top over her head, revealing her bare, tanned torso and high, full breasts. Jack tried not to look as he busied himself taking his own clothes off. He turned away as Summer undid the button fly on her white denim shorts, and by the time he turned around again, she was running, naked, down to the sea. Naked himself now, he ran after her, gasping with pleasure as the refreshing water hit his over-heated body.

Summer, swimming further out, was wondering what the hell had got into her. She couldn't remember ever having felt so happy, so joyously free, so ecstatic in another human being's company. And, she had to admit to herself, so incredibly turned on. Jack had coped effortlessly with the exhausting hike, his long legs making light work of the heights and distances involved, never stopping chatting in that intelligent, educated way of his. He was the perfect mixture of brains and brawn, Summer decided, turning back to face the shore and seeing that he was only a few feet away from her.

'This is glorious!' he shouted. 'Sensational, exquisite, sublime!' He yelled the words out and they echoed slightly around the cove. 'Thank you for bringing me here, Summer.'

'It's my special place,' she said. 'I've never brought anyone here before.' And before she could think any more about it, she swam over to him and kissed him, holding his face in her hands. Jack kissed her back with such ferocity that they both nearly went under, but they soon recovered themselves, and kissed and kissed and kissed, oblivious to everything but the other's mouth and hands and body, just the two of them, alone in the sparkling Mediterranean Sea. Jack's hands, when they weren't holding onto Summer's face like he never wanted to let her go, were roaming around her body, stroking her breasts, waist and buttocks, but never venturing between her legs. Soon she was writhing underneath his touch, silently begging him to touch her there.

By mutual unspoken assent, they started to swim back to shore, collapsing on the sand at the water's edge as they resumed their exploration of each other's bodies. Jack took first one full breast and then the other in his hands, gently sucking and nibbling until Summer was crying out in pleasure, begging him for more. Tentatively, his fingers strayed down to where her thighs met, touching her ever so lightly on the very edge.

'Oh yes, just like that,' Summer breathed, so he moved his head downwards, kissing her flat belly all the way down until he reached the burning skin between her legs. He spread her wide with his fingers, slowly sliding them in and out as he sucked and licked and kissed. Within less than a minute he felt her starting to contract around him, bucking helplessly against his face as the gentle waves lapped around them.

'Oh God, oh don't stop, oh, Jack, oh yes, oh God, ohhhhhh . . .'

Once she'd come to her senses, Summer laughed.

'Sorry, that was a little premature,' she said, sitting up and kissing him, stroking his wet curly head, not wanting to be apart from him even for one second.

'It was beautiful,' said Jack, kissing her back.

She reached out for his cock, rock hard and ready, and bent her head to suck him between her lips, but he pushed her back gently against the sand. 'If you do that, I won't last a second,' he said shakily. 'And for our first time together, I want to come inside you.' Summer's eyes glazed over with lust as she gazed up at him.

'I'm all yours.'

Jack raised himself up on to his elbows and slowly, oh so slowly, began to inch himself inside her, looking her in the eye all the while. She was so wet that it was difficult to do it so slowly, but eventually he had gone as far as he could go, filling her up with every inch of him. Still looking her in the eye he raised his eyebrows slightly, and she nodded. He thrust further, and then they were both lost, crying out in absolute pleasure. Summer wrapped her legs around his back, as he thrust rhythmically into her, again and again and again, his muscular buttocks powering his large cock, bringing her to orgasm again and again and again, as the waves continued to lap around them, the sun beating relentlessly down on their thrashing bodies. At long last, Summer felt Jack grow even further inside her. For a brief moment he was completely motionless, before crying out 'Summer!' as heaving spasms wracked his entire glorious body.

After about thirty seconds, still inside her, he raised himself up on his elbows and looked her straight in the eye again.

'This may be totally crazy, but I think I love you.'

Summer smiled with pure happiness. 'If you're crazy, then so am I. I think I love you too.'

And they started to kiss some more.

'I don't know about you, but I'm starving.' Summer lifted her head from where it had been resting on Jack's broad chest.

'Well, that sure was a good way to work up an appetite.' He tightened his arms around her and she gave a happy sigh.

'Really, though, I could eat a horse. You stay there and I'll set up the picnic.'

They'd moved out of the shallows and had been lying in the shade of the rocks at the back of the beach, making slow and languorous love one more time before drifting off to sleep in each other's arms.

'OK, let's see what you have,' said Jack lazily, watching as Summer clambered to her feet, brushing the sand off, and made her way over to the rucksack, which she'd also left lying in the shade. She was so lithe and supple, he could watch her move for ever.

'First things first.' She grinned. 'Wine!' With a flourish she produced a bottle wrapped in a plastic sleeve. 'Yay! It's still cold. This thing is magic.'

'What is it? Some kind of insulating thermos?'

'Something like that, yeah. I've no idea how it works – the important thing is that it does.'

Jack laughed. Summer uncorked the bottle of rose and poured them a plastic wine-glass each. They clinked glasses.

'To life and love,' said Jack.

'Life and love,' said Summer. 'But we need to talk seriously soon.'

'I know, I know. Can we eat first though?'

'Sure.' Summer smiled at him, unable to refuse him anything.

She laid out the feast on a small gingham cloth on the sand.

'Right, let's get stuck in.'

'This all looks delicious,' said Jack. And it did. Simple, but delicious. Tortilla, tomato salad, jamon Serrano, fresh crusty bread and a couple of enormous ripe peaches.

'Did you make this?' Jack asked, taking a bite of the still warm tortilla.

'Of course! Do you like it?'

'Let's just say I'm seeing more and more advantages to your being a cook.'

Summer laughed. 'Try the tomato salad. And take some bread to mop up the juices.'

The almost overripe tomatoes were thickly sliced and layered with thin slices of sweet Spanish onion, slivers of garlic and torn fresh basil leaves, all drenched in heady extra-virgin olive oil.

'Jeez, this is heaven on a plate!' Jack greedily mopped up the oily, garlicky, fragrant juices with a hunk of crusty bread, washing the whole lot down with a swig of chilled rosé.

'Don't you think the tomatoes taste of the sun?' said Summer, taking a large mouthful herself. Jack looked surprised.

'How funny you should use that phrase. I was thinking only yesterday that you look like the sun.'

Summer smiled. 'What a lovely thing to say.'

'Maybe that's what being Ibiza-grown does to you.'

'I guess that's the only logical reason.' They gazed at one another some more.

'And now you must try this ham,' said Summer, handing him the plate on which she'd laid out the local delicacy, so finely cut it was almost translucent. 'Take a bite of ham, then a bite of peach – the sweetness and saltiness complement one another perfectly.'

'I can't believe I'm being given lessons in how to eat by a beautiful naked Swedish girl in a deserted beach paradise. Whatever else may happen to me for the rest of my life, I will always be thankful that I had this day. Thank you, God!' Jack shouted dramatically, stretching his arms up to the sunny blue sky.

'Shut up and eat!' laughed Summer, before taking an enormous bite of peach. It was so ripe that the juices ran down her chin, and soon they were both so messily covered in sticky sweet peach juice that they had to go back into the sea to wash it off.

'So . . .' said Summer, once they were back on dry land. 'Not wanting to ruin the moment or anything, but I think it's time for that serious talk.' She looked at him hesitantly. 'I don't do this, Jack. I've never knowingly slept with another woman's man before, and it's not something I feel comfortable with – well . . .' she laughed sheepishly. 'Obviously I felt comfortable *doing it* – more than comfortable – oh, you know what I mean!' she added, flushed. 'But I don't like deception. You said you wanted to get to know me better – and I think we can certainly say we've achieved that.' At this, Jack picked up her hand and kissed it. 'But what's to happen next?'

'Even before today happened, I'd decided I was going to break it off with Tamara,' said Jack, taking both her hands in his. 'Now, I'm more certain than ever. But I can't do it until we get back to LA. She's on a major high at the moment about this new movie role, we're on our European vacation, the Press will be everywhere – it would be a total nightmare, and it's not fair on her. I do owe her that, at least. If I wait until we get back home, we can pretend it's an amicable separation, no third parties – hell, she can even say she's moved on from me now that she's a serious actress – I don't care.'

'I understand that. You don't want to make her suffer unnecessarily.' Summer kissed him on the lips. 'But what happens now? You're going to be here another ten days, right? And she's turning up soon. Can we avoid each other all that time? I know Bella and Poppy have already arranged some lunches and nights out . . . I'm not sure I want to avoid you anyway . . .'

'That's good to know.'

'And what happens afterwards? You just talked about going "home". If LA's your home, and Ibiza is most definitely mine, then where does that leave us?'

'I was thinking about this while you were asleep,' said Jack. 'I see how much you love this island, and I would never try and uproot you from what you love. But I'm pretty flexible. I don't have to spend my whole life in LA. I move around anyway, depending on the movie I'm shooting, and I could definitely live part-time in Ibiza. Hell, it worked for Johnny in France.'

'Johnny . . .?'

'Depp.'

Summer gave a sudden snort of laughter.

'What is it?'

'I can't believe I'm having this conversation,' she spluttered. 'I only met you yesterday, and now we're planning our lives together. Today's been so dreamy, I guess the mention of Johnny Depp brought home to me how utterly mad and surreal the whole thing is.'

'It does seem crazy, I know,' said Jack. 'But it's right, isn't it?' He clasped both her hands and looked into her eyes again. 'You know it's right.'

'Yes, I know it's right.' Summer sighed happily. 'So I suppose now we play it by ear, and try to be very discreet.'

'You got it.'

Jack leaned back on his elbows in the sand, turning his face up to the sun. Summer looked appreciatively at his bronzed torso with its scattering of curly chest hair, and the dark line that led down enticingly from his belly button to his groin. God, he was beautiful.

'So tell me about Tamara.'

Jack frowned. He didn't want to badmouth the woman he'd been engaged to for nearly a year, but he didn't want to lie to Summer, either.

'She – uh – she has her moments.'

'What do you mean?' Summer rolled over onto her front and started to play with Jack's feet.

'Hmmm, that's nice. OK, she's – well, let's just say that "high maintenance" is putting it mildly.'

Summer laughed.

'She has tantrums like other people have breakfasts. Shit, that's an appalling analogy.'

'It certainly is. Gets your point across though. She sounds a nightmare.'

'It's not her fault, really. She had a tough upbringing, her parents have only ever been interested in her as a commodity' – Jack found himself unconsciously quoting Tamara's therapist – 'but she's still like a little kid. A very spoilt little kid. We should never have got engaged in the first place.'

'So why did you?'

'God knows.' Jack changed the subject. He didn't think that the answer – 'sex' – would be very tactful after the day they'd just had. 'And what about you? How come there are no guys in your life? You're so beautiful, I'd have thought you'd be fighting them off. You do promise me there's no one, don't you?'

'I promise.' Summer mentally crossed her fingers behind her back. There was no point in sullying this beautiful day by talking about the unfortunate matter of David. She'd tell him it was over as soon as she possibly could, and no harm would be done. 'I guess I've never met the right guy. And now I have.' She crawled across the sand to kiss him again.

'And now you have.' Jack pulled her down on top of him. The time for talking had passed.

14

Sun was streaming through the shutters onto Summer's bed in bright diagonal stripes. She sighed with pleasure as she felt Jack next to her – their legs were entwined in a happy tangle of damp sheets, one of his arms around her waist. She bent her head to kiss his shoulder, breathing in his musky, male smell as she did so.

Jack had spent the last two nights at her flat, sneaking away from Ben and Natalia under cover of darkness, after putting in sterling performances of normality during lunches, respectively, at Playa Las Salinas and Aguas Blancas. The nights had been exquisite; as exquisite, in their own way, as their magical day on the beach. The more time Summer and Jack spent in each other's company, the more convinced they were that they had to be together.

Summer had spent the last two days counting the minutes until he turned up at her door, handsome, always smiling, tearing off what little she happened to be wearing within seconds of setting eyes on her. And afterwards . . . afterwards they had talked for hours, between kisses and more lovemaking, each taking more joy in the other's company than either of them had taken in anything before, their entire lives. It was heady, intoxicating stuff, probably made all the more so by its illicitness, but now it was going to have to stop.

Because today Tamara would be arriving on the island.

Summer felt Jack stir beside her and turned around to smile at him as he drowsily opened his eyes.

'Morning, beautiful.' Gently he drew her down to kiss him on the lips. After a few seconds, she felt his hardness rising against her leg, and she pulled away with regret.

'Oh, Jack, I wish we could, but haven't you got to be at the airport in . . .' she glanced at the alarm clock on her painted wooden bedside table . . . 'less than an hour?'

'Shit,' Jack groaned, sitting up and putting his curly head in his hands. 'Has it really come around so quickly?'

'I don't know how I'm going to bear not being with you every night,' said Summer, leaning over to kiss him again. Then she forced her innate practicality to take over. 'But I guess we'll manage somehow . . .'

Jack smiled ruefully. 'Speak for yourself. It's going to be hell.'

'You go and get showered while I fix us a pot of coffee,' said Summer, throwing back the sheets and leaping out bed. 'And make sure you remove every last trace of me!'

Jack laughed. 'No shower in the world could do that.'

As he walked past her on his way to the bathroom, he put his hands around her waist from behind and nuzzled the back of her neck, breathing in the scent of her hair.

'I'm going to miss you like crazy.'

Jack was waiting for Tamara at one of the two private jet terminals at Ibiza airport, wondering where the hell all these paparazzi had come from, considering he'd largely managed to avoid the paps since setting foot on the White Isle. And then he realized: of course, Tamara must have tipped them off. He wondered if it was something to do with the cryptic text she'd sent him. He took his phone out of his pocket and looked at it again:

Hey baby. Meet me at the airport at midday. I'm bringing you a surprise! Tammy x

He forced himself to smile, feeling foolish as he stood there with his enormous bunch of white lilies and roses, as the paps shot reel after reel of him, shouting questions all the while.

'Over here, Jack!'

'Been missing the missus, Jack?'

'There are rumours that she's been offered the lead in Miles Dawson's new movie. Can you confirm these rumours?'

'You planning anything exciting for your romantic reunion, Jack?'

Oh, for fuck's sake.

'We've been apart less than a week,' he said curtly. He was starting to feel very uncomfortable about seeing Tamara again, and almost wished he could finish it with her as soon as he saw her. After the last two nights at Summer's apartment, he was 100 per cent convinced that she was the only woman for him.

The only ones who knew what was going on were Ben and Natalia, both of whom had been sworn to secrecy. If it hadn't been for the need to explain his repeated absences from Natalia's villa, he wouldn't even have told them. The whole situation was humiliating enough for Tamara as it was, without their entire circle of friends knowing about it.

Ben and Natalia had been sympathetic and agreed to keep up the charade until they all got home. Ben had decided that this was the time to tell Jack about Tamara's abortive attempts to flirt with him, and Jack had been surprised by how little he cared. It did make him feel marginally less guilty, though.

The doors at the back of the arrivals lounge burst open and Tamara made her entrance. Clocking the paps, who were going into raptures at the sight of her, she struck several poses, petite and pretty in a red-and-white polka-dot playsuit, skyscraper scarlet Louboutins, matching glossy pout, and enormous Gucci shades. Then she cried out, 'Jack! Darling!' and ran over to him, throwing herself into his arms.

Feeling a complete fraud, Jack held her tightly, watching over the top of her head as one of her bodyguards pushed her stack of Louis Vuitton cases across the concourse towards them. With increasing disbelief he carried on watching as the doors burst open again to reveal his dad, Filthy Meadows, resplendent in full leathers, despite the soaring temperature, with a red-and-white bandana wrapped around his head.

'Dad?'

'Surprise, Son!'

Jack held Tamara at arm's length. '*This* is the surprise you told me about?'

The paps were beside themselves with excitement now.

'Uh-huh!' She grinned up at him. 'Isn't it great? Filth is playing at Ibiza Rocks in a couple of nights' time, so we thought we'd show up together and surprise you.'

'You made a detour to St Tropez to meet Tamara rather than coming straight here? Hi, Dad,' Jack added, embracing his father.

'We wanted to surprise you,' Filthy repeated. 'And, hey – I haven't been to St Trop since the Eighties. It was a real blast from the past, returning to the scene of so many crimes!' He winked and Tamara giggled.

'Let's talk about it in the car,' said Jack. 'What a fantastic surprise! Great to see you, Dad!' he said loudly for the benefit of the paparazzi. 'Have you got all your stuff? Let's go!'

Once in the car, Tamara, pretty little face glowing, said, 'Isn't this wonderful? It's so cool to see you, Jack. I can't tell you how much I missed you.'

Feeling lower than he'd ever felt in his life, Jack said, 'You too, sweetheart, you too. So, Dad,' he quickly changed the subject. 'Ibiza Rocks? What's the deal with that?'

'I'd never heard of it either, but Tammy – hey, it's your story, babe – you tell him.'

'The night before last' – Tamara was practically bouncing off her seat, so pleased was she with her story – 'I was out with Miles and his friends and we got chatting to these guys who run this gig called Ibiza Rocks.'

Jack nodded. 'Yeah, I've heard of it. Not sure what it's all about, though.'

'Well, a few years ago, they decided that with all the clubbing and dance music, there was a gap in the market for good old-fashioned guitar music.'

'Nothing old-fashioned about guitar music,' said Filth.

'Of course there's not, darling. Just a turn of phrase.' Tamara smiled fondly at her future father-in-law. 'So they started Ibiza Rocks, which is held like once a week and is now *insanely* popular.'

'But what has this to do with Dad?'

'I was coming to that,' said Tamara impatiently. 'The guys were in a major fix as the Arctic Monkeys were gonna to be playing like this Friday but . . .' she paused for dramatic effect, '. . . they bailed, big time!'

'So Tamara stepped in and offered them my services,' grinned Filthy. 'And I, ever the gentleman, was happy to oblige.'

Jack laughed. 'You mean you, with nothing better to do, and able to command an *enormous* fee, were happy to oblige.'

Filthy winked.

'You know me too well, son.'

'Isn't it great?' grinned Tamara again, desperate for approval. 'Didn't I do good?'

Jack felt a sudden and enormous surge of fondness for her. 'Yes, Tammy, you did brilliantly.'

'David Abrahams is unable to take your call right now. Please leave a message and he'll get back to you as soon as he can.'

'Uh – hi, David. It's me, Summer. Could you call me back, please? It's quite important. Thanks.'

Summer gazed at her phone, exasperated. She'd already left David three voicemail messages that morning – two at the office and another on his mobile. She'd texted and emailed and even sent a Facebook message. In fact she'd spent so much time checking and re-checking her phone, emails and Facebook that she'd been incapable of concentrating on the piece she was supposed to be writing – the introduction to her delicious recipe for wild rabbit with lavender, thyme and honey.

She wouldn't dump him by phone, email or Facebook, of course – she was merely trying to arrange to see him, so that she could do so face to face. She knew it wouldn't be the end of the world if she didn't finish the affair with her boss immediately, but it felt like the most important thing in her life right now.

After the last couple of nights with Jack, she felt that they knew each other inside out, mind, body and soul. She couldn't bear the fact that she was keeping this secret from him. Her head was overflowing with images of his handsome, smiling, trusting face, his sincere green eyes as they looked into hers with so much love.

No, there was nothing else for it – if the mountain wouldn't come to Muhammad, Muhammad would have to go to the mountain. Summer shut her laptop and walked inside from the balcony, where she had been working on her article. She threw a navy-and-white Breton-striped halter-necked jersey minidress over her bikini, shoved her feet into a pair of white plimsolls and started to make her way down the hill to the *Island Life* offices.

Bella, Andy, Poppy and Damian were sitting outside, drinking early evening G&Ts. They'd just put Daisy to bed and were getting excited about their night out (Britta had kindly offered to babysit and Bella knew that her little girl would be safe in the Swedish woman's capable hands).

'I'm dying to see Aqua,' said Bella. 'Nice of Shane to extend his invitation to all of us.'

When he'd heard Tamara's prospective arrival date, Shane Connelly had offered a 'welcome to the White Isle' dinner at Aqua for Tamara, Jack, Ben, Natalia, Poppy, Damian, Bella and Andy. They were to sit at the VIP table on the rocks, and Jack and Tamara were to arrive by boat (with a couple of carefully selected paparazzi lurking). He had offered the entire meal on the house, but Jack, thinking of Summer's words, had insisted on paying for them all. She was right – he could afford it a hundred times over.

'Well, he wouldn't have met the celebs without us, would he, Belles?' said Poppy. 'Although, between you and me, I bet he thought we'd make the evening more fun.'

'Of course he did, darling,' said Damian, leaning back in his chair and looking around. 'God, it's beautiful here. I totally understand why you moved.' The garden was cast in its sunset rosy glow, the trees starting to cast long shadows on the shimmering pool. Apart from their voices, the only sound was that of the cicadas, which were at their loudest at this time of day.

'Yes, it's truly gorgeous,' said Poppy. 'Thanks so much again for inviting us.'

'You know you're always welcome,' smiled Bella. '*Mi casa es tu casa.*'

'So you *can* speak Spanish! I was starting to wonder.'

'Oh, piss off, I'm a bit rusty, that's all. I—'

She was interrupted by a familiar voice shouting, 'Surprise!' from the far end of the garden.

'Daddy!'

Bella jumped out of her chair and ran along the length of the pool into her father's outstretched arms.

'Hello, angel face,' Justin said in his weird Cockney mid-Atlantic drawl. 'Hope you don't mind me turning up like this – I know you got guests . . . Hi, guys!' He waved over at the others and they all waved back. 'But I got my hammock and sleeping bag. You know me, I—'

'Like to sleep under the stars. I know, Daddy,' said Bella. 'It's so lovely to see you. Are you here for any particular reason, or did you just decide to pop on the boat at the last minute?' Justin lived in Majorca, a mere ferry's ride away, and was prone to impetuous decisions.

'Isn't wanting to see my beautiful daughter and grand-daughter reason enough?'

Bella laughed. 'Of course it is.'

'You're looking fantastic.' Justin stood back and looked Bella up and down. 'Your mum always used to dress you in pink when you were tiny.' His voice was wistful for a second. Despite the misdemeanours that had given Bella's mother, Olivia, no choice but to divorce him, he still had a soft spot for his ex-wife.

Bella had dressed up for the evening in one of her old pre-pregnancy dresses that she could at last get into again:

205

a pale pink, A-line, Sixties-inspired mini that showed off her nice brown arms and legs. Her long dark hair was loose around her shoulders, and she knew she'd scrubbed up well for once.

'Anyway, enough of this chat.' Justin brandished the large bottle of Fundador brandy he was holding in his right hand. 'I'm gagging for a drink, and I want to see my beautiful granddaughter.'

'Daisy's just gone to sleep,' said Bella as they walked back across the garden, past the lavender bushes, orange trees and scarlet wild poppies. 'But we can go and have a quick look at her if you promise to behave yourself and be quiet.'

The last time Justin had been over, Daisy had been asleep when he arrived, but he'd been so overwhelmed with love that he couldn't resist leaning into her cot to kiss the top of her downy blonde head. Daisy hadn't minded in the slightest, but had failed to get back to sleep for the rest of the night, rendering Bella completely shattered for the whole of the following day.

'Don't worry, darlin', I learned my lesson! Bloody hell, the house is coming on a treat – when did you get the pool filled? All right, Andy? Hello, Poppy gorgeous! Nice to see you again, Damian.'

They all exchanged greetings and Andy went to get a glass to pour Justin his brandy. As soon as they were settled once more around the table, Bella said, 'Dad, lovely as it is to see you, we're going out tonight, to rather a posh do. We'll be leaving in an hour or so. Sorry to have to desert you on your first night, but—'

'What's the do, darlin'?'

'We've been offered the VIP table at a new restaurant called Aqua, owned by a chap by the name of Shane Connelly. He used to be in—'

Justin slapped his thigh, grinning. 'Not old Connors? Gay Aussie Connors?'

Bella started to laugh. She might have known. Her dad knew everybody who was anybody in the Balearics.

'Yup.'

'Well, we go way back. I'll give him a ring and he'll set up another place for me at your posh table. No problemo.'

Summer gazed out over her balcony, looking at the view of higgledy piggledy streets down to the old port, trying to quash the panic inside her. Tamara had arrived. Tamara was with Jack. Tamara Gold, movie star and international sex symbol, was with *her* Jack. The Jack who had brought her to orgasm after intense orgasm, and told her, repeatedly, how much he loved her.

At the time she'd believed him, trusted him implicitly, but now tiny doubts were starting to niggle away at her. What if he'd been playing with her? Summer was neither overly modest nor one to think too highly of herself. Realistically, she knew that she was good at most things and better than average looking, but compared to a movie star? And if she was capable of lying so blatantly to Jack's face about David, what was to stop him lying blatantly to her?

When she'd tried to approach David in the office that afternoon, it had been impossible to get his attention for even a minute. Valentina had told her that he was stressed about end-of-month deadlines, but it almost seemed as though he'd been avoiding her deliberately.

God, the whole thing was such a mess.

Looking down again at the sun setting over the harbour, Summer made up her mind. Tonight she'd go out. These days she only went clubbing a few times a year, having got most of it out of her system in her hedonistic teens, but tonight she wanted to let her hair down, to forget about everything. She'd go up to the bars in the Old Town, meet some of her old friends, have fun, remind herself of what life used to be like.

And then she'd go to Pacha and dance. Yes, she had to get up for the crèche in the morning, but to hell with it – she'd manage. Tonight she needed to lose herself in the music. And what better place to do that than Pacha?

'Oh my God, this is soooo incredible!' said Poppy, flinging her arms around Shane's neck. 'Bonza, bonza and thrice bonza, mate!'

'Try not to rupture yourself, Pops,' said Damian. Poppy swivelled on her heel and gave him the finger. 'But I have to agree. You've got a pretty awesome set-up here.'

'Thanks,' said Shane. 'But just you wait . . .'

They made their way down the whitewashed walkway that led to the VIP table on the promontory, Bella, Andy and Justin a few steps behind them. Justin, who had drunk around half the bottle of Fundador he'd brought from Majorca, was staggering slightly, and Bella was holding onto him tightly – it would be a shame if he fell into the sea.

When they arrived at the enormous, round VIP table, they all laughed in amazement. It couldn't have been more perfect. Cleverly lit, the white-linen-clad table looked as though it was floating above the sea, which they could hear lapping at the rocks, thirty metres or so below.

'Mate,' said Justin, stumbling and giving his old friend an enormous hug. 'This is BONZA!'

'Sorry about Dad,' said Bella. 'He's been on the Fundador.'

'Nothing wrong with that,' said Shane. 'Anything goes in Ibiza.'

'True,' said Bella, feeling happy and free. It was the first time she'd been out partying since Daisy had been born, and she was enjoying herself already. *This is what life used to be like*, she thought.

'Hey, guys,' said Natalia, walking down the whitewashed walkway and looking like Tippi Hedren or Kim Novak; any of Hitchcock's blondes. 'What an *amazing* venue. Congratulations, Shane.'

'Thanks,' said Shane, who had liked Natalia when he'd met her at Bella's pool party; he recognized a fellow grafter. 'Hey, Ben.' He had a slight crush on Ben, who was exactly his type, but his gaydar told him not to go there. It was a shame, but it couldn't be helped.

'Hey, Shane,' said Ben, liking the chap, and all too aware that Shane fancied him. Gay men tended to go for him even more than straight women did, which was saying something. He didn't mind, of course – the pink pound contributed hugely to the box office – but Nat occasionally got a tad arsey about it. 'This is—'

'Look, look, look!' interrupted Poppy, pointing down at the water.

A state-of-the-art speedboat was hurtling across the wine-dark sea towards them. Poppy nudged Shane, winking complicity. He had excelled himself, publicity-wise.

Filthy was standing on the stern, acoustic guitar in hand, singing not, for once 'Sexy Green-Eyed Woman', but his second-most famous hit, a cheesy ballad that was played ad nauseam on Radio 2 at Christmas, 'Best Friends and Lovers'.

Behind him, Jack and Tamara were sitting with their arms around one another's waists, Tamara's head resting on Jack's shoulder, soppy smiles plastered across both their faces.

*

'So you've got the leading role in *Dust Bowl*?' said Bella, unable to take her eyes off the charismatic young beauty sitting the other side of Andy. Despite what Poppy and Damian had told her, she found Tamara utterly charming.

'Uh-huh,' said Tamara, in her element. 'I brushed up on my Steinbeck.'

Andy, clearly also under her thrall, smiled at her. '*The Grapes of Wrath*?'

'Uh-huh. And *East of Eden* and *Cannery Row*.'

'What – in three days?' asked Bella.

'I'm not as stupid as I look, y'know.'

Bella and Andy both laughed.

'You don't look stupid,' they said in unison.

'Oh wow! You two are like sooo cool. I wish Jack and I talked like that,' said Tamara.

'It takes years, and probably a baby,' smiled Bella.

'You got a baby? Boy or girl?'

'A little girl. Her name's Daisy,' said Andy.

'You got photos?' Tamara seemed to be genuinely interested, so Bella took her phone out of her handbag and showed her a couple of the thousands of Daisy photos she had stored.

'Omigod! She is adorable. Look at her little round cheeks! She is so lucky to have you two as parents.' Tamara's voice went small. 'I wish you were my parents.'

'We're not that bloody old,' said Bella, laughing. Andy kicked her under the table.

'Oh no, I didn't mean that . . .' Tamara looked mortified.

'It's OK,' said Andy. 'I remember being in my early twenties. Everybody over thirty seemed ancient to me.'

'Well, that's not entirely accurate in my case,' said Tamara. 'I am engaged to Jack. No, I was just being an idiot. It was a comment on my own parents rather than anything to do with your age.' She seemed so sad for a couple of seconds that Bella wanted to give her a hug.

Tamara had made even more of an effort than usual this evening, dressing up in a figure-hugging, buttock-skimming, strapless dress made entirely of emerald-green sequins. A ton of smoky-eye make-up set off her deepest green contacts, and her shiny dark hair fell in a sleek curtain to her waist. She looked exotic, feline and sexy as hell.

'Looking like that, darlin', you can say anything you like,' said Bella's father, who was sitting the other side of her. Bella felt a brief stab of irritation at his disloyalty. He could be such a dirty old man sometimes.

'That's very kind of you.' Tamara flashed him her most gorgeous smile, enjoying herself again.

Further around the table, Poppy was monopolizing Filthy.

'So you're playing Ibiza Rocks, Filth?' she asked. 'That's sooo cool. You know I'm your biggest fan.' She looked up at him with big, innocent eyes and Filthy laughed.

'Yeah, sure, I'll sort out VIP tickets and backstage passes. Don't I always?'

'Yippee! Thanks so much!' Poppy grinned, completely unabashed, and shouted across the table: 'VIP tickets and backstage passes to Ibiza Rocks on Friday night, everyone!'

As they all raised their glasses and cheered, Jack felt extraordinarily weary. He'd been getting VIP tickets and backstage passes to his dad's gigs his entire life, and now wanted nothing more than to abandon the non-stop party ship. He thought longingly of his and Summer's deserted beach. He missed her so much. What was she doing right this minute, he wondered.

Summer was walking up the Calle de la Virgen, Ibiza's main gay street, stopping to chat to the guys running the shops and bars, most of whom she had known for years.

The ancient winding street was narrow and heaving with people, all out to have a good time. Handsome, ripped guys with caramel tans in skin-tight T-shirts rubbed shoulders with fabulously made-up transvestites, some very camp old queens and plenty of tourists of myriad nationalities who were simply there to gawp. The atmosphere was raucous and jolly, and Summer was cheering up by the second as she high-fived yet another bar owner in a bicep-revealing racer-back vest.

'Hey, Summer!'

'Hey Jürgen!'

Jürgen had come to Ibiza on holiday from his native Hamburg ten years ago, and never gone back.

'Wow, are you looking *fabuloso* tonight!' He gestured flamboyantly, his hands making hourglass shapes in the air.

'Thanks. Thought I'd make a bit of an effort for once. I'm hitting Pacha later.'

She was looking particularly stunning, and totally Ibiza-chic, in her white denim cut-offs paired with a white crochet string bikini top, and simple brown leather flip-flops on her feet. Her hair flowed, loose, straight and streaky blonde over her slim shoulders, and she wore no jewellery save for a delicate silver anklet. After her day frolicking naked on the beach with Jack, she was more deeply tanned than ever, and looked as though she'd walked straight out of a beach fashion shoot for *Vogue*, circa 1967. Every head – male, female, gay and straight – had turned as she walked by.

'Well, it certainly paid off. You are simply *radiant*, darling. You stopping for a drink?'

Summer smiled, 'Yeah, why not?' and perched herself on one of the high stools surrounding a small round table directly to the right of the bar's cavernous entrance. She had plenty of time to kill before Pacha got going. Nobody bothered hitting the clubs until way past midnight.

'So what can I get you?'

'A vodka *limon* would be great, thanks.'

As Jürgen went inside to get her drink, Summer took in the scene around her, watching the colourful promenade. Much as she adored Ibiza's natural beauty, its beaches and olive and pine groves, she did love this aspect of the island too. The nightlife was so exciting and vibrant and cosmopolitan. On an evening like this, the sheer buzz of the place coursed through your veins like a drug.

'So who's the lucky guy?' asked Jürgen as he returned with her drink. She reached into her brown leather shoulder bag to pay, but Jürgen was having none of it. 'No, no – this is on the house. You haven't been out on the scene for ages.'

'Thanks.' Summer smiled and took a sip of her drink. 'What do you mean – lucky guy?' Was it that obvious?

'You have the glow of somebody who has been shagged senseless in the last twenty-four hours,' said Jürgen. 'Not to put too fine a point on it.'

'I wish,' Summer laughed, her heart pounding furiously.

'Oh bless, she's blushing. It's OK, sweetheart – if you don't want to talk about it, you don't want to talk about it. Uncle Jürgen knows the score.' He tapped the side of his nose and Summer laughed again.

'OK, so what have I been missing?' she said, changing the subject. 'What's the latest gossip?'

'Well,' said Jürgen, pulling up a stool and settling in for a good old natter. 'In the last week or so, this island has become celebrity central.'

'Hey, nothing new about that.' Summer cursed herself for asking about gossip. At this time of year it always revolved around who'd seen which celebs, where. 'So who's spotted who? Kate Moss, I guess?'

'Oh yes, Kate's been very visible. Salinas, DC-10 . . . And rumour has it there was a party at her villa that lasted for three days!'

'Good old Kate, she never disappoints.'

'P Diddy's yacht was spotted somewhere near Formentera . . .'

'That hardly counts,' snorted Summer. 'He gets every-where. You can do better than that.' *What the fuck was she doing?* Her mouth was running away with her and she felt as though she had no control over what came out of it.

Jürgen sniffed huffily. 'The boys at El Olivo served dinner to King Juan Carlos the night before last. He didn't leave a tip or say please or thank you once.'

'That's a bit more like it,' smiled Summer.

'And Rihanna was showing off at Blue Marlin, demanding the best table and getting her minders to take photos of her butt in a tiny thong.'

'Better and better . . .'

'I've been saving the best till last,' grinned Jürgen. 'There are rumours that Jack Meadows has been here for a few days, though nobody's actually seen him. What we *do* know is that Tamara arrived today, with – wait for it – Jack's dad, Filthy!'

Summer was momentarily nonplussed. 'Filthy? What's he doing here?'

'Playing at Ibiza Rocks,' said Jürgen. 'You don't seem too surprised about Jamara though . . .?'

Summer thought quickly. Word would probably get around that Jack had been at Bella's party, and it would look weird if she didn't mention that she'd met him.

'That's because I met Jack,' she admitted. 'He was at my friend Bella's pool party a few days ago . . .'

'Well, you are a dark horse.' Jürgen looked at Summer admiringly. 'Why didn't you say something when I was blathering on about P Diddy's yacht?'

'I was saving the best till last,' she said, and he laughed.

'Touché! So – spill, darling, spill! What's he like?'

'He was nice.' Summer took a sip of her drink, willing her body not to betray the emotions flooding through her. 'He was very nice.'

The atmosphere around the table at Aqua was mellow and happy. They'd feasted on exquisite fish soup, followed by the restaurant's signature stuffed sea bass, then nectarines poached in sauternes and filled with the lightest, creamiest zabaglione, all washed down with the best white wines from Shane's cellar. Now they were drinking *hierbas* and chatting about how they were going to spend the rest of their holiday.

'You've *got to* go to Formentera,' said Bella, waving her glass around. 'The colour of the sea there is like nothing you've ever seen before.'

'We'll take the boat out,' said Natalia decisively. 'It's the only way to see it.'

'Cool,' said Tamara. 'Thanks, Nat.'

Natalia ignored the pang of guilt she felt as Tamara smiled at her. She wished Jack hadn't unburdened himself to her and Ben. Jack, for his part, wished that Tamara would stop behaving so sweetly. He almost wanted Nightmare Tantrum Tamara back – this version was unnerving him and making him feel extremely guilty. He suspected it was for Filthy's benefit – Tamara loved the fact that she could wind his dad around her little finger.

At Shane's insistence ('gotta keep things lively'), they'd all swapped places for the pudding, and Filthy was now sitting next to Justin. They were getting on famously, two naughty old boys swapping scandalous anecdotes; it was no surprise to anyone that they shared several acquaintances – to say nothing of a number of old girlfriends.

Justin, older than Filthy by about five years, was more hippy than rocker, this evening sporting fraying denim cut-offs, long dark-grey hair tied back in a ponytail, a v-necked white linen tunic and the shark's tooth on a leather thong that he liked to keep, permanently, around his neck.

'If you'd seen her, Filth, you'd understand,' he'd confided to his new best friend earlier. Filthy had put his arm around Justin's shoulder, a tear forming in his eye. 'No need, my buddy, no need. I understand,' he'd said, and both their minds had drifted back to the young girls they'd squired years ago and still believed themselves in love with, both conveniently forgetting the women they'd loved enough to actually marry.

Filthy, whose hair was so badly dyed black that there was an entire bitchy column in the *Daily Mail* devoted to it, had abandoned his leathers in favour of black jeans and a cherry-red waistcoat with nothing underneath (he was still pretty wiry, with all that jumping about on stage). His earlier red-and-white bandana kept some of the black fluff away from his face.

'So what's the plan for later?' asked Justin.

'Later?' said Filth, downing his *hierbas* in one.

'Yeah, later, mate. Later!' Justin thumped his hand on the table for emphasis. 'This is Ibiza and I wanna hit the clubs!'

'Still the oldest swinger in town,' laughed Bella from across the table. She was on her way to feeling pleasantly pissed. 'It does sound tempting, though. I haven't been clubbing for years . . . Andy?' She looked at him hopefully.

'One of us has to relieve Britta.' He looked into her happy, sparkling eyes and smiled. 'It's OK, Belles, you go out and have fun. I'm cool with calling it a night – I need to get on with the book in the morning anyway.'

'Really?! Oh, I love you so much!' She gave him a huge smacker on the cheek.

'Hey, I'll come clubbin' with ya,' said Filthy. 'See what all the fuss is about.'

'Me too!' Tamara cried, her pretty face lighting up. 'Oh, can we, please, Jack, please?'

All Jack wanted to do was go back to Natalia's villa and dream of Summer, but he figured that a night's clubbing would at least delay the evil moment of having to refuse Tamara's demands for sex. He forced himself to laugh naturally.

'We're in Ibiza, right? 'Course we should be going clubbing. Where do you wanna go, honey?'

'Pacha,' said Tamara decisively. 'I wanna go to Pacha.'

15

Summer walked all the way through the Old Town, through the pretty squares with their lit-up restaurants and boutiques and bars, up past the ancient ramparts and down again where the narrow winding lanes opened out into the harbour. It was a warm evening, and she was enjoying the feeling of her hair swishing against her bare back, the fragrant wisps of breeze on her bare arms and legs. At half past one in the morning, Ibiza Town was still heaving, the traffic around the port almost at a standstill. A lot of people were heading in the same direction as Summer, out past the boats in the marina towards Pacha. Tonight was David Guetta's legendary 'F*** Me I'm Famous' night, and excitement levels were bubbling.

Summer's shorts and bikini top were by no means inappropriate – there was a hell of a lot of flesh on display as hordes of happy holidaymakers stumbled towards their destination. At last it loomed, a whitewashed, cuboid building with multiple terraces flanked by palm trees, its iconic double-cherry logo enticingly symbolic of the hedonistic delights that lay within.

Pacha. Clubbing for beautiful people.

Tamara was enjoying herself enormously. Slinky and gorgeous in her sequinned green dress, she was lapping up adulation from several new admirers (the clientele in Pacha's VIP area were *way* too cool to admit to being fans), not to mention the undivided attention of Justin and Filthy. She didn't care that their joint age was about 510 – not having had a proper father figure, she loved getting attention from older men and never found anything remotely distasteful about it.

Almost as much as the attention, she loved how cool this place was – way cooler than Les Caves in St Trop, which she now recognized as tawdry Eurotrash. No, Pacha oozed real glamour, from the white leather banquettes in the VIP areas to the fabulous open-air terraces to the incredibly beautiful podium dancers on the main dance floor, visible twenty feet below them.

There was a bottle of Absolut vodka sitting in an ice bucket on the white stone table in front of them, but Tamara, whose twin poisons, back in the bad old days, had always been Absolut and coke (not cola), was sticking resolutely to her mineral water. A great roar came up from the dance floor as the DJ segued into another crowd-pleaser and they all grinned around the table at each other.

'Right, I'm ready to get down and dirty,' said Poppy, downing her drink in one and slamming it on the table. 'This VIP stuff's all very well, but you really need to be on the dance floor to get the proper Pacha *"experience"*.' She did air quotes, taking the piss out of herself, and everybody laughed. 'Coming, Belles?'

'Hmmm, dunno. It's awfully comfortable up here. *And* you can hear yourself think.'

'Just listen to yourself! When did you get so old? Come on, Mrs Fuddy Duddy, let's go and show those youngsters how it's done.'

'Oh, all right, twist my arm then,' replied Bella good-naturedly.

'You coming, Damian?'

'Try keeping me away.'

So the three of them made their way towards the velvet rope that cordoned the VIP area off from the plebs. As Filthy launched into one of his scandalous accounts of life on the road, Tamara heard Bella cry, 'Summer! Wow, you look amazing. We're heading down for a bit of a boogie, but the others are over there – big table in the corner. Why don't you join them?'

Tamara turned her head to see who this newcomer was, and watched as the crowds parted, all heads turning, to let through one of the most beautiful girls she had ever seen in her life. Flushed and glowing from her exertions on the dance floor, Summer walked with easy grace towards their table. Her casual sexy ensemble reflected Ibiza's laid-back, beachy vibe perfectly, and made Tamara feel stupidly overdressed in her sequins and six-inch Louboutins.

Ben jumped to his feet, holding out his arms.

'Summer! How lovely to see you again. Come and have a seat and a drink. Now, who don't you know . . .?'

Inside he was thinking *fuck fuck fuck* and wondering how Jack was going to react.

'Hi, Summer,' Jack said coolly, getting up to kiss her on both cheeks. 'Meet my fiancée. Summer, this is Tamara, Tamara, this is Summer – we met her at Bella's pool party.'

'Hi,' said Tamara curtly, looking from one to the other, immediately wary. There was something not quite right in their body language.

'Hi.' Summer smiled and held out her hand. Tamara didn't take it.

'Dad, this is Summer,' Jack continued quickly. 'Summer – my dad, Filthy Meadows.'

'Hi, Filthy.' This time Summer smiled with genuine warmth. 'I love your music.'

'My God,' said Filthy. 'Are you real? Look at her, Justin, can you believe such a girl exists? Goddess of golden youth . . .' His voice went all dreamy and Jack rolled his eyes.

'And this is Justin, Bella's father,' Ben added quickly, seeing the look on Tamara's face.

'Hi, Justin.' Summer smiled warmly again. 'How lovely to meet you. Bella's a great friend of mine.'

'You're a friend of Bella's? My girl's always had good taste! You Swedish, by any chance?'

Summer nodded, laughing.

'Thought so – you've got the look of a young Britt Ekland – I shot her, back in the day, you know – but I'd say you're much more beautiful . . .'

Ben and Natalia exchanged glances. Even though they didn't know the situation, both old men were behaving extremely insensitively, given Tamara's massive insecurities.

Summer just stood there, tall, blonde and serene, smiling at the compliments.

'Come and sit over here, darlin,' Justin continued. 'Budge up, Tamara.'

It was swelteringly hot on the dance floor and you couldn't move for heaving, sweaty bodies.

Poppy shouted something at Bella over the music, but it was impossible to hear her. By the look on her grinning, shiny face as she gyrated in clinging neon-yellow lycra, it was something to do with what a fantastic time she was having.

But Bella wasn't having a great time. It was *too* hot and cramped, her feet hurt, and she felt horribly old and dowdy in her Sixties-inspired frock, compared to the young, outrageously dressed clubbers all around her. Poppy and Damian still seemed to fit in, but she had moved on from this scene, she realized. Above all, she missed Andy and Daisy like hell. It was time to go.

'Listen, Pops,' she shouted in Poppy's ear. 'This isn't really me any more. I'm going to call it a night.'

'WHA . . .?'

'I'M CALLING IT A NIGHT!' Bella shouted even more loudly. Poppy opened her mouth to remonstrate, but Bella shook her head. Poppy gave a rueful grin, shrugging. 'OK THEN. NIGHT, LOVELY.'

'CAN YOU SAY MY GOODBYES TO THE OTHERS – AND TRY NOT TO WAKE DAISY WHEN YOU COME IN.'

Poppy nodded, and Bella smiled and hugged her, relieved she could stop shouting. She kissed Damian goodnight and made her way through the heaving throng of sweaty clubbers towards the exit.

As she looked at the sea of ecstatic, gurning faces, she acknowledged to herself that most of the revellers were off their heads on drugs – that was another difference between this and her old life, where lines of coke and Ecstasy pills had been pretty much obligatory for a night's clubbing.

She was almost at the door when somebody tapped her on the shoulder. She turned around and found herself face-to-face with Jorge.

'Bella!' He grinned, delighted to have bumped into her. 'Wow! You look beautiful!'

'Hardly,' Bella gave an embarrassed laugh, indicating the scantily clad clubbers around her. 'I feel so old!'

'*Pouf* – they are children,' said Jorge with a dismissive shrug. 'You are a very sexy woman.'

Bella smiled. 'Thanks, but right at this moment I just feel like a very tired old mother.'

Jorge laughed.

'I mean it – I'm off now.' Bella indicated the exit with her head.

'You're not going?' Bella was flattered by the disappointment in his voice.

'Yes, but the others are all still here – Poppy and Damian, Ben and Natalia, Jack and Tamara . . .'

'Did you say *Tamara*?' Jorge's eyes lit up.

'Oh, I forgot, you haven't met her yet – yes, upstairs in the first-floor VIP lounge.'

'Thank you, Bella!' Jorge said warmly, kissing her on both cheeks. 'Goodnight, and have a safe journey home.'

Tamara was seething. Summer, after a couple of vodkas, had begun to open up to the assembled company, giving advice about the best beach bars and little-known restaurants around the island in that annoying, candidly humorous way of hers. The old men were hanging on her every word, tongues hanging out, practically drooling. Ben and Natalia tried to keep Tamara in the conversation, for which she was grateful, but she couldn't help but notice how quiet Jack had become since Summer's arrival, nor the fact that he kept glancing over at her when he thought that she, Tamara, wasn't looking.

Just as she was thinking that now may be the time to play the spoilt film star and demand to be taken home, an extremely good-looking man approached the table.

'*Hola!*' he cried out. '*Quelle coincidence, eh*? Ben, Natalia, Jack! Oh my God, it is *you* – Tamara! *The* Tamara Gold! You are even more beautiful in the flesh.'

Tamara smiled. This was more like it.

'Thanks,' she said. 'But who are you?'

'I am Jorge, a friend of Bella's – and I met these guys at Bella's pool party a few days ago.'

'Sounds like it was all happening at Bella's pool party,' said Tamara tartly.

'It was,' said Summer. 'Hi, Jorge.'

'Oh hi, Summer,' said Jorge casually. 'I didn't see you there.'

Yes! At last somebody who seemed immune to Summer's Scandinavian charms. Tamara could have hugged him. Instead, she said, in her most charming voice,

'In that case, it's *lovely* to meet you, Jorge. Why don't you come and sit down here and tell me all about yourself?'

Summer was finding it very difficult to act normally. It had been silly of her not to have envisaged the possibility of bumping into Jack and Tamara, *especially* in one of Pacha's VIP areas, for God's sake. But Ibiza was her territory, and being waved past the hoi polloi, both at the club's entrance, and at the velvet rope, was second nature to her. She was hot and sweaty after dancing her heart out and had needed to escape from the crowds for a while.

When she'd seen Bella, her first thought had been just to say hello to the others, then make her excuses and leave. But Tamara had been so rude to her, refusing even to shake her hand – as if being a film star meant even such basic manners were beneath her – that Summer's stubborn streak had come to the fore. No, she'd stick around, check out the competition.

Tamara was stunning, she had to admit that, but she couldn't see how she could ever have been right for Jack; the intellectual, nature-loving, outdoorsy Jack she knew and loved. Everything about the girl was fake, from her breasts to her lips to her hair. And what a stroppy little madam, too – sitting there with that petulant expression on her face, all because for once she wasn't centre of attention.

Thank God Jorge had turned up to distract her. He did have some uses, she supposed, watching as he flirted outrageously with Tamara, buttering her up, making her prink and preen.

'Why that's sweet of you to say,' she was now saying coquettishly, giggling like Scarlett O'bloody Hara and brushing an imaginary piece of fluff off Jorge's T-shirt.

Being so close to Jack without being able to touch him was torture. She remembered every second of their lovemaking, and as she recalled his mouth on her bare skin, she flushed. She glanced up and saw that he was looking straight at her, smiling slightly. She realized he knew exactly what she was thinking, and she felt a rush of heat to her groin. Any doubts she'd had earlier in the evening had gone. They were meant to be together, and that was that. The Tamara business was unfortunate, but it couldn't be helped. Her brattish behaviour certainly made Summer feel less guilty.

Summer was sitting between Filthy and Justin, who were hilarious company, despite their overt lechery. And it was kinda cool to be chatted up by a Rock God, if a bit weird. A *bit* weird? She laughed at herself internally. This had to be the weirdest situation she'd ever been in. And Jack looked horribly uncomfortable, bless him. She glanced over again, loving the way his curly black hair fell into his thickly lashed eyes, the awkward expression on his gorgeous face. Dressed down in baggy shorts and a plain navy-blue T-shirt, he was, as far as she was concerned, the most handsome man in the world.

'So – Summer.' She jumped as he addressed her directly, speaking quietly, his eyes never leaving her face.

'Uh-huh?'

'Do you have a personal favourite beach here?'

Her heart started beating faster as she glanced over at Tamara, but she seemed to be totally engrossed in whatever Jorge was saying to her. She clasped her hands in her lap and looked back at Jack.

'Yes. Yes, I do.'

'Where's that, babe?' asked Filthy.

She turned to him and smiled.

'It's this tiny little cove, on the northern coast. It's so small it doesn't even have a name, but it's beautiful. I have never been happier than I've been there.'

When she looked at Jack again, he was smiling broadly.

Shit, thought Ben. *These two are sailing perilously close to the wind.*

'So. How do you know Summer?' Tamara's tone was deceptively honeyed.

'Oh, we go way back.' Jorge tried to brush it off, but Tamara was having none of it.

'I said – *how*?'

Madre de dio, she was like a terrier. A very sexy little terrier though. Jorge sighed. 'I guess you could say we were childhood sweethearts.'

'Really? I wouldn't put you two together . . .'

'*Porque no*?' Jorge gave a crooked half-smile.

'Well, not being rude or anything, but isn't she kinda . . . uptight? Loves herself a bit too much? You seem much more of a *free spirit* . . .' Tamara put her perfectly manicured little hand on Jorge's well-muscled thigh and he felt a stirring in his loins.

'That is exactly right! Wow – you are as perceptive as you are beautiful.' Tamara smiled. 'Yes, Summer was too serious, too controlling. She tried to restrict me, but I am – as you say – a *free spirit*.'

'Sounds like me and Jack. He won't let me smoke, even

226

though it's the only vice I have left.' Tamara sounded petulant again.

'*Quieres fumar*?' Jorge's voice was low and conspiratorial. 'I have plenty.' He patted the back pocket of his tight white jeans.

Tamara laughed. 'So have I!' She patted her diamond-studded Gucci clutch bag.

Jorge laughed too, his teeth gleaming in his mahogany face. 'You wanna come upstairs to the roof terrace?'

Tamara gave a little half-bow, Scarlett O'Hara again. 'Why, kind sir, I can think of nothing I'd like more.'

'Ahhh, that's better.' Tamara inhaled deeply on a Marlboro Light and looked around approvingly. They were sitting under the stars in a chill-out area with an almost Moroccan vibe – all silk cushions, low tables, atmospheric lighting and stunning views over the floodlit Old Town. A bikini-clad model sitting in a giant cocktail glass was drawing little attention from the seen-it-all-before clubbers, although a few heads were turning discreetly in Tamara's direction. She was aware of, and enjoying this.

'Cool place,' she said.

'Pacha is always the coolest.' Jorge smiled at her, and she felt something quicken in her chest. He really was handsome, with his limpid dark eyes, wide, high cheek-bones and full, pink lips, his longish dark hair falling around his face. 'But you, Señorita Gold, are the most beautiful woman I have ever seen.' He stared deeply into her eyes and she felt a throbbing sensation begin, low in her stomach. The attention of a handsome man was simply irresistible. Jack treated her more like a naughty little sister than a lover most of the time, and Tamara had always been powerless in the face of temptation. She gazed back at Jorge through dilated pupils, subconsciously licking her lips. Jorge felt himself harden in his tight white jeans.

Jesus, he hadn't seen this coming. He had been more than happy to hang out with the Hollywood stars – to flirt a little, sure – Jorge was a born flirt – but was Tamara Gold actually coming on to him? He didn't have to wait long to find out.

'Jack and I have an – uh – open relationship,' she said coyly, looking up at him from under her eyelash extensions and twirling a lock of shiny dark brown hair around her forefinger.

'*Madre de dio!*' Jorge glanced around, thinking quickly. They practically had the terrace to themselves now, and nobody was paying them much attention. He needed to strike while the iron was hot. 'You wanna come somewhere more private with me?'

'Oh yes, baby.'

Tamara felt powerless, her sex addiction and adrenaline taking over where common sense left off.

'Follow me. And look cool.'

Jorge sauntered towards a door marked *No Entrada* and pushed it open. Tamara followed, her lustful gaze fixed firmly on his tight, white-denim-clad buttocks. Halfway down the narrow, dimly lit corridor he opened another door, switched on a light, then locked the door behind them.

'Where are we?' Tamara asked.

'Store cupboard.' Jorge grinned at her. 'Staff entrance. I worked as a cleaner here when I was a boy, so I know my way around.'

Tamara smiled slowly. 'Well, well. You do take me to the best places.' She was so aroused she felt she might come in her pants if he didn't hurry up and screw her.

'You wanna bit of rough, Señorita Hollywood Princess?'

'Hell, yeah.'

His hands were running up and down her body now as he nuzzled her neck, whispering and breathing in her ear. She could feel his silky dark hair brushing the tops of her breasts.

'You like it hard?' He bit the side of her neck. 'You like it dirty?'

In response, Tamara slithered out of her dress in one quick move. She was wearing nothing underneath and Jorge took a sharp intake of breath at the sight of her incredible young body.

'Bend over.'

She did as she was told, balancing herself against a grubby wall with the palms of her hands. Her flexibility was impressive, and for a couple of seconds Jorge savoured the view of her high, peachy buttocks, before grabbing her by the hips and thrusting roughly inside her.

Within less than a minute, they'd both come, Jorge pulling out at the last minute and shooting his load over Tamara's back.

Tamara sank to the floor, and turned around, wiping her damp sweaty hair away from her face.

'Wow!' she laughed. 'Thanks. That was awesome.'

'Awesome,' Jorge repeated, grinning down at her. He could hardly believe what had just happened. She looked delightfully wanton, naked on the floor of the dingy store cupboard, her hair falling in tendrils over her bouncy breasts.

'But – ewwww.' Tamara jerked her head to indicate the sperm running down her narrow back. 'What are we gonna do about *that*?'

Jorge laughed. 'This is the great advantage of making love in a store cupboard.' He reached up to a shelf to pull down an industrial roll of loo paper, and handed it to her.

'I can't reach,' Tamara pouted. 'Can you do it?'

Well, it wasn't every day you got to wipe your own spunk off a Hollywood starlet's back.

They both got dressed, and Tamara took out her compact to redo her face.

'How do I loo—' she started, stopping when she saw that Jorge had chopped out two chunky lines of coke on one of the cupboard's shelves. 'Erm . . .' she said. 'If that's for me, you're barking up the wrong tree, mister. I've been clean for nearly ten years now.'

Jorge's face fell.

'I thought that was only a story for the Press. Surely everybody likes to indulge occasionally?'

Tamara glanced at the parallel lines, silently calling to her like sirens luring sailors on to the rocks.

'Not me.' She shook her head a little less decisively than she had before.

'This is quality stuff,' Jorge wheedled. 'Wow – you'll feel like you're flying . . . One line won't hurt you . . . No?' He shrugged. 'OK. *De nada*.' He bent his dark head and took a long, deep sniff through a straw. *'Mon dieu. Formidable!'*

As he bent his head to hoover up the second line, Tamara grabbed him by the shoulder.

'Stop! I've changed my mind . . .'

'I have to get to see you again – alone,' whispered Jack to Summer. They had taken advantage of Tamara's disappearance, and the general prevailing drunkenness, to manoeuvre themselves next to one another on the white leather banquette.

'I know – me too – but shhh.'

'I love you,' Jack mouthed.

'I love you too,' Summer mouthed back. It was dark and crowded, even in the VIP area, and nobody seemed to be paying much attention to them, sitting side by side in the Stygian gloom, each of them acutely aware of Summer's naked midriff and thighs – so tantalizingly within Jack's reach.

They didn't notice Tamara coming back to the table until she was almost upon them. Her eyes were glittering, her hair a wild tangle, her scarlet lip-gloss badly applied, way over the edges of her collagen-filled lips.

'Sorry to break up the party,' she said sarcastically, hands on her green sequinned hips. 'But I was under the impression that Jack was *my* fiancé.'

'And where have *you* been for the last hour, *honeybunch*?' asked Jack, immediately on the defensive, but trying to keep his voice down. People were starting to stare at them.

'Checking out the sights.' Tamara cackled madly. 'This is a pretty cool club, as you'd realize if you could tear yourself away from that . . . that . . .' Her voice faltered as she glared at Summer.

'Hey, I'd better be going,' said Summer, getting to her feet. 'It was nice to see you again, Jack.'

'Yeah, you fuck off to wherever you came from, and *leave my fiancé alone!*'

With these words, Tamara grabbed the bottle of Absolut from the low white stone table and poured it into an empty glass, nearly filling it to the brim. She drank about half the neat liquor in one gulp, and Jack jumped up.

'Tammy? What the hell are you doing?'

'What am I doing? I'm having fun for once in my life, you impotent asshole.' She started to laugh again, and Jack winced at all the people around hearing the word impotent, even though it couldn't be further from the truth.

'Honey . . .' He put a restraining hand on her arm, and she pushed him away.

'Fuck off, Jack.'

He watched in horror as she shoved her way through the throngs of people to the other side of the room, scrambled up on top of the white stone bar, via a white stone barstool, and started to dance. The dancing, though drunken and shambolic, was sexy – he had to give her that. Tamara knew how to move well. But . . .

Oh Jesus Christ, she wasn't wearing any underwear. And she was drawing quite a crowd of men, nudging each other as they looked up her skirt. Taking a deep breath, Jack pushed his way through them, clambered up onto the bar himself and tried to tug her skirt down.

'Stop it, Tamara, you're making a complete exhibition of yourself.'

'*Stop it, Tamara, you're making a complete exhibition of yourself!*' she mimicked, pushing him away. 'Don't be such a fucking killjoy, Jack. These guys are all enjoying the show. You're enjoying the show, aren't you, guys?' She blew a kiss to her audience, and a few voices cheered.

'Dad?' Jack yelled. 'Help me, will ya?'

Now it was Filthy's turn to push his way through the crowds.

'Outta my way, you goddamn losers. You oughta be ashamed of yourselves.'

And between them, Filthy and Jack dragged Tamara's writhing, cursing form down from the bar.

'That was your doing, wasn't it?' Summer stared at Jorge, who had reappeared in time to witness the floorshow. The music throbbed around them in the strobe-punctuated near darkness. 'You gave her drugs.'

Jorge shrugged nonchalantly. '*¿Que es Pacha sin drogas?*'

'My God. I knew you were bad, but I thought you were better than that. Don't you know the girl's a recovering addict?'

'She'll be OK. Small hangover maybe. Anyway, I was doing you a favour.'

'I don't know what you mean.' The blood rose in Summer's cheeks and she was glad of the cover of darkness.

'Come on – *Summer, Jack; Jack, Summer.*' Jorge smiled provocatively. 'You know what I mean.'

'All I know is that you have never grown up.' Summer's heart was galloping in her chest. She had to deflect attention. 'What's your fucking problem, Jorge?'

As Summer turned on her heel, not waiting for an answer, Jorge considered her words. What *was* his fucking problem? He wasn't terribly intelligent, but, asked so directly, he realized that it was probably that he'd never really got over Summer.

16

Lars's latest addition to his growing portfolio of eco resorts was situated on a long stretch of perfect white beach backed by gently swaying palms on Mexico's Caribbean coast – sometimes referred to as the Mayan Riviera. He'd flown back from the South of France the previous day, but was so exhilarated by how well the project was coming along that he hardly felt any jet lag. His holiday had been fun, but all things considered he was extremely glad to be back at work. St Tropez's showy, glittery displays of conspicuous consumption could induce nausea that was almost physical, after a while. Although . . . for a moment his mind drifted back to Tamara Gold, her face free of make-up, acting so sweet and charming with the film director at Club 55.

He stood on the little wooden balcony of his *cabaña* and looked out to sea. The waves crashing against the snowy shore were an aquamarine rarely seen outside digitally retouched travel brochures. The sun was rising on the horizon, a lone kite surfer the only other human being for miles around. There would be plenty more people up and about later, but at this hour most of them were still sleeping off their tequila hangovers.

The collection of simple wooden huts with hammocks hanging from palm trees over their outdoor decks had been about to go into receivership, but Lars had seen a fantastic business opportunity and bought out the owner, a local entrepreneur who'd been more than happy to sell. The *cabaña*s were basic, but their location was unsurpassed, and Lars's company had nearly finished renovating them to the highest standards of eco luxury. While not changing the simple, back-to-nature vibe of the resort, every element was to be luxurious: the highest thread count Egyptian cotton on the beds, the fluffiest white towels, the chic-est, most energy-efficient outdoor showers.

The beach bar was to have a relaxed, bohemian vibe, the restaurant would showcase simply spiced seafood cooked over coal, and the spa would feature all the latest therapies, with skilled masseurs and eco-friendly unguents. It was all planned with meticulous attention to the tiniest detail, from the jewelled lanterns that lit up the sandy walkways at night, to the vintage lamps and colourful, Aztec-patterned cushions in the sunken seating areas dotted around the bar.

Lars walked down the wooden steps leading from the deck outside his hut straight onto the powdery beach, and headed for the sea. The clear water was refreshing, and as he looked back to the little cluster of huts and palm trees on the shore, he felt a sense of deep satisfaction that he had never had in all his years of banking. Being made redundant had seemed like the end of the world at the time, but now, with hindsight, he realized it was probably the best thing that had ever happened to him.

'Come along darling, Mummy's got you. Yes, that's right, my angel. Look, Andy, she's swimming!'

Andy, en route to his study and carrying a large mug of

coffee, stopped to watch the two of them with indulgent pride.

'Clever girl, Daisy,' he said, smiling.

Daisy, loving the water, giggled with delight, and suddenly shook off Bella's hands, her little plump legs kicking away madly as she headed under like a tadpole.

'Yay!' said Bella, watching her daughter come up for breath. 'Chip off the old block. No question of her maternity then.'

Andy laughed. 'You look like you're feeling a bit better.'

'Yeah, the water's helping.'

Her hangover was subsiding at last, thank God – even though she'd left Pacha early, she was starting to realize that, as far as she was concerned at least, motherhood and clubbing were, absolutely, mutually incompatible. Poppy and Damian, who had woken both her and Daisy as they'd stumbled in at half past five that morning, were still out for the count.

'Glad you came home when you did?' Andy teased her. He'd been happily surprised to be woken by Bella crawling into bed beside him shortly before 3 a.m. – he hadn't expected her back for several more hours.

'Yes, and I've learned my lesson,' said Bella, scooping Daisy out of the water and planting a kiss on top of her wet head as she cuddled her. 'What we have here is more wonderful than any amount of glamorous nightlife could ever be.'

'Absolutely,' said Andy, and Bella half-walked, half-swam across the pool towards him, Daisy still in her arms, to give him a kiss. 'Right, I'd better get on. See you in a bit.'

He carried on across the garden towards his study, and Bella and Daisy continued to play in the water, both of them giggling with pure pleasure.

'Hey! Bella!' shouted a voice at the back gate.

'Hey, Filthy!' Bella waved at him from the pool, wondering what he was doing there. 'The gate's open, come in.'

'Cool pad you've got here,' said Filthy and Bella grinned. Filthy Meadows thought her house was cool! 'Justin said I should come over, hang out for the day. Hope that's OK?'

'Yeah, of course it's OK.' Naturally her father hadn't consulted her about this, but really, how could she object if Filthy Meadows wanted to come and hang around her finca, bestowing upon it his own particular brand of rock'n'roll coolness?

'Filth!' cried Justin, emerging from the house holding a bottle of Fundador by the neck, looking extremely rough. Grey stubble covered his face, which was half-hidden behind a pair of blackout shades, and his long pewter hair was sticking out in all directions. 'Great to see you mate. Hair of the dog?'

'Now you're talking,' said Filthy with a crooked grin.

'*Hola*, Bella!' called another voice and Bella turned back to the gate.

'Gabriella! How lovely to see you. But . . .'

'Don't worry, this is only a passing visit. I'm meeting some friends in San Carlos, so I thought I'd pop in and say hello, and give you these.' Gabriella, elegant and casual in rolled-up jeans and a man's crisp cotton white shirt, its oversized cuffs turned back at her elbows, held up a basket of eggs. 'Freshly laid this morning.'

Gabriella's grand villa on the north-west coast, close to Benirrás beach, had a Petit Trianon-like farmstead attached to it, with chickens, geese and goats; she took great delight in collecting the still-warm eggs herself – on the few occasions she was out of bed in time to beat her gay middle-aged houseman to it.

'How kind of you,' smiled Bella, thinking it was probably about time she got out of the pool, before any more uninvited guests pitched up. 'Come in and I'll make some coffee . . .'

'Gaby?' her father interrupted, running over to and gazing at the Italian woman in awe. 'Is it really you?'

'Justin! *Madre mia!*' They stood and stared at one another for a couple of seconds, before erupting into gales of laughter and an enormous embrace.

Bella climbed out of the pool, Daisy still in her arms.

'I'd have let you know Daddy was here before, Gaby, but he only turned up last night.'

Filthy, the other side of the pool, gave her a wink.

'Hey, girl, let's leave them to it, huh?'

Tamara groaned, trying to get back to sleep in Natalia's four-hundred-thread-count Egyptian cotton sheets. She hadn't had a hangover for nearly ten years, but the symptoms were still all too familiar. The sheets were drenched with sweat, her head ached, her mouth tasted like somebody had crapped in it and she had a horrible lurking sense of impending doom.

Desperately, she tried to recall the events of the previous night. Aqua. Filthy serenading her and Jack on the boat. Then Pacha. Oh yeah – the handsome Spaniard, Jorge. Screwing in the store room. That had been fun. So everything was cool.

As she lay there, relaxing for a second and wondering why Jack wasn't with her, more memories started to come back to her, one by one. Snorting coke with Jorge, then downing several drinks in quick succession in one of the bars on the roof terrace. Coming downstairs to find Jack and Summer looking far too cosy for her liking . . .

No. Noooooo. Nonononononoooo.

Suddenly, with horrendous clarity, she remembered dancing on the bar, with all the men staring up her dress.

Tamara moaned and put two pillows over her head. Maybe if she could sleep, it would all go away, for ever.

Ben was driving Natalia's silver Porsche convertible into Jesus, the nearest small town to her spectacular villa. It was Natalia's normally efficient housekeeper's day off, and they'd run out of milk. Ben was more than happy to do the errand himself – it was good to get out of the house, and he didn't particularly want to be around when Tamara woke up.

Jack had confided in him that he couldn't stand the situation any longer. He was meant to be with Summer, and after Tamara's behaviour last night, and what Ben had told him about her propositioning him, he didn't feel that he owed her anything any more. If she was capable of flashing herself at a whole load of strange guys *right under his nose*, Christ knew what she was capable of when he wasn't around.

He'd tell Tamara it was over, and they'd issue a dignified joint statement to the Press. Tamara would then fly back to LA (or wherever else in the world she wanted – it was no longer Jack's business), leaving Jack free to spend as much joyous time with Summer as he pleased.

While Ben sympathized whole-heartedly with his buddy, he had a feeling it wasn't going to be quite as simple as that. He did feel sorry for Tamara – the poor girl had serious issues – but he didn't see why Jack should be the one to have to deal with those issues. Having witnessed more of her tantrums than he cared to remember, Ben didn't want to be there to witness this one – no doubt the tantrum to end all tantrums.

As soon as he'd delivered the milk back to the villa, he planned to take Natalia out for a day at the beach. Probably Las Salinas – they could hit the Jockey Club for lunch. Nat loved the Jockey Club, with its relaxed glamour, expensive menu and slightly older clientele, and it would be good for the two of them to have a few hours alone, too. They'd spent far too much time in their friends' pockets since leaving the States, and it was all starting to get extremely claustrophobic.

He pulled up outside Can Pascual, Jesus's small supermarket, and got out of the Porsche. The shopkeeper greeted him cheerfully.

'*Hola*, Señor Jones!' The handsome movie star was a popular and familiar figure in these parts – all the locals knew he was involved with the mysterious Russian woman who owned the enormous modern villa at the top of the hill. With his floppy golden hair, perfect Hollywood teeth and tall, broad-shouldered physique, he exuded expensive glamour, yet was always friendly and approachable.

'*Hola, Pedro. ¿Que tal?*'

'*Muy bien, gracias.*'

As Ben walked over to the chill cabinet to get a couple of pints of semi-skimmed milk, he picked up a copy of the *Ibiza Sun*, the island's main English-speaking newspaper, from the newsstand that stood next to a stall rammed with straw hats, flip-flops, frisbees, buckets and spades. Not looking at the paper properly, he smiled at the buckets and spades. Did kids still make sandcastles? He recalled the freezing beaches of his happy childhood, a sudden memory of building sandcastles with Damian rushing through his mind. The dark grey sand at Llandudno had continually been pounded by the fairly scary waves of the Irish Sea, but they'd loved the beach. Kids always loved beaches, even if they were cold and miserable.

But as the years rolled on it was very easy for one's expectations to change.

Another customer was waiting to be served, so he had a quick look at the front page of the paper.

'Shit!'

The shopkeeper and other customer looked over at him curiously, and he hastily folded the paper, paid for his purchases, and went back outside into the blazing sunshine as quickly as he possibly could. In the relative safety of the Porsche, he unfolded the paper again and started to read:

IBIZA EXCLUSIVE! SENSATIONAL SCANDAL! HOLLYWOOD'S GOLDEN COUPLE ON THE SKIDS!

Jack Meadows pictured in bed with local blonde! Drunken Tamara flashes crowd at Pacha! End of the road for Jamara?

Underneath were two photos.

One looked as if it had been taken on somebody's phone through a gap in a curtain, of Jack and Summer lying naked in bed together – presumably in Summer's flat, Ben thought. Even given the poor quality of the picture, it was quite obvious that they were completely besotted with one another – Jack stroking Summer's face as he gazed into her eyes, her long golden hair fanning out on the pillow. Summer's slender brown legs were wrapped around his in an elegant display of extreme intimacy.

The other photo – oh Jesus, poor Tamara – had been taken at Pacha, and depicted her drunken dancing on the bar. The photo had been shot from below, her nether regions pixelated.

Ben carried on reading.

Clubbers in Pacha were stunned last night when Tamara Gold treated them to a live show they would never forget. Eschewing decorum, the worse-for-wear starlet, who is famously teetotal, climbed onto the VIP bar and started performing her own version of dirty dancing. When it became apparent that she was not wearing underwear, fiancé Jack, ever the gentleman, leapt to her rescue, helped by his father, rock legend Filthy Meadows.

But Jack is not quite the hero he seems. As you can see from the above picture, he has been getting very friendly with a blonde beauty, thought to be local journalist Summer Larsson. The couple are believed to have met at a pool party hosted by an English couple who live near San Carlos, while Tamara was in St Tropez auditioning for a part in a new movie. Contact us on www.ibizasun.es if you know the identity of the English couple.

What will happen next? Will Jack choose the blonde or the brunette? Has Tamara fallen off the wagon for good? And will Ibiza ever recover from the excitement?

Watch this space, guys!

Ben chucked the paper on the passenger seat, turned the car around and put his foot on the gas. He had to get back to the villa as quickly as he possibly could.

Natalia's infinity pool was one of the most extraordinary that Jack had ever swum in, and he'd swum in some extraordinary pools in his time. The gleaming turquoise body of water stretched around the entire villa, like a moat, via a series of waterfalls at the back, so to get to the villa you had to cross a curved stone bridge. At the front, there was an island with three palm trees on it, and it was around this island that Jack was currently swimming, trying to clear his head and prepare himself for what he had to do.

He had a killer hangover – they'd drunk quite a bit with dinner, and then all that vodka at the club – but it was nothing compared to how Tamara must be feeling. How had she managed to get so drunk so quickly? He supposed that your tolerance went way down when you'd been clean for years. In the few words they'd been able to exchange before he escorted Tamara home, Summer had been very quick to blame that disgusting prick Jorge for giving her drugs – and if it was true, it was unforgivable. Tamara's history was well documented, but she was a grown woman, and he was sick of making excuses for her.

With a sigh, Jack prepared to do one final lap before going upstairs to do what had to be done. He was absolutely dreading it, but if it meant he could be with Summer, it would be worth it. As he propelled himself through the water with a strong front crawl, he gradually became aware of some sort of commotion going on outside Natalia's state-of-the-art front gates. The gates were around the other side of the villa, so the noise had to be pretty loud to reach him in the pool. He was swimming to the side of the pool so he could get out and investigate, when he heard Ben's voice, shouting angrily,

'Let me through, you fucking cunts. No, I've got nothing to say, except piss off.'

A few seconds later, he appeared at the French windows that led out to the pool, still carrying two pints of milk and a newspaper. Impatiently, he dumped the milk cartons on a glass-topped table.

'Hey,' said Jack. 'What the hell's going on out there?'

'You'd better sit down, mate.'

Jack picked up a towel and gave himself a quick rub down before perching on the edge of a sunlounger.

'What is it?'

Wordlessly, Ben handed him the folded paper.

'Oh shit. Did some asshole get pictures of Tammy at the club? Jeez, this is the last thing she needs right now.'

'I'm afraid it's worse than that,' said Ben. 'Somebody's also spilt the beans on you and Summer.'

'*What?*'

Jack practically ripped the paper in half as he unfolded it. His eyes widened in horror as he saw the headline, and both photos. Ben put a comforting hand on his shoulder as he started to read. Once he'd finished, he looked up, anguish written all over his handsome face.

'But *how?* – *Who* could have done this? You and Natalia were the only people who knew . . .'

'Mate, I hope you know that—'

'Oh no, no, I'm not accusing you. It's just . . . There's so much detail. Whoever their *source* is' – he drawled out the word with bitter sarcasm – 'knew that we met at Andy and Bella's party.'

'With all due respect, mate, you and Summer haven't been particularly subtle about things. There were loads of people at that party who could have suspected something was going on, and hung out around Summer's flat – I'm assuming that is Summer's flat?' Jack nodded mutely. 'They were just waiting for their moment. That photo has to be worth tens, if not hundreds, of thousands of dollars.'

'More than the photo of Tammy.' Jack winced as he looked at it again.

'I'd say so.'

'So how did the *Ibiza Sun* pay for it?'

'I imagine the editor has an understanding with a bigger paper.' Ben took out his phone and pressed the screen a few times. 'Yup, you've made the Mail Online as an "exclusive" too. Funny interpretation of the word, but . . . Sorry, mate.'

'Fuck.'

'What are you going to do?'

'Well, I guess it's forced my hand, but I'm gonna do what I was going to do anyway. This has just made everything even more difficult and shitty than it already was.'

'Is there anything I can do to help?'

'Maybe. Could you stick around today? I know you wanted a day at the beach, but I've no idea how Tammy's gonna react, and it'll be good to have somebody on my side now Dad's gone awol.'

'Yeah, sure, anything, mate.'

He got up, nervously running his hands through his hair. 'Wish me luck, buddy.'

'Good luck, Jack.'

Jack stood watching Tamara sleep, bracing himself for what he had to do. She looked much younger when she was sleeping, despite the smudged eye make-up that had smeared itself all over Natalia's expensive pillowcases. He remembered how he used to love watching her for a few minutes before she woke up. This was the last time he'd ever do it, he realized. He shook himself. Now was not the time to be getting sentimental.

He sat down on the bed and gave her shoulder a gentle shake.

'Tammy? Wake up, sweetheart . . .'

'Ugh . . . wha . . .' Groggily she opened one eye. 'Oh, hi, Jack.' After about one blissful second of oblivion it all came back to her. 'Oh shiiit. Don't be pissed with me, Jack, please? I'm sorry, OK? I fell off the wagon. It won't happen again.' She pulled a pillow over her face and Jack gently removed it.

'Sit up, sweetheart. There's something I have to tell you.'

As Tamara sat up, holding the sweaty sheet protectively against her breast, she saw the newspaper in Jack's hand.

'Oh no. Oh fuck. Oh, Jack, Jack, they didn't get pictures of me at Pacha, did they? Oh no, please, not that . . .'

She looked so young and frightened that Jack thought his heart might split in two. He could hardly bear to break it to her.

'It's worse than that, honey.'

'Oh, quit stalling, just let me see the goddamn paper.' She snatched it out of his hand. In a way, Jack was relieved – he had been trying to come up with the right words and now he wouldn't have to.

As she read, Tamara's expression changed from frightened to downright furious.

'WHAT? *You've been screwing that uptight cunt Summer?*'

'Summer's not uptight . . .'

'Oh, spare me, please. We mustn't insult little Miss Goody Two-Shoes Summer, now, must we? Little Miss Goody White Bikini Two-Shoes, *who thinks nothing of screwing somebody else's guy.*'

Tamara burst into loud, angry tears.

'Tammy, please – I'm sorry. I was going to tell you when we got home to LA. I didn't want you to find out like this . . .'

'What, so you could carry on screwing her behind my back for the rest of our vacation? Well, how very *noble* of you, sweetheart.'

Jack tried to put his arms around her and she pushed him off violently.

'DON'T TOUCH ME!' she screamed. Outwardly, Tamara was the picture of grief and anger, but inside, her mind was whirring. This certainly took the pressure off her. OK, so the drunken dancing and crotch-flashing was humiliating, but the news that Jack had been cheating on her was, in many ways, a godsend. Jack Meadows, the all-American hero, would be no more. He was the bastard who'd been screwing some unknown blonde behind her back, the bastard who'd caused Tamara Gold to turn to the bottle after years of sobriety. Conveniently Tamara forgot about all of her own infidelities. Yes, this could be spun to her advantage. Taking a deep breath, she buried her hurt and anger somewhere inside.

'Just fuck off and leave me alone, Jack.' This time her voice was cold, measured. 'I'll be leaving this afternoon. I never want to see you again.'

Summer sat curled up in a ball on the floor of her tiny bathroom. The paparazzi all around her front door were terrifying, and this was the furthest away she could hide herself. Even greater than the fear, though, was her anger. Fucking Jorge – she would kill him, as soon as she got out of this hellish situation. She had no doubt whatsoever that he was the one who'd tipped off the Press. He'd been at Bella's party and at Pacha last night; he'd told her he knew about her and Jack; most importantly, it was exactly the sort of amoral, scumbag behaviour he'd stoop to. Jorge thought nothing of trampling over other people's feelings in order to feather his own nest.

She was desperately worried about Jack, too. Bad though this was for her, it was a million times worse for him; he had Tamara to contend with, on top of everything else. And God only knew what damage this would do to his career. She couldn't wait to see him, to kiss away his pain. He'd sent a brief text, earlier, saying he'd come to her later today, but that he had a lot to deal with; he couldn't risk calling her in case their phones had been hacked.

Suddenly, blissfully, she heard his lovely cultured voice outside, above the shouting of the paps.

'Why don't you assholes fuck off and leave her alone!' OK, so the words weren't quite so cultured, but the sentiment was gallant.

'You looking forward to getting your leg over again, Jack?!' shouted one voice.

'She looks a right goer, your Swedish blonde!' chortled another.

'Don't you *dare* talk about Summer like that.'

There was a cry, then a loud thudding sound. Jack had clearly taken a swing at one of the bastards.

'Summer!' cried Jack, banging on her front door. 'It's Jack. Let me in.'

Summer ran out of her bathroom and into her living room. Hiding behind the front door, she opened it a couple of inches and saw one of Jack's eyes through the crack.

'Quick,' she whispered, and Jack dashed through the door, slamming it behind him with an almighty bang.

They stood there, looking at each other, before collapsing in each other's arms, shaking.

'Shit,' said Summer. 'Shit shit shit shit shit.'

'I'm so sorry, my darling,' said Jack. 'If it wasn't for me, you'd never have had to go through that.'

'Don't be silly.' Summer found she was crying, now that he was here and in her arms. 'I love you. But how can *that*' – she nodded in the direction of the front door – 'be legal?'

'I'll never know.' Wearily, Jack ran his fingers through his hair. 'Hey – do you have anything to drink?'

'Sure.' Summer went into the kitchen and produced a bottle of *hierbas* and two glasses. 'We can't even go out on the balcony – they managed to get up there, too.'

'I'll take you back to Natalia's soon. It's huge and we'll be much more secure. I just want to spend a few minutes here with you. Alone.'

'I know. I understand. So . . .' Summer took a sip of her *hierbas*. 'How did Tamara take it?'

'Tears, tantrums . . .'

'To be expected, huh?'

'Yes, but . . . It wasn't as bad as I expected.' Summer raised her eyebrows in silent query. 'I think she's out to ruin me. You see, this – you and me – excuses her behaviour at Pacha, to an extent. Well, it will in the eyes of all the stupid people out there. I'm pretty sure she's going to play the innocent victim, while I'll be the bad guy who messed with her heart. That wounded vulnerability will no doubt be great publicity for the Miles Dawson movie.'

'Shit,' said Summer again. 'I hadn't thought of that. What a fucking bitch.'

'Not really.' Jack shook his curly head. 'Remember, she's been in the movie business since she was a kid. It's only natural she should try to turn this to her best advantage.'

Summer laughed ruefully. 'You are such a good guy, Jack,' she said, putting her arms around him and kissing his forehead. 'That's one of the reasons I love you so much.'

'A lousy idiotic fool is more accurate.'

'Well, you're probably too nice a guy to be in the movie business.'

Jack laughed again at this. 'Yes, I probably am.'

'I could kill Jorge,' said Summer suddenly, getting up and starting to pace angrily around the room. 'Unscrupulous little toad.'

'Are you sure it was him?'

'One hundred per cent. He could easily have taken that upskirt shot of Tamara on his phone last night. He must have seen us at Bella's party, hung out around here until he got a photo of us, and then decided to bide his time until it was right. He gave Tamara drugs last night and waited for the fallout. He—'

She was interrupted by somebody banging on the door.

'Summer – let me in! It's me – David!'

'David?' Jack looked puzzled and Summer felt her heart turn to ice.

'My boss,' she said quietly. 'I don't want to speak to him right now.'

The banging got louder.

'SUMMER! Let me in. Or do you want me to tell these guys some more gossip about you?'

'Summer? What's going on?'

Summer couldn't look him in the eye. Silently praying – what? That David wouldn't tell Jack about her fling with him? That if he did, Jack wouldn't mind? – she opened the door.

David burst into the room.

'When were you planning to tell me?' he demanded, standing with his hands on his hips, his face like thunder. 'How do you think I felt, finding out about you in the *Ibiza* fucking *Sun*?'

'I'm not sure what business it is of yours . . .' Jack started.

David laughed bitterly.

'So she hasn't told you. Why am I not surprised? Let me introduce myself. I'm David Abrahams, editor of *Island Life*. I am also Summer's lover.'

The sudden pain and confusion on Jack's face were more than Summer could bear.

'Jack . . .' she started, laying a hand on his arm. He ignored her.

'Carry on,' he said to David.

'Yes, Summer has been screwing her boss for the last six months. She's a great lay, isn't she?'

Summer waited for Jack to leap to her defence, but he said nothing.

'David, I tried to break it off with you. I did. But you were too busy with end-of-month deadlines to meet me.'

Jack turned to her.

'Was this before or after we met?'

'After, but—'

'So when I asked you – on the beach first, then again

250

and again and again – if there was anybody else, and you said no – you *promised* no – you lied to me?'

'It wasn't like that – I didn't think it was important.'

'Thanks,' said David sarcastically.

'Oh, fuck you, David,' Summer said angrily. 'Jack, that day on the beach was so perfect, I didn't want to sully it by talking about my sordid fling with my boss—'

'Oh this just gets better and better,' said David.

'You lied to my face,' Jack repeated.

'Please, Jack,' Summer pleaded, willing him to understand. 'It was so perfect—'

'So perfect . . . Yet based on a lie.'

'I didn't want you to think badly of me.' Tears had started to fall slowly down Summer's face.

'I thought the world of you, Summer. I thought you were everything that is good and true and honest. I thought *you* were perfect.' Jack's voice cracked, and Summer felt a glimmer hope. But his expression hardened again as he remembered something. 'You actually told me that you *hated deception*.'

Summer winced.

'Please, Jack. Those plans we made—'

'You lied to me.'

'Stop saying that!' Summer cried desperately.

'Looks like she was stringing us both along, buddy,' said David complacently.

'Don't you *dare* call me buddy,' Jack snapped. 'Goodbye, Summer.'

And he walked out of her front door into the heaving mass of paparazzi.

'JACK!' screamed Summer, but he carried on walking, about half a foot taller than all the scumbag photographers around him.

'By the way,' said David. 'You're fired.'

And he followed Jack out of the door.

17

'I hope she's bearing up OK,' Bella mused to Daisy as they drove down the white dirt track that led to the Art Resort. 'Poor Summer.'

'Po Summa,' repeated Daisy solemnly.

After Jack had walked out on her that dreadful afternoon, Summer, even more besieged by the paparazzi, had called her parents in despair. Her father had driven up to the outskirts of the Old Town, pushed his way through the paps, bundled his broken daughter into his ancient 2CV and taken her back to the family home, where she'd been holed up ever since.

Bella was quite happy to get out of *her* house, for once. Fun though it was having guests, things had gone completely tits up after the Jack/Tamara/Summer story had broken in the Press, and she was dying for life to return to normal. Jack had flown back to LA after discovering what he saw as Summer's unforgivable betrayal, but there was no reason for Ben, Natalia, Poppy and Damian to curtail *their* holiday, and Bella found herself catering for large numbers of people at least once a day – dinner if they'd all gone to the beach, or lunch if they'd decided on a pool day. She did love cooking, but it was all a bit full-on.

Her father and Filthy Meadows, who still had his gig at Ibiza Rocks to perform, had become thick as thieves, and were all too frequently to be found in the folly at the bottom of her garden, drinking *hierbas* and Fundador late into the night and keeping Bella (and, worse, Daisy) awake with their impromptu jam sessions. Then there was the matter of the constant paparazzi presence outside the property boundary of the finca, desperate to catch a glimpse of the couple who had introduced Jack Meadows to his Swedish blonde.

Yes, for all that she felt guilty to admit it, Bella would be quite happy when her friends had buggered off back home.

In the meantime, though, there was Summer to look after. Britta had sounded terribly concerned when she'd phoned her that morning.

'I don't know how to get through to her,' she'd said. 'I've never seen her like this. My happy-go-lucky, free-spirited daughter has gone. In her place is . . . I don't know. Could you bear to come and see her, Bella? Maybe talking to somebody who met this Jack guy will help.'

Bella hadn't thought twice about it, scooping Daisy up and telling the others she'd see them on the beach later. But now she felt slightly apprehensive as she climbed the stone steps that led up from the beach to the little white house on the hill. She was dreading seeing Summer broken-hearted, and felt guilty that her party had been the catalyst for the heart-break – had Summer never met Jack, she'd still be the cool, happy-go-lucky free spirit that her mother so missed.

'Bella!' Britta jumped out of the purple paisley deckchair in which she was reclining in her overgrown front garden. She was barefoot in tie-dye indigo and turquoise harem pants and a plain white vest top that showed off her sinewy yoga arms; her wrists and ankles jangled with ethnic jewellery. Her silver-threaded blonde hair hung in plaits to just below her shoulders, and her kind blue eyes crinkled in her deeply tanned face as she smiled. 'Thank you so much for coming. Hello, Daisy!' She kissed the little girl on top of her head.

'It's the least I can do,' Bella smiled back. 'Summer's been a wonderful friend to me the last couple of months. I wouldn't have settled in nearly so well without her help.'

'She's a good girl,' said Britta sadly. 'Anyway, what can I get you? I discovered some wonderful new herbal teas in Anichas.' She name-checked the latest health-food shop to open in San Carlos.

'That would be great, thanks. Whatever you recommend.'

Bella followed Britta into the house. She had only ever seen it before from the beach, and was curious to have a peek inside. It was bigger than it looked, with terracotta-tiled floors and simple whitewashed walls. Brightly coloured Indian throws were slung casually over sofas, and artefacts from all around the globe – Swedish painted wooden dolls, Indian statues, South American wall hangings – gave it a welcoming, if slightly cluttered air. Wind chimes tinkled in the very slight breeze coming off the sea.

'Summer's in her old bedroom, in there . . .' Britta nodded towards a wooden door with S-U-M-M-E-R spelt out in red-and-white-painted wooden lettering. 'Why don't you go and say hi, while I make the tea? She'll be glad to see you.'

Bella carried Daisy across the room (she'd had to leave her buggy at the bottom of the steep stone steps) and opened the door. She blinked in surprise. The room was in complete darkness, the curtains drawn so tightly that not a chink of light could get in.

'Summer?' she enquired gently.

'Bella?'

'Bella *and* Daisy, as you'd see if you weren't lying in total darkness. Do you mind if I open the curtains a bit? It's a beautiful day out there.'

'So what's new?' Summer's voice was listless.

Bella ignored her and went to open the curtains. The light that flooded the room revealed its near-squalor. Dirty clothes lay where they'd been dropped on the floor; used mugs, and plates scattered with half-eaten slices of wholemeal toast littered every surface. The almond butter (Bella was getting an eye for these things) on the toast was attracting loads of insects.

'Would you mind taking Daisy for a bit? My arms are absolutely killing me.'

Summer, who was lying on a single bed facing a wall, sat up slowly. She was wearing what looked like the bottom half of a pair of shortie pyjamas and a grubby black vest top. Her hair was scraped back in a greasy ponytail and her eyes were red and swollen from crying. She still managed to look beautiful, but it was as if somebody had turned down the dimmer switch on her usual golden glow.

'Hey, Daisy,' she said softly, holding out her arms.

'Summa.'

'My God.' Summer gave a slight smile for the first time in days, as she took Daisy from Bella. 'She said my name.'

'She's been chattering away non-stop, ever since she said her first word at my party.'

Oh, for chrissakes, you stupid cow!

'Y-your party,' Summer stammered, her eyes filling with tears, and before Bella knew it, she was sobbing her heart out, huge gulping, snotty sobs convulsing her slender body.

'Oh, sweetheart,' said Bella in anguish, sitting down next to her to give her a hug. 'Just let it all out, and then you can tell me all about it.'

'Doh ky, Summa,' said Daisy, from somewhere inside the two women's arms. At this, Summer started to laugh through her tears, wiping her face on the back of her hand.

'Sorry, Daisy, I'm drenching you.'

'Let me take her,' said Bella. 'And cry all you want. I'm in no hurry.'

Summer took a couple of deep breaths. 'It's OK, I'm done crying. I'm sorry. I know I've gotta get a grip. I'm behaving like a total idiot, but I've never felt this way before.'

'Wha—' Bella started, but was interrupted by Britta pushing through the door, carrying two delicately painted cups of herbal tea.

'Hey, darling,' she said.

'Hey, *Mamma*.' Summer smiled weakly.

'Don't worry, I'm not going to interrupt you two gals. Just brought you some calming lavender tea.'

'Thanks, Britta,' said Bella, taking one of the fine bone china cups with her left hand and putting it on the tiled floor. Summer took the other.

'Holler if you need anything else.' Britta shut the door quietly behind her.

'So . . .' Bella turned to Summer with a sympathetic smile. 'Do you want to tell me all about it?'

'This has to have been the worst week of my life,' said Summer slowly. Bella squeezed her hand. 'Maybe that means my life has been too sheltered – I don't know. But after feeling so happy when I first met Jack, I guess it's all come as a bit of a shock.'

'The Press have been pretty bloody horrible,' said Bella. Despite the fact that Jack had dumped her, Summer had been predictably vilified in the tabloids as the heartless scarlet woman who had split up Hollywood's golden couple. All the journalists agreed that Jack's return to LA was merely a ruse to put them off the scent before he and Summer got back together. 'And as for that boss of yours – what a piece of lowlife scum!'

Yes, David had kissed and told, painting Summer as a cruel nymphomaniac who used men for sex before discarding them like used condoms. He'd shared intimate photos and even described her favourite positions in bed to some of the seedier tabloids.

'He's not my boss any more. But yes – God knows what I ever saw in him. The very thought of him makes my flesh crawl now.'

'Not surprised. And of course he's not your boss any more – no way could you carry on working for a creep like that!'

'No, Bella. He's not my boss any more because he fired me.'

'*What?* The cunt can't do that.' Bella automatically put her hands over Daisy's ears. 'Surely there are employment laws here? You were brilliant at that job.'

'Thanks.'

'And just because he couldn't handle the fact that you preferred a handsome film star to him (for which, big kudos, by the way – Jack Meadows – YUM!), that's no grounds for giving you the sack. You could probably sue him.'

'I don't know.' Summer shrugged sadly. 'Maybe I could. But you're right, I could never work there again. Shame, because I loved that job.' She took a swig of lavender tea. 'But all my old workmates would be laughing behind my back. Those photos, those sordid details he decided to share with the whole fucking world . . . FUCKING SHITHOLE BASTARD!' she suddenly shouted.

'That's a bit more like it,' smiled Bella. 'Listen, why don't we continue this outside? It's so beautiful out there and you don't look as if you've seen fresh air in days.'

'I haven't. OK, you're right – let's get out there. It's not nice for you and Daisy to have to wallow in my miserable pit.'

'Oh, it's not that – I . . .'

'I know.' Summer smiled and stood up, shoving her feet

into an old pair of flip-flops that were lying on the floor next to her bed. 'You have my best interests at heart, and I appreciate it. Thanks for coming.'

'It's nothing. It's nice to see you again. Tell you what, though. Do you think your mum would mind looking after Daisy, so we can have a proper uninterrupted chat?'

'I can think of nothing she'd like more.'

Bella and Summer were sitting in adjacent deckchairs in the shade of a fragrant lemon tree. The uninterrupted view down to the Art Resort in its beautiful bay was spectacular. Several boats with pristine white sails bobbed on the glittering sea, and shoals of brightly coloured fish were visible beneath the crystal-clear waters, even from this distance.

'I honestly thought he was the real deal,' said Summer, not taking her eyes from the bay. 'That day we had, Bella. Those nights. It was like something out of a fairy tale. Beyond magical. I lost count of the number of times he told me he loved me.'

'It does sound incredibly romantic.' Bella kept her own gaze fixed on the horizon.

'Well, he can't have loved me, can he? Not if he was willing to throw it all away over a creep like David. He clearly is a *really good actor*. In fact, it was an Oscar-winning performance.' Her eyes filled with tears again and she angrily swiped them with the back of her hand.

'Jack seemed like a genuine guy to me,' said Bella gently. 'But he *is* a man. God, bloody men and their stubborn pride – they can be infuriating sometimes!'

Summer snorted. 'Tell me about it.'

'You know they have that stupid Madonna/whore thing going on . . . And he'd put you on a pretty high pedestal by the sound of it.'

'He can hardly have had me down as the Madonna type.'

Summer gave another snort of laughter. 'We screwed on our first date.'

'You were screwing *him*.' Bella pointed out. 'He wouldn't have minded that. But I can see how an Alpha male like Jack wouldn't take too kindly to *his woman*, as I bet he had started to think of you – in a stupid, male, Neanderthal way – shagging somebody else' – Bella was on a roll now – 'especially somebody as distinctly Beta male as your horrible hairy ex-boss!'

Summer couldn't help but giggle.

'Oh, Summer, what could have possessed you? Seriously? Weird little ape-like creature . . .' Bella was giggling too, now. 'Those little hairy arms and legs . . . Those stubbly little hairy fingers . . . I bet he had a hairy back, too! Oh God, look at you! He did, he did, he did, didn't he?!'

Soon they were both laughing hysterically, shoulders heaving as they clutched the sides of their deckchairs.

'Oh God oh God oh God,' Summer eventually gasped. 'Thank you, Bella. I can't tell you how good it feels to laugh again.'

'It's good to see you laugh.'

As quickly as their laughter had bubbled up, it subsided, and they both gazed out to sea. After a while, Summer turned to Bella, her eyes blazing.

'You know who else I could kill, though?'

'David's parents, for creating him?'

'Jorge.'

'What's poor Jorge got to do with it?' Bella had a soft spot for Jorge and couldn't understand certain people's – well, Summer's and Andy's, anyway – antipathy towards him.

'He sold the first story to the Press.'

'What?' asked Bella in shock. 'How do you know?'

'He was the only one who knew all the details. He was

there at your party *and* at Pacha that night, he gave Tamara drugs, he took the upskirt photo—'

'Whoa whoa, stop right there! He gave Tamara drugs? What the fuck?'

Summer laughed, not unkindly.

'Oh, Bella, Bella, you can be naïve sometimes. Haven't you realized yet? Jorge is one of the biggest dealers on the island!'

'Oh. My. God.' Bella slapped herself on the forehead. Of course, it all made sense. The description of himself as an 'odd-job man', the flashy wheels, the constant texting, the whispered conversations with that coked-up bastard Jamie Cavendish. 'How can I have been so stupid?'

'Hey, don't worry about it. He can be very charming. I know – I fell for it myself.'

'So what *is* the story with you two? What happened all those years ago, Summer?'

Summer sighed.

'We kind of grew up together. We used to play on the beach as kids. When I was about thirteen and he was sixteen, I started to notice how handsome he was, and developed a huge crush on him.'

'God, I can imagine.'

'He realized. Of course he did. And to give him credit, he didn't take advantage of me then – I was still a geeky kid, in his eyes. But when I turned fifteen . . .'

' . . . and he was eighteen? God, you must have been a beautiful pair of teenagers.'

'Thanks. But yeah, he was my first time. Nothing wrong with that – I was totally up for it.'

'I can't tell you how soft porn this is sounding!'

Summer laughed. 'Yeah – I guess. But I adored him. He was the love of my life – and I his, or so I thought.'

'What happened?'

'It turned out he was already dealing. Small-time stuff in those days. Mainly pills to English package tourists in San Antonio. And I don't want to be rude about your compatriots, but Jeez, some of those girls . . .'

'Yeah, I know. We Brits abroad don't have a terribly good reputation.'

'He said they just *threw themselves at him*, that he couldn't help himself . . .'

The sunset had been particularly spectacular that night. Summer had sat with thousands of tourists outside Café Del Mar, drinking cocktails and listening to chill-out music. She'd only been to San Antonio a few times before, as she'd been brought up to appreciate Ibiza's gentler charms, but one of the holistic therapists at the Art Resort had offered her a lift across the island on his moped.

Now, as excitement rose as the glowing red orb sank slowly into the sea, culminating in a communal roar of approval and round of applause that rippled all the way down the strip, San An's more obvious, brazen appeal sent thrills through her teenage heart.

Jorge had recently started an evening job handing out flyers up and down the strip, and would generally drive back across the island afterwards to see her on the beach, where they would make love under the stars. But tonight Summer wanted to surprise him – she had managed to blag a couple of free tickets to a foam party at Es Paradis; at the grand old age of sixteen she looked just grown-up enough to get past the bouncers if she wore make-up.

As it got darker, the crowds started drifting away from the beach and one of Café del Mar's barmen, noticing the beautiful, over-made-up young blonde sitting alone on the beach with her arms wrapped around her legs, made his way over to her.

'Is everything OK, señorita?' In San An, where most of the punters were foreigners, English was the lingua franca.

'Yes, thanks.' Summer smiled at him. Wow, she was exquisite. 'But – I don't suppose you happen to know a man' – how she loved saying this – 'called Jorge Dupont? Dark hair, handsome – he works here on the strip.'

The barman frowned slightly.

'Jorge? Yes, I know him.'

'I've been here all evening and I haven't seen him. Perhaps he's not working tonight?'

'Oh yes, he's working tonight.' The barman's voice had taken a grimmer tone as he saw Summer in a different light. How much younger could these druggie slappers get? 'But the strip isn't his patch. Look, if you walk down there' – he pointed away from the beach – 'and take the third right, followed by the second left, you should find him quite easily.'

'Oh, thank you so much!' Summer jumped to her feet and gave him a spontaneous kiss on the cheek, before setting off in the direction he'd indicated.

It was decidedly seedier away from the beach, with loud, neon-lit bars advertising half-price drinks all night and 'English breakfast just like mother makes it.' Groups of pissed, sunburnt lads vomited in the streets and girls clearly totally off their tits stumbled from bar to bar, make-up smeared across their faces. Summer was starting to feel more and more uncomfortable. This wasn't the Ibiza she knew; why was Jorge working here?

She turned another corner into a completely dark, deserted cul-de-sac, and frowned. Surely this couldn't be right? But then she heard noises at the dead-end of the street and carried on walking in the darkness, her heart pounding as she started to make out shadowy figures in the gloom.

When she finally identified one of them, she cried out in horror.

Jorge was standing against the wall, with his jeans around his ankles. On her knees in front of him, a plump girl whose low-slung shorts exposed an unsightly tattoo on her love handles was giving him a blow-job. He was simultaneously snogging another girl and fondling the tits of a third girl with cheap peroxide hair and long black roots.

She threw up on the spot.

'He broke my heart.'

'But you forgave him?'

'I grew up. I went away to university, I had more boyfriends. This is a small island, I couldn't avoid him for ever. It was easier just to be polite.'

'And now?'

'He broke my heart once. I'm not going to let him get away with doing it twice.'

'But how can you be sure it was him?' Bella was reeling from the revelations about the man who'd spent all summer being so kind and helpful and – OK, she had to admit it – flirtatious with her.

'He as good as admitted it, Bella! He told me, that night at Pacha, that he knew about me and Jack. He admitted that he'd given Tamara drugs. And the very next day, it all comes out in the Press? A bit too much of a coincidence, to my mind.'

'It does sound like it.' Bella was disappointed. 'Why am I always such a crap judge of character?'

Summer smiled. 'You're just a nice person, who likes to give people the benefit of the doubt.'

'That's true.' Bella smiled back. 'But now down to the nitty gritty. Would it be horribly insensitive of me to ask about the sex on the beach with Jack? I am gagging to know the filthy details!'

Summer laughed. 'I thought you'd never ask.'

'Hello, darling.' Andy's voice was warm but slightly distracted as he answered his phone. 'How is she?'

'She's OK. I'll tell you later,' said Bella, glancing at Summer, who was sitting across the rickety outdoor wooden table from her. 'Listen, sweetheart, Britta's invited me and Daisy to stay for lunch. She's doing her fantastic raw-food lasagne.'

'Sounds delicious,' said Andy drily.

'It is. But it means I won't see the others at Benirrás until after lunch, and it also leaves you car-less. You don't mind cadging a lift with one of them, do you?'

'Are you mad?!' Bella could hear the sudden elation in his voice. 'This gives me the perfect excuse to stay at home and get on with my book! God, I need a day off from this constant lotus-eating.'

'You and me both.' Bella laughed. 'OK, I'll see you back at the ranch. Can you let the others know?'

'Sure. I love you.'

'I love you too.'

'Give Daisy a kiss from me?'

'Of course.' As she ended the call, Bella plonked a great big smacker on Daisy's lips. 'That was from Daddy.'

'Daddy,' said Daisy, her face lighting up.

'You three are so cute,' said Summer, smiling wistfully.

'We have our moments. Anyway, Summer, I've had a thought.' Bella swiftly changed the subject. 'You said you hadn't seen daylight for days. So what's been happening with Britta's crèche?' Bella hadn't been to any yoga classes since her house guests had arrived; that was one more thing she was missing.

'Ah – well, you see . . .' Summer looked embarrassed. 'That's another of the reasons I haven't been out. If I'd had something to get up for, I'd have done it, however miserable I was feeling. But several of the *yummy mummies*' – the bitterness in her voice was palpable – 'told Mom that they'd be taking their business elsewhere if I was still in charge of the creche.'

'*What*?!'

'Yeah, they didn't want their precious babies being looked after by some nymphomaniac home-wrecker – that's me, in case you hadn't realized.'

'Oh, the stupid fucking stuck-up bitches!' She covered Daisy's ears again, looking guilty.

'That's what I said to the first one who called,' said Britta, coming outside with her serving dish of organic raw-food lasagne. 'How dare they talk about my daughter like that? But then Summer made me realize that we can't afford to be losing customers.'

'So what are you doing instead?'

'For the time being, I've hired a girl from an agency, but she's expensive, and not very nice with the kids.'

'Why don't I do it?' Bella said suddenly.

Two blonde heads swivelled in her direction.

'You?'

'Yeah, why not? Only until all this rubbish blows over and Summer is back in favour again.'

'I don't see that happening soon,' said Summer morosely.

'You wait. People have short memories.' Bella smiled.

'You'd do that for me?' asked Britta.

'I'd love to.'

'I'll pay you, of course. And you won't have to miss out on your own yoga as I'll be happy to give you private sessions after you've done the crèche.'

'Well, it looks like I'm onto a winner then.' Bella held out her hand. 'Let's shake on it. It's a deal.'

'Sa dil,' repeated Daisy, grinning.

*

Tamara was also grinning as she drove along the Californian coastal road in her white convertible Mercedes, the sound of the enormous Pacific waves pounding the shore just audible over the smooth purr of the engine. The meeting with her agent had gone better than she could have imagined – well, it was about time the bastard earned his 15 per cent.

The campaign they'd concocted between them was comprehensive enough to blacken Jack's name for good. For a minute she felt a pang of guilt, then hardened her heart as she recalled the absolute humiliation she'd felt when she'd seen him looking so cosy in the corner of Pacha's VIP lounge with that blonde bitch Summer. That was what had tipped her over the edge, what had caused her to flash herself at a roomful of strangers. Wincing as the memories hit her, she denied responsibility for her own actions like the addict she was.

'California Girls' by the Beach Boys came on the radio. Tamara smiled again and, turning it up, started to sing along at the top of her voice.

'Oh God, that's good,' panted Tiffany in a throaty voice as Jamie rammed his cock inside her, right up to the hilt.

'You love that, don't you?' Roughly, he pulled her long dyed red hair, jerking her head back. 'Tell me how much you love it.'

'Fill me up, fuck me harder. Deeper, harder. Oh God, oh yeah, oh, Jamie, oh, fuck me, deeper, deeper, harder, faster. Your cock's so big and hard. Oh God, yeah.'

'You've been a very naughty girl.' Jamie felt Tiff stiffen beneath him and his cock got even harder. 'And what happens to naughty girls?'

'They get punished. I've been a very naughty girl,' Tiffany parroted. 'Please teach me a lesson.'

Jamie gave her peachy arse an almighty thwack with

the length of bamboo cane he was holding in his right hand. Tiff winced.

Bloody hell, that was painful, even by his standards. She had to make him come more quickly.

'You know what your little Tiffany's missing, Jamie?'

'What's that, baby?'

'She wants it up the special place, where only you can go . . .'

As soon as she said the words, before he could even take action, Jamie came, pumping his load inside her.

'Oh God, that was good,' she sighed, relieved that the ordeal was over, and wondering what her reward would be this time. Last time he'd given her a pair of diamond earrings. She'd immediately had them valued and discovered they were worth over £20,000. Now that had to be worth a bit of a sore bum, in anybody's money.

'Yeah, it was, wasn't it?' Jamie preened himself. 'If only everybody appreciated me like you do, Tiff.' He gave her arse a perfunctory kiss and looked around her flat. It was an exceptionally seedy dive, with a mattress on the floor and one bare light bulb hanging from a wire from the ceiling. He liked the seediness, though. It emphasized the difference in their circumstances and made him even hornier than Tiff herself did.

What he didn't know was that Tiffany had sold half the jewellery he'd given her and was now living in a far more salubrious apartment in Ibiza Town. She only rented this dive by the night when she knew she was going to see Jamie. She and the landlord had an understanding.

Jamie's phone beeped.

Get yourself down Aqua tonight if you want in on some celebrity action, he read. *Bonza mate.*

Jamie smiled to himself as he pressed delete. Aqua it was, then.

18

'It must have been heartbreaking when you found out your fiancé had been cheating on you,' gushed Kandi. The TV presenter had blonde hair like a helmet and make-up that appeared to have been lacquered on. In fact, thought Tamara, she looked as if somebody had sprayed a can of super-strong hairspray all over her head *and* her face.

Trying not to giggle, she said, 'Heartbroken is putting it mildly. But the thing is, Kandi – is it OK if I call you that?'

'It's my name!' Another simpering grin. Tamara simpered back.

'It wasn't *entirely* a surprise.'

'You mean you had your suspicions?' The fact that Kandi looked permanently surprised rendered her fake look of surprise redundant. The reason it was fake was that Tamara had already been down exactly the same route on five other chat shows, but the scene had to be played out.

'Too right I did.' Tamara leaned in conspiratorially towards the TV presenter. 'We women *know* when something's not right, don't we, Kandi?'

'We sure do, honey.' Kandi put a sympathetic hand on Tamara's denim-clad knee. She was dressed down today, in skinny jeans, sneakers and a clinging white T-shirt, going for the all-American clean-cut preppie look to distinguish her further from that Swedish blonde slut.

'And when I saw Jack – *my* Jack – with that . . . that . . .' she stammered, as though she could hardly bring herself to speak Summer's name.

'It's OK, honey, we know who you mean. Don't we?' Kandi turned to the audience, who booed loudly.

'Thanks.' Tamara smiled sweetly. 'Well, when I saw them together, that night – they were all over each other, Kandi – they didn't even have the decency to wait until they were alone . . .'

Boooo!

'. . . well, I guess something snapped inside me. I lost control. I'm not proud of what happened next. Oh Lord Almighty, do I rue the day I ever set foot in that den of iniquity.' She turned to face the camera. 'Don't go to Ibiza, guys. It's just as bad as they all say.' She gave a stifled sob, and Kandi handed her a tissue. 'None of this would have happened if we'd never left America.'

At this, there was a loud cheer from the redneck audience, and the band started playing the 'Star-Spangled Banner'.

'Jesus. Laying it on a bit thick, isn't she?' said Ben, taking a swig from his can of Bud. He and Jack were sitting on Jack's enormous leather sofa, their feet up on his glass coffee table, watching Jack's vast wall-mounted plasma-screen TV.

'She's good,' said Jack morosely. 'She's very good.'

They had taken a break from discussing their latest movie project to watch Tamara on daytime TV, and now they both wished they hadn't. The movie, a sentimentally macho Vietnam buddy-flick, was a proper jobs-for-the-boys project, with a screenplay written by Damian, and Jack and Ben in the two lead roles.

'Poor Summer,' said Ben, glancing at his friend. 'It's really not fair for her to be painted in such a harsh light.'

Jack's expression closed over.

'Don't talk to me about Summer.'

'Come on, mate. It's obvious you're missing her like crazy. All you have to do is pick up the phone.'

'She lied to me.'

'Jesus!' Ben slammed down his empty beer can in frustration and walked over to the big silver fridge in the corner of the den to get another one. Jack could be infuriatingly pig-headed at times. As Ben snapped the ring-pull on his fresh beer, his phone beeped in his pocket. His heart beating fast in anticipation, he took it out and read the message.

Sorry, Ben. Studio heads adamant. No go if JM on board. Are you gonna tell him or should I? Bx

Shit shit shit. Earlier that day, he'd had a meeting with Belinda, his and Jack's agent, who had warned him that there had been concern amongst the studio heads about Jack's involvement in the movie. His reputation was now so tarnished that they feared the puritanical, narrow-minded movie-going public would boycott any project with his name attached to it. The fact that his part was to have been the clean-cut, patriotic all-American hero was the death knell as far as Jack was concerned.

I'll tell him, he typed back. But you tell them that if they don't want Jack, they can't have me.

He looked over at his friend, whose curly dark head was bent over his script. This was going to be tough. Since flying back from Ibiza, Jack had thrown himself into the movie, immersing himself in the music of the period and watching a seemingly never-ending stream of 'Nam flicks. Ben suspected that it was the only thing keeping his mind off both Summer, and his constant vilification in the Press.

Taking another swig of his beer, Ben walked back over to the leather sofa and sat down next to Jack.

'Mate,' he said. 'We need to talk . . .'

In the airy wooden *cabaña* that he was using as an office, Lars switched off the TV and threw down the remote, swearing under his breath. What a hypocritical little bitch. Vividly he recalled Tamara's dishevelled, scared, defiant, then ultimately mocking appearance after he'd caught her in the men's toilets at Les Caves du Roy. That seedy liaison had certainly not been a one-off.

OK, so it couldn't have been nice for her seeing Jack's infidelity splashed all over the papers, but neither Jack nor his stunning blonde had said anything to the Press, each preferring to maintain a dignified silence. Tamara's brazen, blatant attempt to destroy him was despicable. Lars didn't think he'd ever met anybody he disliked more, however alluring he continued to find her – the interview he'd just watched had been enough to reconfirm that.

He swore again. Why the fuck was he letting her get to him like this? He'd only met her twice.

Time to get back to work. He turned to his laptop and stared once more at the pictures his Ibiza contact had emailed him. The location was perfect, on one of the still unspoilt north-western beaches – the sunsets would be phenomenal – and the infrastructure already there. It would need quite a bit of work to turn it into one of the eco retreats in which his company specialized, but it might prove his biggest success to date. The island's popularity never seemed to wane, and there was a huge market there for his brand of environmentally friendly luxury.

Funny that it was in Ibiza that all the Tamara/Jack shit had happened.

Stop thinking about her, you fool. She's bad news, poison, a horrible, warped fantasy.

He looked again at the email and made up his mind. Yes, it was definitely worth a recce. And if he was planning to fly to the White Isle in the next month or two, who better to hook up with than his old friend Bella? He checked his watch – it would be nearly 9 p.m. there, not too late to give her a ring.

'Hello?'

Lars smiled at the sound of her familiar, slightly school-girlish tones.

'Bella? It's Lars!'

'Lars! What an unexpected treat!'

'Is this a good time to talk?'

'Yes, perfect, we put Daisy to bed about an hour ago and I'm making our dinner. Wait a sec, though – our reception's crap inside. Darling, could you take over the risotto for a bit? Hold on, Lars, don't go anywhere, I'm topping up my glass and making my way outside . . . That's better!' He could hear her smiling down the phone. 'So – where are you calling from? From what I gather from Poppy, you could be colonizing the moon right now!'

Lars laughed. 'We both know how Poppy likes to exaggerate. I'm in Mexico, overseeing the work on my latest project.'

'Coooool. All eco luxe *à la playa*, right?'

'Right.'

'So how's it going?'

'It's going good. So good that I think soon I can leave it in the hands of my team here and move on to my next project.'

'Such a high flier – *literally*!' Lars laughed again. 'So

where will this next project take you? The Seychelles? Maldives? Outer Hebrides?'

'Aha – that's why I'm calling you. Bella, do you think Ibiza is ready for yet *more* eco luxe *à la playa*?'

'You're expanding to Ibiza? Coming here? Oh yayayayayyy! Yup, we're always ready for more – as long as it's done *tastefully*, and *sympathetically to the environment*, of course,' she added, with a hint of irony. 'In fact, I think we're more popular than ever in groovy eco circles . . .'

Lars smiled to himself at the words 'our' and 'we' and the pride in Bella's voice. She sure had re-domiciled quickly.

'Especially after our great celebrity scandal this summer!'

'You mean the great scandal that started at your party?' Lars asked innocently.

'What other great scandal would I be talking about?' Bella laughed. 'Though I wouldn't have thought celeb gossip was your thing.'

'Well no, of course it is not, not usually.' Lars hoped he didn't sound as flustered as he suddenly felt. 'But when my old friends are involved, it is impossible not to take some notice. And I did meet Jack and Tamara.'

'Oh God, yeah! How stupid of me. St Tropez, right, just before they came here? What did you make of them? I have to admit I was completely taken in by Tamara. What a fucking little bitch she's turned out to be. She's making poor Summer's life an absolute nightmare.'

'Jack's too, if you believe what you read in the Press. I thought he seemed a good guy . . .'

'He is.'

'. . .Tamara, not so much. She . . .' Lars stopped himself, not wanting to let Bella know about the incident at Les Caves du Roy – though why he should feel any loyalty to Tamara was beyond him.

'She what?' Bella asked curiously.

'Nothing. It doesn't matter.' He swiftly changed the subject. 'So what's she like, your friend – Summer, is it?'

'Yeah, your compatriot Summer. She's lovely, even more gorgeous in real life than she is in the photos – I'm assuming you've seen the photos, given how avidly you seem to have been following the story?!'

'Uh-huh.' Lars felt himself colouring slightly and was glad Bella couldn't see him.

'And so kind and sweet and – well, about as far from *up herself* as you'd expect somebody that beautiful to be.'

'She sounds great.' Lars hadn't really been listening, his mind still on the entirely vexing matter of Tamara.

'She is – you'd LOVE her!' Bella suddenly sounded excited, matchmaking opportunities whirring around her brain. Summer wasn't over Jack yet, but maybe, given time – Lars was one of the most decent chaps she knew, they were both Swedish, he'd be spending a lot of time in Ibiza, they might be *perfect* for one another. 'Oooh, actually . . . I'll introduce you when you're here. There isn't a special woman in your life at the moment, is there?' The question was almost rhetorical – Lars had been single for as long as Bella had known him. 'When did you say you're flying over?'

'I didn't, and I don't need you to set me up with anybody,' Lars laughed. 'But it will probably be within the next month or so.'

'If you need somewhere to stay, well – you know – *mi casa es tu casa*, as they say here.' Bella was suddenly dying to show off the finca to someone new, and it would be nice to have some company while Andy finished his bloody book, all memory of her over-staying guests forgotten.

'Thanks, Bella, but I think I'll be staying on site.'

'In that case, we'll just have to have you round for dinner every night instead! So where is this site? I know the island pretty well now, you know . . .'

After Lars hung up, he walked over to the edge of the *cabaña* and looked out to sea, feeling his loose T-shirt flapping against his body in the wind. Talking to Bella had fired him up about his Ibizan venture and he was starting to feel the delicious thrill that coursed through him every time he began a new project. But why did angry thoughts about Tamara keep intruding on his excitement? An image of her sexy, taunting face popped into his mind.

'Do you want me, Lars? Do you want to kiss me?'

Dammit, this was absurd. Without a second thought, he pulled the snowy white T-shirt over his head, revealing his enormous tanned chest and shoulders, and strode down to the water's edge. It was very blowy at this time of day, the swirling waves crashing against the pristine white shore, and Lars took a deep breath as he plunged into them, his strong front crawl powering him effortlessly out to sea.

He had no idea how long he'd been swimming, and when he finally turned back to face the shore, the cluster of *cabaña*s was barely visible. But at least he was thinking straight again.

Tamara's hair extensions took four hours to apply, but the end result was worth it. Her gay personal hairdresser, Anton, was of Hispanic origin and spoke with a pronounced lisp. Tamara liked him but today he was getting ever so slightly on her tits.

'Babychile, you have played the Preth perfectly. *Perfectly!*' He grinned as he attached another silky dark brown lock to her own dyed mop. 'Jack's name is *mud* in thith town, I tell you – *mud!*'

'Yeah – whatever.'

The reason Tamara sounded so sulky was that she was starting to feel guilty that her campaign to blacken Jack's name was going so well. Given the fact that she had been screwing around on him for the duration of their relationship, it didn't seem fair that, on account of one solitary indiscretion, nobody in Hollywood would now touch him with a bargepole. The news that his 'Nam project had collapsed had spread through town like wildfire, and Tamara knew how excited he had been about it. She had loved him once, and couldn't bear to think of his hurt pride and professional despair.

On top of feeling guilty, she was absolutely terrified that word of *her* indiscretions would come out. After all, she hadn't exactly been discreet about them (which was probably why they were called indiscretions, she thought, laughing hollowly to herself). She cringed as she remembered the student jock at Coachella, the Eurotrash stud in St Tropez, the handsome Jorge in Ibiza. Not to mention her blatant come-ons to Ben Jones.

And on top of the guilt and the terror, there was a third unwelcome emotion in Tamara Gold's world: loneliness. She had grown used to hanging around in a gang with Jack, Poppy, Damian, Ben and Natalia, and she missed them all – even that stuck-up cow Natalia, she realized. They were an intelligent, close-knit group of friends, and she found her old crowd of hangers-on exceptionally vapid by comparison. She let out a sigh.

'Wathammatter, thweetcheeks? Don' look tho low. You have the world at your pretty little feet right now.'

'Yeah . . . I guess.' Tamara forced a smile and was rewarded by the sight of her perfect veneers in the mirror. 'Hey, Anton. Fancy hitting the town tonight?'

It was one of those beautiful, slightly hazy late summer LA evenings where the jasmine-scented air hung heavy with promise. Tamara smiled to herself as she pulled up outside The Ivy in her white convertible Mercedes. Maybe life wasn't so bad after all. She was dressed casually in a pretty pale pink sundress, flat leather sandals and enormous Gucci shades, her new glossy hair extensions flowing freely over her shoulders.

She got out of the car and pushed open the white picket fence that surrounded the restaurant's terrace. Ivy (what else?) clambered up the walls, and fresh flowers of every conceivable hue on every white linen-clad table gave an impossibly pretty country garden ambience to the place. Each table was shaded with a pristine white parasol, under which Hollywood's movers and shakers schmoozed, clinched deals and pushed salads around their plates.

Tamara spotted Jennifer Aniston, in her usual casual attire of slim-fitting jeans and strappy vest, chatting over what looked like Bellinis with her old friend Courteney Cox. Kim Kardashian and Kanye were suitably bling-tastic at a very prominent table . . . ah! There he was! Tamara waved as she caught sight of Anton, who was channelling his inner hipster in the West Hollywood uniform of jeans, T-shirt and blazer, topped off with a black fedora.

People pretended not to notice – heads left studiously unswivelled – as Tamara sauntered through the tables, but she could tell by the way the buzz of conversation had suddenly increased by several decibels that her entrance had caused a stir.

'Thweetcheeks.' Anton rose to his full five foot six to kiss Tamara on both cheeks. 'You look wavithing.' He had recently been cultivating a pencil moustache that, combined with the fedora, made him resemble a diminutive 1930s gangster.

'Thanks, Anton.' Tamara smiled as she sat down. Within seconds, a waiter had appeared, brandishing menus and taking drinks orders. Anton ordered a Gimlet, Tamara a Virgin Mary.

'Back off the thauthe, huh?' He raised his perfectly threaded eyebrows.

'Can't risk it.' Tamara grimaced. 'That – uh – episode in Ibiza showed me how dangerous it is for me. Once an addict, always an addict.'

'Tough, huh?' Anton tried to look sympathetic as he took a swig of his Gimlet.

'Not really. It's easier than the alternative.' Tamara shuddered as she remembered how she'd felt that morning in Ibiza, the memory of flashing her crotch to a load of strangers slowly coming back to her in painful – no, agonizing – detail.

'Tho tell me again when filming thtarts?'

Tamara had been pretty monosyllabic during the four hours it had taken for Anton to create her (though he did say so himself) stupendous new head of hair, and he hoped she'd prove better company this evening. Not that he would ever have entertained turning her invitation down – being seen with her always did wonders for business.

'Only a couple weeks now!' Tamara grinned, visibly excited at the prospect. 'I can't wait! I've learned all my script and everything!'

Anton smiled. She was quite sweet when she was enthusiastic about stuff – although she could be a complete pain in the butt when she wasn't.

The hubbub of conversation suddenly reached new heights. Tamara and Anton turned their gaze towards the entrance, to be confronted by the sight of Ben, Natalia, Poppy, Damian and – oh Jesus Christ – Jack, approaching one of the best tables on the terrace. Such a blatant display of loyalty towards Jack from her former friends was painful for Tamara to witness – though she couldn't blame them, she supposed.

'Sheeet,' said Anton.

'Sheet indeed.'

The waiter arrived to take their order.

'I'll have the Maryland soft-shell crab,' she said quietly, not wanting to draw attention to herself.

'Just a Caethar thalad – hold the drething – for me,' said Anton.

'You sure you don't want more?' Tamara looked at him quizzically.

'Darling, I'm developing a paunch.'

Tamara laughed. Anton was tiny.

'Theriously. You wouldn't want to thee me naked.' He winked and she laughed again.

At the large round table in the middle of the terrace, the conversation was low-pitched and furious.

'Oh, for fuck's sake, they could have let us know,' said Poppy. This night out, this public display of solidarity, had been planned for nearly a week, and now Tamara was here to ruin it?

'She probably only booked at the last minute,' said Jack. 'Look at her – sitting in that shitty corner table, with her *hairdresser*, for chrissakes.' Despite everything, he felt slightly touched by how young, lonely and vulnerable she looked. Poor Tamara. It wasn't her fault that he'd been bewitched by Summer, after all. 'Maybe we should ask her to join us.'

The look of incredulity on the four faces that immediately turned in his direction was priceless.

'*What?!!!*'

'Listen, mate,' said Ben, laying a steadying hand on his friend's arm. 'There's being a good guy, and there's being a complete fucking sap. She's been trying to ruin you. In fact, she's ruining all of us.' He was starting to get angry now. 'If it wasn't for her, *Saigon Summer* would still be a viable project.'

'Exactly!' said Natalia, furious. 'And I am going to tell her so.'

She marched across the terrace to the corner table – a terrifying, vengeful Slavic goddess in her white Lanvin minidress and four-inch silver Jimmy Choos.

'Hey, Nat.' Tamara tried to sound casual, friendly even.

'Don't you "Hey, Nat" me.' Natalia deliberately spoke loudly so the other diners could hear. 'You should be ashamed of yourself. What you have been doing is *despicable*.'

'What?' said Tamara, angry herself now. 'Jack cheated on me!'

'Oh, quit the Little Miss Innocent act. Like *you* didn't send Ben photos of your stupid fake breasts?!'

The restaurant went suddenly silent. In an instant Ben was at Natalia's side. 'Nat, that's enough,' he said. 'Let's go and enjoy our dinner.'

As they walked back, a ripple of applause went through the assembled diners. The movie-going public may have been taken in by Tamara, but Jack Meadows was popular in Hollywood, and most movie-industry insiders had been horrified to see his star fall so rapidly.

Tamara gave a sob (this time a real one) and leapt up from the table.

'Sorry, Anton,' she said. 'I gotta go.' She took her platinum Amex out of her purse and handed it to him. 'Have dinner on me. And invite anyone you want to.' She ran out of the restaurant.

After driving at breakneck speed all the way back to her old Beverly Hills mansion, the first thing that Tamara did was crack open a bottle of vodka.

19

Summer shut her laptop with a sigh, her heart like lead. Still no responses to any of her exploratory job-seeking emails. On an island as small as Ibiza, there weren't an enormous number of openings for food and drink writers, and she was starting to realize what a privileged position she had been in before, with her job on *Island Life*.

She could freelance, of course – she had a good enough portfolio of work to start sending it out to publications on the mainland, or even in different countries, but it would be a long time before she managed to put together sufficient regular gigs to support herself financially, and she couldn't live off her parents for ever.

Just as the yummy mummies on the beach had not wanted their precious offspring to be looked after by a homewrecker, so the wives of the rich men who had previously paid her to cook for their glamorous parties had put their feet down. The husbands were keener than ever to see her again, of course, but in such matters it was still the women who ruled the roost.

The only way she had been able to pay this month's rent was by subletting her apartment to an old friend from

Barcelona who was staying in Ibiza for the summer. She was glad to stay at her parents' home for the time being – the flat held far too many painful memories of Jack – but the summer would soon be over, and besides, subletting was strictly against the terms of her contract.

She supposed she could get a job in a bar, but she couldn't bear the idea of people sniggering at her behind her back: the ridiculous slapper who had been stupid enough to fuck a famously engaged movie star; the once successful journalist and cook who was now reduced to this, in order to support herself.

She put her head in her hands in despair. What on earth was she going to do?

Andy sat in the morning sun outside Café Madagascar, perusing the papers the café provided over a pot of delicious black coffee. After giving Bella a lift to the crèche at the Art Resort, he had decided to make the most of his early start to drive into Ibiza Town – there were certain boring but essential things to do with revenue and Spanish law that could only be dealt with in the island's capital.

And now he found he still had nearly an hour to kill before any of the official departments opened. Not such a hardship, he thought, smiling to himself as he closed the *International Herald Tribune* and opened the *Ibiza Sun*, flicking through its tawdry pages until something in the gossip column caught his eye.

He had never been one for celebrity gossip, but having been exposed to so much of it this summer was willing to give the luridly illustrated piece more than a cursory glance. It was a particularly juicy story, about a barely legal American popstrel disgracing herself at one of the clubbing after-parties with a still-handsome matinee idol nearly forty years her senior. He was wondering where these hacks got their information when he felt a tap on his shoulder.

'Andy, mate!'

Andy looked up to see the tall, panama-hatted figure of Shane Connelly silhouetted against the morning sun.

'Shane.' He stood up to shake his hand.

'OK if I join you?'

'Of course, go ahead.' They both sat down.

'Bonza morning, eh?'

'Yes, it's absolutely beautiful,' Andy agreed, gesturing to the waitress for more coffee and wondering what was coming next. Shane seemed strangely uneasy, as though something was bothering him.

'Er – I hope you don't mind, but I couldn't help noticing what you're reading there.'

'Ah.' Andy laughed, slightly embarrassed to be caught looking at such trash. 'Not my usual choice of reading matter, but—'

'Don't worry about that, mate!' Shane grinned, but Andy could see the anxiety etched on his face. 'I . . . Oh God . . . Is it OK if I share something with you?'

'Go ahead.' Andy looked the other man right in the eye, even though this situation was so far out of his comfort zone as to be laughable.

'That story . . . well . . . *those two* were in Aqua last night, and . . .'

'The story's not about Aqua though, is it?' Andy took another quick look at the paper to be sure.

'No, but . . . Oh jeez, mate – can you keep a secret?' Before Andy had a chance to answer, Shane continued, 'I gave the tip-off that they'd be there, at Aqua . . . My contact must have followed them to the after-party, and—'

'Wait, wait,' said Andy, frowning. 'I don't understand. Aqua's not mentioned at all. Why would you tip off the

Press if it's not doing you any good, publicity-wise?' He was disappointed – he liked Shane and hadn't thought he would stoop so low. The girl in the story was barely out of nappies.

'I haven't been tipping off the Press.' Shane looked Andy in the eye. 'Well, not unless the celebs ask me to.'

Andy nodded, thinking of the night Filthy had serenaded Jack and Tamara on the speedboat.

'I've been tipping off somebody else who asked me for a heads-up on any celeb action going down at Aqua. I reckoned it was harmless enough, that he was just a bit of a sad cunt, to be honest, who got off on hanging around famous people.'

'But now you think he's been selling stories to the Press?'

Shane nodded. 'I'm sure of it. Most of the scoops that have been published this summer have originated from Aqua, one way or another. If it gets out, it'll ruin me. I've always prided myself on my discretion.'

Andy's face was the picture of incredulity. 'Then why on *earth* have you been tipping this man off?'

'Because he's one of my biggest investors, and I can't afford not to keep him happy.'

Cycling through the woods en route to her special beach was meant to make Summer feel better, but today it had only intensified her longing for Jack. She remembered every moment of their first bike ride together, how he had made her laugh and gasp with shock at his tales of Hollywood life; the look in his candid hazel-green eyes as they'd roamed across her face; the absolute ease she had felt in his company.

'It's not fair,' she shouted up to the sky as she reached the clearing in the woods that led to the hike down to the beach. 'Why did I ever meet you, Jack? What have I ever done in my life to deserve this?'

She dismounted and walked over to the side of the cliff, with its view down to the beautiful little cove. As she gazed down at the turquoise water gently lapping the white sandy shore, she was overcome by memories so painfully strong that she found her entire body was trembling. She clenched her fists and squeezed her eyes tightly shut, but not before a single tear had slipped down her cheek.

And all of a sudden it occurred to her: it would be so easy. All it would take would be one step, and all this pain would be over. One step . . .

No!

Utterly horrified that the thought should even have entered her mind, she scrambled up the hillside until she was a safe distance from the edge.

As Summer cycled back the way she had come, she tried to think positive, of ways to get her life back on track. But the sad reality was that it was only the thought of her parents' grief that had stopped her from jumping. She didn't believe she had anything else to live for any more.

'*Merde*,' whispered Jorge, who had been taking a stroll along the cliff path himself, ducking into the undergrowth the moment Summer appeared. It had been one of their favourite walks as kids, and it cut his heart like a knife when he saw how close she had been to jumping. He had been about to leap out to stop her when she came to her senses.

As he turned and walked back towards the main road, Jorge suddenly knew exactly what he had to do.

Bella was enjoying filling in for Summer at the crèche, though it hadn't been so easy getting up at the crack of dawn three times a week when she'd still had house guests. It had been sad saying goodbye to all her friends when they'd finally departed for LA, but getting back to normal had been pretty bloody heavenly. On crèche days, Summer would come down from the little house on the hill to look after Daisy after the class, and Bella would do an hour's one-on-one yoga with Britta. They'd then all – including Daisy – have a quick dip in the sea, before eating breakfast at the Art Resort.

Try as she might, Bella couldn't interest Summer in anything else. Convinced that everybody on the island was laughing at her, she refused to go anywhere more public than her parents' house, although Britta had confided in Bella that she often ventured out on her own to cycle northwards along the white track that led to the secluded cove where she'd spent that blissful day with Jack.

It broke Bella's heart, remembering how perfect she'd thought Summer's life was when she'd first met her.

As she was thinking this, a very unwelcome figure walked into the creche.

'Jorge.' She looked at him with open hostility, thinking that if he hadn't spilled the beans to the Press, none of this would have happened; Summer could even, conceivably, be living happily ever after with Jack right now. And she, Bella, wouldn't be feeling so bloody stupid, having let him flirt with her all summer. 'What do you want?'

'I need to talk to Summer.' Jorge tried to grasp Bella's hand, but she pulled away. 'She won't answer my calls . . .'

'I don't think she has anything to say to you.'

'Please, Bella. I know she thinks that I went to the newspapers, but I didn't. I promise.'

'Why should Summer believe anything that comes out of your mouth?' Bella snapped, when a little girl ran up to her in tears, and started tugging at her skirt. 'Oh, darling, what's the matter?' She crouched down and stroked the little girl's head, glancing up to say, 'Listen Jorge, if it's that important, you can meet me outside in forty-five minutes' time. Now isn't convenient.'

'You'll hear me out?' Jorge smiled his handsome smile, looking relieved, and Bella felt herself wavering slightly. 'Thank you, Bella, *merci*, *gracias*. You won't regret it, I promise you. And neither will Summer.'

Bella waited until the last yummy mummy had finally gone before rushing out onto the beach with Daisy in her arms.

'Summer's not here yet, is she?' she asked Britta.

'No, not yet – why?'

'Jorge's out front. He's got something he wants to tell me. He says it's important. Something to do with Summer. Could you please take Daisy and – I dunno – tell Summer I'm in the loo or I've nipped out for a minute?'

Britta looked doubtful.

'Are you sure this is a good idea?'

'He seemed genuine. I think I should at least see what he has to say.'

'OK then. I trust your judgement. Hello, Daisy,' Britta added as she took her from Bella. 'Aren't you looking pretty today?'

'Yes,' said Daisy, and Bella and Britta both laughed.

Jorge was leaning against the whitewashed wall at the front of the Art Resort, hands in his jeans pockets. When he saw Bella, he straightened up.

'OK, fire away,' said Bella, hands on her hips.

'I guess Summer's told you about our past?' Jorge looked rueful.

'She has indeed.' Bella raised her eyebrows.

'We were young, Bella. I had too many opportunities. But I have remained very fond of her ever since.'

'I'm not sure what this has to do with anything. Come on, Jorge, cut to the chase.'

Jorge drew something out of his pocket and handed it

to Bella. It was a slightly crumpled newspaper cutting, dated a few days previously, about Jack Meadows's career being on the rocks.

'Poor bugger,' said Bella. 'It doesn't seem fair that he and Summer should have taken so much flak . . .'

'*Mais exactement!*' Jorge practically shouted, banging his hand on the wall. 'And that is why—'

'Bella? Jorge? What's going on?'

Summer was standing at the entrance to the Art Resort, her eyes large and hurt, more forlorn-looking than ever.

'I thought you were my friend,' she added accusingly to Bella.

'Oh, sweetheart, I am.' Bella took her hand. 'I'm not sure what Jorge's trying to tell us, but for what it's worth, I don't think he sold those pictures to the Press.'

'Yeah, right,' Summer snorted.

'I didn't, *carita*. I promise. I wouldn't do that to you.'

Britta appeared behind Summer in the doorway.

'Why don't you come to the café and talk about this over some camomile tea?

'You did *what*?' Summer looked at Jorge incredulously.

'*Si si*, I know, I am not proud of it. But it was her idea, truly. She told me that she and Jack had an "open relationship", and it *definitely* wasn't the first time she'd done something like that.'

'And the little bitch has been going on all these chat shows, taking the moral fucking high ground?' Britta didn't usually swear, but now she was a lioness, enraged on behalf of her cub.

'*Exactement*. So you see, I couldn't have sold those photographs. Whatever you think of me, Summer, I couldn't have done that to you – and I couldn't have done it to her, either, not after we'd just made love.'

'If that's what you call it!' But Summer was starting to look less hostile.

'Whatever.' Jorge shrugged. 'I am not that low.'

'You gave her drugs, knowing she's an addict,' Britta pointed out.

Jorge shrugged again. '*Drogas – Ibiza –* I thought I was doing her a favour.'

At that moment, all three women realized that whatever screwed morality Jorge had, his years as a dealer meant that it genuinely hadn't occurred to him that he'd been doing anything wrong.

'So what happens now?' asked Bella.

'What happens now is that I set the record straight,' said Jorge. 'I want to make up for hurting you all those years ago, Summer.'

And for the first time in weeks, Summer smiled.

Jack poured himself another large slug of JD and staggered over to the desk drawer where he kept the yellowing newspaper cuttings – the newspaper cuttings in which that cunt David Abrahams had kissed and told about Summer.

He spread them out over his coffee table and started to re-read, bitterly. There was no doubting the man was telling the truth: he recognized every graphic description of Summer's sexual preferences; every snide innuendo rang true. How could he have been so stupid as to think that she would only have responded like that to him?

Even worse than the descriptions were the photos. Summer's lovely smiling face as she sat up naked in bed, her breasts pixelated out; Summer blowing a sultry kiss to the camera, presumably naked again, given her bare shoulders; Summer writing on her balcony, wearing only a bikini.

He hadn't been out of the house for four days now, existing on a diet of JD and tortilla chips. He alternated between listening to loud classical music, torturing himself with thoughts of Summer, and – when he couldn't bear it any longer – watching hours of bad TV.

He was pouring himself the third finger of whisky in half an hour when the door burst open and Ben marched in, straight over to Jack's state-of-the-art sound system. He switched off Rachmaninov, which was blaring out at full blast.

'Hi, buddy.' Jack didn't look up from the cuttings. Ben had a key and the password for the electronic gates at the front of his house, so he wasn't particularly surprised to see him.

'Jack, you've got to stop this,' said Ben bluntly, taking in his friend's dishevelled, unshaven appearance. He was wearing baggy grey track pants that hung off his lean hips and a grubby Princeton T-shirt that smelt as if he'd slept in it.

'Why? Look at me. Washed-up loser. No career, no prospects, no—'

'No Summer?'

'I don't want Summer! She lied to me . . .'

Realizing that there was no getting through to him about Summer, Ben sat down next to his friend and put an arm around his broad shoulder.

'This blip in your career is just that – a blip,' he said, more gently this time. 'Something will come up soon, I know it will.'

Jack snorted derisively. 'Yeah, like what?'

20

More nervous than he'd ever felt in his life, Jorge took a sip of water in the Green Room. Having discussed it at length with his father, he had decided that the best place for setting the record straight would not be the *Ibiza Sun*, but one of the many MTV-like Spanish satellite channels, all of whose offices and studios were in Madrid. The very first one he'd rung had been so keen, and offered him so much money, that he'd almost been tempted to take it, but his father had steered him away from that direction.

'You are not selling your story, you are setting the record straight. You must remember the difference,' he had said.

So the two of them had flown to Madrid that morning (at the TV channel's expense – Henri had decreed that expenses *were* allowed), and here he was, trying not to sweat through the heavy foundation the flirtatious make-up girl had plastered all over his face.

He looked at his watch. Still fifteen minutes to go. Fifteen minutes before he would be *on air, live, in front of millions of people*.

On an impulse he picked up his phone and pressed the screen.

'Jorge?' asked Summer. 'Is everything OK? Aren't you about to do your interview?'

'Yes, yes.' Jorge said nervously. 'I am in the Green Room now.'

'Then why are you calling me?' asked Summer incredulously. 'You should be – I don't know – preparing, resting your voice, or something!'

'I want to tell you what made me do this, *carita* . . .'

'I thought you wanted to do the right thing?' Summer was instantly on guard, her voice accusing. 'Please don't tell me that even in this you have an ulterior motive? *Jorge* . . .'

'No, no, I do want to do the right thing. But the reason . . . I saw you, Summer.'

'You saw me?'

'On the edge of the cliff. You looked so sad. I . . . I could not bear to think of your pain, *carita*.'

'Oh, Jorge.' Summer's voice was much softer now. 'In that case, all I can say is thank you, from the bottom of my heart, and good luck. But you must get off the phone! Get ready to face your public! Go now! Go!'

'OK, boss,' said Jorge, instantly feeling much happier. Talking to Summer had always had that effect on him.

'And now we have a WORLD EXCLUSIVE!' Paloma, the exquisite presenter, was almost beside herself with excitement. This was going to be the scoop of her career. They had somehow managed to keep what was about to happen a secret, and she knew that the reaction would be explosive.

'Do you remember, ladies and gentlemen, the big scandal that happened on La Isla Blanca, our very own Ibiza, this summer? Jack Meadows, the blonde vixen, poor, poor Tamara Gold?'

There were boos and cheers and shouts of '*La pobre!*'

'Well, we have it on good authority that not everything is as it seems . . .' Paloma paused for a few seconds to allow her words to sink in. Sure enough, the audience gasped as one. 'And here, to set the record straight, is one of us, a local boy. Please welcome, ladies and gentlemen – Jorge Dupont!'

There was a round of applause and Jorge walked onto the stage, looking extremely handsome in a black suit and open-necked white shirt, yet boyishly, *endearingly*, nervous.

'*Hola*, Jorge.' Paloma got up to shake his hand.

'*Hola*, Paloma.' Jorge flashed her a charming grin and they both sat down.

'Before we start,' said Paloma. 'I think we should make it clear to the ladies and gentlemen that you have not accepted any money for this interview, that you are not *selling your story.*'

Jorge shook his head adamantly. 'No, no, I could not do that. In fact, I feel uncomfortable enough *telling my story* . . .' There was a ripple of laughter through the crowd. 'But it is something I must do.'

'And why is that?' asked Paloma.

'Because I hate injustice.'

Aaaaah.

Already he had the crowd, which was mainly made up of women of a certain age, eating out of his hand.

'So Jorge, where do you want to start?'

'Maybe at the party where Jack Meadows met my friend, Summer Larsson?'

'Sure. So why was Jack Meadows at a party with non-celebrity people?'

Jorge shrugged. '*Es* Ibiza!' Another ripple of amusement. 'The hostess of the party, Bella, is a neighbour and good friend of mine. She has the most beautiful baby. *Hola*, Daisy!' He waved at the camera, and there was another '*aaaah*' from the audience. 'She is old friends with Ben Jones, who brought Jack Meadows to the party. Tamara was not there. Summer met Jack that day, and I think they liked each other . . .'

'And how do you know Summer?' asked Paloma gently.

'We are old friends. Oh, OK, we were childhood sweethearts.' Another gasp from the audience. 'But that is why I feel I must speak up. It is not fair for Summer to take all the blame for what I fully admit is a fairly sordid situation.'

'Okaaay,' said Paloma, enjoying herself thoroughly. 'So let's fast-forward a few days. Can you tell us what happened that night at Pacha, please, Jorge?'

Jorge took a sip of his water. 'Before I start this bit, I want you to know that I am not proud of my part in it. But I feel I have no alternative but to speak out.'

'It's OK, Jorge,' said Paloma sympathetically, putting a hand on his knee. She wondered if he'd be up for a drink later. 'We understand.'

'OK, so there I am, in the VIP lounge, when who should I see but my old friend Summer, with all the Hollywood people I met at Bella's party.'

'Small world,' smiled Paloma.

'*Es* Ibiza,' said Jorge again, shrugging and striking gold for the Ibiza tourist board. 'So I join them, and then I see her. Tamara Gold. She is beautiful, such a beautiful girl in the flesh.'

'Even better than the pictures?'

'Much better than the pictures.' Jorge nodded emphatically. 'So we get talking, and then we both go upstairs for a cigarette, and then I notice . . .'

'What did you notice, Jorge?'

'I noticed that she was *flirting* with me!' Another gasp from the audience.

'And what form did this – uh – *flirting* take?'

'She told me that she and Jack Meadows had an *open relationship.*'

The excitement in the studio was now at an all-time high. People were gasping, chattering excitedly, texting their friends this momentous piece of news.

'Shhh shhh, quiet in the studio please!' shouted Paloma, in the manner of a judge shouting 'order, order!' in a courtroom. She didn't think she'd ever had so much fun in her life. She turned her attention back to Jorge.

'And so what happened then?'

'Well . . .' Jorge looked down at his feet. 'This is the bit that I'm not proud of.' He looked up again. 'But I have to set the record straight. Tamara and I – she is very beautiful, you must remember, and a famous film star – hard for a simple Spanish boy to say no to – we . . . uh . . . we made love in a store cupboard . . .'

'You were absolutely brilliant,' said Paloma, pushing her silky long black hair away from her face and looking Jorge straight in the eye. 'They loved you.'

'Really?' Once he'd got over his nervousness, Jorge had found himself hugely excited by the whole showbiz experience.

'Sure they did. Hey,' Paloma touched him lightly on the arm. 'Can I buy you a drink later?'

'*Si – me gusta mucho!*' Jorge smiled back into Paloma's eyes. '*Pero* – I have to take my dad out to dinner. I owe him for making me refuse the money. Perhaps you'd like to join us . . .?'

'I'd love that,' said Paloma, thinking that this boy just got cuter and cuter by the second.

'Well, how cool was that?!' Bella turned to Andy with a large smile.

'Cool?' Andy, who'd been silent for most of the show, sounded incredulous.

'Yeah . . . cool,' Bella repeated, a hint of uncertainty entering her voice. 'Tamara's going to get her comeuppance, Jack and Summer will be off the hook – I mean, if he and Tamara had an open relationship . . .'

'But they didn't,' said Andy. 'You know they didn't.' He switched the TV off with the remote and started to pace around their lovely airy living room. 'I can't believe that you think something so sordid is cool.'

'Oh, for fuck's sake, stop being so bloody pompous.' Bella was getting angry herself now. 'Look how miserable Summer's been since the shit hit the fan – I'd have thought you could agree that anything that might help her would be cool . . . ?'

'Of course I don't want Summer to be unhappy' – Andy's voice grew softer for a second – 'but I really don't think that airing your dirty laundry on TV is the right way to go about it. I mean – shagging in a store cupboard? It's so seedy and undignified . . .'

'Oh, what would you suggest as an alternative? You've never liked Jorge, and now you just can't bear it, knowing he's done the right thing . . .'

'DONE THE RIGHT THING? No, I never have liked him, Bella, and for a good reason. He's a DEALER, remember? An amoral scumbag, who happens to have designs on the mother of my child.'

'He's never had designs on me,' said Bella, impatiently brushing aside the fact that she had almost hoped he had, once.

'Jorge had designs on you from the moment we first met him, and you loved it,' Andy shouted, surprising both of them. 'And that's why you're defending him.'

'I'm defending him because he did the right thing by Summer.'

'I can't be bothered to argue about it any more.' Andy sounded defeated. 'I'm going to my study. Let me know when dinner's ready.'

He walked out of the French windows and Bella stared at his tall, retreating frame.

'You can make your own bloody dinner.'

21

High in the sky over the Atlantic, Lars shifted uncomfortably in his seat. Flying, even Business Class (Economy was out of the question for a man of his size) was always an endurance test, but something in his liberal Swedish upbringing wouldn't let him spend the obscene amounts required to fly First Class. Which was faintly ridiculous, given how much he was now earning, and the number of hours he had to endure in airplanes, but it couldn't be helped, not when that money could be spent on so many more worthwhile things.

He was glad he had the wherewithal, for example, to have paid for the drug and alcohol rehabilitation of one of the staff in his company's headquarters in Albuquerque, New Mexico. The New Horizons Clinic had sorted the man out to the extent that he was now back with his wife and able to start repaying Lars – which he didn't need, but knew was important for his employee's self-esteem.

Now, though, it wasn't only the size of the seat that was making Lars uncomfortable. He looked again at the small article that had even made the international version of *The Times*, about some Spanish boy screwing Tamara Gold in a store cupboard. Jesus, she picked some seedy places. Store cupboards? Toilets? What was wrong with the girl? He shook his big blond head in exasperation.

He felt nothing but contempt towards the lowlifes who treated her so ungallantly – and how many more of them would surface after this, eager to make a quick buck from her humiliation? His heart constricted at the thought. Now, it appeared, in addition to the aggravating mixture of lust, anger, frustration and protectiveness that he felt towards this near stranger, he had to add another emotion: compassion.

Yet again, he had to force her out of his mind, and instead tried to focus on Ibiza, where he was currently flying, and his potential new eco retreat on the north-west coast. It would be great to see Bella and Andy again, too, and to meet their little girl, whom Poppy had described to him as 'just the most deliciously cute bundle of adorableness you could possibly imagine'.

Bella had invited him to dinner at their new home in a couple of days' time, and he was thoroughly looking forward to it. He'd been working away from home for so long that a little bit of domestic bliss, however vicarious, was exactly what he needed.

Glass of red wine in hand, Bella walked out through the French windows and joined Andy and Daisy at the table he'd carried out from under the bougainvillea-covered balcony, so that they could eat under the stars. Dusk was slowly falling, the candles Andy had lit flickering gently in the fading light.

'Everything under control?' He smiled, looking up from his crossword.

'Yup, for the moment at least.' Bella smiled back, sitting down next to him. The steaks were marinating in red wine, garlic, rosemary and thyme, the potatoes wrapped in foil, ready for the oven, the big mixed salad prepared and waiting to be dressed. It wasn't exactly fancy fare, but she knew that Lars, who was very much a red meat sort of guy, would love it.

'Oh, I hope they like each other,' she suddenly blurted out, unable to contain her excitement. Things already seemed to be looking up a tiny bit for Summer: that very morning, a couple of Britta's yoga veterans had asked kindly after her – in marked contrast to the snotty attitude they'd previously displayed. It seemed that Jorge's TV appearance was starting to do the trick, but Bella was doing her best not to talk to Andy about it, determined to keep the uneasy truce they'd formed.

'You and your mad matchmaking.' Andy gave her knee an affectionate pat. 'They might hate each other on sight.'

Bella laughed. 'How could anyone possibly hate Summer on sight?'

'Fair point.'

'Summa!' piped up Daisy from her high chair, her little face lighting up.

'Yes, darling, Summer's on her way,' said Bella. 'And my old friend Lars – that's why we're letting you stay up past your bedtime. I'm hoping they're going to be very good friends. Wouldn't that be nice, my angel?'

'Yes,' Daisy agreed solemnly.

'See?' Bella looked over at Andy, who laughed, shaking his head.

'Do you really think Summer's going to be interested in other men so soon after . . .?'

'Not immediately, no. But you know, baby steps . . . They'll become good friends first, and then – well, friendship is one of the best foundations for romance,' said Bella with optimistic conviction. 'I mean – look at us!'

'Look at us indeed,' smiled Andy. 'Glad you've got it all worked out. Well, let's hope you're right – it would be great to see her happy again.'

'Oooh, wouldn't you just know it,' said Bella triumphantly. 'She's looking happier already!'

Andy followed her gaze to the bottom of the garden, where Summer and Lars were walking through the gates, chatting and smiling, apparently entirely at ease in one another's company. They looked, somehow, right together, both exactly the same shade of Scandi-blonde, Summer's height making Lars's six foot seven seem less outlandish.

'Well well well,' said Andy. 'You may be right after all.'

'So what do you think of Lars?' asked Bella casually, as Summer reduced the strained marinade and whisked in some butter to make a simple sauce for the thick griddled steaks, which were now resting, perfectly rare, on the side.

'Oh, he's great,' Summer smiled. 'What a nice guy. And how funny that we're probably distantly related.'

'Yes, isn't it?' said Bella, not wanting particularly to dwell on this new development. It had transpired over drinks by the pool that Lars and Summer both had relatives in the same small fishing village on the east coast of Sweden. 'And he really is *such a nice guy*!'

'Sure,' said Summer distractedly as she worked alongside her. 'How's this?' she added, offering Bella a teaspoon to taste the vinaigrette she'd been whisking up.

'Divine,' said Bella, drinking the whole spoonful. 'Sorry, I'm disgusting, but your culinary magic never ceases to amaze me. Anyway, back to Lars . . .'

'*Bella* . . .' Summer gave her a look. 'You're not trying to set me up with him, are you?'

'Don't be silly, lovey, I just thought that you two would like each other – you know, as friends.'

'We do. What's not to like about Lars?'

'Exactly. And what's not to like about you?'

Summer laughed. 'Your transparency is cute, but it's not going to work. I can't think about another man when I'm still so stupidly hung up on that handsome movie-star bastard.'

Almost to her surprise, it seemed, her eyes filled with tears.

'Oh, Summer, sorry sorry sorry,' said Bella, giving her a hug. 'But don't – I don't know – dismiss him out of hand?'

'No dismissing out of hand going on here,' said Summer, holding up both her hands, then wiping away a stray tear. 'Right, shall we get this food on the table?'

Inevitably, the conversation turned to Jorge's TV appearance.

'He's been a useless shit for a lot of his life, but he's helped me now.' Summer took a huge gulp of her red wine, more drunk than was usually her wont.

'How?' asked Lars, who was also quite drunk on Andy and Bella's hospitality and free-flowing wine. The cicadas chirruped more loudly, seeming to change key as one; the air smelled of mountain herbs.

'Surely it's obvious?' said Bella. 'If Jack and Tamara had an open relationship – *as I know they didn't*, before you say anything, Andy, but she *said* they did – then Summer's not the EVIL VIXEN that the stupid-cunt tabloids have made out.'

'Lovely turn of phrase, darling,' said Andy. 'And I'm glad that things are getting better for you, Summer. But, I don't know, it's all so sordid. I've never liked the man – I'd say that "useless shit" is a perfectly apt description.'

'Actually, I take it back,' said Summer, feeling guilty. She had been genuinely touched by Jorge's phone call from the Green Room. 'I guess that was the wine talking! No,

I think he just lost his way a bit over the years – it was sweet of him to help me the way he did.'

'Selling your story is not gentlemanly behaviour,' said Lars.

'He didn't sell it!' Summer and Bella said simultaneously. There was a pause during which the cicadas changed key again.

'But . . . you know . . . I can't help feeling a little sorry for Tamara now,' added Summer.

'Seriously? The bitch who's made your life hell?' asked Bella.

'Hey, I screwed her fiancé. *I* made my life hell. I've probably made her life hell.' Summer finished the dregs of her wine and poured more into her glass. 'And I know what it's like to read shit about yourself in the Press, to know that people are talking about you, laughing about you . . .'

She looked so bleak that Bella leaned across the table to squeeze her hand.

'She didn't do herself any favours, appearing on all those talk shows,' Bella pointed out. 'In a way, you almost have to admire her chutzpah. I'm guessing that Jorge wasn't the only one.'

Lars, who knew that Jorge wasn't the only one, said nothing.

'She must have been shit-scared that something like this would come out,' Bella continued.

'Yeah, well, that's why I'm starting to feel sorry for her,' said Summer.

'What a sweet girl you are,' smiled Andy.

'Almost too sweet for your own good!' Bella, who was as drunk as the rest of them, poured herself some more red wine. 'Isn't she, Lars? Isn't Summer just sweetness personified?'

'Bella . . .' said Summer.

'You really are incredibly unsubtle, darling,' laughed Andy.

'Yes, I think Summer is very sweet,' said Lars.

'And incredibly beautiful?' Bella persisted.

'Bella, stop it!' Summer protested.

'And incredibly beautiful, yes,' Lars concurred, smiling at her. He said something in Swedish and they both started to giggle.

'What?' asked Bella. 'What's so bloody funny?'

Summer responded to Lars in Swedish, then added, 'Oh, Bella, Bella, I'm sorry, this is rude of us, but . . .'

'. . . we both understand that you would like us to be together, and we both appreciate it,' smiled Lars.

'But it's not going to happen,' added Summer. 'I like Lars very much indeed.'

'Likewise,' said Lars. 'But I'm afraid there is no chemistry whatsoever. You only have to take a look at us! If anything, Summer is like the sister I never had.'

'Oh bollocks,' said Bella, and they all burst out laughing.

22

'Listen, Lily, life ain't fair. Nothing is fair.' It wasn't difficult for Tamara to start crying, sobbing her heart out as she handed the little girl over to the sour-faced magistrate. 'The sooner you learn that, the better.'

Lily just wailed even louder, clinging to her like a limpet. Man, this child actress was good. And Tamara knew a thing or two about child actresses.

'Now you gotta be strong.' Briefly Tamara wrapped her arms tightly around the sobbing little body, planting a big kiss on top of her grubby little head. 'It won't be for ever, I promise you.' She pulled away and looked Lily straight in the eye. 'You hear that darlin? I *promise* ya. I'll be back for you, and before you know it we'll be one big happy family again.'

And she turned abruptly on her heel as if she couldn't bear to prolong the moment.

'CUT!' shouted Miles.

Tamara carried on walking in the direction of her trailer, tears still streaming down her cheeks. Miles hurried after her.

'That was fantastic, Tamara. My heart was breaking.' He put his hand on her shoulder and turned her around to face him. 'You OK, hon?' His kind hazel eyes searched her tear-stained face.

'Sure.' Tamara forced a bright smile. 'I'm fine. Just the pathos of the scene got to me, I guess.'

'Hey. Let's take this to your trailer.' Miles turned to the rest of the crew and shouted, 'Break for fifteen minutes, guys!'

They were in the second week of shooting *Dust Bowl*, on location in Texas's panhandle. An incredibly realistic set of poverty-stricken shanties had been built on miles of scrubby wasteland; the cast was word-perfect, all the crew assembled. And then the shit had hit the fan.

Jorge's interview on Spanish TV had turned him into an overnight celebrity, his dark good looks and innate charm proving surprisingly telegenic. The gullible public loved the fact that he hadn't accepted any money for telling his story, that he 'hated injustice' and 'only wanted to set the record straight'. He was also being papped a lot with the stunning TV presenter, Paloma, who had interviewed him. Reporters had been clamouring for Summer's side of the story, too, but to give her her due, she had kept fully schtum, only ever managing a tight-lipped 'No Comment' to the hordes of paparazzi who had started to hound her anew.

Jack's fortunes seemed to be on the rise, the studios now falling over themselves to get him on board, his 'Nam project fully back on track. God, the movie industry was a fickle, shallow, horrible business.

As for Tamara, she had become an international laughing stock. If only she hadn't milked the Jack and Summer situation quite so relentlessly, she might have gotten off more lightly. Instead she was the butt of every joke, material for every second-rate comedian who thought they could impersonate her 'wronged little girl' act, segueing at the last moment into raving nympho. It was hideous.

And once Jorge had spoken out, others had started to crawl out of the woodwork. First up was the Eurotrash stud she'd screwed in the toilets in St Tropez, next the student jock from Coachella. She wouldn't be surprised if Ben bloody Jones decided to tell *his* 'Tamara's a slut' story. Of course her fucking bloodsucking parents had jumped on the bandwagon, giving interview after interview about how her sex addiction was clearly linked to all her other addictions. There had even been speculation that she'd been screwing Filthy Meadows, for fuck's sake, with so-called 'journalists' poring obsessively over footage of him serenading her with 'Sexy Green-Eyed Woman'.

The only good thing in her life at the moment was Miles Dawson, her director, who had stayed staunchly loyal from the minute the story first broke, saying that her personal life had nothing to do with him, or the movie. He had banned all newspapers from the set, which was as closely guarded as Fort Knox, so the constantly prowling paparazzi couldn't get so much as a long-lens shot of any of the cast. But still Tamara could hear the other cast members sniggering behind her back. It was all she could do to get out of bed every morning, let alone give the performance of a lifetime.

Safely inside Tamara's trailer, Miles sat down on the edge of her flimsy camp-bed and said, seriously, 'You know, this trial-by-media thing sucks, majorly, but you mustn't let it get to you. They'll find somebody else to write about before long, and as soon as this movie comes out, everything'll be forgiven and forgotten. Just you wait and see.'

'Thanks, Miles.' Tamara took a tissue out of the box on her makeshift dressing table and blew her nose. 'That's sweet of you. But I brought it on myself. I tried to use the media to my advantage – I can hardly complain when the tables are turned.'

'You're being very strong, and I'm proud of you.' Miles was far too professional to admit it, let alone act on it, but he'd developed a major crush on Tamara in the last couple of weeks. Oh, he knew her reputation all right, but with him she'd never been anything but sweet, hard-working and eager to please. Her longing to be taken seriously as an actress was incredibly endearing, as far as he was concerned. And even dressed in rags, with no discernible make-up and dirt smeared all over her face, she was still immensely, staggeringly beautiful.

'You gotta ride this out, hon. *Dust Bowl* is gonna be the making of you.' He planted a chaste kiss on the top of her head and made to leave the trailer. 'Back in five? Just to give you time to get yourself together?'

'Thanks, Miles.' Tamara smiled gratefully at him again. 'What would I do without you?'

Once he'd gone, she checked her appearance in the mirror, wiped away the smudges under her eyes and fiddled with her hair a bit. Then she pulled the bottle of vodka out from where she'd hidden it under the camp-bed and took a hearty swig. She needed Dutch courage to get through the rest of the scene.

'I never thought I'd say this – *Dad*,' Tamara spat at her co-star, the famously hell-raising ex-Shakespearean actor Peter O'Flanagan. 'But I am ashamed to be your daughter.'

Peter grabbed her by her narrow wrists.

'Don't you dare talk to me that way! I won't have it! D'ya hear me? I won't have it!'

'I don't see how you consider yourself in a position to tell me what to do,' Tamara said quietly, extricating herself from his grasp. 'Just look at you.'

Peter looked down, but not before catching a glimpse of his dishevelled form reflected in the camera's lens; the bare feet, the skinny shoulders, the makings of a beer gut pushing its way through the string vest. Yeah, he'd been method acting, but he was sick of playing such a fucking loser. He was a vain peacock of a man in real life – all cravats and well-rehearsed one-liners. And Tamara, despite the grubby garb, still looked good enough to eat (or, more accurately, to fuck). With a roar of anger that was almost real, he pulled back his arm to hit her. Instead of the planned near-miss, he whacked her squarely on the shoulder.

'CUT!' shouted Miles.

'Fuck you, Peter. That hurt,' said Tamara crossly, rubbing the bruise that was already starting to form.

'Sorry, darling,' Peter smirked. 'We all have to suffer some war wounds in the name of our craft.'

'Don't be a dick, Peter,' said Miles sharply.

'Well, sorreee for trying to get a bit of authenticity on set,' huffed Peter.

'It's possible to make the rushes *look* authentic, without them actually *being* authentic. We are in the business of make-believe, smoke and mirrors. Nobody needs to be hurt, do they? You're actors, goddammit, not soldiers! Can we take it from the top again, this time *acting* pain, rather than inflicting it?'

Miles winked at Tamara and she gave him a grateful smile.

Tamara was lying on her camp-bed, staring at the ceiling of her trailer. It was funny – she didn't mind the lack of luxury one tiny bit. In fact, she was almost getting off on it, as she took another swig from the vodka bottle and slid her hand between her legs. Hmmm. She looked around for something else with which to arouse herself. Oh yeah – that ylang-ylang massage oil would do nicely. She poured some into the palm of her hand, and started to rub both hands over her breasts, down to her waist, then lower. Shutting her eyes, she tried to imagine that it was somebody else doing this to her, somebody with large, capable, masculine hands.

She was starting to get into it when there was a rap on her trailer door. Assuming it was Miles (well, who else would want a chat in the middle of the night?), she hastily replaced the lids on the bottles of both vodka and oil, shoved them out of sight under the bed, wrapped herself in her favourite emerald-green silk robe and opened the door.

Peter O'Flanagan, eyes glittering and mean with booze, pushed his way in.

'Hullo, *darling.*' He slammed the flimsy door behind him and Tamara instantly felt scared.

'Hey, Peter. Uh – I'd just gone to bed?'

Peter laughed nastily.

'Oh yeah? And what were you doing, in that tiny bed of yours?'

'I was trying to sleep? Until you barged in!' Tamara faced him bravely.

'Yes, of course you were.' Peter smirked.

'Please, Peter, you're making me feel uncomfortable. Can we talk about this in the morning?' Tamara was doing her best to be as grown up as she possibly could, considering all the booze and emotional turmoil churning through her veins.

'Talk about what? Your little problem? OUR little problem? Takes one to know one, Tammy.' As he said this, breathing into Tamara's face, his breath significantly fouler than hers, Peter pushed her down onto her camp-bed. 'I could smell the booze on you earlier. I can smell it now.' Roughly he tore her robe apart, starting to breathe more heavily as it revealed her large round breasts, still glistening with ylang-ylang oil.

'Please, Peter – don't . . .' Both his legs were between hers, now, prising them apart. His greasy grey hair was dangling in her face, and – whatever anybody might ever think about her – she really, really, *really* didn't want this.

'Oh, come on, darling. You're the one with the sex addiction. I'm doing you a favour, aren't I? Oh yes, you slut. You fucking disgusting little whore. You love that, don't you?'

Tamara had always assumed that if anybody had tried to rape her she'd fight them off, but what she hadn't reckoned with was the sheer, superior strength of a man. However much she struggled to push him away, he was always one step ahead, laughing at her pathetic attempts to defend herself, shoving his sweaty hand over her mouth when she tried to scream. Eventually, it was easier just to give in, however much she hated herself for it, and however many tears trickled down her cheeks into her hair as she lay there, defenceless and letting him do what he wanted to do.

Peter got off her with a self-satisfied groan, wiping himself on her beautiful emerald silk robe.

'Nice tits,' he said. 'But for a sex addict, you could have done better. *Nul points*, I'd say, for enthusiasm.'

'Fuck off, Peter,' Tamara whispered, barely able to move her head from the pillow. 'Just fuck off out of my life for good.'

'Easier said than done, my angel! I'll be seeing you bright and breezy on set tomorrow, oh darling daughter of mine.' Peter winked, making Tamara feel even sicker. Once he'd left her in relative peace again, she whispered,

'That's what you think.'

*

'Where the fuck is she?' Judd Mason, the handsome young actor playing Tamara's teenage brother, was starting to get pissed off. Having got up at the crack of dawn to get ready for today's filming, the whole cast and crew had now been kept waiting for nearly an hour by Tamara's failure to show. Miles wouldn't have put up with that kind of behaviour from anybody else, and people were starting to make resentful murmurs about what they perceived as the leading lady's preferential treatment.

'I'll go and see what's keeping her,' Miles said eventually, his heart sinking. He hoped she was OK. He'd felt desperately sorry for her yesterday as she'd sobbed her heart out in her trailer.

Peter, who was hungover as hell, was starting to feel extremely uncomfortable. He guessed that maybe he'd been a bit rough with Tamara last night, and hoped that she wouldn't kick up a fuss. Still, he consoled himself, it was her word against his, the word of a known junkie and sex addict against that of a thrice Oscar-winning Shakespearean actor – who would believe her if she started bleating that the sex hadn't been entirely consensual?

'Tamara!' Miles rapped loudly on her trailer door. 'Are you OK in there? We really need to get going . . .'

No answer.

'Tamara!' He shouted more loudly, growing more worried by the minute. 'Are you OK?' He rattled the handle, expecting it to be locked from the inside, but to his surprise the door swung open – revealing an empty trailer. His heart thudding, Miles took a quick look around. Most of her clothes were still hanging from the rail that acted as a makeshift wardrobe, and an untidy jumble of shoes cluttered up one corner. But her toiletries had all gone, her dressing table was empty save for an envelope addressed to him, in rounded, girly writing. Frantically, Miles tore it open.

I'm so sorry for letting you down, but I can't do this any more. Please don't think too badly of me. Tamara x

Miles sat down on the camp-bed with a groan and put his head in his hands. What the fuck was he going to do now?

Hiding behind an enormous pair of Chanel shades, with a Pucci silk scarf wrapped turban-style around her glossy brown hair, Tamara channelled her inner Liz Taylor and defiantly ignored the discreet stares of the other first-class passengers as she got stuck into her second bottle of Dom Perignon.

She felt dreadful about abandoning Miles (and probably her last chance of a proper career), but all she had to do was recall Peter's loathsome voice sneering, 'I'm doing you a favour, aren't I, you fucking disgusting whore,' as he jabbed his horrible cock inside her, for any such regrets to vanish.

They all think I'm a whore, a total screw-up, anyway, she thought bitterly. *I might as well have some fun living up to my reputation.*

She took out her iPad and looked again at her Twitter feed. It cheered her up, a bit.

Tamara may have become somebody to be mocked in conventional, *boring* society, but her stock was high, it seemed, in the LGBT community. She was up there with proper gay icons like Judy Garland, Barbra Streisand, Liza Minnelli and – yes! – Elizabeth T herself.

But where is my Richard? she asked herself, slightly self-pityingly, as she swigged some more of the expensive champagne and tweeted back to one of her biggest transvestite fans:

@IbizaDusty. On my way, honey. I only wanna be with you xxx

Lars and Summer were sitting outside the Rock Bar in Ibiza Town, just behind the waterfront. The bar, a favourite with the hedonistic international clubbing crowd, was packed with scarily cool people; it was taking for ever to catch the waitress's eye to replenish their vodka limons.

Although Bella's attempt at matchmaking had failed, Lars and Summer had become firm friends over the last few weeks, meeting for drinks or dinner after Lars had finished his daily rounds of meetings with surveyors, lawyers and local environment officers. Bella and Andy met him for lunch whenever they could, but weren't so flexible in the evenings due to Daisy.

It was great for Lars to have some company on the island, and his friendship was helping to take Summer's mind off Jack, if only for a few hours a time. Thanks to Jorge, things were gradually improving for her. She no longer thought that people were sniggering at her behind her back, and at long last felt able to show her face in public again.

Tonight Lars had taken her out for dinner at El Olivo, a fantastic (and very expensive) restaurant with a beautiful outdoor terrace situated high up in the Old Town.

'You can take me out when you have another job,' he had said, and Summer had gratefully accepted his generosity, happy to enjoy a bit of luxury after the misery of the past couple of months. The post-dinner drinks at the Rock Bar were on her.

'So you're really not going to go through with it?' Summer couldn't disguise the disappointment in her voice. She had grown used to Lars's company and had taken it as a given that he would be a more or less permanent fixture on the island for some time.

Lars shook his head slowly.

'I am afraid that after a lot – a hell of a lot – of consideration, it just won't be cost-effective. I'm sad about it – the location is so beautiful, and already I have been seduced by the magic of Ibiza . . .'

'It does get to you, doesn't it?' Summer smiled.

'Uh-huh. But the costs are simply too high – the site needs much more work than I initially thought – and remember, I am used to Central and South American prices.'

'What a waste of your time and money over the last few weeks.'

'The money is factored in. It's important to do a proper investigation before starting any new project, and sometimes the projects don't prove viable. And it certainly hasn't been a waste of my time.' Lars smiled at Summer affectionately. 'It's been great catching up with Bella and Andy again, getting to know the island . . .' He paused and Summer raised her eyebrows. 'And getting to know you, of course.'

Summer leaned over to kiss him on the cheek.

'Hey, look over there,' he added, pointing towards a fabulous procession of models in bikinis and bewigged transvestites, some on stilts, handing out flyers for one of the clubs. 'Quite a spectacle!'

'Ah, the parade,' said Summer, with the air of somebody who'd seen it all before. 'Can you see what they're promoting?'

As they both looked closer, they became aware of a tiny figure at the heart of the procession, prancing through the streets in a bright violet bikini and brandishing a bottle. Two transvestites minced along behind her, imitating her drunken dancing as she spun and twirled and swigged from the bottle, her bikini becoming ever more wonky, one large, firm breast almost completely exposed by the time that Lars saw who it was.

'Fuck.'

'Lars? What is it? Shit,' added Summer. 'Tamara.'

They watched in horror as the transvestites, one of whom was dressed like Dusty Springfield, pranced and pulled faces behind Tamara's back, taking the piss on a massively bitchy scale. Tamara, totally oblivious to the unkind laughter she was drawing from the growing crowd of holidaymakers snapping photos on their phones, continued dancing, swigging and whooping, clearly completely off her head.

'We've got to stop her,' said Lars, without a second thought. Surprising herself, Summer agreed with him – it was horrible to see somebody so hell-bent on self-destruction – although she wasn't sure why Lars was reacting quite so strongly. As far as she could recall, he had only met Tamara once.

'If you can get her away from those . . . people,' said Summer, who had known the Dusty drag queen, and her vicious reputation, for years, 'we can take her to my flat. My friend who's staying there won't mind, once I explain the situation.'

'Good idea,' said Lars, smiling briefly at her. 'Wish me luck,' he added, before striding purposefully into the fray.

Summer's apartment was blissfully quiet and private. Her friend, who was out drinking and clubbing, hadn't minded them using it at all, as long as she had somewhere to sleep when she was done partying. As Lars planned to take Tamara back to wherever she was staying once he'd managed to sober her up a bit, this wasn't a problem.

It had been no mean feat, dragging her away from the trannies, but after Lars had pointed out, bluntly, that 'these people are not your friends; friends do not encourage you to make a ridiculous fool of yourself, then mock you behind your back,' whatever had been buoying her up seemed to deflate and she had allowed herself to be led up the winding backstreets to Summer's flat.

Summer, guessing that the sight of her wouldn't help matters, had given Lars directions and her spare set of keys, before going back to her parents' house. She still didn't know what Tamara was to Lars, but she knew she couldn't be in better hands.

Now that they were safely inside the flat, Lars looked even more upset than he had the time he'd caught her screwing in the toilets in St Tropez, and Tamara, despite the quantity of neat tequila inside her, was feeling just the tiniest bit scared. But she was damned if she was going to show it.

'So,' she said sarcastically, standing with her hands on her hips as she squared up to him, swaying slightly. 'My knight in shining armour shows up out of the blue again. What is it with you, Lars? Have you been stalking me?'

'Don't be ridiculous. I have no idea why I have the bad luck to bump into you all over Europe.' Tamara snorted at this. 'But I am ONLY TRYING TO HELP YOU!' He grabbed her narrow wrists and shook them slightly. 'Don't you understand, you stupid girl? The way you are acting, anything could happen to you . . .'

At this all the fight went out of Tamara and she slumped down onto the floor, her head bowed, her body shaking.

'Tamara?' Lars's voice was more gentle now, as he knelt down beside her, jack-knifing his enormous frame. 'Tamara?' He lifted her chin with his forefinger and was horrified to see tears streaming down her cheeks. 'Shhh, shhh, it's OK baby, it's OK. You're safe with me.' He cradled her head against his chest, stroking her hair and letting her cry it all out, not asking any questions, just soothing her with his masculine presence.

After about ten minutes, her sobbing abated, and Lars handed her a tissue. She blew her nose.

'Thanks,' she said. 'I needed that.'

'So,' said Lars. 'Do you want to tell me what happened?'

'I ran away from the set. I thought the transvestites were my friends – they've been tweeting me for ages to come join in their processions. They said I was a gay icon, that I should return to Ibiza, where I have this *huge cult following*. I thought they were my *friends*,' she repeated, faltering. 'What a fucking *idiot*.' She looked so sad that Lars would have done anything, at that moment, to make her feel better. 'I've let Miles down. I've let everybody down. In fact, I think I've completely fucked up my life.' She put her head in her hands. 'Jesus. What have I done?'

'Why did you run away, Tamara? Did somebody hurt you?'

Tamara nodded and took a deep breath.

'He . . . he . . . came to my trailer . . . in the middle of the night . . .'

'Who came to your trailer?'

'Peter O'Flanagan. He's an actor – one of my co-stars in *Dust Bowl*. He . . . forced himself on me. I tried to fight him off, but he was too strong for me.' She looked directly into Lars's eyes, desperately willing him to believe her. Something in his expression told her that he did. 'It was awful, Lars. Just horrible. The things he was saying . . .'

'You don't have to tell me if you don't want to.'

'I think I do want to.' Tamara's voice was very small. 'He said that he was doing me a favour, because . . . because I'm a sex addict, and a disgusting whore, and . . .'

Lars tightened his arms around her, cradling her head to his chest again so she wouldn't see the anger in his eyes. He was so furious that he actually felt he could kill Peter O'Flanagan with his bare hands if he walked into the flat right now.

Tamara was relishing the delicious safety of being in

Lars's strong arms. Despite it being a deeply inconvenient moment, she had a sudden, crazy urge to kiss him. But for once, she let her rational side take over. In Lars, she sensed she had at last found a proper friend, somebody who, for whatever reason, had her best interests at heart. She would not fuck it up with him.

'You know what?' she said, suddenly determined, and trying to sound sober. 'I'm sick of being a screw-up. Thank you for looking out for me tonight, Lars. I appreciate it. But now I need to take charge of my life. I'm going to get clean, and this time I'm going to stay clean.'

'In that case,' said Lars, feeling unaccountably proud as he saw the resolve in her pretty, tearstained face, the stubborn set of her chin. 'I know exactly the place for you.'

23

It was pleasantly cool, sitting under the vines on the partially covered terrace of Bar Anita, despite the heat outside. It was also packed to the rafters, with a combination of locals, and tourists dressed for the beach, in kaftans over bikinis, shorts and T-shirts. The waiters were rushed off their feet.

Bella absolutely loved Anita's; it had become her new home from home. The lively yet laid-back atmosphere, the friendliness, the mouthwatering home-cooked food, the sense of Ibicenco history in its whitewashed walls and defunct old phone box – she could happily go there every single day, and frequently did, even if it was only for one drink or a *café*.

Today she and Daisy had popped in for lunch after stocking up on some basics in the tiny *supermercado* next door. Bella's swordfish steak with garlic and parsley butter, home-made chips and huge mixed salad were exactly what she wanted to eat in this climate, at this time of day; Daisy was devouring her tiny portion of spaghetti Bolognese, chopped up small by one of the good-natured chefs.

'Bella!'

She looked up from her food to see Jorge, tanned and handsome, standing in front of her, smiling.

'Jorge! How lovely to see you. It's been ages,' she said warmly, getting up to kiss him on both cheeks. Since his newfound notoriety, Jorge had become a considerably less conspicuous figure in the local community – spending half his time at glittering celebrity-studded parties in Madrid, if you were to believe the local tabloids.

He sat down in the empty chair opposite her and smiled self-deprecatingly. '*Si, si*, I have lots to tell you, Bella. My life has changed so much in the last month – thanks to Paloma.'

Was he actually blushing?

'Oooh, Paloma,' Bella teased. 'So, is it serious with her? She's a stunning girl.'

'Yes, she is,' Jorge concurred. 'But also she is smart. Very smart. She thinks I could get my own chat show on her cable network.' He leaned in conspiratorially. 'Maybe I do not need to sell *drogas* for the rest of my life.'

'Oh my God, that's fantastic news,' cried Bella, leaning over to give him a hug. 'Congratulations! So how—'

'Bella?'

Andy was standing above them, his face like thunder. He'd been in a meeting at the bank and had dropped by Anita's to grab a sandwich before driving Bella and Daisy back to the finca: his deadline was looming, and stopping for a proper lunch was a luxury too far for the next few weeks.

'Hello, darling.' Oh shit, Andy was so bloody touchy about Jorge. Bella, feeling a prickle of guilt about her previous, *harmless* fantasies, hoped he wasn't going to make a scene.

'Have you finished?' Andy demanded, completely ignoring the younger man. 'If so, can we get going? I need to get on.' He gestured to a waiter for the bill, which he paid, then practically frogmarched Bella and Daisy out of the bar. Bella gave Jorge an apologetic look over her shoulder, which he acknowledged with a smiling shrug.

Once they were all safely ensconced in the jeep, Andy turned on Bella. 'Looks like I interrupted something.'

'What do you mean?'

'You were almost snogging him!'

'I wasn't!' Bella was indignant. 'If you must know, I was congratulating him.'

'On what? A particularly lucrative deal?' said Andy sarcastically.

'Oh, stop being like this! He was telling me he might be getting his own TV chat show, thanks to his new girlfriend Paloma . . .'

Andy gave a hollow laugh. 'Yeah, right, as if any TV network would touch him with a bargepole. Ibiza's most prolific drug dealer? His background would be public knowledge within weeks!'

'Actually that probably wouldn't be such a bad thing,' mused Bella. 'There are loads of – oh, I don't know . . . rappers! – who've come clean about their drug-dealing pasts, and the fact that he's a reformed dealer might even work in his favour. His colourful past might give the show a bit more depth.'

'DEPTH? Reformed? Now you really are taking the piss!'

'He is, though! He was telling me that he's going to give up deal—'

Andy interrupted her. 'And you fell for that?! Bella, you are *the* most ridiculous, gullible—'

Bella felt the anger bubbling up inside her.

'Can you stop being so fucking patronizing?'

'Can you not swear in front of our daughter?'

Feeling her fists balling, Bella took a couple of deep breaths to steady herself.

'Why do you refuse to believe anything good about him?'

'Because he's amoral scum – and you're so bloody besotted with him, you can't see what should be obvious to anybody with half a brain.'

'Can you please not swear in front of our daughter? And how bloody DARE you?'

The row continued for the whole journey home, and by the time they reached the finca Daisy was bawling her eyes out, hating the sound of her parents shouting at each other.

'Now look what you've done!' said Bella angrily, scooping Daisy out of her car seat and showering her little face with kisses. 'Shh, shh, it's OK, darling, Mummy's here now. Sshh shhh shhh.'

Andy stared at them both.

'Look what *I've* done? I don't believe this. I'm going out for a bit. And I've no idea what time I'll be home.'

With that he got back into the jeep and sped off down the driveway with not so much as a backwards glance.

Bella, standing at the gate with her sobbing daughter in her arms, began crying too, quietly at first, but soon it turned into full-on wailing, almost as though she and Daisy were trying to out-wail each other. Once she realized the ridiculousness of the situation, she started to laugh through her tears, and Daisy, influenced by her mother's mood, giggled too.

'Come on, darling, let's take this stuff inside.' Bella kissed the top of Daisy's silky head. 'Daddy'll come to his senses soon enough.'

'Toon nuff.' Daisy smiled up through her long, wet eyelashes.

'. . . so you've no idea where he's gone?' asked Poppy at the other end of the phone.

Bella was pacing around the pool, Daisy half-crawling,

half-toddling about at her feet – they'd have to sort out some kind of pool guard soon, now that Daisy was so mobile. Several hours had passed since Andy had stormed off, and she was starting to feel worried. It was most unlike him to behave so irrationally.

'None whatsoever, and he's switched his phone off. Talk about a bloody overreaction – how am I meant to avoid Jorge altogether? He's our neighbour, for God's sake!'

'Sounds like the good old-fashioned green-eyed monster. Oh, I'm sure he's worked himself up into a state of high moral dudgeon, convincing himself that he doesn't like Jorge because he's a dealer, but I bet there's a healthy dollop of jealousy there too. Come on, be honest, Belles, he does flirt with you, doesn't he?'

'Oh all right. Yeah, he does. But it's perfectly harmless, and anyway, it's the first time anybody's flirted with me for as long as I can remember.'

'Hmmm. Well, if I were you I'd carry on as normal – get Daisy's supper ready, put her to bed. He'll come home soon enough.'

'I know, it's just – I hate to think of him all on his own somewhere, festering with resentment . . . oh, sorry, Pops, hang on a sec . . . Daisy, stop that!' The little girl was grinning as she licked on a leaf she'd picked from the beautiful pink-flowering bush that grew next to Bella's largest orange tree. She had no idea what it was, but the flowers were gorgeous.

Daisy's happy expression changed to one of revulsion, her round face screwed up in an impressive display of negative emotion, and Bella knelt down to prise the leaf out of her plump hand. 'Come on, darling, give that to Mummy . . .' She turned back to the phone. 'Listen, Pops, I'd better go. Time's marching on and Daisy's obviously starving! Thanks for listening to me rant on.'

'You know you can always rant away at me.' Poppy laughed. 'Let me know how it all goes – I'm sure it'll work itself out.'

'I hope so. Bye! Love you!'

'Love you too.'

Bella smiled as she hung up. Talking to Poppy always made her feel better.

'Come on, darling, let's go and have supper.'

Bella knelt down to pick Daisy up, noticing, as she did so, how pink her daughter's cheeks were, how glassily shiny her enormous brown eyes. Panicking slightly, she put her hand against one of her soft little cheeks, and felt it burning.

'Oh, my dearest angel, I'm so sorry. I should have looked after you better today,' she said, trying to stay calm as she carried her into the house. 'It's just a bit too much sun, isn't it? We'll have some food, and some milk, and you'll be right as rain in no time.'

But Daisy wasn't right as rain. In fact, she rapidly got worse and worse, her little body burning up in her mother's arms. When she spontaneously vomited all over Bella's chest, it became clear that the natural maternal abilities, on which she'd hitherto relied, were not going to cut it this time.

She picked up her phone, and dialled the number of the only doctor in San Carlos, with whom they'd registered when they first moved in, but got a recorded message. Of course, the surgery was closed between one and six. She tried Andy again, without much hope, and swore in exasperation when it went straight to voicemail. She tried the local taxi firm, but at this time of year it was always busy.

'Shhh, shhh, my darling, it's going to be OK, I promise.' Her voice faltered and she blinked back the tears, trying to be strong for her little girl as she cuddled her. She felt totally impotent, trapped in her beautiful home, with no car in which to take Daisy to a doctor, and nobody answering their fucking phones. 'You're going to be OK, I promise, I promise.'

'Tummy hurt, Mummy,' said Daisy, very quietly, heavy lids drooping over her eyes.

Oh God, what was wrong with her? Could it be – she could hardly bear to let the thought into her mind – meningitis? Was that leaf she'd licked poisonous? She'd go back and have another look at the bush with the beautiful pink flowers, but she didn't want to leave Daisy alone again for a single second.

In desperation, she picked up her phone with her left hand and pressed the screen.

'Hey, Bella,' Summer answered.

'Oh, Summer, I'm sorry to call you like this, but I don't know who else to turn to . . .'

'Shit, is everything OK?'

'No, it's not . . . it's . . .' Bella, almost incoherent with fear, could hardly get the words out. 'It's Daisy. She's not well, and I can't get hold of the doctor, and Andy's stormed off with the car, and he's not answering his phone, and . . . and . . . I'm really scared it might be something serious. Could you please give me a lift to the hospital in Santa Eulalia?'

'I'm on my way.'

Summer was better than her word. As she started up her Fiat, she dialled Dr Rosado's mobile – he was a family friend and had adored her ever since he'd delivered her into the world, twenty-five years ago. She woke him from his siesta, and as soon as he heard her story, he asked for Bella's address and told Summer he'd see her at the finca.

He got there first and banged loudly at the heavy wooden door.

Bella, who'd had a call from Summer telling her the doctor was on his way, opened the door with relief.

'Oh thank God you're here. I don't know what to do . . . she's getting worse, I think . . . Please, please tell me she's going to be OK? Please, Dr Rosado?'

'Let me examine her first. It's probably nothing worse than a mild infection,' said the doctor reassuringly, but the look on his face changed when he saw the little girl, who was now bright red all over, her little body writhing about on the sofa, eyes screwed up in discomfort as she scratched ineffectually at her face.

'Mummy, it hurt.'

He examined her gently for a few minutes, stroking her hair back from her damp little brow, then turned to Bella. 'It may be an allergic reaction. Has she eaten or drunk anything different today?'

'Boiled egg, toast and fruit for breakfast, spaghetti Bolognese for lunch, milk, juice . . .' said Bella automatically, and idiotically. 'Oh God, sorry, I'm not thinking straight. She licked a leaf, earlier, from a flower bush in the garden. But it was only a couple of seconds before I took it out of her mouth.'

'Can you show me this bush?'

'I . . .' Bella looked over at Daisy.

'It's OK,' said the doctor impatiently. 'She will be fine for a minute or two. It's more important that I identify this leaf, so I know how to treat her.'

'Follow me.' Bella ran outside, all the way around the pool, the doctor hot on her heels. He stopped as he saw the luscious flower bush, with its shiny dark leaves and beautiful pink blooms.

'What is it?' Bella asked, panicking again.

Dr Rosado turned to her, his eyes serious. '*La adelfa*. In English, you call it, I think, oleander.'

'Oleander.' Bella was happy with the name – it had a comforting, familiar ring to it. 'So it's not poisonous?'

'No, you misunderstand me. *La adelfa* is one of the most poisonous plants in the world.' He started running back to the house.

'What? How poisonous? Not properly poisonous? Not from just licking a leaf?' Her voice was increasing in both speed and volume as she ran alongside the doctor. 'Please tell me it's not possible? Surely people would know about it? Why is such an evil thing growing in my garden anyway?'

'First I must give her a simple emetic,' said the doctor, not answering any of her questions directly. 'It's important to remove all the poison from her body.'

'She's already been sick a couple of times.' The hope in Bella's voice touched the kind doctor's heart. 'That has to be good, doesn't it? Doesn't it?'

'That is good.' He gave her a brief smile. 'I will attempt to make her sick some more, and give her something to relieve the discomfort.'

'And then?'

'And then we must take her straight to the hospital.'

Jorge, driving his BMW back down the motorway from Santa Eulalia, was trying to decide what to do for the best. He had seen Andy sitting morosely in the corner of the bar in which he'd been having a meeting with one of Paloma's contacts. After the scene he'd witnessed at Anita's, he guessed that he and Bella had had a row and that Andy had subsequently stormed off. Why else would such a strait-laced, upstanding sort of guy have been downing whisky after whisky in a bar on his own in the middle of the afternoon?

Jorge had a sneaking suspicion that he had been the reason for the row, and it was this that gave rise to his dilemma. Ever since his epiphany on seeing Summer standing on the cliff-edge, he had become mildly obsessed with the idea of 'doing the right thing'. If his instincts were correct and Andy had stormed out because of a row, Bella would no doubt be out of her mind with worry by now. Lunch at Anita's had been hours ago.

He sighed. Most probably, he shouldn't get involved. Why interfere in other people's problems? But then again, he genuinely liked Bella and didn't want to think of her unhappy.

He put his phone on speaker and pressed the screen.

'What is it?' Bella sounded even more distracted and distraught than he'd anticipated.

'Uh, I just saw Andy in Santa Eulalia. I thought maybe you would like to know—'

'Oh thank you thank you thank you. Oh, thank God. Please, Jorge, can you go and get him? Daisy's sick – maybe very sick – and we're taking her to the hospital now.'

'*Madre de dio, no.*' Jorge slammed his hand on the steering wheel. He adored that little girl. 'But – she will be OK, yes?'

'We don't know yet,' said Bella, with a sob in her voice. 'Dr Rosado has done all he can, but – she's been poisoned, and it's all my fault . . .'

Andy was starting to regret his anger and stubbornness as he looked morosely across the quiet bar's terrace at the happy families on the beach below. Any one of those happy families could have been him and Bella, with Daisy. He needn't have stormed off like that, he supposed; the large volume of neat whisky in his bloodstream was making him question, to an extent, hitherto strongly held beliefs.

Drug dealers were bad guys, right? After Bella had told him what Summer had told her about Jorge's past (and present), Andy had been slightly ashamed of the relief he'd felt. Vindication! At long bloody last, Bella would stop looking at the runty little low-life with such stupid affection.

But it hadn't worked out that way. Bella and Poppy had led such bohemian lives, compared to his own relatively conventional one, that they didn't automatically think of dealers as the scum of the earth; they'd met enough of them over the years to consider them as – well, not friends, exactly, but certainly individuals with their own personalities, and not just an amorphous group of amoral parasites.

The bastard had homed in on Bella, sensing her insecurity about her appearance after giving birth. Andy couldn't believe she'd fallen for it; surely he gave her enough compliments for her not to need the extra ego-boost afforded by Jorge's slimy flattery? It was absolutely infuriating. He loved her and Daisy so much, their life at Ca'n Pedro couldn't be any more perfect – why had they let such a stupid, petty thing get in the way?

He wished he was back at the finca now, but he'd drunk too much to be able to drive home, and it would be hellish getting hold of a taxi at this time of day. He was trying to get a handle on his jumbled thoughts, when who should appear in the bar but the very cause of all the friction.

'Jorge?' Was he so drunk that he was hallucinating, imagining his nemesis was standing in front of him? 'What are you doing here?'

'It's Daisy – she is sick. Very sick.'

'What? Daisy? My daughter Daisy?' Andy jumped to his feet, stumbling slightly. 'What's wrong with her?'

'She ate something poisonous from the garden, she—'

The words weren't making sense.

'Is she OK? For Christ's sake, man, tell me she's OK.'

'I don't know. The doctor is with her, but he thinks it could be bad.' All the blood drained from Andy's face, and Jorge put a steadying hand on his arm. 'They have taken her to the hospital. We must go now.'

'We?'

'I will take you in my car – much quicker than taxi.' Jorge tactfully didn't allude to the fact that Andy was in no fit state to drive himself.

'Thank you, Jorge.' Andy swallowed. 'I'll call Bella en route.'

The traffic was murder. Both men were sweating, from the heat and with anxiety. Andy, craning his neck out of the window, his fingers drumming impatiently against the dashboard, suddenly shouted, 'What's the fucking hold-up?'

Jorge looked at the road ahead and made a snap decision.

'OK, we go a different route.' He revved the Beemer's engine and made a dramatic, and totally illegal, U-turn. 'I have a better way. Local knowledge.'

The U-turn was so illegal that soon a police car was chasing them, siren blazing, but it was a much clearer road to the hospital. Jorge put his foot down.

'Do not worry about them,' he said to Andy, nodding at the rear-view mirror. 'I will deal with them. The most important thing is we get you there as fast as we can.'

Andy, looking over his shoulder at the police car gathering speed behind them, said, 'Thanks again, Jorge – especially after I was so rude to you earlier.'

'*Ah, es no importante.* I love Daisy. She is a beautiful little girl, and her father should be with her right now. *Vamos.*'

He shifted up a gear. As they hurtled around the corner, the hospital loomed up in front of them. Jorge screeched to a halt immediately outside, and Andy, looking back again at the police car screeching to a halt behind them, hesitated.

'I said I'd deal with them,' said Jorge, pushing Andy out of the car. 'Just go!'

*

Bella sat holding Daisy's hot little hand, her eyes never leaving her flushed face. Having handed her over to the hospital staff, Dr Rosado had had to return to his own practice in San Carlos, but he had told Bella to call him if she needed him. Daisy was unconscious now, on an intravenous drip and wired up to a contraption that would apparently alert the skilled team on the emergency ward to any changes in her condition.

In the meantime, all they could do was wait.

Summer, sitting next to Bella and holding her other hand, gave it a gentle squeeze. Bella, incapable of speech, squeezed back.

Her mind was a jumble of terror, guilt and anguished hope, as again and again she made pacts with a God she'd never believed in.

Please let her be OK. I don't care about anything else in the world. I'll do anything, anything . . .

Why didn't I look after her better? I'm so sorry, my beautiful little angel. I'll never forgive myself if . . . no no no . . . don't even think it . . .

Hurry up, Andy, please. I can't do this without you.

As if on cue, the door burst open revealing a sweaty, panting Andy.

'How is she?'

'I don't know – just look at her! Oh, Andy . . . our little girl.' Suddenly the tears that Bella had been holding back were pouring down her face. As Andy held her tightly in his arms, she sobbed, 'Please don't let her die, God, please.'

'Shh, shh, she's going to be OK,' he said, with more conviction than he felt, anxiously scanning Daisy's dear little body, with all the wires coming out of it, over Bella's shoulder. 'I'm so sorry I wasn't there when it happened. I'm sorry for everything.'

'I'm sorry for everything too . . .' Bella's words were muffled against his broad chest. 'None of it matters. Nothing matters apart from Daisy getting better.'

'She will, darling. I promise you she will.'

Beeeeep. Beeeeep. Beeeeep.

Bella and Andy sprang apart, and Summer leapt out of her chair at the sound of the alarm.

'What is it? What the fuck is it? Oh Jesus, what's the matter? Where's the doctor?' Bella was out of her mind with fear now, and Andy opened the door and ran down the hospital corridor, shouting, 'Somebody come, please, please!'

Within seconds a female doctor was at Daisy's bedside, checking the monitors and lifting her eyelids to gauge the reaction.

'Her temperature has dropped rapidly. Before it was very high . . .'

'Yes, I know,' Bella practically screamed at her. But as she looked at Daisy's face she saw that instead of being flushed and sweaty, it was now deathly pale.

'What's happening? Why?' asked Andy, in more measured but no less urgent tones than Bella's.

'Sometimes the poison affects the body this way,' said the doctor gently. 'We need to monitor her heart, now.'

'What?'

But already the doctor was summoning nurses, who with impressive speed arrived in the room with a scary-looking contraption that they proceeded to strap to Daisy's little chest.

'What is it?' asked Summer.

'It's an electrocardiogram – an ECG,' said one of the kind nurses. 'You must not worry, it is only to monitor her heart rate, because her temperature has dropped so rapidly.'

'Jesus Christ, this can't be happening,' sobbed Bella. 'I want my little girl back.'

24

The New Horizons Drug and Alcohol Rehab Centre was situated right on the edge of the Chihuahuan Desert in New Mexico, overlooked by the Guadalupe mountain range. The warm rust-coloured adobe buildings that housed the centre were designed to look like Native American pueblos, surrounded by spiky cacti and bathed in rich sunlight. There was a strong holistic, spiritual emphasis throughout, an emphasis on treating the body, mind and soul as one, which made the whole business of rehabilitation a lot less nightmarish than it might have been.

Yes, as rehab went, it was pretty cool, thought Tamara, as one of the Native American therapists put another hot stone on her back. The actual detox had been as horrible as it always was – hot sweats, nightmares, violent shakes and vomiting, the full-on self-hatred shebang – but she had to admit that Lars had found her a good place in which to recover.

Lars had been very kind to her – probably kinder than anybody had ever been in her entire life. He had told Miles Dawson why Tamara had gone AWOL, and exactly who was to blame. Miles – and Tamara could scarcely believe this – had actually agreed to schedule filming around

Tamara's rehab, to film all the scenes she wasn't required in first, and to wait until she'd fully recovered to shoot hers. He really must value her acting, she thought in awe, and with enormous gratitude.

What's more, he had fired Peter O'Flanagan, replacing him with another, equally well respected (but far kinder) veteran actor. He had sworn all the cast and crew to secrecy, stressing that anybody who leaked anything to the Press would be out on their ear as swiftly as O'Flanagan had been dispatched.

Miles had visited her at New Horizons a couple of times, as had Lars, but other than that she hadn't had any visitors. She hadn't bothered telling her parents where she was – as far as they were concerned she was still on the *Dust Bowl* set. Had she confided in them, they would only have seen the information as something else with which to feather their unscrupulous nests.

The recovery programme comprised regular, delicious and healthy meals, yoga at dawn, meditation twice a day, an afternoon hike in the mountains, spa therapies ranging from hot stone to acupuncture, aura cleansing to crystal healing, and counselling. God, was there a lot of talking! Tamara's regular sessions with her therapist back in LA meant that she was used to talking about herself, but never before had she admitted to her sex addiction. And once the floodgates had been opened, there was no going back.

The counsellors suggested that the reason she behaved the way she did was because she was desperate for the love she had never received from her parents. It was so fucking obvious, when you thought about it, it was almost insulting that she hadn't recognized it before. They helped her dissociate meaningless sex with random strangers from the concept of love. Most of all, they encouraged her to love herself.

'Are you sure I don't love myself too much already?' Tamara had joked to the counsellor who had first mooted this, a kind-eyed Cherokee in his mid-sixties.

'My child, nobody as hell-bent on self-destruction as you have been could be considered to love herself,' had been his reply. He had a point, she supposed.

While she would once have scoffed at all the New Age baloney, she had to admit that, as a package, it was incredibly effective. And soothing. Soothing was the word, she thought. She had been soothed. The only element she didn't like was the insistence on group sessions, in which one had to open up to the other drunks and addicts in the time-honoured 'My name is Tamara and I'm an alcoholic' fashion. Having been outed in the Press as a sex addict, it felt way too raw and painful to be opening up to a roomful of strangers about her deeply embarrassing and personal problems.

Here, Lars had intervened on her behalf.

'I think these sessions may be doing her more harm than good, huh?' he had said to the counsellor in his mild manner after he'd found Tamara in tears on one of his weekly visits. 'I know you say they are a part of the recovery plan that everybody must go through, but not everybody has had to endure having their personal problems exposed by the media. Can you think about making an exception?'

And amazingly, they had.

Lars. Oh, Lars. Tamara's mind went all dreamy at the thought of him. She looked forward to his visits more than anything. She owed him everything. He had turned her life around. And – she had to admit it, now she was being honest with herself – she had developed an enormous crush on him. He was so big and strong and male – the memory of how it felt to be wrapped up in his arms still made her shiver with delight. Nobody, not even Jack, had made her feel that safe. In fact, she realized, the reason she had resented Jack so much was that she had expected him to make her feel safe, but he hadn't.

Nothing could come of it, of course. How could Lars ever desire her after seeing her hit rock bottom so spectacularly? But oh how she relished those precious hours in his company.

Summer was starting to get her life back on track. Having witnessed Bella's and Andy's total devastation at the prospect of losing Daisy, she realized she had to stop feeling so sorry for herself over what she now recognized as having been nothing more than a brief fling. A few days of great sex. A grubby little interlude. Whatever.

She had started working at the crèche again, Jorge's revelation about Jack and Tamara's 'open relationship' having relaxed the attitudes of Britta's customers towards her. Now that the paparazzi had lost interest she had been able to move back into her flat and – despite the memories of Jack – it was good to be home, to feel independent again.

She had managed to land a couple of freelance commissions – for an inflight magazine and a rival English-language website to *Island Life*. But she missed the freedom of having her own column, so she'd decided to start a food and travel blog, which already had an impressive following. At least her fling with Jack had done her some good, she supposed, under no illusions that her celebrity-by-association wasn't partly responsible for the blog's instant popularity.

In truth, she was doing herself a disservice. The blog attracted followers not because of her notoriety but because she was a terrific writer and her years at *Island Life* had given her a good eye for what made a visually appealing site. The blog had a clean, unfussy style, with vividly coloured photos springing from a stark white background, and a humorous, chatty tone.

Now, at half past five on an early September afternoon, she was strolling along the length of Playa Las Salinas, en route to meet Jorge, who had suggested a drink at Sa Trinxa, one of the coolest beach bars on the island. By any standards, Las Salinas was stunning. The mile-long, crescent-shaped stretch of powdery white sand backed by a small pine forest behind the dunes was packed with beautiful people wearing very little indeed. The sea was gin-clear here, the music pumping out from the string of chic bars running along the beach giving a feeling of pure summer happiness, all day long.

Sa Trinxa was an Ibiza institution, built up on a wooden platform at the back of the beach, sheltered from the still-fierce Balearic sun under a canopy of bamboo and banana leaves. DJ Jon spun classic tunes to a chilled-out, glamorous crowd, many of whom had come ashore via speedboats from yachts moored further out in the glimmering turquoise bay.

'*Hola*, Summer!' cried Luis, the head waiter and bar manager, delighted to see her again after her virtual disappearance from the scene for the latter part of the season. '*Que guapa*!'

'*Hola, Luis, y gracias,*' Summer smiled. '*¿Jorge es aqui?*'

'*Si, si.*' Luis nodded to the far end of the bar, where Jorge was in deep conversation with an extremely wealthy-looking middle-aged man – all bare barrel chest, mahogany tan, Gucci shades and Patek Philippe watch.

Summer gave a wry smile. For all his talk of retirement from his lucrative source of income, it didn't seem as if Jorge was in any hurry. Oh well, it was none of her business, hadn't been for years, and it wasn't as if his customers didn't know what they were letting themselves in for.

'*Hola*, Summer.'

'*Hola*, Jorge.'

The wealthy stranger got to his feet, smiling, and Jorge introduced them.

'*Hola, Summer. ¡Que bonita!*'

'*Si, si, Summer es muy bonita*,' laughed Jorge, rolling his eyes as she sat down with them at the corner table.

Forty minutes later Summer was eating her internal words. Yup, she had to admit she'd done Jorge a serious injustice. The man was head of one of Spain's biggest cable channels and he did, indeed, think that Jorge had the potential to host his own chat show. He had also taken an enormous shine to Summer, and tried to persuade her to do a screen test too, but Summer was adamant – she could think of nothing she'd like less, especially after her experience with the paparazzi earlier that year.

'So – shall we take a walk?' Jorge asked, after the TV exec had gone back to the large and riotous table he'd been lunching at.

'Sure,' said Summer, wondering what was coming next.

Sa Trinxa was the last bar at that end of Salinas, and as they walked further the crowds thinned out, until it was just the two of them, Jorge and Summer, barefoot under the deep blue sky.

Jorge scrambled up a sandy dune, closely followed by Summer.

'Do you remember the first time we came here, when we were kids?' said Jorge, sitting down and looking out to sea.

'Sure I do,' said Summer casually, sitting down next to him. 'It was the first time we kissed.'

Jorge turned to look her in the eye.

'I have never said sorry to you for what happened back then.'

Summer shrugged. 'It was a long time ago.'

'You were sixteen years old, *carita*. For you to see . . . that night . . . after everything we had together . . .'

'Yeah, well, it kinda forced me to grow up quickly.' Summer gave a dismissive laugh. 'Maybe not such a bad thing.'

'I loved you very much,' said Jorge sadly. 'Sometimes I wonder, if I had not been so stupid—'

'Don't . . .'

'Oh, I know, it is too late. Anyway, now I have Paloma, and maybe a new life, in Madrid . . .'

'You would leave all this?' She gestured down at the view of the white sandy beach, the expanse of glittering sea. The sound of happy chatter and mellow beats from Sa Trinxa came in waves across the salty air.

'You did.

'But I—'

'Yes, I know, you returned. But you did leave, you saw what else was out there. I think maybe I need to do that, maybe to grow up . . .?' He gave her a beseeching smile.

'So you did listen to what I said that night.'

'I always listen to what you say. And . . . I just want to say that I'm sorry.'

Summer smiled. 'Apology accepted.'

'And also . . .' Jorge paused, 'that I will always love you.'

'You know what, Jorge.' Summer smiled again. 'I think I will always love you too.'

And for the first time in nearly ten years, they hugged.

'How is she?' asked Andy, walking into Daisy's nursery with two mugs of tea.

'Fine, I think,' said Bella, stroking their daughter's soft cheek through the bars of her cot with one hand and accepting one of the mugs with the other. 'Thanks.'

They had been back from the hospital for a week now, all the medical staff agreeing that it was perfectly safe for Daisy to go home, but that didn't stop both parents checking her condition anxiously at intervals throughout the night, and as soon as they woke up every morning.

Bella looked around the sunny little nursery, with its yellow-and-white gingham curtains, painted cot and Beatrix Potter hardbacks lined up neatly on their shelves, and felt her chest constrict so much she could barely breathe.

Andy, seeing the look on her face, gently put both their mugs of tea down on the wooden floorboards, helped Bella to her feet and put his arms around her.

'I know,' he said. 'I know.'

'Just imagine . . .'

'No need to do that. She's safe now.' He tightened his arms around her and Bella took a few deep breaths before repeating, almost like a mantra,

'She's safe now. She's safe now.'

24

India Cavendish was sunbathing on one of the large terraces of her opulent modern villa, trying to read *Vogue*. But none of the autumn/winter fashions featured within were of any interest or relevance to her, and she was too preoccupied with her own misery to be able to concentrate anyway.

She had a dreadful hangover and coke comedown and it was taking all of her internal resources not to pick herself up with another couple of lines and a drink. But she knew that that would only prolong the agony. Jamie was being meaner than ever, if that were possible, and it had got to the stage where Milo was too scared to be in the same room as his father. Today she'd asked the nanny to take him to the beach, out of harm's way.

She knew her husband was screwing that little slut that he'd introduced her to at Pacha (Tiffany? Something ghastly and common anyway), but India was beyond caring about that. Let somebody else cater to his warped fantasies. The one thing she did care about was getting out of this hellish sham of a marriage. Bella and Andy's words kept ringing in her ears, and she knew she should be contacting her family lawyer, for both her own *and* Milo's sake. But she was too depressed and permanently exhausted.

Raised voices from inside the house made her sit up straight, and she strained to make out what was being said. She had been keeping tabs on her husband's dodgier business practices of late, hoping the information would prove useful when it came to the divorce. Determined to eavesdrop, she tied a fringed batik sarong around her near-skeletal body and crept through the French windows into the large, sunny downstairs sitting room, which was adjacent to Jamie's study.

'Listen, Jamie, we need to cool off a bit in New York,' said a voice that India recognized as belonging to David Abrahams. 'My contact is starting to ask questions.'

'Well, you'll have to field them, won't you?' Jamie drawled back. 'Listen, you little toad, you owe me big-time for all the leads I've given you this summer. Your photo of that Summer whore with the film star must have netted you more than a year's crappy journo wages.'

India froze. *David* took the photo of Summer with Jack Meadows? And then went on to kiss and tell himself, painting her as a brazen slag to the rest of the world? What an absolute shit.

'Yeah, man, I know, I owe you for that one.' David's voice was wheedling.

'And for Miley Jackson with Jared Salter, and for . . .' As Jamie's voice droned on and on, listing celebrity after celebrity, India understood what had been going on. It looked as though her husband had been giving David leads on celebrity gossip in return for information from New York. Whatever this information was, she'd bet her bottom dollar it wasn't legal. *Yes!* This might, at last, be the information she needed to have him by the short and curlies. *Yes!* She and Milo would finally be free. *Yes!*

Such was India's elation that she forgot the necessity for absolute silence. She must have made some sort of noise, because the next moment the sitting-room door burst open and the tall, menacing figure of Jamie loomed into view.

'What have we here?' he said in a voice silky enough to turn her heart to ice. 'Been eavesdropping, have we, *darling wife*?'

'Oh no, Jamie, I promise, I just came in to get myself a drink,' India babbled, almost incoherent with fear, walking over to the cut-glass drinks tray to prove her point. She could see David entering the room, tentatively, behind her husband.

'David, go home,' said Jamie, not turning around. 'And don't come back until you've got me the information I need.' As David stood there, seemingly uncertain of what to do, Jamie looked over his shoulder and bellowed at the top of his voice, 'I said, FUCK OFF OUT OF MY HOUSE!'

Looking almost as terrified as India felt, David turned on his heel and ran.

Jamie shut the door behind him, then locked it for good measure.

'Right, so how am I going to make sure that you remember nothing of what you just heard, eh? How do you suggest I do that, you spying, dried-up old bitch?'

And with that, he delivered the first blow.

It was a peaceful afternoon at the finca. After a lazy late lunch of grilled sardines and salad, Andy had returned to his study to continue work on his book, Daisy was sleeping soundly in her nursery, and Bella was painting the view of their house from the back of the garden. Summer, who had joined them for lunch, was splashing about in the pool.

Bella dipped her paintbrush into a tiny bit of purple paint and mixed it into the pink on her easel, capturing yet another shade of the bougainvillea climbing the bright white wall.

The relief that Daisy was OK, back to the happy, healthy little girl she had always been, had made both Bella and Andy appreciate everything they had afresh. Never again would she take for granted the wonderful life they had together, Bella thought, snapping her eyes shut in an attempt to block out the memory of Daisy lying there with all those wires coming out of her poor poisoned little body.

Andy had been so full of remorse that he hadn't been there when Daisy had been taken so horribly ill that the floodgates had finally opened.

'I'm so, so sorry, Belles. I should have been here with you,' he'd said, almost crushing her in his arms, his tears dropping hotly on her shoulders. 'What kind of man am I? Our little girl. Jesus fucking Christ.'

Bella had found herself crying too, just holding onto him, happy that she had him back again.

'My *bloody book* should never have taken precedence over you and Daisy,' Andy had added.

'It's OK,' Bella had responded. 'I know you've got to write your bloody book – and I'll stop calling it that from now on, I promise. I love the fact that you're so *obscenely* clever that you're writing a history book . . . I'm so proud of you . . . I love you so much . . .' She was kissing him in between the broken-up sentences. Then she laughed. 'And it's going to pay for everything from now on, innit?'

'Innit?' Andy had laughed back, kissing her tear-soggy face.

'Yeah, innit. And I'm sorry too.'

'Hey,' called Summer from the pool. 'Did you see Jorge and Paloma in the gossip column again this morning?'

Bella nodded. 'Yup – so his chat show's really going to go ahead.'

'Good for him.'

'Do you mean that?'

'Sure I do.'

'I mean, I'll always be grateful that he went to pick Andy up when Daisy was ill' – even now Bella couldn't bear to talk about it – 'but I thought that maybe, with your history . . .'

'No, that's all water under the bridge. My life has almost got back to normal since he told his story.' She didn't tell Bella about their moment on the dunes behind Las Salinas – it seemed like a betrayal, somehow. 'And I think leaving Ibiza will do him good, even if it's only for a short time. You know, sometimes life here can be a little *too* intense?'

Bella was about to respond when they were interrupted by somebody rapping at the high, wrought-iron gate at the bottom of the garden.

'*¡Si, entrar – es abierto!*' Bella called back.

The gate opened to reveal the bruised, bloodied and barely recognizable body of India Cavendish, propped on the shoulder of a man who looked local, probably a cab driver.

'India?' Bella leapt out of her chair and ran across the garden to her. 'Jesus Christ, are you OK? Sorry, what an idiotic question. Can you talk? Where did you find her?' she asked the man, who responded in such a torrent of Spanish that it was difficult to follow, though the gist of it was that India had hailed him on the road outside her villa. He had wanted to take her to the hospital, but she'd insisted on being brought here, to Ca'n Pedro.

'It's OK – we'll look after her now.' Bella reached into her pocket for some money to pay the driver and thrust several notes into his hand. '*¿Es OK?*'

'*Si si.*'

'*Muchas gracias, señor.*'

She half-carried India across the garden, calling out to Summer – who had climbed out of the pool and was making her way over to them with a horrified look on her lovely face – 'Could you get Andy from the study, sweetheart?'

'Of course.' Summer immediately ran off in the direction she'd just come.

Once they'd reached the shade of the patio, Bella laid India down on a sunlounger.

'I don't want to bleed all over your lovely white cushions.'

They were the first words India had spoken since she'd got there.

'Don't be silly.' Bella smoothed India's hair away from her brow, trying to be as gentle as she possibly could. 'OK, so – are you up to talking?'

India nodded.

'First things first – we need to make sure you're not seriously hurt. I've got the number of Dr Rosado in San Carlos . . .'

'I'll call him now,' said Andy, who had just reached them, his face a mixture of anger and concern.

'What hurts the most?' Bella asked, her eyes raking over India's face and body. She had two black eyes, one of which was so puffed up that she couldn't open it, a split lip, a deep gash on her forehead, and cuts and bruises all over her frail body. Her light brown hair was matted with blood, her fringed batik sarong torn and stained.

'Everything.' India gave a feeble attempt at laughter, then clutched her ribs. 'Owww. Especially here.'

'Jesus. I simply cannot imagine how anybody could do this to another human being. It was Jamie, wasn't it?'

India nodded again.

'Please tell me you're never going back to him.'

'I'm never going back to him.' Even in her weakened

state, India's voice was firm. 'I've got the goods on him now.'

'What do you mean?'

'Dr Rosado's on his way,' said Andy. 'Why don't you tell us everything once he's checked you out and made sure the bastard has done no permanent damage? You might also want to think about calling the police.'

Luckily, apart from a couple of extremely painful fractured ribs, it appeared that India had managed to escape serious injury. The expression on the doctor's kind face turned grimmer and grimmer as he examined her, noting the number of punches and kicks Jamie had thrown at his fragile wife.

'*Bastardo*,' he muttered under his breath, before turning to Andy and speaking quietly to him in Spanish. Since Daisy's accident, the two men had become friends, often meeting for a coffee or beer at Anita's on days Andy needed to pop into San Carlos.

'The doctor thinks we should take some photos of your injuries. They'll help you in court,' he told her sympathetically.

'Go ahead,' said India. 'The more ammunition I can collect against that fucker, the better.' She took a swig of the large brandy that Bella had given her, wincing as it stung her cut lip. It was combining with the strong pain-killers the doctor had prescribed to numb the fiery agony in her ribs and face – the two places that hurt the most, although every single part of her body hurt, really.

So Andy took out his phone and, trying to be as non-intrusive as possible, slowly walked around her, snapping her poor, beaten-up face, a heel imprint in the small of her back, the sickening legions of cuts and bruises on her arms and legs.

Once the doctor had gone, India sat up straight on the sofa and looked at Bella, Andy and Summer, in turn.

'There's something I need to tell you all,' she said. 'I'm glad you're here today, too, Summer.'

Not wanting to interrupt, Summer raised her eyebrows encouragingly.

'The reason Jamie got so angry—' she started.

'There can be no *reason* for this,' said Andy with venom.

'I'm not trying to justify it,' said India wearily.

'Let her speak, darling,' said Bella, shooting Andy a look.

'Sorry. Carry on.'

'I overheard a conversation he was having, with David Abrahams.'

'David?' said Summer in surprise. 'What's he got to do with anything?'

'An awful lot, I'm afraid.' India turned and looked Summer directly in the eye. 'Summer, it was David who took that photo of you and Jack Meadows. Jamie must have seen the two of you at Bella's party, and tipped him off about it.'

'What?' Summer could hardly take it in at first. 'And he deliberately set out to ruin things between me and Jack, pretending he'd only found out himself through the Press?' She was so angry she looked as though she might explode. 'The fucking lying bastard – I'm going to KILL him!'

'But why would Jamie tip David off?' Bella asked, giving Summer a worried glance. 'It doesn't make sense.'

'It appears that my darling, noble husband and that charmless moron David have had some kind of scam going on,' said India, trying not to spit blood – neither literally nor figuratively. 'whereby Jamie gives David the heads-up on local celebrity gossip, which David then sells to the Press, presumably for large sums of money, in return for – well, this is what I'm not so sure of – but I heard them mention information from New York.'

'David used to be a financial journalist in New York,' said Summer, her fury abating as tentative excitement took over. 'And – oh my God, I saw a bunch of folders on his computer, all called NY something. He walked in on me as it came up on screen – I'd never seen him so angry.' She looked around at them all with shining eyes. 'Do you suppose it could be some sort of insider dealing?'

Underneath the cuts and bruises, India's face lit up. 'My God, it could, couldn't it? And that's like really, really illegal? Like, the vicious shit could be put away for a long time?'

'An extremely long time,' said Andy. 'An awful lot longer than he'd get for what he's done to you – which is bloody ridiculous, as far as I'm concerned.' Bella tried not to smile – it was such a typically Andy thing to say. 'I have to say that insider dealing is exactly what it sounds like, but . . .'

'I can get proof,' said Summer excitedly. 'The security guards at the *Island Life* offices still know me, I know the password to David's Mac – I'll access those files and get proof. Oh yes, that scheming fucker is finally going to get his comeuppance.'

And Summer smiled the biggest, sunniest smile that any of them had seen on her in a long time.

'*Hola*, Miguel.' Summer leaned forward to kiss the surprised security guard on both cheeks, deliberately flashing him a glimpse of tanned cleavage. It so wasn't her style, but she would do anything it took to get her revenge on David.

'¡*Hola*, Summer!' Miguel flushed with pleasure. All the security guards – in fact, practically all the staff – at *Island Life* had been sad to see Summer go. Her sunny presence used to light up the offices, and she had been sorely missed. 'Long time no see.'

Summer pulled a sad face, and Miguel gave her a sympathetic tap on the shoulder. 'Is it OK if I come in? I left some things behind when Mr Abrahams fired me' – Miguel's face darkened at the mention of David's name – 'and I haven't felt up to collecting them until now.'

'*Si, si,* of course.' Miguel smiled as he gestured for her to continue over to the lifts. She was such a sweet girl. And so beautiful.

Upstairs, Summer entered the dark open-plan office and switched the light on. She looked around the still-familiar surroundings with a pang of nostalgia. Despite her only ever coming in a couple of times a week, there had been a fun camaraderie, still evident in the casual shambles left behind by her ex-colleagues. The cleaners would be in early tomorrow morning, and the unwashed coffee cups, piles of magazines, newspapers, empty wine bottles and several glasses, were proof of another fun and productive day at work.

She walked over to David's weird glass cubicle and opened the door. God, it was horrible, the very essence of him practically seeping into her pores, even now.

Jesus, what was I thinking? she asked herself, for the thousandth time.

She sat down at his desk, switched on his Mac, praying that he hadn't changed his password in the last couple of months, and started to type.

humanchains

Yuck. She'd thought the password was cool and literary before, when, stuck in Barcelona, he'd phoned and asked her to pull up the latest advertising revenue figures from his hard drive. But now? Creepy didn't do it justice.

Yay! Summer's heart soared as the computer sprang into life. What a fucking idiot not to have changed his password – although he'd probably forgotten he'd given it to her, back in the days before his lust for her turned to hatred. And how would he know she had the means to use it against him, anyway?

She scrolled through the folders and opened NY1 – as good a place to start as any. Seeing that it contained one Word and one Excel file, each with the same name, she made her way through the rest – which now went all the way up to 93. She opened the NY93 Excel spreadsheet and started to laugh, quietly, to herself.

David and Jamie were well and truly screwed.

Jamie was pretty fucking pissed off. After walking out and leaving India in a bloody mess on the marble floor yesterday afternoon, he'd headed straight for Tiff's flat in Playa d'en Bossa, without bothering to call her first. But when he'd arrived there, there'd been no sign of her, and the landlord had pleaded ignorance of her very existence. Enraged, Jamie had called her mobile but heard only a recorded voice, in Spanish, telling him that that number was no longer in use. What he didn't know was that Tiffany had found herself another sugar daddy, one who gave her the jewels without the sore bum. Deciding that life was too short to pander to Jamie's warped fantasies any more, she'd sold the last of the jewellery he'd given her, changed her phone, and asked the landlord at the crummy Playa d'en Bossa flat to deny she'd ever existed. After a particularly good blow-job, he'd been putty in her cheap French-manicured hands.

Jamie had spent the rest of the night on a coke-fuelled bender around the hooker bars of San Antonio, and now, discombobulated from all the booze and drugs, was speeding back home in a taxi. Even he wasn't stupid enough to drive in his condition. Dispassionately he wondered whether India had managed to drag herself up from where he'd left her. He wasn't worried that she'd tell anybody about the beating – his wife was far too scared of him for that – and besides he had too much power and influence on the island. But he thought he'd probably taught her the lesson that it would be wise to keep her mouth shut, silly bitch, if indeed she had heard anything of his conversation with David.

It was only when the taxi turned into the drive that he saw the phalanx of grim-faced – and very heavily armed – Guardia Civil standing outside his house.

25

Lars's Albuquerque headquarters, in a beautiful old Spanish Colonial building, had huge windows offering spectacular views of the rugged, russet Sandia Mountains, whose grandeur generally both moved and inspired him. Today, though, the mountains were the last thing on his mind as he sat at his teak desk, reading and rereading two emails that had arrived in his inbox within hours of each other.

Hey Lars,
Greetings from sunny rehab! How's the real world? Life here continues at its gentle, soothing pace, though a couple of the new inmates are real nutjobs, which has livened things up a bit! One of them has popped so many ludes he thinks he's Elvis (which almost makes me wish I was still doing the group sessions – only almost, though: his 'Jailhouse Rock' sucks).
The other is like this trust-fund hippy chick who's so full of vegan bullshit she's in danger of turning into a mung bean – she's only been caught trying to smuggle crack and meth in three times! Something tells me that chick don't wanna get clean . . .

But hey, who am I to mock? I was fucked up enough to think the transvestites were my friends. Aaaargh! That still makes me cringe so badly every time I think of it. I know I've said it before, but thank you so, SO much for coming to my rescue. God only knows what gutter I'd have ended up in.

Anyway, enough of the self-pity! The good news is that they think I'm nearly ready to be unleashed on the unsuspecting public!!! Yippee! Fantastic as this place is, I can't wait to get back to work. Miles came to see me yesterday and it sounds as though filming's going great so far. And he says the actor now playing my dad is a really nice guy, which should make shooting this time round a helluva lot more enjoyable, shall we say!

I hope we'll be able to stay in touch once I'm out. I know we'll both be busy but it would be nice to hook up from time to time if our oh-so-busy, important schedules allow it!!!

With loads of love and gratitude, as ever
Tamara x

Over the last few weeks, Tamara and Lars's friendship had deepened, and he realized that what he had felt for her before had been nothing more than a glorified crush, an intense physical attraction based on the briefest acquaintance. Now, though . . . Well, he had to admit to himself that he adored everything about her. Her bravery, her brutally honest self-criticism, her humour, her excitement about getting back to work. He didn't need her gratitude, but couldn't deny that it touched him.

He hoped she meant it about staying in touch, post-rehab, but she was still a world-famous movie star and sex symbol, for all her problems. He smiled at the words 'our oh-so-busy, important schedules', as if his work was on a par with hers, and tried not to feel too encouraged by 'loads of love', which was surely nothing more than an affectionate, girly way of signing off.

Unsure what to do for the best, he took another look at Summer's email. On the one hand – well, she was absolutely right about his feelings. What a lovely, perceptive girl – and indeed, what a very good friend *she* was turning out to be. They'd been in email contact since he moved back to Albuquerque and he was glad to hear that her life was, slowly but surely, getting back to normal, though there remained an air of sadness about her.

He read the last couple of sentences again.

If you don't tell her, you'll never know if she feels the same way you do. And you know – after everything you've done for her, I have a tiny inkling that she might! Lars, life is too short – if there's even the slightest possibility of finding happiness you should grab it with both hands. Believe me, I know. Good luck, and be sure to tell me how it goes.

Love
Summer xxx

Jack was sweating from his hike when he finally reached the summit of Griffith Park's Mount Hollywood. He was in extremely good physical shape, but the heat was fierce, even though it was nearly October. On a rare, smog-free day like today, the 360-degree panoramic views never failed to thrill him – eye level with the iconic Hollywood sign, you could see everything from the hazy Verdugo Mountains to the LA basin leading to the glittering downtown skyline to the magnificent Pacific, shimmering deep blue in the distance.

It wasn't particularly sensible to hike in the midday sun, but Jack had felt the need for a punishing workout, to sweat out some of the sadness that sometimes threatened to overwhelm him. By day, mostly, he could throw himself into his work – even now he was listening through his iPod speakers to classics from the late Sixties and early Seventies, to keep himself in *Saigon Summer* mode. The 'Nam buddy project was now fully underway, and due to start filming in a couple of months' time. But by night, his dreams were full of his Summer – some happy, some sad, some disturbingly erotic.

He took a swig from his water bottle and paused for one last look at the spectacular view before making his way back down the mountain.

By the time he got home he was ready for lunch, and after a quick shower, started to prepare himself some chili beef fajitas with extra onions and red and green peppers. Jack liked to eat, and he liked to cook – fresh, healthy food in decent, man-sized portions, often with a hearty chili kick (he attributed his love of chili to his mother's Hispanic roots).

While the vegetables and beef were sizzling away on the hob in his huge all-white state-of-the-art kitchen, Jack poured himself a glass of sweet, tangy blood-orange juice, downed it in one and poured another. He tasted the fajita mix, adjusted the seasoning, then plonked the lot onto a warm flour tortilla, adding a dollop of sour cream for good measure. As he carried his plate and glass over to the large glass-topped table in the centre of the room, Jack felt a wave of sadness that he would never have the chance to cook with Summer. A vivid image of her happy face as she told him how to take a slice of ham, followed by a bite of peach, came into his mind. Again he pushed it aside.

She lied to you, man. Stop being such a dope.

It had been a huge surprise to all of them when that wanker Jorge had told his story about screwing Tamara in the store cupboard, but Jack supposed he should thank him, really. After all the other creeps had crawled out of the woodwork with their stories about Tamara, Jack's star had started to rise again in direct proportion to Tamara's falling. He was surprised by how little he cared that he had been so comprehensively, and publicly, cuckolded. He just thought: poor Tamara. There had been rumours about her abandoning the set of *Dust Bowl*, of yet another stint in rehab, of Miles Dawson having to halt filming and the rest of the cast being fed up to the back teeth with her, but it was all being kept very hush hush.

Whatever Ben and the others thought, Jack hoped that Tamara was OK, and resolved to check up on her once she'd finished filming. He was taking his final, delicious bite of fajita, when the video intercom buzzed. He went to answer it and was surprised to see Poppy waving back at him from the driver's seat of her shiny pillar-box-red convertible Sixties Alfa Romeo.

'Hey, Pops.' He smiled. 'To what do I owe this honour?' He would always have a bit of a soft spot for Poppy.

'Hey, Jack! Buzz me in, won't you? I've got some exciting news!'

'Intriguing. Come on in – I'm in the kitchen.'

The electronic gates parted to let the glamorous little red car through, and a minute or so later, Poppy rushed through the sliding glass doors, arms outstretched for a hug. Dressed down today in white skinny jeans and a pale yellow slouchy off-the-shoulder T-shirt, she epitomized laid-back LA cool.

'Can I get you anything? Coffee? Juice?'

'I'm fine,' said Poppy, so impatient she was practically bouncing on her old-skool Adidas trainers. 'Sit down and listen.'

'Whoa!' Jack put his hands up, laughing. 'I don't see what can be so urgent that we can't have some coffee or juice.'

'I've just got off the phone to Bella – she told me the most *shocking* news,' said Poppy, stopping Jack in his tracks as he walked towards the fridge.

'What is it?' he said, in a blind panic all of a sudden. 'Has something happened to Summer? Please, for God's sake Poppy, tell me that Summer's OK?'

'So you *do* care,' Poppy teased, sounding pleased with herself. Watching the dark blush suffuse his handsome face, she decided to put him out of his misery. 'Don't worry, mate, Summer's fine. Well, physically anyway.'

Jack scowled. 'What do you mean by that?'

'You know exactly what I mean by that. ANYWAY, do you want to hear the gossip from the White Isle or not?'

Jack sat down on his white leather sofa. 'Sure.'

'Do you remember that horrible man Jamie Cavendish who was at Bella's party?'

Jack had a vivid flashback to sitting in Bella's folly with Summer, their tentatively romantic conversation interrupted by the odious Englishman.

'Uh-huh.'

'Well, yesterday, his wife India turned up at the finca bleeding, battered – *half dead*, by the sound of it.' Poppy did like to embellish a story.

'The bastard did that to her?'

Poppy nodded. 'Of course. But it's the reason he did it that's so interesting.'

'I don't think there can ever be a reason,' Jack started, the same way Andy had, in Ibiza.

'OK, bad choice of words. The reason he got so *angry*' – Poppy emphasized the word – 'was that India had overheard a conversation.' She paused for dramatic effect. 'Between him and David Abrahams.'

'David Abrahams,' Jack repeated. 'You mean that asshole – Summer's boss? The one that she was screwing?'

'Yes.' Poppy sighed and looked out of the window. 'Don't you think it's time for you to lighten up, you misogynistic bastard? You were ENGAGED to Tamara, for fuck's sake!'

'Summer knew that. Hell, who on the whole planet didn't know I was engaged to Tamara? But I had no idea that Summer was screwing her boss.'

'Has is ever occurred to you that she might have been ashamed of it?'

'She lied to me.' Jack's face was a mask.

'Oh, stop being such an utter dick, and listen to me.'

Jack looked up.

'What India overheard,' Poppy said, 'was enough to put both her husband AND that shit David Abrahams behind bars. And that isn't all. It was *David* who took the picture of you and Summer in her flat.'

'What?' Jack stood up and started pacing around his kitchen. 'But . . . how?'

'Jamie saw you two together at Bella's party. I *told you* you weren't being very subtle about it.'

'Poppy . . .'

Poppy put up an imperious hand. 'Hear me out, Jack. Jamie told David, who hung around outside Summer's flat waiting until he could get a photo of you. And what a photo he got!'

'So *he* sold the photo, and then came marching into Summer's flat, all indignant that he'd had to find out about us in the Press?'

'Yup.' Poppy nodded her shiny blonde head vigorously.

'What a creep.'

'Yup.' Poppy nodded again.

'It may be despicable, but it's not illegal. I don't see how that could get him arrested.'

'Ah – this is where it starts getting interesting. You know I said Jamie tipped him off?'

'Uh-huh.'

'Well, he wasn't doing it out of the kindness of his heart. And you weren't the only unlucky celeb to have been caught with his pants down in Ibiza this summer.' Poppy paused. 'Jamie and David had this racket going. Jamie's so loaded that he had access to all the VIP areas on the island. He kept his ear to the ground, tipped David off every time anybody remotely famous did something scandalous – which tends to happen a lot in Ibiza – and David sold the stories.'

'I still don't get how that's illegal?'

'I'm coming to that!' said Poppy impatiently. 'In return for this lucrative sideline, David gave Jamie some even more lucrative information from his old financial contacts in New York. Basically, insider dealing.'

Jack was starting to smile. 'Man, that's heavy shit. And they can prove it?'

'This is the best bit. Your lovely Summer got the proof. She snuck into the *Island Life* offices in the dead of night' – Poppy was getting carried away again – 'and found the incriminating files on David's computer.'

Jack looked at Poppy incredulously. 'Summer did that?'

'Fantastic, isn't it? Not just a pretty face!'

Jack ignored this. Something had occurred to him. 'Wait a minute. What about the – ahem – upskirt photo of Tammy? I don't recall seeing the Abrahams loser at Pacha that night.'

'They reckon that was probably some random clubber on the make with their phone. Surely you run the risk of things like that happening every time you're out in public?'

Jack nodded. 'I guess we do. Especially if we choose to dance on tables with no underwear.'

Poppy laughed. 'It must have made the *Ibiza Sun*'s editor's day to have both photos land on his desk at the same time.'

'Yeah, well, I'm glad somebody benefited from it.'

'Jack . . .'

'What?'

'Don't you think it's time you stopped being so ridiculously stubborn and pig-headed? You obviously miss Summer like mad, and Bella said that she's never seen anybody so unhappy as that poor girl.'

'She said that?'

'And a whole lot more. Apparently Summer's been saying that you must be a really good actor, as she believed you when you said you loved her. *And* that if you truly loved her, you wouldn't have thrown it all away over that creep David Abrahams . . .'

'But I do love her!'

The words were out before Jack knew it.

26

Tamara was sitting in the shade in her section of the wild and beautiful gardens of New Horizons, listening to the sound of pan pipes over a tinkling fountain. Each of the residents, as the patients/inmates were known, had his or her own section of garden – a policy that worked well as nobody was gated, or fenced off in any way, but respected the others' need for solitude. There was a group section for those that felt inclined to have company.

She was trying to focus on her script, but finding it difficult to concentrate as today was Friday, and Lars was on his way. Her usual excitement at seeing him was laced with sadness, as she was checking out of rehab next week. The therapists all considered her ready to be unleashed into the real world – which was great, of course, but it did mean that this would be the last time Lars visited her. She hoped they'd stay friends, but she couldn't expect weekly visits any more; he wouldn't feel the need to look after her (wherever in his enormous heart that had come from) now that she was well, and able to look after herself.

She sighed and put the script down, gazing out at the magnificent mountains. She was itching to get back to work, and determined to be as hard-working and un-diva-like as possible, to make up to Miles and the rest of the cast and crew for mucking them around. But without Lars . . .

'Tamara.' His deep voice made her jump up, out of her seat. She turned and, with the sun in her eyes, could only make out his enormous frame, silhouetted against the desert.

'Lars? You're early. I mean – hey! It's great to see you. But . . .' She was babbling, overjoyed but suddenly insanely shy at the sight of him. Tamara Gold – shy? Had she not been feeling so – well, shy – she'd have laughed out loud at herself.

He bent over to give her a brief hug, kissing her on both cheeks. Was she imagining it, or did his lips brush the corner of her mouth? Finding she was trembling, Tamara took a step back. She had to get a grip.

'Yes, I am a little early. I hope you don't mind?'

'Hell no!' *Oh great, very ladylike, Tammy.* 'I mean, of course not. It's lovely to see you. Let me have them send up some herbal tea.'

'That is OK.' Lars had moved around her, now facing the sun, so Tamara could see his face more clearly. 'I was wondering . . .' He paused, his voice hesitant, almost shy himself, it seemed. 'If you would care to take a drive in the desert with me?'

'Oh wow!' Tamara practically bounced up and down with delight and Lars smiled. 'I'd love that – thanks,' she added, trying to sound a bit cooler. 'But – am I allowed out?'

'I checked with the management and they say it's fine.'

'Well, in that case, wait a minute while I go put some proper clothes on.' Tamara gestured down at the shortie pyjama and vest-top combination she was wearing, and Lars tried not to stare at her body. 'Thank you so much!' And she stood on tiptoes to give him another kiss on the cheek.

*

'So you go back to work next week, huh?' Lars turned his head briefly from the dusty desert road to smile at Tamara, who was looking cute and fresh-faced in white denim shorts and a green-and-white stripy T-shirt that didn't match her eyes. There wasn't much point in wearing coloured contacts in rehab, and the softness of her natural hazel was actually extremely appealing.

'I do! And it's all thanks to you.' Tamara tentatively put a small hand on Lars's thigh as she smiled back at him. 'I cannot thank you enough, Lars. God knows what would have happened to me if I hadn't bumped into you when I did.'

Trying to ignore the pleasure her hand on his leg gave him, Lars said, 'Well, maybe I was the catalyst, but you did the hard work. You have sorted yourself out, and you should be proud of yourself. I am very proud of you.' Without thinking, he leaned over and put his hand on her bare thigh. She gave a just audible sigh of pleasure and they both, realizing simultaneously what an intimate position they were in, snatched their hands away.

Lars stared fixedly at the road for about half a minute, trying to regain his equilibrium, before adding, 'And Miles Dawson believes in you. He is a good man . . .'

'He sure is,' said Tamara excitedly. 'And he's a real good director.'

'So do you not see what that says about you, Tamara? The fact that he believes in you?'

'That I'm unbelievably lucky and don't deserve it?' Tamara joked.

'Never say that,' said Lars, drawing his Land Rover to a halt in a red sandy clearing on the side of the road. He turned to stare at her for what seemed an eternity, before adding, 'Oh, Tamara.'

And before she knew what was happening, Lars had leaned over and taken her face in his hands, kissing her on the lips with surprising tenderness, given his size and strength. Tamara let her mouth open under his, her arms wind around his neck, and soon they were kissing the life out of one another, hands entwined in each other's hair, lost in their emotions as the desert sun beat down on the Land Rover's roof, the ancient rugged mountains watching over them.

After some time they stopped and simply gazed at one another, smiling, laughing slightly, touching each other's faces.

'Did that just happen?' asked Tamara in awe, her eyes wide as she gazed at Lars's kind, open face.

'I'm sorry,' said Lars. 'I had it all planned, I was going to make a speech, to tell you how I felt, to see if there was any way that you could return my feelings, before . . .'

'Before?' Tamara smiled.

'Well, before – that. I'm sorry,' he repeated. 'I couldn't help myself.'

'Oh, you silly . . . beautiful . . . wonderful . . . man.' Tamara had taken his face in her hands again and was showering it with kisses between words. 'Don't you know that I adore you? That your visits have been keeping me going these last few weeks? That you are the reason I was determined to get better? I couldn't let you down, not after everything you've done for me.'

Lars was smiling more widely with every word she uttered, with every kiss she planted on his broad, handsome face.

'I've been kidding myself that I wanted to protect you because you were damaged,' he said. 'That it was my duty as one human being to another. But do you know the real reason I wanted to protect you?'

'No,' she said, leaning back with her hands clasped around his neck, looking up at him from under her eyelashes, loving every second of it.

Lars laughed. 'Of course you do. But I'm going to tell you anyway. It is because I love you.'

Tamara hadn't realized it was possible to be so happy.

'I love you when you are sweet, like this,' Lars continued.

Tamara gave a little bow of acknowledgement, tightening her hold on the back of his neck.

'I loved you when you were stroppy . . .'

Tamara shook her head sadly. 'Mad.'

'Hell, baby, I even loved you when you were drunk and borderline psychotic.'

And they started to kiss again.

'I can't believe you've actually finished it,' said Bella, raising her champagne glass. 'Congratulations, darling.'

'Layshons, Daddy,' added Daisy, lifting up her beaker of diluted juice, and both adults smiled indulgently.

Andy had taken them all out for a late Sunday lunch to celebrate completing the second draft of his book – which had been no mean feat after the eventful summer they'd had. Aside from Daisy's poisoning, which neither of them wanted to think about, there had been the moving in, the renovations, their boisterous house guests, the pool party, Summer, Jack and the constantly lurking paparazzi, India's beating and the subsequent arrests of both Jamie and David Abrahams. It had hardly been the peaceful retreat, conducive to writing an intellectually demanding history book, that Andy had been looking forward to.

But he had done it. And where better to celebrate than Benirrás, the most beautiful west-facing beach on the island? It was here that the hippies famously still came to do their drumming on Sunday afternoons, as the sun set over the dramatic fist-shaped rock to which only the heartiest of swimmers would attempt a journey at this time of year.

Now that it was nearly November, there were only a few locals eating and drinking at Elements, the eco-chic bar to the right of the beach as you looked towards the sea, but the hippies were out in force as usual – several about to pack up their backpacks and drift off to Goa, or Thailand, or Bali for the winter months.

Benirrás was a smallish cove surrounded on all sides by high, steeply descending forest. A few years previously, one sizzlingly hot summer, a dreadful fire, which had lasted the best part of a week, had devastated a large proportion of the forest. There had been speculation that it had been caused by a careless tourist throwing a cigarette butt out of a car window – that would have been enough, so tinder-dry had the landscape been that year – but it had, in fact, been due to a couple of the hippies lighting a campfire in a cave.

The ambitious reforestation plan had been so successful that the forest now actually looked like forest again, rather than the desperately sad swathe of burnt terracotta stubble that had backed the beach for the first couple of years after the fire.

The beach was sandy, but rocky once you were in the water, which was incredibly clear as a result. As well as the hippies, and tourists who came to watch them in high season, the beach was very popular with families with small children, and Bella now waved to a forty-something yummy mummy she recognized as a new attendee at Britta's yoga classes.

'Don't think we're going to get much of a sunset today,' said Andy, looking out at the dark clouds gathering over the sea. As he spoke there was a clap of thunder, and Bella laughed.

'No flies on you, darling.'

In response to the thunder, the hippies began drumming, and within minutes heavy rain was lashing down onto the beach. Bella, Andy and Daisy, sitting outside but protected by the large white awning over their heads, watched, enthralled.

'It's beautiful, isn't it?' said Bella.

'So are you,' said Andy, seriously.

'Hey, what's brought this on?' she laughed, pleased.

'I just want you to know that you and Daisy mean everything to me . . . my girls . . .'

'Aw, thanks, darling.' Bella smiled.

'I mean it. After we nearly lost Daisy, I started to realize how stupid I've been, so stubborn and proud with my ridiculous aversi—'

'Your ridiculous what . . .?' Bella's smile was getting wider, her heart thumping. He couldn't mean what she thought he meant, could he? Surely not, not after all these years.

Waves were pounding the shore now, rain thundering into the sea, all the boats in the lovely little bay bobbing madly. The hippies were drumming wildly, demonically almost, which added to the eerie, frenetic atmosphere.

As if he'd finally made his mind up about something, Andy hailed the nearest waiter, and indicating Daisy, who was watching her parents curiously, asked him to look after her for a few minutes. The waiter nodded, smiling.

'Come with me,' said Andy, taking Bella by the hand. Laughing, she followed him, running onto the beach, which was now deserted save for the mad drumming hippies.

Once they were almost at the water's edge, halfway across the beach, Andy dropped to one knee on the wet sand. The rain was pelting down on both their heads, and down inside Andy's glasses, which he took off as he delved into his jeans pocket and produced a ring.

Bella looked down at his dear, familiar, dripping face and smiled, more happy laughter bubbling up from somewhere deep inside her.

'Bella, I love you more than I love life itself. Will you please do me the honour of becoming my wife?'

27

Summer had approached the *Island Life* offices with some trepidation, not sure what kind of reception she was going to get. She had shopped the editor to the police, for one thing; trespassed on company property, for another. And she was still cringing at all the details about her sex life that David had thought fit to spill all over the Press.

But as she walked through the glass swing doors, her former colleagues gave her a standing ovation.

'Welcome back, Summer!'

'*¡Bienvenido querida!*'

'*¡Hola, guapa!*'

The sight of all the friendly, smiling faces relaxed her and she smiled back.

'*Muchas gracias, todos,*' she replied, and made her way over to her old desk, the one that she used to share with the part-time weddings editor.

She logged onto the Macbook and smiled as she saw her desktop wallpaper ping onto the screen – the breathtaking view from her parents' house – along with easily accessible shortcuts to her various folders: Restaurants, Recipes, Seasonal Ingredients, etc.

'Hey,' she called out, to nobody in particular, 'how come everything's exactly as I left it?'

Valentina walked over to the desk and whispered, 'David ordered me to get rid of all traces of you, but after he kissed and told about you like that I just thought *Fuck him!* – disgusting little man. There was no way he could tell whether I'd done it or not – he was useless at all the technical stuff.'

Summer felt almost tearful at such loyalty. 'Thanks, Val,' she whispered. 'You've made my life so much easier. You fancy lunch today?'

'I'd love it,' smiled Valentina. 'It's great to have you back. We've all missed you.'

That evening, as Summer walked the short distance between the *Island Life* offices and her pretty little flat in the Old Town, it started to rain. Only a few tiny droplets to begin with, but still – rain, proper rain. It was funny, every summer was long, and hot, and every late October the farmers would bemoan the lack of rain, claiming it had been the longest, hottest summer ever and that their crops were going to suffer, and they'd keep on moaning until the rain set in. For a little rock of an island that the rest of the world associated with year-round sunshine, the seasons were actually very important. She'd heard it had rained in the west yesterday, but it hadn't hit Ibiza Town until now.

Summer couldn't resist breaking into a little dance. Arms outstretched, palms upward to feel the drops drizzling, and very shortly afterwards, plopping onto them, she began humming the tune from *Singin' in the Rain*. *Do do do do do, do do do do do dooooh* . . .

Oh wow, this was going to make her next article so easy. She'd been wanting to write about the deliciously bosky wild mushrooms that you could find in some of the forests in the centre of the island – how to forage for them, while still respecting the environment; how to prepare them, getting rid of any creepy crawlies, and identifying any poisonous ones; and, most crucially of all, how to cook them. There were loads of ways, but the simplest, and probably the most delicious, was just with butter, garlic and lots of parsley.

But without the rain there would be no fungi. OK, she corrected herself, automatically subbing her piece already: fungi would exist, but probably underground, and not very tasty – if indeed edible at all. By this time the rain was pouring down, and Summer broke into a run up the narrow winding street that led to her flat. She was nearly home now, laughing and crying at the same time. Laughing because the rain was exhilarating, because it was good for the land, because it meant she could write about wild mushrooms (and eat them). And crying because . . .

Well, because of Jack, of course. She still cried about him on a daily basis, though she'd hoped that today, her first day with her old life properly back on track, might have been different. It hadn't. OK, she supposed it had, to an extent – in that she felt she could actually have a functioning life again, a life in which she wasn't continually obsessing in some idiotic teenage fashion over a movie star who treated adult women the way rock stars treated groupies.

Jack had been linked to several Hollywood starlets since he'd been restored to flavour of the month in Hollywood, and each one hurt Summer more than the last. She couldn't believe she'd been stupid enough to fall for everything – anything – he'd told her. She almost felt sorry for David Abrahams, as at last she understood, for the first time in her life, what it was to yearn, physically, for somebody who quite clearly could take you or leave you. But she'd never lied to David. She'd never said that she loved him, whereas Jack had told her constantly, from just after they'd first made love on their beautiful little beach, that he loved every single thing about her.

He really was a very good actor, Summer thought cynically, as she let herself into her flat and walked out onto her balcony, enjoying the feeling of the rain on her skin. Yeah, that was what made him such a successful movie star. The handsomeness helped, of course (she tried not to think about how much his handsomeness helped) – but the ability to appear genuine while you were lying your gorgeous ass off? The ability to look into the camera with the same (false) sincerity with which he'd looked into her eyes?

Oh, he was bloody good at his job, no doubt about it. Quite possibly he'd been rehearsing for his next role as they'd rolled around in the shallows together that first time. Maybe he was up for Burt Lancaster's part in a remake of *From Here to Eternity*? The thought brought tears tumbling down her face again, but this time she didn't bother brushing them away as by now the storm was so heavy that her tears were being washed away by the rain.

Summer climbed the stairs and let herself into her flat, then went straight out to her balcony and looked down at the view towards the harbour, the view that used to make her so happy. There was a proper storm brewing now and the sea was very choppy – although all the boats bobbing about in the harbour seemed to be OK.

'Fuck you, Jack,' she said, letting the wind and the rain wash the tears from her face. It didn't seem to work. The more the wind and rain did their washing and blowing business, the more her tears flowed. She tried to focus on the harbour, over the winding backstreets, on the boats that looked so small from here, but were in fact enormous yachts. Local housewives dressed in black were leaning out of windows, struggling to pull in the flapping, sodden washing that they'd hung up on lines earlier in the day.

'Fuck you, Jack!' This time Summer shouted it out, wanting to feel free from him, wanting her every waking moment not to be dominated by his handsome, famous face. 'I hate you, I hate you, I HATE YOU!' She sank to her knees, crying, on her sodden, windswept balcony, not caring about the cold and the wet, her mind too full of Jack – remembering how it felt to fuck him, to kiss him, to plan the rest of her life with him.

'Please just get out of my head!' Summer cried, huddled on the slippery terracotta tiles. 'Stop making me hate my life. I want to be happy again.'

'I'll make you happy again, if you'll let me,' said a lovely, cultured, beautifully familiar voice.

Slowly Summer sat up and turned around, the wind whipping her wet blonde hair across her face, her drenched clothes clinging to her body.

'Jack? How did you get here?'

It really was him. Tall, soaked to the skin and just as handsome as she remembered him, standing right behind her on her balcony.

'Can you ever forgive me?' he asked simply, holding out his arms to her.

Summer hurled herself into them, banging her fists against his chest, sobbing harder than ever.

'You lousy, lying, cheating, rotten BASTARD!'

'I'm sorry. I'm so sorry, Summer. Please forgive me? Please? I love you.'

'It's been months,' Summer sobbed.

'I know. And there hasn't been a moment when I haven't been thinking of you. Hey – let's get out of the rain.' Still

374

with his arms around her shivering shoulders, he led her into the warmth of her flat.

'I'm sorry,' Jack repeated. 'What more can I say? I was a stupid, pig-headed buffoon. I was jealous . . .'

'You were jealous? You were fucking engaged! And how do you think I've felt recently, seeing you in the papers with – now let's see, who was the last one? Oh yeah, Amy Lascelles – or was she the one before? You have no idea—'

'Summer, shhh, shhh, they were all publicity stunts, set up by the studios. You know how it—'

'Actually, no, I don't!' Summer's voice was rising, becoming more bitter and sarcastic with each word, all the pent-up hurt and anger pouring out in a torrent of bile. 'Because I'm not from your world. I'm not a famous fucking movie star! Or had you forgotten that?'

'Jeez, what do I have to do to stop you shouting at me?' In exasperation, Jack took her in his arms and kissed her. It worked.

Jack and Summer curled up in front of the wood-burning stove on Summer's little two-seater sofa, every single bit of their bodies entwined. One of Jack's hands was stroking the back of her neck, the other her slender thigh. They had changed out of their wet clothes and couldn't stop gazing at each other. Every few minutes they stopped their conversation to kiss again.

'I'm sorry I didn't tell you about David,' said Summer. 'I was ashamed. He was such . . . oh God – there's so much to tell you!'

'About Abrahams' and Jamie Cavendish's little scam? I know. And well done getting the proof – that was very cool work.' Jack kissed the top of her arm – the part of her currently closest to his mouth – unable to relinquish body contact for more than a few seconds.

'But how can you know? It was hardly global news.'

Jack laughed. 'Haven't you forgotten the Bella–Poppy grapevine? News sure travels fast on that plant.'

Summer laughed too. 'Those girls!' Then she frowned. 'How creepy, though, to think of him lurking right outside that window, waiting for a photo opportunity.' Spontaneously, she jumped up and pulled the curtains together more tightly.

'I should never have let him come between us,' said Jack seriously. 'I'm so sorry.'

'It's OK. You've said it.' Summer smiled back into his eyes and kissed him, pulling him down onto the sheepskin rug on the floor beside her. 'All that matters is that you're here now. And I'm never going to let you go again.'

'Oh, Summer,' said Jack softly as he undid the tie on her towelling bathrobe, pushing it off her shoulders. 'How I've dreamt about this.' Taking one golden breast in both hands and then the other, he licked and sucked her nipples, gently at first and then harder, until she was throwing her head back and crying out with joy.

'Please, Jack. I don't think I can wait any longer.'

He knelt back on his heels, undoing his own robe and exposing the finely muscled torso that she remembered in such exquisite detail, the broad shoulders, the scattering of curly dark hair, the dark line leading enticingly down from his navel to . . .

Oh God, that cock.

And now he was thrusting it inside her, filling her with the most exquisite sensations, kissing her as though she were the most precious thing on earth. Covering her face and body with kisses as he thrust and thrust and thrust, breathing how much he loved her.

'I love you, Summer, I love you, I love you, I love you.' It was so quiet that nobody but the two of them would have been able to hear.

'Oh God I love you, oh God that feels so good, oh yeah, oh God I love you, Jack.'

Again and again they gave each other pleasure with all the love and lust that had built up, unsatiated, over the last few months.

Afterwards, feeling him throbbing still inside her, Summer kissed Jack on his damp, sweaty shoulder, so happy that tears were starting to form in her eyes. There had been so many tears today. But these were good ones.

'Welcome home, my darling.'

Eight months later . . .

Can Talaias stood on top of a hill, a few kilometres outside San Carlos. The dilapidated old finca had been discovered in the late Sixties by ex-RAF pilot, louche film star and professional cad Terry-Thomas, he of the moustache, gappy teeth and catchphrase '*Jolly good show*'. He had been horse riding in the unspoilt countryside with his wife when he'd come across it, and had been so captivated by its incredible location, with views all the way down to the sea, that he'd snapped it up pretty much on the spot.

Fabulously quirky and glamorous renovations followed, including the addition of a circular tower (Terry's private suite), an enormous crazily paved terrace, a swirly, irregularly shaped swimming pool and three levels of tropical gardens. Rumours abounded of deliciously decadent and scandalous parties at Can Talaias when Terry was still alive, and now his former home had been turned into one of the most beautiful and captivating boutique hotels in Ibiza.

It was the perfect place for a wedding.

'Are you sure nobody's going to mind about the dress code?' Bella asked, last-minute nerves starting to freak her out again.

'I told you, it's fine,' smiled Summer. 'In fact, it's great.'

'And it's a bit late to start worrying about that now,' laughed Poppy.

'It doesn't seem too poncy? I mean, surely people should be allowed to wear what they want to, at weddings? I never thought I'd tell people what to wear at my wedding . . .'

'What about Black Tie, or Morning Dress?' said Poppy. 'Far more prescriptive, and anyway – it's your wedding, and you can *ask* them to wear what you bloody well like.'

The dress code, written in colourful calligraphy by Bella on her hand-painted parchment invitations, was 'Anything But Black'.

'And stop being so bloody silly,' added Poppy. 'Who'd want to wear black here, anyway? It's hardly as if you've invited them all to a funeral.'

They were getting ready in the circular Terry-Thomas suite, at the top of the tower. Andy and Bella would be staying there that night, having spent the previous night apart, in time-honoured fashion. Bella had stayed at the finca with Daisy and her mother, Andy at Ben and Natalia's with his best man, Bella's brother Max.

'So who do you think will be the first guests?' asked Poppy, trying to quell Bella's nerves, as she and Summer did up the pearl buttons that ran down the back of her long lace dress.

'Jorge and Paloma,' said Summer. 'He never wants to miss out on any part of a party – or the free drinks, of course.' She picked up the enamel-inlaid binoculars lying next to one of the windows, the one that looked down the hill to a white rubbly track that now held a snaking line of vehicles, and smiled. 'Guess what, guys? Looks like I'm right!'

'Do I look OK?' Jorge asked Paloma, checking his reflection yet again in the rear-view mirror of the violet-sprayed

Maserati he'd hired to match his Dior bespoke silk shirt, unbuttoned and untucked over very tight white jeans.

'Relax, sexy, you always look OK,' said Paloma languidly, running her hands down over her silky long black hair. 'And me?' She generally wore black for sophisticated occasions such as this, but with deference to the dress code had settled, somewhat sulkily, on a slinky amethyst ankle-length gown that perfectly complemented Jorge's violet silk.

Jorge smiled. 'You always look beautiful.'

Back down the hill, under the vines at Bar Anita, some of the wedding guests were starting to cause quite a stir amongst the other customers.

'That's Ben Jones!' whispered a twenty-something trust-fund babe to her equally over-privileged friend, trying not to gawp. 'And Jack Meadows,' the friend whispered back.

Ben, in keeping with his screen persona as the ultimate British gent, was wearing a lightweight navy-blue linen jacket over a sky-blue cotton shirt with stone-coloured, immaculately tailored trousers. Natalia, ever by his side, was in a Swarovski crystal-embossed powder-blue chiffon minidress that showed off her endless legs. Even in the comparative shade of the vines, their blondness gleamed.

'I do love this colour thing,' said Damian, whose pale pink shirt was great against his dark complexion.

'Poncy git,' said Ben.

'He has a point, though,' said Natalia, waving a languid hand at the rainbow-clad guests all around them. A lot of the men had taken the opportunity to unleash their inner peacock, with white suits and brightly coloured shirts being the most popular sartorial choice. 'So far, it is beautiful.'

'And we haven't even got up the hill yet,' added Jack, who was missing Summer already. She'd driven up to Can

Talaias several hours earlier to do her bridesmaid's stuff. 'Should we think about making a move?'

'Missing her already?' teased Ben. 'Yeah, sure, let's get going. I'm dying to see what Terry-Thomas's old place is like.' He drained his beer and went into the bar to pay their bill.

Shane Connelly and Gabriella were driving up the hill in Gabriella's battered old Bentley.

'Can Talaias,' she said. 'How well I remember the parties . . .'

'You didn't really go to Terry Thomas's parties, did you?' Shane chuckled. 'You're a legend, Gabs!'

'Oh yes,' smiled Gabriella, outrageously glamorous in scarlet silk and real diamonds. 'Denholm Elliott and Ann Margret disgracing themselves in the pool, Orson Welles and his naked cabaret . . . it was a different time, Shane.' She looked wistful for a second. 'But it is still the most beautiful location.'

'I guess Justin probably remembers a thing or two from those days too, eh?'

'Oh yes,' replied Gabriella with a twinkle in her eye. 'And he is more than happy that his daughter should be getting married there.'

Bella was looking out of the window in the tower at her guests milling about on the huge open terrace below. Summer and Poppy had gone down to mingle, and she was having a few quiet moments on her own. Chairs with rainbow-coloured ribbons streaming behind them had been positioned to form a makeshift aisle facing the edge of the terrace that looked down over the sea, several kilometres below. A jungle of lush plants in striking pinks, reds and oranges clashed vividly with both sky and sea, and large spherical white balloons tied to trees with ribbons added an air of ethereal other-worldliness to the happy scene.

Summer and Poppy were both dressed in short, strappy dresses comprising two layers of cornflower-blue and pale-green chiffon. Poppy's outer layer was green, Summer's blue (to match their eyes), and the effect was just gorgeous. They looked like a couple of beautiful blonde mermaids or nymphs or something, Bella thought fondly, watching them smile and twinkle as they charmed her guests.

She couldn't quite believe that this day had actually come.

She turned to look at herself again in the full-length mirror and smiled. Her intricate white lace, halter-neck, low-backed dress was slim fitting with a very slight fishtail effect from the knee down – which meant she could actually walk. She never wanted to take it off! Suddenly overcome with excitement, she started to dance around the room, singing to herself, her long dark hair swinging around her shoulders.

'I'm getting married in the morning!'

'Afternoon, actually, darling,' said her mother, Olivia, walking into the room hand-in-hand with Daisy. 'Oh my God, you look beautiful.' Tears started welling in her eyes and Bella rushed over to give her a hug.

'Thanks, Mum, but you shouldn't have come in. I'm not completely ready! I wanted to make my grand entrance!'

'I know you did, darling, and sorry, but Daisy was insistent.'

Bella rolled her eyes. Her mother could deny Daisy nothing.

'So what do you think?' she asked, striking a pose. But Daisy was standing stock-still, gazing at her, open-mouthed.

'Mummy's a princess,' she said, eventually.

'That's the right reaction!' Bella cried, rushing over to pick Daisy up and kiss her. 'And don't you look like the most beautiful little fairy?'

Daisy's white chiffon dress was simplicity itself, falling from her shoulders to below her knees in soft gathered folds. Barefoot, with a couple of Marguerite daisies nestling in her silky blonde hair, she could have stepped right out of the pages of one of the Flower Fairy books Bella had loved as a child.

'Yes,' said Daisy.

Nearly all the guests were seated when Tamara and Lars eventually rolled up, flushed and slightly out of breath. The drive from the airport had been a lot quicker than they'd anticipated, so Tamara, unable to resist Lars in his sand-coloured safari suit, had instigated a quickie in the surrounding countryside. 'So, Mr Indiana Jones, are you going to show me how it's done?' had been her husky opening gambit.

Unwelcome worries about being late had faded as soon as Tamara had wriggled out of her tight little dress. Eight months on, he still found her as irresistible as she found him, and neither of them could quite believe their luck in finding one another.

Trying to regain some composure, Tamara walked to their seats arm-in-arm with Lars, smiling at everybody she knew – and everybody she didn't know, too. Well, they had to know her, right? Every inch the glamorous movie star, in an emerald-green Hervé Léger bandage dress and huge Oliver Peoples shades, she slipped into a free chair close to the front of the aisle.

'Hey, Tammy.'

Tamara looked over her shoulder at the man sitting behind her.

'Hey, Jack.'

'Are we cool?'

'My God, you do pick the most inappropriate moments! This is Bella and Andy's *wedding*. Of course we're cool. Talk later, sweetie.'

She winked, and Jack, Lars and everybody around them relaxed.

'I've never seen you look more beautiful, darlin',' said Justin, resplendent in a bright orange tunic over white linen trousers and fuchsia-pink espadrilles.

'For once, I have to agree with you, Justin,' said Olivia, whose fuchsia-pink maxidress was an uncanny match to her ex-husband's footware. 'Utterly gorgeous, darling.'

'Thanks, Mummy, thanks, Daddy,' said Bella, her eyes shining. 'I love you both so much!' She took a couple of deep breaths. 'I guess this is it then.'

In one corner of the terrace, behind a carob tree, a lone guitarist started to play the opening bars of 'Dream A Little Dream Of Me' by the Mamas and the Papas. Nobody realized, yet, that the hidden musician was Filthy Meadows himself.

Bella looked out at it all from the white arched doorway of the main building. It was almost too beautiful to be real. She hesitated.

'Get a move on, Mummy,' Daisy said loudly, and as both Bella's parents started laughing, she pulled herself together and walked out onto the terrace, clutching her father's arm with one hand, her vivid pink, scarlet and orange bouquet of peonies, roses and lilies in the other.

Andy was waiting for her out there.

The song came to an end as Bella reached Andy, so tall and upright in his white linen suit, perfectly silhouetted against the sea and sky, both such a deep blue that it was difficult to tell where the horizon began. Seeing the tears, easily visible behind his glasses, in his clever dark eyes, she reached out to hold his hand.

'You look beautiful,' he mouthed.

'I love you,' she mouthed back.

'Ahhhhh' sighed the crowd, and they both looked over their shoulders, giggling slightly guiltily. They'd been so engrossed in the moment that they'd forgotten that their guests who, not sitting that far away from them, would be able to lip-read pretty well.

The vows went with no mishap, apart from Daisy saying 'yay!' and clapping after each of them, and all too soon it was time for them to walk back past all their friends and family, to the strains of 'Here Comes The Sun', played, again, by Filthy, still hidden beneath his tree.

'You could have timed it a bit better, Belles,' said Poppy, mock-reproachfully as she took a sip of elderflower cordial. 'I can't believe I'm not getting pissed at your wedding.'

Bella smiled and gave Poppy's barely discernible bump a little pat.

'It'll make it stand out from all the others you've been to.'

'It already does. It's yours!' Poppy threw her arms around Bella's neck and hugged her again. 'And it's wonderful. Living up to your expectations so far?'

'More than. It hardly seems real. I keep getting that out-of-body thing – "Is this happening to me?" – that you mentioned.'

'Told you so.'

'Must you always be right?'

Poppy tilted her golden head to one side to consider. 'Yeah, probably.'

'So, Pops – any idea yet what your little one's going to be?'

'You tell me. You're going to be its godmother.'

'One of thousands,' Bella laughed, and Poppy did too. Half of Hollywood had already been asked to god-parent her unborn child.

'A boy,' Bella added. 'I'm sure you're going to have a beautiful little boy. But you let him anywhere near Daisy and I'll kill you.'

'Congratulations, both of you,' said India Cavendish, approaching Bella and Andy with a smile. She had a glass of champagne in one hand and Milo's hand in the other. 'What an absolutely gorgeous day, and you look beautiful.'

'Thanks, India,' said Bella, kissing her on both cheeks 'So do you.'

It was true. India had put on a bit of weight and, no longer gaunt, looked tanned, healthy and happy in a prim-rose-yellow lace minidress.

'So how is everything?' asked Andy, smiling at her and marvelling at the transformation from the desperate battered woman who had turned up at the finca that after-noon last year.

'Absolutely wonderful, thanks.' India gave another radiant smile. 'And I've got some fantastic news – but you know, *pas devant.*'

Daisy, who Bella was beginning to suspect was almost scarily perceptive for her age, suddenly piped up, 'Why don't you come and play with me, Milo?' All three adults smiled indulgently as they watched their children walk off hand-in-hand, Milo in his little white suit and Daisy in her little white dress, chattering all the way.

'So what is it?' Bella turned back to India, eager for gossip.

'Actually, I've just realized it's probably completely inappropriate to tell you on your wedding day, but—'

'Sod appropriate!' said Bella impatiently. 'Tell us!'

'Oh, OK! The decree nisi finally came through today! I'm officially free!'

'Fantastic news! Yay, India!'

There were high fives and hugs all around, drawing curious glances from some of the other guests.

'And I've got half the bastard's money!'

'Including the house?' asked Bella, high-fiving her again.

'Yup, but I'm selling it. Ghastly monstrosity – Jamie never did have any taste, and it's much too big for me and Milo. Although . . .'

'Although what? Oooh, look at you – there's a new man on the horizon, isn't there? Yes, you do look—'

'Bella, stop it, you're embarrassing the poor woman,' laughed Andy.

'It's OK, there is somebody, but it's early days yet. He's, um – Milo's sports teacher . . .' Bella and Andy both smiled. '. . . and he's ten years younger than me.'

Bella and Andy continued their rounds of the gardens, stopping to chat to guests as they drank champagne and hibiscus cocktails and nibbled on tapas – the main meal wouldn't be served for another hour or so.

'Blimey, we did it,' said Bella.

'We did it,' said Andy, smiling at her.

'And isn't it all just *fabulous*?' she added triumphantly, struck yet again by the incredible beauty of their surroundings. Pretty little wrought-iron tables and chairs were dotted, apparently at random, in clearings in the lush foliage, and hammocks, also apparently at random but actually calculated to give the best view down to the sea or over the pool, were strung up between trees.

It was in one of these hammocks that they came across Tamara, posing for all she was worth in her tight green dress, as Lars snapped away at her.

'Oh!' she sat up straight when she saw them. 'Shit, how embarrassing! I hope you don't mind?'

'Why would we mind?' asked Andy, smiling at her. 'We'd mind if people didn't want to take photos – it's so beautiful here.'

'Sure is,' Tamara concurred excitedly, dark curls bouncing as she tried to balance in the hammock.

'It is phenomenal,' said Lars, reaching out to shake Andy's hand, and kiss Bella. 'I don't think I've congratulated you both properly yet.'

'Of course you have,' said Bella. 'And you've given us the best present anybody possibly could have!'

'Ah – I hope you enjoy it,' smiled Lars. The wedding present was two weeks at his Mexican resort for their honeymoon.

'We can't wait,' said Andy, grinning boyishly. 'I've never been to Mexico.'

'So how are you?' Bella asked Tamara. 'I can't wait to see *Dust Bowl*. It hasn't reached Ibiza yet, but you've had some fantastic reviews.'

'Thanks,' said Tamara. 'At long last my brilliance has been recognized.'

'I'm so proud of my girl,' beamed Lars.

'You know I couldn't have done it without you.' Tamara jumped nimbly out of the hammock and stood on tiptoes to kiss him on the cheek. 'Anyway, enough of posing here on our own, and keeping the *beautiful* bride and groom from the rest of their guests! This is a party – let's go mingle!'

Summer and Jack were sitting on the ledge of the terrace, legs dangling, looking out to sea.

'Have I ever told you how beautiful you are?' said Jack, stroking Summer's smooth brown cheek.

'Loads of times,' she said, smiling into his eyes. 'But I never tire of hearing it. Isn't this a wonderful day? I don't think I've ever seen Bella so happy.'

'It's fabulous,' Jack agreed. 'I'm going to miss you like crazy the next couple of weeks though.'

'You'll manage.' Summer leaned over to kiss him. 'And you'll be so busy the time will fly by.'

Much as she loved her life in Ibiza, Summer had discovered that she couldn't bear to be apart from Jack for too long, so she found herself flying out to LA, or Saigon, or wherever he happened to be filming; the rest of the time he flew back to be with her, in Ibiza. It was an extremely happy arrangement, and the travelling gave her loads of material for her blog, which now had a global following. She managed to keep her *Island Life* column going, too – she could file her copy from anywhere in the world – and either Bella or India Cavendish would take over at the crèche during her absences.

For the next two weeks, though, Summer and Britta had promised to look after Daisy while Bella and Andy were on their honeymoon. Although Britta was perfectly capable of doing it on her own, Bella had confided that she would be even happier if Summer was there for Daisy – 'I've never even been apart from her for one night before, and she absolutely adores you.'

Well, how could she possibly refuse?

'Oh look, there's the happy couple!' Summer turned and waved at Bella and Andy, who were approaching them through the crowds.

'What an amazing day,' said Jack sincerely, swinging his long legs back over the ledge and standing up to shake

Andy's hand and kiss Bella on the cheek. 'Congratulations to you both.'

He looked so absurdly glamorous, so off-duty film star, that Bella had to give herself a metaphorical pinch. Was this man really a guest at her wedding? He was wearing a slim-cut white suit over a plain navy-blue T-shirt with navy-and-white old-skool Adidas sneakers and vintage Ray-Bans.

'Thanks so much for flying all the way from Saigon.'

'It's my absolute pleasure,' said Jack. 'Although my director's not best pleased that his two leading men had to halt filming to fly to Ibiza for the weekend,' he added with a smile.

'Oh God, I hadn't thought of that!' Bella couldn't quite believe what she was hearing. 'Um – maybe pass on my apologies to him?'

'I wouldn't have missed it for the world. It's a wonderful day. And if it wasn't for you and Andy, I'd never have met Summer.'

Later, the grounds were lit up by lanterns in the trees, dotted along pathways and on the white linen-covered round tables that filled the lovely terrace. Everybody had eaten and drunk like kings, and there was a magical feeling of happiness in the warm night air. Stars twinkled in the inky sky and cicadas chirruped insistently, a constant background to Ella Fitzgerald singing classic Cole Porter through hidden speakers.

Suddenly the music stopped, and the faint strains of live guitar music could be heard, wafting up from the curvy, irregularly shaped pool. Bella turned to Andy with a puzzled look on her face. This hadn't been in the plan – they'd decided against a first dance, as all four of their feet were of the leftish persuasion. Andy shook his head at her, shrugging. He patently had no idea what was going on either. Taking her by the hand, he walked to the edge of the terrace so they could see the pool, and one by one their guests followed suit.

The music, which they now heard was classic Spanish guitar, with a hint of flamenco, was getting louder, and Bella started to smile even more broadly as she took in the scene.

Sitting on stools at the far end of the iridescently lit pool were her father and Filthy Meadows, playing, in perfect harmony, the most beautiful music Bella had ever heard. Nothing could be better suited to their surroundings.

'Daddy?'

'Surprise, darlin'!' He didn't stop playing. 'Hope you don't mind. Filth and I have been practising for months!'

'Mind? It's wonderful!' Bella and Andy ran, hand in hand, down the shallow stone steps that led to the pool, and over to where the old boys carried on strumming away under an ancient silvery olive tree.

'What are you waiting for, girl?' said Filthy with a wink. 'Just dance!'

So Bella and Andy, and gradually all their guests, started to dance. Around the pool, on the terraces, in the gardens, twirling and twirling with joy and laughter, as the guitars played on through the magical warm night air.

As ever, the island wove its spell around them.

'It was always you, from the first moment I saw you,' she said. 'You must have known?'

'I knew that it was you, for me. I was never sure that it was me, for you.'

They reached for each other, on their beautiful beach, the moon bathing their lovely bodies in exquisite silvery light. They were perfect together; they knew that now.

'I love you, Jack.'

'I love you, Summer.'

And the sea glistened like mercury, rolling in gentle waves against the burnished platinum shore.

Acknowledgements

To my amazing editor Kim Young and the equally wonderful Martha Ashby, for your fantastic advice, ideas and all-round editorial brilliance. To Anne O'Brien, for your clever way with words and the ability to polish some occasionally very plodding prose – I'm still cringing at the amount of repetition in the first draft. To the rest of the team at HarperCollins, especially the lovely Claire Palmer, for all your hard work behind the scenes.

To my agent, Annabel Merullo, and Laura Williams at PFD for your constant support.

To all the friends I've ever partied with in Ibiza – you know who you are! To my beloved family – can't wait to celebrate publication with you all on the White Isle this summer.

And as ever, to Andy, with happy sunshiny memories of our honeymoon there, and the hours we spent in Anita's Bar.